Scottish Stories of Fantasy & Horror

Scottish
Stories of
Fantasy
&
Horror

EDITED BY PETER HAINING

FOREWORD BY ANGUS WILSON

BONANZA BOOKS
NEW YORK

Dedicated to the memory of my grandfather
Alexander Haining
and
"Tir nam Beann, 's nan Gleann, 's nan Gaisgeach."

Originally published as *Clans of Darkness*

Selection and original material copyright © MCMLXXI by Peter Haining
Foreword copyright © MCMLXXI by Angus Wilson

This 1988 edition is published by Bonanza Books,
distributed by Crown Publishers, Inc.,
225 Park Avenue South, New York, New York 10003,
by arrangement with Peter Haining and Euro-Features Limited.

Printed and Bound in the United States of America

Library of Congress Cataloging-in-Publication Data

Scottish stories of fantasy and horror / edited by Peter Haining ;
foreword by Angus Wilson.
        p.   cm.
    Originally published: The clans of darkness. London : Gollancz,
1971.
    ISBN 0-517-65500-4
    1. Fantastic fiction, Scottish.   2. Horror tales, Scottish.
3. English fiction—Scottish authors.   I. Haining, Peter.
II. Title.
[PR8676.5.F35C5 1988]
823'.0872—dc19   88-4287
                                                                          CIP

ISBN 0-517-65500-4
h g f e d c b a

CONTENTS

ACKNOWLEDGMENTS

The Editor wishes to extend his thanks to the following authors (or their executors, trustees or agents) and publishers for permission to include copyright material in this book: the estate of Neil Munro for 'Red Hand' from *The Lost Pibroch*; The executors of Sir Arthur Conan Doyle for 'Through The Veil'; the estate of John Buchan for 'The Outgoing of the Tide' from *The Watcher by the Threshold*; Messrs A. P. Watt for 'The Wolves of God' by Algernon Blackwood; The Porpoise Press, Edinburgh, for 'The Clock' by Neil Gunn from *Hidden Doors*; the author's agent for 'Tam Mackie's Trial' by Hugh MacDiarmid; Messrs A. M. Heath and the *Reader's Digest* for 'The Strange Meeting' by A. J. Cronin; Messrs A. M. Heath for 'Music When Soft Voices Die . . .' by John Keir Cross from *The Other Passenger*; Messrs A. D. Peters for 'Sealskin Trousers' by Eric Linklater; and Alex Hamilton for his story, 'Dead Men Walk'. I am also grateful to Angus Wilson who made time in his busy life to pay his own tribute to the worlds of Scottish fantasy.

'In Scotland, railways, roads, newspapers and tourists are slowly but surely doing their accustomed work. They are driving out romance; but they are not driving out the popular creed as to supernaturals. That creed will survive when the last remnant of romance has been banished, for superstition seems to belong to no one period in the history of civilisation, but to all. It is as rife in the towns as it is amongst the hills, and it is not confined to the ignorant.'

J. F. CAMPBELL

FOREWORD

by Angus Wilson

Fairyland, an insubstantial replica of our own human realm, where delights are greater, emotions more volatile, personality more ambiguous and fleeting than the grinding, bounded, convention ridden world we live in, has been a very general need of human imagination throughout the world. Yet nowhere, probably, have the fairies offered their tempting, mischievous, even dangerous lures more potently than in the Border Country of lowland Scotland. Here in this lawless, violent, beautiful yet mournful hill country with its glorious, perilous rocky seashore the need of the fairy kingdom was most needed to offset the precarious, harsh life of a people peculiarly endowed with imagination and strange fancy. Even the most prosaic tourist must have his moment of Gothick romance when faced with the ruins of Caerlaverock or Sweetheart or Melrose or the many other castles and abbeys that speak for the now mouldered attempts to impose order, feudal or spiritual, upon this history-burdened country. It is no surprise that Border men and women should have seen the fairy folk to tempt them to a sweeter way of life. But, of course, it is only by the degenerate Edwardian days of Sir James Barrie that Lowland imagination with its strong measure of spiritual awe (whether Catholic or Calvinist) tried to make the elfin world into something sweetly fit for Kensington Gardens children. The great border ballads, the medieval men themselves, knew that this beguiling fairy realm was but one, though most powerful, of the deceitful lures of the Evil One. Whosoever supped with the dainty Queen of the Fairies would pay for his delights by sacrificing his soul to the Prince of Darkness. Fairies and elves (all those strange, necessary human fancies now debased further than even Sir James supposed into the cuteness of Disneyland) lay very close to the world of witches and warlocks and familiars. And the man or woman who supped from thistledown cups should not be suffered to live.

Mr. Haining, then, very properly begins this anthology with an anonymous account of that first great Scots historian of the fairy realm, Thomas the Rhymer. We can have no doubt from the beginning of the sinister nature of the beguiling other world of Scotland. The very titles of the two seventeenth-century pieces that follow tell us how the Kirk viewed the insubstantial—'The Secret Commonwealth', and Satan's Invisible World Discovered'. Then follows one of the finest pieces of writing of that strange, ambiguous, great man Sir Walter Scott—and for all his Tory romanticism he makes no compact with the wicked Sir Robert Redgauntlet and his horrid companions in hell: Lauderdale, handsome Claverhouse and all the other persecutors of the faithful Covenanters. From then on Mr. Haining's anthology is not only an illustration of the riches of the writings of Scotland—Galt, James Hogg, Allan Cunningham, R.L.S. in unusual but splendid moral allegorical form, John Buchan at his very good best, a touching magical MacDiarmid piece, and Linklater subtle and clever—but an excellent illustration of the changing approach to the supernatural through the nineteenth and twentieth centuries.

Theology gives place to sheer Gothic sensation, sensation becomes increasingly psychological, the supernatural becomes associated with history when in Conan Doyle's story the present collides with the last stand of the Roman legions at the Wall, it takes a science fiction plunge with Eric Linklater, and, at the last, with Alex Hamilton's 'Dead Men Walk' is used to rebut the vulgar scepticisms of a London newspaper voice. But not only does the mood of horror change, but the change of styles that succeed one another in this fascinating selection must immediately strike every reader who has a feeling for words. Myself, I am in no doubt that, even taking into account John Buchan's extraordinary gift for pastiche and Hugh MacDiarmid's poetic power, Walter Scott stands out among these authors

10

for his control of language, with a dialogue that assists the swift moving story and a story that never engulfs the living people that take part in it.

One point only may surprise the English reader—the predominance of the Border over the Highlands in this occult legendary scene. It is late before the Highlands appear, and even then it is the far off Orkneys that predominate. I guess that this is a linguistic affair, in which England is the loser of a rich mass of Gaelic verbal legend. Nevertheless, that the Highlands of Scotland stand in the world's eye as one of the great northern sources of primitive story is surely proved by the work of James Macpherson. If ever Voltaire's saying about God has been proved it is surely in the invention of Ossian.

INTRODUCTION

'She had the largest collection in the country of tales and songs concerning devils, ghosts, fairies, brownies, witches, warlocks, spunkies, kelpies, elf-candles, dead-lights, wraiths, apparitions, cantraips, giants, enchanted towers, dragons and other trumpery. This cultivated the latent seeds of poetry, but had so strong an effect on my imagination, that to this hour, in my nocturnal rambles, I sometimes keep a sharp look-out in suspicious places; it often takes an effort of philosophy to shake off these idle terrors.'

So wrote Robert Burns in a letter (1787) to his friend, Dr. Moore, explaining the debt his work owed to an old woman who had lived in his home when he was a child These formative circumstances behind the poet's work differ little, in fact, from those of many other of Scotland's great writers of ballads and stories who similarly grew up surrounded by hearthside legends and in countryside that sheltered all manner of demons, bogies and spirits.

Not without reason has Scotland been described as being 'more prone to superstition and old fears than any other nation in the world', and this is naturally reflected in its literature from the heroic legends of the earliest times through Scott and Stevenson right to the present day. Indeed from the many dark corners of the Highlands and the strange places of the rambling Lowlands have come a host of *Seanachas* (traditional tales) evolved from myth and epic and woven by generations of skilful story-tellers into a rich tapestry of fantasy. To them have been added stories of witches and warlocks developed from the terrible persecutions which numbered Scotland second only to Germany in the fury of her witchcraft hysteria; the ghosts and fairies of haunted castles and vales; the fearful monsters of remote lochs and glens; the dark superstitions and fears born in ignorance and kept alive in compromise between heart and learning; and the horrors which only man can inflict upon man in bitterness and a desire for revenge. All these elements—and more—form Scotland's unique vein of macabre literature.

It is a literature so voluminous and gifted, in fact, that attempting to be merely *representative* as one is in a collection such as this is almost impossible and an apology from the editor for failing to include this tale or that legend is perhaps requisite before we begin. Yet, I am not here to plead forgiveness for my failings but to set you on the path through a selection of great stories in fact and fiction which together I believe cover most of the elements of Scottish fantasy and horror.

My guidelines in selection have been simple: quality, a feeling for the 'grue' (as Stevenson called the facility of 'thrilling by means of the weird'), a diversity of subject, and material not already anthologised or easily available. This, coupled with the fact that I was primarily interested in the work of Scottish writers who are household names, called for exhaustive research and a rigorous and continuous pruning of the material. Because of this, too, a great many writers and stories that should be present have found themselves on the editor's spike and I can do no more than apologise for my taste (hopefully stifling the protests of those who feel their favourite writer or writers have been overlooked) and say that I *did* want to include items by such as Robert Burns—his poem 'Tam O'Shanter' is certainly a classic of macabre verse—Andrew Lang, R. B. Cunninghame-Graham, Norman Macleod, 'Christopher North', William Sharp, George Macdonald, S. R. Crockett, Norman Douglas, and many, many more. (There was also a particular story with the irresistible title of 'The Man Who Travelled to Learn What Shivering Meant' and even that had to go one desolate morning!) But space and an international readership are hard task-masters.

This 'international readership', I hasten to add, has always been very much in my mind because the Scots are great travellers and are to be found at the ends of the earth. Yet no man of the North ever completely forgets his homeland and in noting the slight bias of this collection in favour of the 'wandering Scots', I can perhaps do no better than use the words of Eric Linklater who wrote recently that 'blood is thicker than the estranging seas and on two noisy nights of the year in a hundred towns from Auckland to Seattle there are many thousands of otherwise orthodox and disciplined citizens who, in a vast emotional confession, proclaim the breeding that environment, often happily, occludes'. As the grandson of a Scottish tailor who did just that the words have a special meaning for me—as they doubtless will for a great many other people.

But enough of sentiment—this is a book of dark deeds for dark nights. Like any anthologist I am sorry in a way my task is now over for there are few more rewarding experiences than ploughing the genius of great writers and coming across some forgotten gem; except that in restoring the item to print someone else may also experience the same exhilaration of discovery and enjoyment. I should like to add, finally, that if the reader finds certain threads of similarity running through many of the stories, this should not be put down to plagiarism on the part of the authors but a careful observance of tradition and a very real belief that there is nothing so strange as fact—Scottish in particular.

So here, then, are the Clans of Darkness, tramping the night paths of imagination, which I give to you with a caution to steady your nerves and the words of John Buchan, 'It is of the back-world of Scotland that I write, the land behind the mist and over the seven bens, a place hard of access for the foot-passenger but easy for the maker of stories'.

PETER HAINING.

15

Scottish Stories of Fantasy & Horror

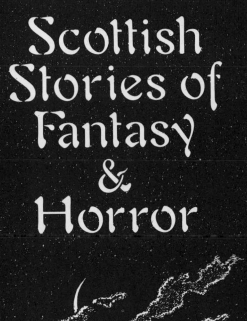

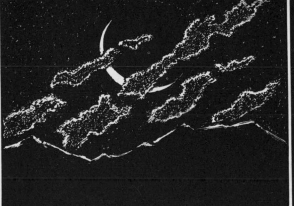

THOMAS THE RHYMER

(Traditional)

THOMAS RYMOUR OF ERCILDOUN (circa 1220–1297), widely immortalised as 'Thomas The Rhymer', is credited with having written the first piece of verse known to exist in the English language. He was also held to be a prophet of remarkable skill and his pronouncements were much sought after by nobility and peasantry alike—the latter nicknaming him 'True Thomas'. He lived for the greater part of his life in a tower (still standing) in Earlston, and from there gave out his thoughts on both the futures of individuals and on national events. It has also been suggested that Thomas was a minstrel, but this story may well have arisen in later years through the mis-spelling of his name: Rymour being a comparatively common name in Berwickshire. None the less his whole life is enveloped in mystery and many Scottish writers and chroniclers have referred to him—notably Sir Walter Scott who included a ballad about him in his Minstrelsy of the Scottish Border. *(Scott owned a valley not far from Earlston known as 'Rhymer's Glen' and according to one biographer, 'spent many of his happiest times in this place with its associations with the shadowy past'.) Several stories of Thomas' life are in existence, but this anonymous piece—which is probably several hundred years old—seems to me to best conjure up the mystique of one of Scotland's first great fantasy figures.*

Thomas, of Ercildoun, in Lauderdale, called the Rhymer, on account of his producing a poetical romance on the subject of Tristrem and Yseult, which is curious as the earliest specimen of English verse known to exist, flourished in the reign of Alexander III of Scotand. Like other men of talent of the period, Thomas was suspected of magic. He was also said to have the gift of prophecy, which was accounted for in the following peculiar manner, referring entirely to the lore of superstition.

As Thomas lay on Huntly bank (a place on the descent of the Eildon Hills, which raise their triple crest above the celebrated monastery of Melrose), he saw a lady so extremely beautiful that he imagined she must be the Virgin Mary herself. Her appointments, however, were those rather of an amazon, or goddess of the woods. Her steed was of the highest beauty, and at its mane hung thirty silver bells and nine, which were music to the wind as she paced along. Her saddle was of 'royal bone' (ivory), laid over with 'orfeverie' (goldsmith's work). Her stirrups, her dress, all corresponded with her extreme beauty and the magnificence of her array. The fair huntress had her bow in hand and her arrows at her belt. She led three greyhounds in a leash, and three raches, or hounds of scent, followed her closely.

She rejected and disclaimed the homage which Thomas desired to pay her; so that, passing from one extremity to the other, Thomas became as bold as he had at first been humble. The lady warned him he must become her slave if he wished to prosecute his suit. Before their interview terminated, the appearance of the beautiful lady was changed into that of the most hideous hag in existence. A witch from the spital or almshouse would have been a goddess in comparison to the late beautiful huntress. Hideous as she was, Thomas felt that he had placed himself in the power of this hag, and when she bade him take leave of the sun, and of the leaf that grew on the tree, he felt himself under the necessity of obeying her. A cavern received them, in which, following his frightful guide, he for three days travelled in darkness, sometimes hearing the booming of a distant ocean, sometimes walking through rivers of blood, which crossed their subterranean path. At length they emerged into daylight, in a most beautiful orchard. Thomas, almost fainting for want of food, stretched out his hand towards the goodly fruit which hung around him, but was forbidden by his conductress, who informed him that these were the fatal apples which

20

were the cause of the fall of man. He perceived also that his guide had no sooner entered this mysterious ground and breathed its magic air than she was revived in beauty, equipage, and splendour, as fair or fairer than he had first seen her on the mountain. She then proceeded to explain to him the character of the country.

'Yonder right-hand path,' she says, 'conveys the spirits of the blest to paradise. Yon downward and well-worn way leads sinful souls to the place of everlasting punishment. The third road, by yonder dark brake, conducts to the milder place of pain, from which prayer and mass may release offenders. But see you yet a fourth road, sweeping along the plain to yonder splendid castle? Yonder is the road to Elfland, to which we are now bound. The lord of the castle is king of the country, and I am his queen; and when we enter yonder castle, you must observe strict silence, and answer no question that is asked you, and I will account for your silence by saying I took your speech when I brought you from middle earth.'

Having thus instructed him, they journeyed on to the castle, and, entering by the kitchen, found themselves in the midst of such a festive scene as might become the mansion of a great feudal lord or prince.

Thirty carcasses of deer were lying on the massive kitchen board, under the hands of numerous cooks, who toiled to cut them up and dress them, while the gigantic greyhounds which had taken the spoil lay lapping the blood, and enjoying the sight of the slain game. They came next to the royal hall, where the king received his loving consort; knights and ladies, dancing by threes, occupied the floor of the hall; and Thomas, the fatigue of his journey from the Eildon Hills forgotten, went forward and joined in the revelry. After a period, however, which seemed to him a very short one, the queen spoke with him apart, and bade him prepare to return to his own country.

'Now,' said the queen, 'how long think you that you have been here?'

'Certes, fair lady,' answered Thomas, 'not above these seven days.'

21

'You are deceived,' answered the queen; 'you have been seven years in this castle, and it is full time you were gone. Know, Thomas, that the archfiend will come to this castle tomorrow to demand his tribute, and so handsome a man as you will attract his eye. For all the world would I not suffer you to be betrayed to such a fate; therefore up, and let us be going.'

This terrible news reconciled Thomas to his departure from Elfinland; and the queen was not long in placing him upon Huntly Bank, where the birds were singing. She took leave of him, and to ensure his reputation bestowed on him the tongue which *could not lie*. Thomas in vain objected to this inconvenient and involuntary adhesion to veracity, which would make him, as he thought, unfit for church or for market, for king's court or for lady's bower. But all his remonstrances were disregarded by the lady; and Thomas the Rhymer, whenever the discourse turned on the future, gained the credit of a prophet whether he would or not, for he could say nothing but what was sure to come to pass.

Thomas remained several years in his own tower near Ercildoun, and enjoyed the fame of his predictions, several of which are current among the country people to this day. At length, as the prophet was entertaining the Earl of March in his dwelling, a cry of astonishment arose in the village, on the appearance of a hart and hind, which left the forest, and contrary to their shy nature, came quietly onward, traversing the village towards the dwelling of Thomas. The prophet instantly rose from the board, and acknowledging the prodigy as the summons of his fate, he accompanied the hart and hind into the forest, and though occasionally seen by individuals to whom he has chosen to show himself, he has never again mixed familiarly with mankind.

THE SECRET COMMONWEALTH

by Robert Kirk

REVEREND ROBERT KIRK (circa *1630–1692*) *gave Scotland probably its first great work of fantasy with* The Secret Commonwealth, *a detailed study of fairies and the fairy world written in 1691. Kirk, a seventh son and as such believed to be specially gifted in matters of the supernatural, was a church minister serving first at Balquhidder and then at Aberfoyle—a spot familiar to all readers of* Rob Roy. *Little is known of his life except that he was twice married and made a Gaelic translation of the Bible. The area in which he lived and worked is especially steeped in the 'lore of Elfinland', and R. B. Cunningham Graham has remarked: 'No doubt the congregation that the ingenious minister served were most of them devout believers in fairy love . . . for they sucked it in with their mother's milk and held it, not by conviction, for they had never reasoned on it, but quite naturally, as part and parcel of themselves; and in such surroundings it was not strange the writer of the book also believed in them.' As far as can be ascertained, the Reverend Kirk completed his study in 1691, but it seems to have remained in manuscript form until 1815— certainly no edition before that date has been traced. A local legend in Aberfoyle has it that the worthy minister did not die, but while out walking in 1692 was seized on a* dun-shi (*fairy hill*) *by the little people whose biographer he had become, and spirited away to Fairyland where he is held to this day. Commenting wryly on this in 1893, the Scottish authority on folk lore and mythology, Andrew Lang, wrote: 'Mr. Kirk has not yet been restored to us—and this is extremely to be regretted as he could now add matter of much importance to his treatise.' In the version of 'The Secret Commonwealth' which follows, some slight anglicisation has been effected to make reading simpler for those not familiar with the Scottish dialect.*

The Siths, or Fairies, they call *Sleagh Maith* (or the Good-people, it would seem, to prevent the dint of their ill attempts), are said to be of a middle nature betwixt man and angel, as were demons thought to be of old, of intelligent studious spirits, and light changeable bodies (like those called astral), somewhat of the nature of a condensed cloud, and best seen in twilight. These bodies be so pliable through the subtlety of the spirits that agitate them, that they can make them appear or disappear at pleasure. Some have bodies or vehicles so spongeous, thin, and pure that they are fed by only sucking into some fine spirituous liquors, that pierce like pure air and oil; others feed more gross on the abundance or substance of corn and liquors, or corn itself that grows on the surface of the earth, which these fairies steal away, partly invisible, partly preying on the grain, as do crows and mice; wherefore in this same age they are sometimes heard to break bread, strike hammers, and to do such like services within the little hillocks they most do haunt; some whereof of old, before the Gospel dispelled Paganism, and in some barbarous places as yet, enter houses after all are at rest, and set the kitchens in order, cleansing all the vessels. Such drags go under the name of Brownies. When we have plenty, they have scarcity at their homes; and, on the contrary (for they are not empowered to catch as much prey everywhere as they please), their robberies, notwithstanding, oft-times occasion great ricks of corn not to bleed so well (as they call it), or prove so copious by very far as was expected by the owner.

Their bodies of congealed air are sometimes carried aloft, other whiles grovel in different shapes, and enter into any cranny or cleft of the earth where air enters, to their ordinary dwellings; the earth being full of cavities and cells, and there being no place, no creature, but is supposed to have other animals (greater or lesser) living in

24

or upon it as inhabitants; and no such thing as a pure wilderness in the whole universe.

We then (the more terrestrial kind have now so numerously planted all countries) do labour for that abstruse people, as well as for ourselves. Albeit, when several countries were uninhabited by us, these had their easy tillage above ground, as we do now. The print of those furrows do yet remain to be seen on the shoulders of very high hills, which was done when the campaign ground was wood and forest.

They remove to other lodgings at the beginning of each quarter of the year, so traversing till doomsday, being impotent of staying in one place, and finding some ease by so journeying and changing habitations. Their chameleon-like bodies swim in the air near the earth with bag and baggage; and at such revolution of time, seers, or men of the second sight* (females being seldom so qualified) have very terrifying encounters with them, even on highways; who, therefore, awfully shun to travel abroad at these four seasons of the year, and thereby have made it a custom to this day among the Scottish-Irish to keep church duly every first Sunday of the quarter to *seun* or hallow themselves, their corn and cattle, from the shots and stealth of these wandering tribes; and many of these superstitious people will not be seen in church again till the next quarter begins, as if no duty were to be learnt or done by them, but all the use of worship and sermons were to save them from these arrows that fly in the dark.

They are distributed in tribes and orders, and have children, nurses, marriages, deaths, and burials in appearance, even as we (unless they so do for a mock-show, or to prognosticate some such things among us).

They are clearly seen by these men of the second sight to eat at funerals and banquets. Hence many of the Scottish-Irish will not taste meat at these meetings, lest they have

* The facility of foreseeing future events which is supposed to belong to certain individuals in the Scottish Highlands. The belief in second sight dates back to a very early period in the history of these regions and is still far from extinct in many parts. Lewis Spence, *Encyclopedia of Occultism.*

communion with, or be poisoned by, them. So are they seen to carry the bier or coffin with the corpse among the middle-earth men to the grave. Some men of that exalted sight (whether by art or nature) have told me they have seen at these meetings a double man, or the shape of some man in two places; that is a super-terranean and a subter-ranean inhabitant, perfectly resembling one another in all points, whom he, notwithstanding, could easily distinguish one from another by some secret tokens and operations, and so go and speak to the man, his neighbour and familiar, passing by the apparition or resemblance of him. They avouch that every element and different state of being has animals resembling those of another element; as there be fishes sometimes at sea resembling monks of late order in all their hoods and dresses; so as the Roman invention of good and bad demons, and guardian angels particularly assigned, is called by them an ignorant mistake, sprung only from this original. They call this reflex man a co-walker, every way like the man, as a twin brother and companion, haunting him as his shadow, as is oft seen and known among men (resembling the original), both before and after the original is dead; and was often seen of old to enter a house, by which the people knew that the person of that likeness was to visit them within a few days. This copy, echo, or living picture, goes at last to his own herd. It accompanied that person so long and frequently for ends best known to itself, whether to guard him from the secret assaults of some of its own folk, or only as a sportful ape to counterfeit all his actions. However, the stories of old witches prove beyond contradiction that all sorts of people, spirits which assume light airy bodies, or crazed bodies coacted by foreign spirits, seem to have some pleasure (at least to assuage some pain or melancholy) by frisking and capering like satyrs, or whistling and screeching (like unlucky birds) in their unhallowed synagogues and Sab-baths. If invited and earnestly required, these companions make themselves known and familiar to men; otherwise, being in a different state and element, they neither can nor will easily converse with them. They avouch that a *heluo* or great eater has a voracious elve to be his attender, called a

26

joint-eater or just-halver, feeding on the pith and quintessence of what the man eats; and that, therefore, he continues lean like hawk or heron, notwithstanding his devouring appetite; yet it would seem they convey that substance elsewhere, for these subterraneans eat but little in their dwellings, their food being exactly clean, and served up by pleasant children, like enchanted puppets.

Their houses are called large and fair, and (unless at some odd occasions) unperceivable by vulgar eyes, like Rachland and other enchanted islands, having fir lights, continual lamps, and fires, often seen without fuel to sustain them. Women are yet alive who tell they were taken away when in child-bed to nurse fairy children, a lingering voracious image of.them being left in their place (like their reflection in a mirror), which (as if it were some insatiable spirit in an assumed body) made first semblance to devour the meats that it cunningly carried by, and then left the carcass as if it expired and departed thence by a natural and common death. The child and fire, with food and all other necessaries, are set before the nurse how soon she enters, but she neither perceives any passage out, nor sees what those people do in other rooms of the lodging. When the child is weaned, the nurse dies, or is conveyed back, or gets it to her choice to stay there. But if any superterraneans be so subtle as to practise sleights for procuring the privacy to any of their mysteries (such as making use of their ointments, which, as Gyges' ring, make them invisible or nimble, or cast them in a trance, or alter their shape, or make things appear at a vast distance, etc.), they smite them without pain, as with a puff of wind, and bereave them of both the natural and acquired sights in the twinkling of an eye (both these sights, when once they come, being in the same organ and inseparable), or they strike them dumb. The tramontanes to this day place bread, the Bible, or a piece of iron, to save their women at such times from being thus stolen, and they commonly report that all uncouth, unknown weights are terrified by nothing earthly so much as cold iron. They deliver the reason to be that hell lying betwixt the chill tempests and the firebrands of scalding metals, and iron of the north

27

(hence the loadstone causes a tendency to that point), by an antipathy thereto, these odious, far-scenting creatures shrug and fright at all that comes thence relating to so abhorred a place, whence their torment is either begun, or feared to come hereafter.

Their apparel and speech is like that of the people and country under which they live; so are they seen to wear plaids and variegated garments in the Highlands of Scotland, and *suanachs* (plaids) therefore in Ireland. They speak but little, and that by way of whistling, clear, not rough. The very devils conjured in any country do answer in the language of the place; yet sometimes the subterraneans speak more distinctly than at other times. Their women are said to spin very fine, to dye, to tossue, and embroider; but whether it be as manual operation of substantial refined stuffs, with apt and solid instruments, or only curious cobwebs, unpalpable rainbows, and a phantastic imitation of the actions of more terrestrial mortals, since it transcended all the senses of the seer to discern whether, I leave to conjecture as I found it.

Their men travel much abroad, either presaging or aping the dismal and tragical actions of some amongst us; and have also many disastrous doings of their own, as convocations, fighting, gashes, wounds, and burials, both in the earth and air. They live much longer than we; yet die at last, or at least vanish from that state. 'Tis one of their tenets that nothing perisheth, but (as the sun and year) everything goes in a circle, lesser or greater, and is renewed and refreshed in its revolutions; as 'tis another, that every body in the creation moves (which is a sort of life); and that nothing moves but has another animal moving on it; and so on, to the utmost minutest corpuscle that's capable of being a receptacle of life.

They are said to have aristocratical rulers and laws, but no discernible religion, love, or devotion towards God, the blessed Maker of all: they disappear whenever they hear His name invoked, or the name of Jesus (at which all do bow willingly, or by constraint, that dwell above or beneath, within the earth), (Philip. ii. 10); nor can they act ought at that time after hearing of that sacred name. The Taiblsdear

28

or seer, that corresponds with this kind of familiars, can bring them with a spell to appear to himself or others when he pleases, as readily as the Endor Witch did those of her own kind. He tells they are ever readiest to go on hurtful errands, but seldom will be the messengers of great good to men. He is not terrified with their sight when he calls them, but seeing them in a surprise (as often as he does) frights him extremely, and glad would he be quit of such, for the hideous spectacles seen among them; as the torturing of some wight, earnest, ghostly, staring looks, skirmishes, and the like. They do not all the harm which appearingly they have power to do; nor are they perceived to be in great pain, save that they are usually silent and sullen. They are said to have many pleasant toyish books; but the operation of these pieces only appears in some paroxysms of antic, corybantic jollity, as if ravished and prompted by a new spirit entering into them at that instant, lighter and merrier than their own. Other books they have of involved, abstruse sense, much like the Rosicrucian style. They have nothing of the Bible, save collected parcels for charms and counter-charms; not to defend themselves withal, but to operate on other animals, for they are a people invulnerable by our weapons, and albeit werewolves' and witches' true bodies are (by the union of the spirit of nature that runs through all echoing and doubling the blow towards another) wounded at home, when the astral assumed bodies are striken elsewhere—as the strings of a second harp, tuned to a unison sound, though only one be struck—yet these people have not a second, or so gross a body at all, to be so pierced; but as air which when divided unites again; or if they feel pain by a blow, they are better physicians than we, and quickly cure. They are not subject to sore sicknesses, but dwindle and decay at a certain period, all about an age. Some say their continual sadness is because of their pendulous state (like those men, Luke xiii. 2–6), as uncertain what at the last revolution will become of them, when they are locked up into an unchangeable condition; and if they have any frolic fits of mirth, 'tis as the constrained grinning of a mort-head (death's-head), or rather as acted on a stage, and moved by another, than by cordially coming of

29

themselves. But other men of the second sight, being illiterate, and unwary in their observations, differ from those; one averring those subterranean people to be departed souls, attending a while in this inferior state, and clothed with bodies procured through their alms-deeds in this life; fluid, active, ethereal vehicles to hold them that they may not scatter nor wander, and be lost in the totum, or their first nothing; but if any were so impious as to have given no alms, they say, when the souls of such do depart, they sleep in an inactive state till they resume the terrestrial bodies again; others, that what the low-country Scotch call a wraith, and the Irish *taibhse*, or death's messenger (appearing sometimes as a little rough dog, and if crossed and conjured in time, will be pacified by the death of any other creature instead of the sick man), is only exuvious fumes of the man approaching death, exhaled and congealed into a various likeness (as ships and armies are sometimes shaped in the air), and called astral bodies, agitated as wild-fire with wind, and are neither souls nor counterfeiting spirits; yet not a few avouch (as is said) that surely these are a numerous people by themselves, having their own politics, which diversities of judgment may occasion several inconsonancies in this rehearsal, after the narrowest scrutiny made about it.

Their weapons are most-what solid earthly bodies, nothing of iron, but much of stone, like to yellow soft flint spa, shaped like a barbed arrowhead, but flung like a dart, with great force. These arms (cut by art and tools, it seems, beyond human) have somewhat of the nature of thunderbolt subtlety, and mortally wounding the vital parts without breaking the skin; of which wounds I have observed in beasts, and felt them with my hands. They are not as infallible Benjamites, hitting at a hair's-breadth; nor are they wholly unvanquishable, at least in appearance.

The men of the second sight do not discover strange things when asked, but at fits and raptures, as if inspired with some genius at that instant, which before did work in or about them. Thus I have frequently spoken to one of them, who in his transport told me he cut the body of one of those people in two with his iron weapon, and so escaped this onset, yet he saw nothing left behind of that appearing divided; at other times he out-wrestled some of them. His neighbours often perceived this man to disappear at a certain place, and about an hour after to become visible, and discover himself near a bow-shot from the first place. It was in that place where he became invisible, said he, that the subterraneans did encounter and combat with him. Those who are *unseund*, or unsanctified (called fey), are said to be pierced or wounded with those people's weapons, which makes them do something very unlike their former practice, causing a sudden alteration, yet the cause thereof unperceivable at present; nor have they power (either they cannot make use of their natural powers, or asked not the heavenly aid) to escape the blow impendent. A man of the second sight perceived a person standing by him (sound to other's view) wholly gored in blood, and he (amazed-like) bid him instantly flee. The whole man laughed at his *airt* (notice) and warning, since there was no appearance of danger. He had scarce contracted his lips from laughter when unexpectedly his enemies leaped in at his side and stabbed him with their weapons. They also pierce cows or other animals, usually said to be Elf-shot, whose purest substance (if they die) these subterraneans take to live on, viz. the aerial and ethereal parts, the most spirituous matter for prolonging of life, such as aquavitae (moderately taken) is amongst liquors, leaving the terrestrial behind. The cure of such hurts is only for a man to find out the hole with his finger, as if the spirits flowing from a man's warm hand were antidote sufficient against their poisoned darts.

As birds, as beasts, whose bodies are much used to the change of the free and open air, forescc storms, so these invisible people are more sagacious to understand by the books of nature things to come, than we, who are pestered with the grossest dregs of all elementary mixtures, and have our purer spirits choked by them. The deer scents out a man and powder (though a late invention) at a great distance; a hungry hunter, bread; and the raven, a carrion; their brains, being long clarified by the high and subtle air, will observe a very small change in a trice. Thus a man of the second sight, perceiving the operations of these forecasting invisible people among us (indulged through a stupendous providence to give warnings of some remarkable events, either in the air, earth, or waters), told he saw a winding shroud creeping on a walking, healthful person's leg till it came to the knee, and afterwards it came up to the middle, then to the shoulders, and at last over the head, which was visible to no other person. And by observing the spaces of time betwixt the several stages, he easily guessed how long the man was to live who wore the shroud; for when it approached the head, he told that such a person was ripe for the grave.

There by many places called fairy-hills, which the mountain people think impious and dangerous to explore or discover, by taking earth or wood from them superstitiously believing the souls of their predecessors to dwell there. And for that end (say they) a mole or mound was dedicate beside every churchyard to receive the souls till their adjacent bodies arise, and so became as a fairy-hill; they using bodies of air when called abroad. They also affirm those creatures that move invisibly in a house, and cast huge great stones, but do not much hurt, because counter-wrought by some more courteous and charitable spirits that are everywhere ready to defend men (Dan. x. 13), to be souls that have not attained their rest, through a vehement desire of revealing a murder or notable injury done or received, or a treasure that was forgot in their lifetime on earth, which, when disclosed to a conjuror alone, the ghost quite removes.

In the next country to that of my former residence, about the year 1676, when there was some scarcity of grain, a marvellous vision strongly struck the imagination of two women in one night, living at a good distance from one another, about a treasure hid in a hill called *Sithbruthach*, or fairy-hill. The appearance of a treasure was first represented to the fancy, and then an audible voice named the place where it was to their awakening senses, Whereupon both rose, and meeting accidentally at the place, discovered their design; and jointly digging, found a vessel as large as a Scottish peck full of small pieces of good money, of ancient coin; and having betwixt them, they sold in dishfuls for dishfuls of meal to the country people. Very many of undoubted credit saw and had of the coin to this day. But whether it was a good or bad angel, one of the subterranean people, or the restless soul of him who hid it, that discovered it, and to what end it was done, I leave to the examination of others.

These subterraneans have controversies, doubts, disputes, feuds, and siding of parties; there being some ignorance in all creatures, and the vastest created intelligences not compassing all things. As to vice and sin, whatever their own laws be, sure according to ours, and equity, natural, civil, and revealed, they transgress and commit acts of injustice and sin by what is above said, as to their stealing of nurses to their children, and that other sort of plaginism in catching our children away (may seem to heir some estate in those invisible dominions) which never return. For swearing and intemperance, they are not observed so subject to those irregularities, as to envy, spite, hypocrisy, lying, and dissimulation.

As our religion obliges us not to make a peremptory and curious search into these abstrusenesses, so the histories of all ages give as many plain examples of extraordinary occurrences as make a modest inquiry not contemptible. How much is written of pigmies, fairies, nymphs, syrens, apparitions, which though not the tenth part true, yet could not spring of nothing; even English authors relate of Barry Island, in Glamorganshire, that laying your ear into a cleft of the rocks, blowing of bellows, striking of hammers, clashing of armour, filing of iron, will be heard distinctly ever since Merlin enchanted those subterranean wights to a solid manual forging of arms to Aurelius Ambrosius and his Britons, till he returned; which Merlin being killed in a battle, and not coming to loose the knot, these active vulcans are there tied to a perpetual labour.

SATAN'S INVISIBLE WORLD DISCOVERED

The story of William Barton, a Warlock

by George Sinclar

GEORGE SINCLAR (circa *1624–1696*), *like the minister of Aberfoyle, Robert Kirk, provided Scotland with a work of enduring fame with the publication of his* Satan's Invisible World Discovered *in 1685. The book is notable, too, in that for a time it was one of the most important 'textbooks' on witchcraft and much used in the trials and examinations of those suspected of practising the dark arts. However, its indiscriminate mixing of fact and fantasy and narrow-minded viewpoint caused it in due course to be discredited, and copies are now of considerable rarity. None the less, its stature in occult literature is undeniable. Sinclar was Professor of Philosophy and Mathematics at the University of Glasgow from 1654–1696, but as a perfatory note in an 1871 edition of his book states, 'Of the parentage, place of birth or early life of that singular character but well-known mathematical writer, George Sinclar, no particulars have been ascertained.' He first came to public attention through a book about recovering sunken treasure,* Hydrostatical Experiments, *in which he described a diving bell of his own invention. His ingenuity was further revealed when he was among the first to attempt the measurement of mountains with a crude barometer. Sinclar was frequently involved in violent controversies through his work and once his inventions were derided in a paper by a fellow professor who wrote, 'It seems ye do all these wonders by Magick, for ye have the ordinair principles of none of these Sciences.'*

Sinclar at first planned to reply to these attacks, but abandoned this idea as he became increasingly involved in preparing his masterwork on witchcraft which set out to prove the actuality of 'devils, spirits, witches and apparitions'. The book was an immediate success and, according to one report, was 'for a long time a constituent part of every cottage library in Scotland'. In it Sinclar recorded famous stories of witchcraft and occult 'happenings' from all over Europe and devoted particular attention to Scotland's own most famous male practitioners, Dr. John Fian and Major Weir. Both their stories are so familiar and widely recorded that rather than them I have selected from the book another episode dealing with an equally unsavoury, but less known, warlock, William Barton. It is illustrative, too, of the whole tone and bias of Sinclar's book.

About thirty years ago, more or less, there was one William Barton *apprehended for* Witch-Craft. *His confession was first,* that if he had twenty Sons, he would advise them to shun the lust of uncleanness. *For said he,* I never saw a beautiful Woman, Maid, nor Wife, but I did covet them, which was the only cause that brought me to be the Devil's Vassal.

One day, says he, going from my own house in *Kirkliston,* to the *Queens Ferry,* I overtook in *Dalmeny Muire,* a young Gentlewoman, as to appearance beautiful and comely. I drew near to her, but she shunned my company, and when I insisted, she became angry and very vexed. Said I, since we are both going one way, be pleased to accept of a convoy. At last, after much entreaty she grew better natured, and at length we came to that Familiarity, that she suffered me to embrace her, and to do that which Christian ears ought not to hear of. At this time I parted with her very joyful.

The next night, she appeared to him in that very same place, and after that which should not be named, he became sensible that it was the Devil. Here he renounced his Baptism, and gave up himself to her service, and she called him her beloved, and gave him this new name of John Baptist, *and*

35

received the Mark. *She likewise bestowed fifteen pounds Scots upon him in the name of* Tocher-good, *and so parted.*

After he had gone a little way off, she calls him back and gave him a Merk-piece *in good and sufficient money which She bad him spend at the* Ferry, *and desired him to keep entire and whole the* 15. *pound, which he declared was real and true Money. He confest that they never met together, but they plaid their Pranks.*

After this Confession he begged Liberty to sleep a little, which the Judges granted to him. After he had slept a short time, he awakened with a great Laughter. The Judges inquired the reason. He replyed, being seriously urged, that the devil had come to him, and rebuked him with anger, and threatened him most furiously, that he had confessed, and bad him deny all, for he should be his Warrand.

After this, he turned obdured, and would never to his dying hour acknowledge any thing, for the Devil had persuaded him, even from his first ingaging, that no man should take his life, *which promise he firmly believed, to the very last.*

When they told him in the prison-house, that the Fire was built, and the Stake set up, and the executioner coming to bring him forth: he answered he cared not for all that, for said he I shall not die this day. *But the* Executioner *got presently orders to lead him forth, and he stepping in at the Prison door in an instant* shot to dead, *as they say, and never stirred again.*

In this strait, they appointed the Executioner's *Wife to strangle him, which she did willingly, a reward being promised to her. When the* Warlock *heard this, that a* Woman *was to put him to death, O,* crys he, how hath the Devil deceived me? Let none ever trust to his Promises.

All this was done at Kirkliston *before famous witnesses. The Executioner's name was* Andrew Martain *and his wife's name* Margaret Hamilton, *who when her Husband died clapt her hands, and cryed often,* Dool for this parting, my dear burd Andrew Martin.

This Barton's *Wife had been likewise taken with him,*

36

Who Declared, that She never knew him to have been a Warlock before; *And he likewise declared*, That he never knew her to have been a Witch before. *She confest* that malice against one of her Neighbours, moved her to ingage in the Devils service. *She renounced her* Baptism *and did postrat her Body to the* Foul-Spirit, *and received his* Mark, *and got a new name from him, and was called* Margaratus. *She was asked, if she had any pleasure in his company,* never much says she.

But one Night going to a dancing upon Pentland-hills, he went before us in the likeness of a rough tanny-Dog, playing on a pair of Pipes. The Spring he played (*says she*) was, The silly bit Chiken, gar cast it a pickle and it will grow meikle. And coming down the hill when we had done which was the best sport, he carried the candle in his bottom under his tail, which played ey wig wag, wig wag. *She was burnt with her husband.*

There is one thing remarkable in this Story, that he bestowed so much money upon the Warlock, *which proved good and sufficient Coin? 'Tis seldom he is so liberal. But surely he would be more liberal if the* Lord *would suffer him to steal, or make use of Treasures lying in the Ground, or in the Bottom of the Sea. If this liberty were granted, he might deceive the most part of men and women in the world, with his gifts.*

A NIGHT IN THE GRAVE

or

The Devil's Receipt

by Sir Walter Scott

SIR WALTER SCOTT (*1771–1832*). *From the country's most famous general work on witchcraft, it is only appropriate that we should next turn to the story which must surely be the finest piece of* diablerie *in Scottish fiction. It is apposite, too, that it should be the work of the man widely regarded as Scotland's greatest novelist, Sir Walter Scott. Scott's life, and indeed his predilection with the supernatural, has been dealt with at such length and by so many distinguished scholars as to need no mention here. He knew the Border Country and the Highlands well through spending much of his early life there, and could magnificently evoke their people, atmosphere and superstitions in his tales. Selecting from the body of his work a story or tale not widely known is almost impossible because of Scott's continuing popularity and the constant reprinting of his prose and poetry. However, the tale here is something of a rarity in this form: it is in fact an extract from the novel* Redgauntlet (*1824*), *and another version has several times been reprinted under the title, 'Wandering Willie's Tale'. This particular printing is taken from a volume of Gothic stories,* Legends of Terror *published in 1826 and consisting in the main of stories from the German. The editors of the volume selected this item to illustrate that 'English writers' [sic] could 'equal—if not excel— in diabolism most of those yet produced from the German school'. They had Scott make some slight textural changes so that a knowledge of the whole story was not essential and called the result 'one of the finest "auld warld stories" which his pen has produced'. It is interesting to note, too, that according to the great expert on Scott's work, Professor C. O. Parsons, the author was influenced by Sinclar's* Satan's Invisible World Discovered *and indeed probably referred to the book while actually writing this tale.*

Ye maun have heard of Sir Robert Redgauntlet of that Ilk, who lived in these parts before the dear years. The country will lang mind him; and our fathers used to draw breath thick if ever they heard him named. He was out wi' the Hielandmen in Montrose's time; and again he was in the hills wi' Glencairn in the year saxteen hundred and fifty-twa; and sae when King Charles the Second came in, wha was in sic favour as the Laird of Redgauntlet? He was knighted at Lonon court, wi' the king's ain sword; and being a redhot prelatist, he came down here, rampauging like a lion, with commissions of lieutenancy, and of lunacy for what I ken, to put down a' the Whigs and Covenanters in the country. Wild wark they made of it; for the Whigs were as dour as the Cavaliers were fierce, and it was which should first tire the other. Redgauntlet was aye for the strong hand; and his name is kenn'd as wide in the country as Claverhouse's or Tam Dalywell's. Glen, nor dargle, nor mountain, nor cave, could hide the puir hill-folk when Redgauntlet was out with bugle and bloodhound after them, as if they had been sae mony deer. And troth when they found them, they didna mak muckle mair ceremony than a Hieland man wi' a roe-buck—It was just, 'Will ye tak the test?'—if not, 'Make ready—present—fire!'—and there lay the recusant.

Far and wide was Sir Robert hated and feared. Men thought he had a direct compact with Satan—that he was proof against steel—and that bullets hopped off his buff-coat like hail-stones from a hearth—that he had a mear that would turn a hare on the side of Carrifragawns—and muckle to the same purpose, of whilk mair anon. The best blessing they wared on him was, 'De'il scowp wi'

Redgauntlet!' He wasna a bad master to his ain folk though, and was weel aneugh liked by his tenants; and as for the lackies and troopers that raid out wi' him to the persecutions, as the Whigs ca'ad these killing times, they wad hae drunken themsels blind to his health at ony time.

Now ye are to ken that my gude-sire lived on Redgauntlets grund—they ca' the place Primrose-Knowe. We had lived on the grund, and under the Redgauntlets, since the riding days, and lang before, It was a pleasant bit; and I think the air is fresher there than onywhere else in the country. It's a' deserted now; and I sat on the broken door-cheek three days since, and was glad I couldna see the plight the place was in; but that's a' wide o' the mark. There dwelt my gudesire, Steenie Steenson, a rambling, rattling chiel' he had been in his young days, and could play weel on the pipes; he was famous at 'Hoopers and Girders'—a' Cumberland couldna touch him at 'Jockie Lattin' . . . and he had the finest finger for the back-lill between Berwick and Carlisle. The like o' Steenie wasna the sort that they made Whigs o'. And so he became a Tory as they ca'it, which we now ca' Jacobites, just out of a kind of needcessity, that he might belang to some side or other. He had nae ill-will to the Whig bodies, and likedna to see the blude rin, though, being obliged to follow Sir Robert in hunting and hosting, watching and warding, he saw muckle mischief, and maybe did some, that he couldna avoid.

Now Steenie was a kind of favourite with his master, and kenn'd a' the folks about the castle, and was often sent for to play the pipes when they were at their merriment. Auld Dougal Mac Callum, the butler, that had followed Sir Robert through gude and ill, thick and thin, pool and stream, was specially fond of the pipes, and aye gae my gude-sire his gude word wi' the Laird; for Dougal could turn his master round his finger.

Weel, round came the Revolution, and it like to have broken the hearts baith of Dougal and his master. But the change was not a'thegether sae great as they feared, and other folk thought for. The Whigs made an unca crawing what they wad do with their auld enemies, and in special wi' Sir Robert Redgauntlet. But there were ower mony great folks dipped in the same doings, to make a spick and span new warld. So Parliament passed it a' ower easy; and Sir Robert, bating that he was held to hunting foxes instead of Covenanters, remained just the man he was. His revel was as loud, and his hall as weel lighted, as ever it had been, though maybe he lacked the fines of the non-conformists, that used to come to stock larder and cellar; for it is certain he began to be keener about the rents than his tenants used to find him before, and it behoved them to be prompt to the rent-day, or else the laird wasna pleased. And he was sic an awsome body, that naebody cared to anger him; for the oaths he swore, and the rage that he used to get into, and the looks that he put on, made men sometimes think him a devil incarnate.

Weel, my gudesire was nae manager—no that he was avery great misguider—but he hadna the saving gift, and he got two terms rent in arrear. He got the first brash at Whitsunday put ower wi' far words and piping; but when Martinmas came, there was a summons from the grand-officer to come wi' the rent on a day precese, or else Steenie behoved to flitt. Sair wark he had to get the siller; but he was weel-freended, and at last he got the whole scraped thegether—a thousand merks—the maist of it was from a neighbour they ca'ad Laurie Lapraik—a sly tod. Laurie had walth o' gear—could hunt wi' the hound and rin wi' the the hare—and be Whig or Tory, saunt or sinner, as the wind stood. He was a professor of religious music in this Revolution warld, but he liked another sound and a tune on the pipes weel eneugh at a bye-time; and abune a', he thought he had gude security for the siller he lent my gudsire over the stocking at Primrose-Knowe.

Away trots my gudsire to Redgauntlet Castle wi' a heavy purse and a light heart, glad to be out of the Laird's danger. Weel, the first thing he learned at the castle was, that Sir Robert had fretted himself into a fit of the gout, because he did not appear before twelve o'clock. It wasna a'the-gether for the sake of the money, Dougal thought; but because he didna like to part wi' my gudsire aff the grund. Dougal was glad to see Steenie, and brought him into the

41

great oak parlour, and there sat the Laird his leesome lane, excepting that he had beside him a great, ill-favoured jack-an-ape, that was a special pet of his; a cankered beast it was, and many an ill-natured trick it played—ill to please it was, and easily angered—ran about the whole castle, chattering and yowling, and pinching, and biting folk, especially before ill-weather, or disturbances in the state. Sir Robert ca'ad it Major Weir, after the warlock that was burned; and few folk liked either the name or the conditions of the creature—they thought there was something in it by ordinar—and my gudesire was not just easy in mind when the door shut on him, and he saw himself in the room wi' naebody but the Laird, Dougal Mac Callum, and the Major, a thing that hadna chanced to him before.

Sir Robert sat, or, I should say, lay, in a great armed chair, wi' his grand velvet gown, and his feet on a cradle; for he had baith gout and gravel, and his face looked as gash and ghastly as Satan's. Major Weir sat opposite to him, in a red laced coat, and the Laird's wig on his head; and aye as Sir Robert grinned wi' pain the jack-an-ape grinned too, like a sheep's-head between a pair of tongs— an ill-faur'd, fearsome couple they were. The Laird's buff-coat was hung on a pin behind him, and his broad sword and his pistols within reach; for he keepit up the old fashion of having the weapons ready, and a horse saddled day and night, just as he used to do when he was able to loup on horseback, and sway after any of the hill-folk he could get speerings of. Some said it was for fear of the Whigs taking vengeance, but I judge it was just his auld custom— he wasna gien to fear onything. The rental-book wi' its black cover and brass clasps, was lying beside him; and a book of sculduddry songs was put betwixt the leaves, to keep it open at the place where it bore evidence against the Goodman of Primrose-Knowe, as behind the hand with his mails and duties. Sir Robert gave my gudesire a look, as if he would have withered his heart in his bosom. Ye maun ken he had a way of bending his brows, that men saw the visible mark of a horse-shoe in his forehead, deep-dinted, as if it had been stamped there.

42

'Are ye come light-handed, ye son of a toom whistle?' said Sir Robert. 'Zounds! if ye are—'

My gudesire, with as gude a countenance as he could put on, made a leg, and placed the bag of money on the table wi' a dash, like a man that does something clever. The Laird drew it to him hastily—'Is it all here, Steenie, man?'

'Your honour will find it right,' said my gudesire.

'Here, Dougal,' said the Laird, 'gie Steenia a tass of brandy down stairs, till I count the siller and write the receipt.'

But they werena weel out of the room, when Sir Robert gied a yelloch that shook the castle rock. Back ran Dougal—in flew the liverymen—yell on yell gied the Laird, ilk ane mair awfu' than the ither. My gudesire knew not whether to stand or flee, but he ventured back into the parlour, where a' was gaun hirdy-girdie—naebody to say 'come in', or 'gae out'. Terribly the Laird reared for cauld water to cool his feet, and wine to cool his throat; and Hell, hell, hell, and its flames, was aye the word on his mouth. They brought him water, and when they plunged his swoln feet into the tub, he cried out it was burning; and folks say that it did bubble and sparkle like a seething cauldron. He flung the cup at Dougal's head, and said he had given him blood instead of burgundy; and sure aneugh, the lass washed clottered blood off the carpet the next day. The jack-an-ape they ca'ad Major Weir, it jibbered and cried as if it was mocking its master; my gudesire's head was like to turn—he forgot baith siller and receipt, and down stairs he banged; but as he ran, the shrieks came faint and fainter; there was a deep-drawn shivering groan, and word gaed through the castle, that the Laird was dead.

Weel, away came my gudesire, wi' his finger in his mouth, and his best hope was, that Dougal had seen the money-bag, and heard the Laird speak of writing the receipt. The young Laird, now Sir John, came from Edinburgh, to see things put to rights. Sir John and his father never gree'd weel—he had been bred an advocate, and afterwards sat in the last Scots Parliament and voted for the Union, having gotten, it was thought, a rug of the compensations—

43

if his father could have come out of his grave, he would have brained him for it on his own hearth-stone. Some thought it was easier counting with the auld rough Knight than the fair-spoken young ane—but mair of that anon.

Dougal Mac Callum, poor body, neither grat nor graned, but gaed about the house looking like a corpse, and directing, as was his duty, a' the order of the grand funeral. Now, Dougal looked aye waur and waur when night was coming and was aye the last to gang to his bed, whilk was in a little round just opposite the chamber of dais, whilk his master occupied while he was living, and where he now lay ina state as they ca'ad it, well-a-day! The night before the funeral, Dougal could keep his awn counsel nae langer; he came doun with his proud spirit, and fairly asked auld Hutcheon to sit in his room with him for an hour. When they were in the round, Dougal took ae tass of brandy to himsel, and gave another to Hutcheon, and wished him all health and lang life, and said that, for himsel, he wasna lang for this world; for that, every night since Sir Robert's death, his silver call had sounded from the state chamber, just as it used to do at nights in his lifetime, to call Dougal to help to turn him in his bed. Dougal said, that being alone with the dead on that floor of the tower (for naebody cared to wake Sir Robert Redgauntlet like another corpse), he had never daured to answer the call, but that now his conscience checked him for neglecting his duty; for 'though death breaks service', said MacCallum, 'it shall never break my service to Sir Robert; and I will answer his next whistle, so be you will stand by me, Hutcheon'.

Hutcheon had nae will to the wark, but he had stood by Dougal in battle and broil, and he wad not fail him at this pinch; so down the carles sat over a stoup of brandy, and Hutcheon, who was something of a clerk, would have read a chapter of the Bible; but Dougal would hear naething but a song of Davie Lindsay, whilk was the waur preparation.

When midnight came, and the house was quiet as the grave, sure aneugh the silver whistle sounded as sharp and shrill as if Sir Robert was blowing it, and up got the two auld serving-men, and tottered into the room where the dead man lay. Hutcheon saw aneugh at the first glance; for

44

there were torches in the room, which shewed him the foul fiend, in his ain shape, sitting on the Laird's coffin! Over he cowped as if he had been dead. He could not tell how lang he lay in a trance at the door, but when he gathered himself, he cried on his neighbour, and getting no answer, raised the house, when Dougal was found lying dead within two steps of the bed where his master's coffin was placed. As for the whistle, it was gaen anes and aye; but many a time was it heard on the top of the house in the bartizan, and amang the auld chimnies and turrets, where the howlets have their nests. Sir John hushed the matter up, and the funeral passed over without mair bogle-wark.

But when a' was over, and the Laird was beginning to settle his affairs every tenant was called up for his arrears, and my gudesire for the full sum that appeared against him in the rental-book. Weel, away he trots to the Castle, to tell his story, and there he is introduced to Sir John, sitting in his father's chair, in deep mournng, with weepers and hanging cravat, and a small walking rapier by his side, instead of the auld broadsword that had a hundred-weight of steel about it, what with blade, chape, and basket-hilt. I have heard their communing so often tauld ower, that I almost think I was there myself, though I couldna be born at the time. However my grandfather in a half flattering, half conciliating tone, addressed the Laird, who, during the commencement of the conversation, often sighed deeply, and hypocritically lifted his napkin to his eyes. My grandfather had, while he spoke, his eye fixed on the rental-book, as if it were a mastiff-dog that he was afraid would spring up and bite him.

'I wuss ye joy, Sir, of the headseat, and the white loaf and the braid lairdship. Your father was a kind man to friends and followers; muckle grace to you, Sir John, to fill his shoon—his boots, I suld say, for he seldom wore shoon, unless it were muils when he had the gout.'

'Aye, Steenie,' quoth the Laird, sighing deeply, and putting his napkin to his face, 'his was a sudden call, and he will be missed in the country; no time to set his house in order—weel prepared God-ward, no doubt, which is the root of the matter—but left us behind a tangled hesp to

45

wind, Steenie.—Hem! hem! We maun go to business, Steenie; much to do, and little time to do it in.'

Here he opened the fatal volume; I have heard of a thing they call Doomsday-book—I am clear it has been a rental of back-ganging tenants.

'Stephen,' said Sir John, still in the same soft, sleekit tone of voice—'Stephen Stevenson, or Steenson, ye are down here for a year's rent behind the hand—due at last term.'

Stephen. 'Please your honour, Sir John, I paid it to your father.'

Sir John. 'Ye took a receipt then, doubtless, Stephen; and can produce it?'

Stephen. 'Indeed I hadna time, an it like your honour; for nae sooner had I set doun the siller, and just as his honour, Sir Robert, that's gaen, drew it to him to count it, and write out the receipt, he was ta'en wi' the pains that removed him.'

'That was unlucky,' said Sir John, after a pause. 'But ye maybe paid it in the presence of somebody. I want but a talis qualis evidence, Stephen. I would go ower strictly to work with no poor man.'

Stephen. 'Troth, Sir John, there was naebody in the room but Dougal Mac Callum the butler. But, as your honour kens, he has e'en followed his auld master.'

'Very unlucky again, Stephen,' said Sir John, without altering his voice a single note. 'The man to whom ye paid the money is dead—and the man who witnessed the payment is dead too—and the siller, which should have been to the fore, is neither seen nor heard tell of in the repositories. How am I to believe a' this?'

Stephen. 'I didna ken, your honour; but there is a bit memorandum note of the very coins; for, God help me! I had to borrow out of twenty purses; and I am sure that ilk man there set down will take his grit oath for what purpose I borrowed the money.'

Sir John. 'I have little doubt ye borrowed the money, Steenie. It is the payment that I want to have some proof of.'

Stephen. 'The siler maun be about the house, Sir John.

And since your honour never got it, and his honour that was canna have taen it wi' him, maybe some of the family may have seen it.'

Sir John. 'We will examine the servants, Stephen; that is but reasonable.'

But lackey and lass, and page and groom, all denied stoutly that they had ever seen such a bag of money as my gudesire described. What was waur, he had unluckily not mentioned to any living soul of them his purpose of paying his rent. One quean had noticed something under his arm, but she took it for the pipes.

Sir John Redgauntlet ordered the servants out of the room, and then said to my gudesire, 'Now, Steenie, ye see you have fair play; and as I have little doubt ye ken better where to find the siller than any other body, I beg, in fair terms, and for your own sake, that you will end this fasherie; for, Stephen, ye maun pay or flitt.'

'The Lord forgie your opinion,' said Stephen, driven almost to his wits' end—'I am an honest man.'

'So am I, Stephen,' said his honour, ' and so are all the folks in the house, I hope. But if there be a knave amongst us, it must be he that tells the story he cannot prove.' He paused, and then added, mair sternly, 'If I understand your trick, Sir, you want to take advantage of some malicious reports concerning things in this family, and particularly respecting my father's sudden death, thereby to cheat me out of the money, and perhaps take away my character, by insinuating that I have received the rent I am demanding. Where do you suppose this money to be?—I insist upon knowing.'

My gudesire saw every thing look so muckle against him, that he grew nearly desperate—however, he shifted from one foot to another, looked to every corner of the room, and made no answer.

'Speak out, Sarah,' said the Laird, assuming a look of his father's, a very particular one, which he had when he was angry—it seemed as if the wrinkles of his frown made that self-same fearful shape of a Horse's shoe in the middle of his brow—'Speak out, Sir! I will know your thoughts—do you suppose that I have this money?'

'Far be it frae me to say so,' said Stephen.

'Do you charge any of my people with having taken it?'

'I wad be laith to charge them that may be innocent,' said my gudesire; and if there by any one that is guilty, I have nae proof.'

'Somewhere the money must be, if there is a word of truth in your story,' said Sir John; 'I ask where you think it is—and demand a correct answer?'

'In hell, if you will have my thoughts of it,' said my gudesire, driven to extremity—'in hell! with your father and his silver whistle.'

Down the stairs he ran (for the parlour was nae place for him after such a word) and he heard the Laird swearing blood and wounds behind him, as fast as ever did Sir Robert, and roaring for the baillie and the baron-officer.

Away rode my gudesire to his chief creditor (him they ca'ad Laurie Lapraik), to try if he could make onything out of him; but when he tauld his story, he got but the warst word in his mouth—thief, beggar, and dyvour, were the softest terms; and to the boot of these hard terms, Laurie brought up the auld story of his dipping his hand in the blood of God's saints, just as if a tenant could have helped riding with the Laird, and that a Laird like Sir Robert Redgauntlet. My gudesire was, by this time, far beyond the bounds of patience, and, while he and Laurie were at de'il speed the liars, he was wanchancy aneugh to abuse his doctrine as weel as the man, and said things that gar'd folks flesh grew that heard them; he wasna just himsell, and he had lived wi' a wild set in his day.

At last they parted, and my gudesire was to ride hame through the wood of Pitmarkie, that is all full of black firs, as they say. I ken the wood, but the firs may be black or white for what I can tell. At the entry of the wood there is a wild common, and on the edge of the common, a little lonely change-house that was keepit then by an ostler-wife, they suld hae ca'd her Tibbie Faw, and there puir Steenie cried for a mutchkin of brandy, for he had had no refreshment the whole day. Tibbie was earnest wi' him to take a bite of meat, but he couldna think o't, nor would he take his foot out of the stirrup, and took aff the brandy, wholey, at twa draughts, and named a toast at each: the first was, The memory of Sir Robert Redgauntlet, and might he never lie quiet in his grave till he had righted his poor bond-tenant; and the second was, A health to Man's Enemy, if he would but get him back the pock of siller, or tell him what came o't, for he saw the whole world was like to regard him as a thief and a cheat, and he took that waur than even the ruin of his house and hauld.

On he rode, little caring where. It was a dark night turned, and the trees made it yet darker and he let the beast take its ain road through the wood; when, all of a sudden, from tired and wearied that it was before, the nag began to spring, and flee, and stend, that my gudesire could hardly keep the saddle. Upon the whilk, a horseman, suddenly riding up beside him, said, 'That's a mettle beast of yours, friend; will you sell him?'—So saying, he touched the horse's neck with his riding-wand, and it fell into its auld heigh-ho of a stumbling trot; 'But his spunk's soon out of him, I think,' continued the stranger, 'and that is like many a man's courage, that thinks he wad do great things till he come to the proof.'

My gudesire scarce listened to this, but spurred his horse, with 'Gude e'en to you, friend.'

But it's like the stranger was ane that does na lightly yield his point; for, ride as Steenie liked, he was aye beside him at the selfsame pace. At last my gudesire, Steenie Steenson, grew half angry; and, to say the truth, half feared.

'What is it that ye want with me, friend?' he said. 'If ye be a robber, I have nae money; if ye be a leal man, wanting company, I have nae heart to mirth or speaking; and if ye want to ken the road, I scarce ken it mysell.'

'If you will tell me your grief,' said the stranger, 'I am one that, though I have been sair misca'ad in the world, ain the only hand for helping my freends.'

So my gudesire, to ease his ain heart, mair than from any hope of help, told him the story from beginning to end.

'It's a hard pinch,' said the stranger; 'but I think I can help you.'

'If you could lend the money, Sir, and take a lang day—
I ken nae other help on earth,' said my gudesire.

'But there may be some under the earth,' said the stranger.
'Come, I'll be frank wi' you; I could lend you the money
on bond, but you would, maybe, scruple my terms. Now,
I can tell you, that your auld Laird is disturbed in his
grave by your curses, and the wailing of your family, and—
if ye dare venture to go to see him, he will give you the
receipt.'

My gudesire's hair stood on end at this proposal, but
he thought his companion might be some humoursome
chield that was trying to frighten him, and might end with
lending him the money. Besides, he was bold wi' brandy,
and desperate wi' distress; and he said, he had courage to
go to the gate of hell, and a step farther, for that receipt.
The stranger laughed.

Weel, they rode on through the thickest of the wood,
when, all of a sudden, the horse stopped at the door of
great house; and, but that he knew the place was ten miles
off, my father would have thought he was at Redgauntlet
Castle. They rode into the outer court-yard, through the
muckle faulding gates, and aneath the auld portcullis; and
the whole front of the house was lighted, and there were
pipes and fiddles, and as much dancing and deray within
as used to be in Sir Robert's house at Pace and Yule, and
such high seasons. They lap off, and my gudesire, as seemed
to him, fastened his horse to the very ring he had tied him
to that morning, when he gaed to wait on the young Sir
John.

'God!' said my father, 'if Sir Robert's death be but a
dream!'

He knocked at the ha' door, just as he was wont, and
his auld acquaintance, Dougal Mac Callum, just after his
wont, too, came to open the door, and said, 'Piper Steenie,
are ye there, lad? Sir Robert has been crying for you.'

My gudesire was like a man in a dream—he looked for
the stranger, but he was gaen for the time. At last, he just
tried to say, 'Ha! Dougal Driveower, are ye living? I
thought ye had been dead.'

"Never fash yoursell wi' me,' said Dougal, 'but look to

50

yoursell; and see ye tak naething frae onybody here, neither meat, drink, or siller, except just the receipt that is your ain.'

So saying, he led the way out through halls and trances that were weel kenn'd to my gudesire, and into the auld oak parlour; and there was as much singing of profane sangs, and birling of red wine, and speaking blasphemy and sculduddry, as had ever been in Redgauntlet Castle when it was at the blythest.

But, Lord take us in keeping! what a set of ghastly revellers they were that sat round that table!—My gudesire kenn'd many that had long before gone to their place. There was the fierce Middleton, and the dissolute Rothes, and the crafty Lauderdale; and Dalyell, with his bald head and a beard to his girdle; and Earlshall, with Cameron's blude on his hand; and wild Bonshaw, that tied blessed Mr. Cargill's limbs till the blude sprung; and Dumbarton Douglas, the twice-turned traitor baith to country and king. There was the Bluidy Advocate Mac Kenyie, who, for his worldly wit and wisdom, had been to the rest as a god. And there was Claverhouse, as beautiful as when he lived, with his long, dark, curled locks, streaming down to his laced buff-coat, and his left hand always on his right spule-blade, to hide the wound that the silver bullet had made. He sat apart from them all, and looked at them with a melancholy, haughty countenance; while the rest hallooed, and sung, and laughed, that the room rang. But their smiles were fearfully contorted from time to time; and their laughter passed into such wild sounds, as made my gudesire's very nails grow blue, and chilled the marrow in his bones.

They that waited at the table were jast the wicked serving-man troopers, that had done their work and wicked bidding on earth. There was the Land Lad of the Nethertown, that helped to take Argyll; and the Bishop's summoner, that they called the Deil's Rattlebag; and the wicked guardsmen, in their laced coats; and the savage Highland Amorities, that shed blood like water; and many a proud serving-man, haughty of heart and bloody of hand, cringing to the rich, and making them wickeder than they would be; grinding the poor to powder, when the rich had broken them to fragments. And many, many mair were coming ganging, a' as busy in their vocation as if they had been alive.

Sir Robert Redgauntlet, in the midst of a' this fearful riot, cried wi' a voice like thunder, on Steenie Piper, to come to the board-head where he was sitting; his legs stretched out before him, and swathed up with flannel, with his holster pistols aside him, and great broadsword rested against his chair, must as my gudesire had seen him the last time upon earth—the very cushion for the jack-an-ape was close to him, but the creature itsell was not there—it wasna its hour, it's likely; for he heard them say as he came forward, 'Is not the Major come yet?' And another answered, 'The jack-an-ape will be here be times in the morn.' And when my gudesire came forward, Sir Robert or his ghost, or the devil in his likeness, said, 'Weel. Piper, hae ye settled wi' my son for the year's rent?'

With much ado my father got breath to say, that Sir John would not settle without his honour's receipt.

'Ye shall hae that for a tune of the pipes, Steenie,' said the appearance of Sir Robert—'Play us up "Weel hoddled, Luckie".'

Now this was a tune my gudesire learned frae a warlock, that heard it when they were worshipping Satan at their meetings; and my gudesire had sometimes play it at the ranting suppers in Redgauntlet Castle, but never very willingly; and now he grew cauld at the very name of it, and said for excuse, he hadna his pipes wi' him.

'Mac Callum, ye limb of Beelzebub,' said the fearfu' Sir Robert, 'bring Steenie the pipes that I am keeping for him!'

Mac Callum brought a pair of pipes that might have served the piper of Donald and of Isles. But he gave my gudesire a nudge as he offered them; and looking secretly and closely, Steenie saw that the chanter was of steel, and heated to a white heat; so he had fair warning not to trust his fingers with it. So he excused himself again, and said, he was faint and frightened, and had not wind aneugh to fill the bag.

52

'Then ye maun eat and drink, Steenie,' said the figure; 'for we do little else here; and it's ill speaking between a full man and a fasting.'

Now these were the very words that the bloody Earl of Douglas said to keep the king's messenger in hand, while he cut the head off Mac Lellan of Bombie, at the Threave Castle; and that put Steenie mair and mair on his guard. So he spoke up like a man, and said he came neither to eat or drink, or make minstrelsy; but simply for his ain— to ken what was come o' the money he had paid, and to get a discharge for it, and he was so stout-hearted by this time, that he charged Sir Robert for conscience-sake—(he had no power to say the holy name)—and as he hoped for peace and rest, to spread no snares for him, but just to give him his ain.

The appearance gnashed its teeth and laughed, but it took from a large pocket-book the receipt, and handed it to Steenie. 'Here is your receipt, ye pitiful cur; and for the money, my dogwhelp of a son may go look for it in the Cat's Cradle.'

My gudesire uttered mony thanks, and was about to retire, when Sir Robert roared aloud, 'Stop though, thou sack-doudling son of a whore! I am not done with thee. Here we do nothing for nothing; and you must return on this very day twelvemonth, to pay your master the homage that you owe me for my protection.'

My father's tongue was loosed of a suddenty, and he said aloud, 'I refer myself to God's pleasure, and not to yours.'

He had no sooner uttered the word than all was dark around him; and he sunk on the earth with such a sudden shock, that he lost both breath and sense.

How lang Steenie lay there he could not tell; but when he came to himself, he was lying in the auld kirkyard of Redgauntlet parishine, just at the door of the family aisle, and the scutcheon of the auld knight, Sir Robert, hanging over his head. There was a deep morning fog on grass and gravestone around him, and his horse was feeding quietly

53

beside the minister's twa cows. Steenie would have thought the whole was a dream, but he had the receipt in his hand, fairly written and signed by the auld Laird; only the last letters of his name were a little disorderly, written like one seized with sudden pain.

Sorely troubled in his mind, he left that dreary place, rode through the mist to Redgauntlet Castle, and with much ado he got speech of the Laird. 'Well, you dyvour' was the first word, 'have you brought me my rent?'

'No,' answered my gudesire, 'I have not; but I have brought your honour Sir Robert's receipt for it.'

'How, Sirrah?—Sir Robert's receipt!—You told me he had not given you one.'

'Will your honour please to see if that bit line is right?'

Sir John looked at every line, and at every letter, with much attention and at last, at the date, which my gudesire had not observed—*From my appointed place,*' he read, '*this twenty-fifth of November*'. 'What!—That is yesterday!—Villain, thou must have gone to hell for this!'

'I got it from your honour's father—whether he be in heaven or hell, I know not,' said Steenie.

'I will debate you for a warlock to the Privy Council!' said Sir John. 'I will send you to your master, the devil, with the help of a tar-barrel and a torch!'

'I intend to delate mysell to the Presbytery,' said Steenie, 'and tell them all I have seen last night, whilk are things fitter for them to judge of than a borrel man like me.'

Sir John paused, composed himself, and desired to hear the full history; and my gudesire told it him from point to point, as I have told it you—word for word, neither more nor less.

Sir John was silent again for a long time, and at last he said, very composedly 'Steenie, this story of yours concerns the honour of many a noble family besides mine; and if it be a leasing-making, to keep yourself out of my danger, the least you can expect is to have a redhot iron driven through your tongue, and that will be as bad as scauding your fingers wi' a red-hot chanter; But yet it may be true,

54

Steenie; and if the money cast up, I will not know what to think of it.—But where shall we find the Cat's Cradle? There are cats enough about the old house, but I think they kitten without the ceremony of bed or cradle.'

'We were best ask Hutcheon,' said my gudesire; 'he kens a' the odd corners about as weel as—another serving-man that is now gane, and that I wad not like to name.'

Aweel, Hutcheon, when he was asked, told them, that a ruinous turret, lang disused, next to the clock-house, only accessible by a ladder, for the opening was on the outside and far above the battlements, was called of old the Cat's Cradle.

'There will I go immediately,' said Sir John; and he took (with what purpose, heaven kens), one of his father's pistols from the halltable, where they had lain since the night he died, and hastened to the battlements.

It was a dangerous place to climb, for the ladder was auld and frail, and wanted ane or twa rounds. However, up got Sir John, and entered at the turret door, where his body stopped the only little light that was in the bit turret. Something flees at him wi' a vengeance, maist dang him back ower—bang gaed the knight's pistol, and Hutcheon that held the ladder, and my gudesire that stood beside him, hears a loud skelloch. A minute after Sir John flings the body of the jack-an-ape down to them, and cries that the siller is found, and that they should come up and help him. And there was the bag of siller sure aneugh, and many other things besides, that had been missing for many a day. And Sir John, when he had riped the turret weel, led my gudesire into the dining-parlour, and took him by the hand, and spoke kindly to him, and said he was sorry he should have doubted his word, and that he would hereafter be a good master to him, to make amends.

'And now, Steenie,' said Sir John, 'although this vision of yours tends, on the whole, to my father's credit, as an honest man, that he should, even after his death, desire to see justice done to a poor man like you, yet you are sensible that ill-dispositioned men might make bad constructions upon it, concerning his soul's health. So, I think, we had better lay the whole dirdum on that ill-deedie creature, Major Weir, and say naething about your dream in the wood of Pitmurkie. You had taken ower mickle brandy to be very certain about anything; and, Steenie, this receipt (his hand shook while he held it out)—it's but a queer document, and we will do best, I think, to put it quietly in the fire.'

'Od, but for as queer as it is, it's a' the voucher I have for my rent,' said my gudesire, who was afraid, it may be, of losing the benefit of Sir Robert's discharge.

'I will bear the contents to your credit in the rental-book, and give you a discharge under my own hand,' said Sir John, 'and that on the spot. And, Steenie, if you can hold your tongue about this matter, you shall sit, from this term downward at an easier rent.'

'Many thanks to your honour,' said Steenie, who saw easily in what corner the wind sat; 'doubtless I will be conformable to all your honour's commands; only I would willingly speak wi' some powerful minister on the subject, for I do not like the sort of summons of appointment whilk your honour's father—'

Do not call the phantom my father!' said Sir John, interrupting him.

'Weel then, the thing that was so like him,' said my gudesire; 'he spoke of my coming back to him this time twelvemonth, and it's weight on my conscience.' 'Aweel, then,' said Sir John, 'if you be so much distressed in mind, you may speak to our minister of the parish; he is a douce man, regards the honour of our family, and the mair that may look for some patronage from me.'

Wi that, my father readily agreed that the receipt should be burnt, and the Laird threw it into the fire with his ain hand. Burn it would not for them, though; but away it flew up the chimney, wi' a long train of sparks at his tail, and a hissing noise like a squib.

My gudesire gaed down to the Manse, and the minister when he had heard the story, said, it was his real opinion,

56

that though my gudesire had gaen very far in tampering with dangerous matters, yet, as he had refused the devil's arles (for such was the offer of meat and drink) and had refused to do homage by piping at his bidding, he hoped, that if he held a circumspect walk hereafter, Satan could take little advantage by what was come and gane. And, indeed, my gudesire, of his ain accord, lang forswore baith the pipes and the brandy—it was not even till the year was out, and the fatal day passed, that he would as much as take the fiddle, or drink usquebaugh or tippenny.

Sir John made up his story about the jack-an-ape as he liked himself; and some believe till this day there was no more in the matter than the filching nature of the brute. Indeed ye'll no hinder some to threap, that it was nane o' the Auld Enemy that Dougal and my gudesire saw in the Laird's room, but only that wanchancy creature, the Major capering on the coffin; and that, as to the blowing on the, Laird's whistle that was heard after he was dead, the filthy brute could do that as weel as the Laird himself, if no better. But heaven kens the truth, whilk first came out by the minister's wife, after Sir John and her ain gudeman were baith in the moulds. And then my gudesire, who was failed in his limbs, but not in his judgment or memory— at least nothing to speak of—was obliged to tell the real narrative to his friends, for the credit of his gude name. He might else have been charged for a warlock.

THE BLACK FERRY

by John Galt

JOHN GALT (*1779–1839*), *though a contemporary of Sir Walter Scott, felt himself constantly overshadowed by the older man and indeed wrote in his declining years, 'What a cursed fellow that Walter Scott has been to drive me out of my original line.' None the less, Galt was a man of considerable literary skill as well as a pioneer settler in the best Scottish tradition. Born in Irvine and educated at Greenock, he was forced to travel for health reasons and in the Levant met Lord Byron (of whom he was to write a distinguished biography in 1834). On his return he began a prodigious flow of novels and drama, the most outstanding of these being* The Annals of the Parish *published in 1821. He was deeply interested in Scotland's 'rich stock of goblin lore' and also in tales of witchcraft and superstition and this is evident in quite a number of his stories. In 1826 Galt went to Canada where he founded the town of Guelph and played a minor part in settling new colonists and administering immigration. However, the work sadly brought about his financial ruin and three years later he was forced to return to Scotland where he lived out his remaining years in Greenock. John Galt is probably best remembered for his ability in portraying the 'feeling' of humour and pathos which is so much a part of life in small Scottish towns and villages. In 'The Black Ferry' he demonstrates, also, his skill at depicting terror of the unknown and mastery of the 'grue'.*

I was then returning from my first session at college. The weather had for some time been uncommonly wet, every brook and stream was swollen far beyond its banks, the meadows were flooded, and the river itself was increased to a raging Hellespont, insomuch that the ferry was only practicable for an hour before and after high tide.

The day was showery and stormy, by which I was detained at the inn until late in the afternoon, so that it was dark before I reached the house, and the tide did not serve for safe crossing until midnight. I was therefore obliged to sit by the fire and wait the time, a circumstance which gave me some uneasiness, for the ferryman was old and infirm, and Dick his son, who usually attended the boat during the night, happened to be then absent, the day having been such that it was not expected any travellers would seek to pass over that night.

The presence of Dick was not, however, absolutely necessary, for the boat swung from side to side by a rope anchored in the middle of the stream, and, on account of the strong current, another rope had been stretched across by which passengers could draw themselves over without assistance, an easy task to those who had the sleight of it, but it was not so to me, who still wore my arm in a sling.

While sitting at the fireside conversing with the ferryman and his wife, a smart, good-looking country lad, with a recruit's cockade in his hat, came in, accompanied by a young woman who was far advanced in pregnancy. They were told the state of the ferry, and that unless the recruit undertook to conduct the boat himself, they must wait the return of Dick.

They had been only that day married, and were on their way to join a detachment of the regiment in which Ralph Nocton, as the recruit was called, had that evening enlisted, the parish officers having obliged him to marry the girl. Whatever might have been their former love and intimacy, they were not many minutes in the house when he became sullen and morose towards her; nor was she more amiable towards him. He said little, but he often looked at her with an indignant eye, as she reproached him for having so rashly enlisted, to abandon her and his

59

unborn baby, assuring him that she would never part from him while life and power lasted.

Though it could not be denied that she possessed both beauty and an attractive person, there was yet a silly vixen humour about her ill calculated to conciliate. I did not therefore wonder to hear that Nocton had married her with reluctance; I only regretted that the parish officers were so inaccessible to commiseration, and so void of conscience as to be guilty of rendering the poor fellow miserable for life to avert the hazard of the child becoming a burden on the parish.

The ferryman and his wife endeavoured to reconcile them to their lot; and the recruit, who appeared to be naturally reckless and generous, seemed willing to be appeased; but his weak companion was capricious and pettish. On one occasion, when a sudden shower beat hard against the window, she cried out, with little regard to decorum, that she would go no farther that night.

'You may do as you please, Mary Blake,' said Nocton, 'but go I must, for the detachment marches tomorrow morning. It was only to give you time to prepare to come with me that the Captain consented to let me remain so late in the town.'

She, however, only remonstrated bitterly at his cruelty in forcing her to travel, in her condition, and in such weather. Nocton refused to listen to her, but told her somewhere doggedly, more so than was consistent with the habitual cheerful cast of his physiognomy, 'that although he had already been ruined by her, he trusted she had not yet the power to make him a deserter'.

He then went out, and remained some time alone. When he returned, his appearance was surprisingly changed; his face was of an ashy paleness; his eyes bright, febrile and eager, and his lip quivered as he said:

'Come, Mary, I can wait no longer; the boat is ready, the river is not so wild, and the rain is over.'

In vain she protested; he was firm; and she had no option but either to go or to be left behind. The old ferryman accompanied them to the boat, saw them embark, and gave the recruit some instruction how to manage the ropes, as it was still rather early in the tide. On returning into the house, he remarked facetiously to his wife:

'I can never see why young men should be always blamed, and all pity reserved for the damsels.'

At this moment a rattling shower of rain and hail burst like a platoon of small shot on the window, and a flash of vivid lightning was followed by one of the most tremendous peals of thunder I have ever heard.

'Hark!' cried the old woman, starting, 'was not that a shriek?' We listened, but the cry was not repeated; we rushed to the door, but no other sound was heard than the raging of the river, and the roar of the sea-waves breaking on the bar.

Dick soon after came home, and the boat having swung back to her station, I embarked with him, and reached the opposite inn, where I soon went to bed. Scarcely had I laid my head on the pillow when a sudden inexplicable terror fell upon me; I shook with an unknown horror; I was, as it were, conscious that some invisible being was hovering beside me, and could hardly muster fortitude enough to refrain from rousing the house. At last I fell asleep; it was perturbed and unsound; strange dreams and vague fears scared me awake, and in them were dreadful images of a soldier murdering a female, and open graves and gibbet-irons swinging in the wind. My remembrance, has no parallel to such another night.

In the morning the cloud on my spirit was gone, and I rose at my accustomed hour, and cheerily resumed my journey. It was a bright morning, all things were glittering and fresh in the rising sun, the recruit and his damsel were were entirely forgotten, and I thought no more of them.

But when the night returned next year, I was seized with an unaccountable dejection; it weighed me down; I tried to shake it off, but was unable; the mind was diseased, and could no more by resolution shake off its discomfort, than the body by activity can expel a fever. I retired to my bed greatly depressed, but nevertheless I fell asleep. At midnight, however, I was summoned to awake by a hideous and undefinable terror; it was the same vague consciousness of some invisible visitor being near that I had once before experienced, as I have described, and I again recollected Nocton and Mary Blake in the same instant; I saw—for I cannot now believe that it was less than apparitional—the unhappy pair reproaching one another.

As I looked, questioning the integrity of my sight, the wretched bride turned round and looked at me. How shall I express my horror, when, for the ruddy beauty which she once possessed, I beheld the charnel visage of a skull; I started up and cried aloud with such alarming vehemence that the whole inmates of the house, with lights in their hands, were instantly in the room—shame would not let me tell what I had seen, and, endeavouring to laugh, I accused the nightmare of the disturbance.

This happened while I was at a watering-place on the west coast. I was living in a boarding-house with several strangers; among them was a tall pale German gentleman, of a grave impressive physiognomy. He was the most intelligent and shrewdest observer I have ever met with, and he had to a singular degree the gift of a discerning spirit. In the morning when we rose from the breakfast-table, he took me by the arm, and led me out upon the lawn in front of the house; and when we were at some distance from the rest of the company, said:

'Excuse me, sir, for I musk ask an impertinent question. Was it indeed the dream of the nightmare that alarmed you last night?'

'I have no objection to answer you freely; but tell me first why you ask such a question?'

'It is but reasonable. I had a friend who was a painter; none ever possessed an imagination which discerned better how nature in her mysteries should appear. One of his pictures was the scene of Brutus when his evil genius summoned him to Phillipi, and strange to tell, you bear some resemblance to the painted Brutus. When, with the others, I broke into your room last night, you looked so like the Brutus in his picture that I could have sworn you were amazed with the vision of a ghost.'

I related to him what I have done to you.

'It is wonderful,' said he, 'what inconceivable sympathy hath linked you to the fate of these unhappy persons. There is something more in this renewed visitation than the phantasma of a dream.'

The remark smote me with an uncomfortable sensation of dread, and for a short time my flesh crawled as it were upon my bones. But the impression soon wore off, and was again entirely forgotten.

When the anniversary again returned, I was seized with the same heaviness and objectless horror of mind; it hung upon me with bodings and auguries until I went to bed, and then after my first sleep I was a third time roused by another fit of the same inscrutable panic. On this occasion, however, the vision was different. I beheld only Nocton, pale and wounded, stretched on a bed, and on the coverlet lay a pair of new epaulettes, as if just unfolded from a paper.

For seven years I was thus annually afflicted. The vision in each was different, but I saw no more of Mary Blake. On the fourth occasion, I beheld Nocton sitting in the uniform of an aide-de-camp at a table, with the customary tokens of conviviality before him; it was only part of a scene, such as one beholds in a mirror.

On the fifth occasion, he appeared to be ascending, sword in hand, the rampart of a battery; the sun was setting behind him, and the shadows and forms of a strange land, with the domes and pagodas of an oriental country, lay in wide extent around. it was a picture, but far more vivid than painting can exhibit.

On the sixth time, he appeared again stretched upon a couch; his complexion was sullen, not from wounds, but disease, and there appeared at his bedside the figure of a general officer, with a star on his breast, with whose conversation he appeared pleased, though languid.

But on the seventh and last occasion on which the horrors of the visions were repeated, I saw him on horseback in a field of battle; and while I looked at him, he was struck on the face by a sabre, and the blood flowed down upon his regimentals.

Years passed after this, during which I had none of these dismal exhibitions. My mind and memory resumed their healthful tone. I recollected, without these intervening years of oblivion, Nocton and Mary Blake, occasionally as one thinks of things past, and I told my friends of the curios periodical returns of the visitations to me as remarkable metaphysical phenomena. By an odd coincidence, it so happened that my German friend was always present when I related my dreams. He in the intervals sometimes spoke to me of them, but my answers were vague, for my reminiscences were imperfect. It was not so with him. All I told he distinctly recorded and preserved in a book wherein he wrote down the minutest thing that I had witnessed in my visions. I do not mention his name, because he is a modest and retiring man, in bad health, and who has long sequestered himself from company. His rank, however, is so distinguished that his name could not be stated without the hazard of exposing him to impertinent curiosity. But to proceed.

Exactly fourteen years—twice seven it was—I remember well, because for the first seven I had been haunted as I have described, and for the other seven I had been placid in my living. At the end of that period of fourteen years, my German friend paid me a visit here. He came in the forenoon, and we spent an agreeable day together, for he was a man of much recondite knowledge. I have seen none so wonderfully possessed of all sorts of occult learning.

He was an astrologer of true kind, for on him it was not a pretence but a science; he scorned horoscopes and fortune-tellers with the just derision of a philosopher, but he had a beautiful conception of the reciprocal dependencies of nature. He affected not to penetrate to causes, but he spoke of effects with a luminous and religious eloquence.

He described to me how the tides followed the phases of the moon; but he denied the Newtonian notion that they were caused by the procession of the lunar changes. He explained to me that when the sun entered Aries, and the other signs of the zodiac, how his progression could be traced on this earth by the development of plants and flowers, and the passions, diseases, and affections of animals and man; but that the stars were more than the celestial signs of these terrestrial phenomena he ridiculed as the conceptions of the insane theory.

His learning in the curious art of alchymy was equally sublime. He laughed at the fancy of an immortal elixir, and his notion of the mythology of the philosopher's stone was the very essence and spirituality of ethics. The elixir of immortality he described to me as an allegory, which, from its component parts, emblems of talents and virtues, only showed that perseverance, industry, goodwill, and a gift from God were the requisite ingredients necessary to attain renown.

His knowledge of the philosopher's stone was still more beautiful. He referred to the writings of the Rosicrucians, whose secrets were couched in artificial symbols, to prove that the sages of that sect were not the fools that the lesser wise of later days would represent them. The self-denial, the patience, the humility, the trusting in God, the treasuring of time by lamp and calculation which the venerable alchymists recommended, he used to say, were only the elements which constitute the conduct of the youth that would attain to riches and honour; and these different stages which are illuminated in the alchymical volumes as descriptive of stages in the process of making the stone were but hieroglyphical devices to explain the effects of well-applied human virtue and industry.

To me it was amazing to what clear simplicity he reduced all things, and on what a variety of subjects his bright and splendid fancy threw a fair and effecting light. All those demi-sciences—physiognomy—palmistry—scaileology, etc., even magic and witchcraft, obtained from his interpretations a philosophical credibility.

In disquisitions on these subjects we epent the anniversary. He had by them enlarged the periphery of my comprehension; he had added to my knowledge, and inspired me with a profounder respect for himself.

He was an accomplished musician, in the remotest, if I may use the expression, depths of the art. His performance on the pianoforte was simple, heavy, and seemingly the labour of an unpractised hand, but his expression was beyond all epithet exquisite and solemn; his airs were grave, devotional, and pathetic, consisting of the simplest harmonic combinations; but they were wonderful; every note was a portion of an invocation; every melody the voice of a passion or a felling supplied with elocution.

We had spent the days in the fields, where he illustrated his astrological opinions by appeals to plants, and leaves, and flowers, and other attributes of the season, with such delighful perspicuity that no time can efface from the registers of my memory the substance of his courses. In the evening he delighted me with his miraculous music, and, as the night advanced, I was almost persuaded that he was one of those extraordinary men who are said sometimes to acquire communion with spirits and dominion over demons.

Just as we were about to sit down to our frugal supper, literally or philosophically so, as if it had been served for Zeno himself, Dick, the son of the old ferryman, who by this time was some years dead, came to the door, and requested to speak with me in private. Of course I obeyed, when he informed me that he had brought across the ferry that night a gentleman officer, from a far country, who was in bad health, and whom he could not accommodate properly in the ferry-house.

'The inn,' said Dick, 'is too far off, for he is lame, and has an open wound in the thigh. I have therefore ventured to bring him here, sure that you will be glad to give him a bed for the night. His servant tells me that he was esteemed the bravest officer in all the service in the Mysore of India.'

It was impossible to resist this appeal. I went to the door where the gentleman was waiting, and with true-heartedness expressed how great my satisfaction would be if my house could afford him any comfort.

I took him in with me to the room where my German friend was sitting. I was much pleased with the gentleness and unaffected simplicity of his manners.

He was a handsome middle-aged man—his person was robust and well formed—his features had been originally handsome, but they were disfigured by a scar, which had materially changed their symmetry. His conversation was not distinguished by any remarkable intelligence, but after the high intellectual excitement which I had enjoyed all day with my philosophical companion, it was agreeable and gentlemanly.

Several times during supper, something came across my mind as if I had seen him before, but I could neither recollect when nor where; and I observed that more than once he looked at me as if under the influence of some research in his memory. At last, I observed that his eyes were dimmed with tears, which assured me that he then recollected me. But I considered it a duty of hospitality not to inquire aught concerning him more than he was pleased to tell himself.

In the meantime, my German friend, I perceived, was watching us both, but suddenly he ceased to be interested, and appeared abosrbed in thought, while good manners required me to make some efforts to entertain my guest. This led on to some inquiry concerning the scene of his services, and he told us that he had been many years in India.

'On this day eight years ago,' said he, 'I was in the battle of Borupknow, where I received the wound which has so disfigured me in the face.'

At that moment I accidentally threw my eyes upon my German friend—the look which he gave me in answer caused me to shudder from head to foot, and I began to ruminate of Nocton the recruit, and Mary Blake, while my friend continued the conversation in a light desultory manner, as it would have seemed to any stranger, but to me it was awful and oracular. He spoke to the stranger on all manner of topics, but ever and anon he brought him back, as if without design, to speak of the accidents of fortune which had befallen him on the anniversary of that day, giving it as a reason for his curious remarks that most men observed anniversaries, time and experience having taught them to notice that there were curious coincidences with respect to times, and places, and individuals—things which of themselves form part of the great demonstration of the wisdom and skill displayed in the construction, not only of the mechanical, but the mortal world, showing that each was a portion of one and the same thing.

'I have been,' said he to the stranger, 'an observer and recorder of such things. I have my book of registration here in this house; I will fetch it from my bed-chamber, and we shall see in what other things, as far as your fortunes have been concerned, how it corresponds with the accidents of your life on this anniversary.'

I observed that the stranger paled a little at this proposal, and said, with an affectation of carelessness while he was evidently disturbed, that he would see it in the morning. But the philosopher was too intent upon his purpose to forbear. I know not what came upon me, but I urged him to bring the book. This visibly disconcerted the stranger still more, and his emotion became, as it were, a motive which induced me, in a peremptory manner, to require the production of the book, for I felt that strange horror, so often experienced, returning upon me; and was constrained, by an irresistible impulse, to seek an explanation of the circumstances by which I had for so many years suffered such an eclipse of mind.

The stranger seeing how intent both of us were, desisted from his wish to procrastinate the curious disclosure which my friend said he could make; but it was evident he was not at ease. Indeed he was so much the reverse, that when the German went for his book, he again proposed to retire, and only consented to abide at my jocular entreaty, until he should learn what his future fortunes were to be, by the truth of what would be told him of the past.

My friend soon returned with the book. It was a remarkable volume, covered with vellum, shut with three brazen clasps, secured by a lock of curious construction. Altogether it was a strange, antique, and necromantic-looking volume. The corner was studded with knobs of brass, with a small mirror in the centre, round which were inscribed in Teutonic characters words to the effect, 'I WILL SHOW THEE THYSELF'. Before unlocking the clasp, my friend gave the book to the stranger, explained some of the emblematic devices which adorned the cover, and particularly the words of the motto that surrounded the little mirror.

Whether it was from design, or that the symbols required it, the explanations of my friend were mystical and abstruse; and I could see that they produced an effect on the stranger, so strong that it was evident he could with difficulty maintain his self-possession. The colour entirely faded from his contenance; he became wan and cadaverous, and his hand shook violently as he returned the volume to the philosopher, who, on receiving it back, said:

'There are things in this volume which may not be revealed to every eye, yet to those who may not discover to what they relate, they will seem trivial notations.'

He then applied the key to the lock, and unclosed the volume. My stranger guest began to breathe hard and audibly. The German turned over the vellum leaves searchingly and carefully. At last he found the record and description of my last vision, which he read aloud. It was not only minute in the main circumstances in which I had seen Nocton, but it contained an account of many things, the still life, as it is called, of the picture, which I had forgotten, and among other particulars a picturesque account of the old General whom I saw standing at the bedside.

'By all that's holy,' cried the stranger, 'it is old Cripplington himself—the queue of his hair was, as you say, always

crooked, owing to a habit he had of pulling it when vexed—
where could you find the description of all this?'

I was petrified; I sat motionless as a statue, but a fearful
vibration thrilled through my whole frame.

My friend looked back in his book, and found the description of my sixth vision. It contained the particulars of
the crisis of battle in which, as the stranger described, he
had received the wound in his face. It affected him less
than the other, but still the effect upon him was impressive.

The record of the fifth vision produced a more visible
alarm. The description was vivid to an extreme degree—
the appearance of Nocton, sword in hand, on the rampart—
the animation of the assault, and the gorgeous landscape
of domes and pagodas, was limned with words as vividly
as a painter could have made the scene. The stranger
seemed to forget his anxiety, and was delighted with the
reminiscences which the description recalled.

But when the record of the fourth vision was read,
wherein Nocton was described as sitting in the regimentals
of an aide-de-camp, at a convivial table, he explained, as
if unconscious of his words:

'It was on that night I had first the honour of dining
with the German general.'

The inexorable philosopher proceeded, and read what I
had told him of Nocton, stretched pale and wounded on
a bed, with new epaulettes spread on the coverlet, as if
just unfolded from a paper. The stranger started from his
seat, and cried with a hollow and fearful voice:

'This is the book of life.'

The German turned over to the second vision, which he
read slowly and mournfuly, especially the description of my
own feelings, when I beheld the charnel visage of Mary
Blake. The stranger, who had risen from his seat, and was
panting with horror, cried out with a shrill howl, as it
were:

'Oh that night as I was sitting in my tent, methought her
spirit came and reproached me.'

I could not speak, but my German friend rose from his

70

seat, and holding the volume in his left hand, touched it with his right, and looking sternly at the stranger, said:

'In this volume, and in your own conscience, are the evidences which prove that you are Ralph Nocton, and that on this night, twice seven years ago, you murdered Mary Blake.'

The miserable stranger lost all self-command, and cried in consternation:

'It is true, the waters raged; the rain and the hail came; she bitterly upbraided me; I flung her from the boat; the lightning flashed, and the thunder—Oh! it was not so dreadful as her drowning execrations.'

Before any answer could be given to this confession, he staggered from the spot, and almost in the same instant fell dead upon the floor.

THE BROWNIE OF THE BLACK HAGGS

by James Hogg

JAMES HOGG (*1770–1835*), *known in Scotland as the* '*Ettrick Shepherd*' *because of his rural upbringing, is probably better known to the world at large as the author of the remarkable* Private Memoirs and Confessions of a Justified Sinner (*1824*), *which in its portrayal of a man with a split personality anticipated so many tales to follow. Hogg, born in Ettrick, Selkirkshire, had scant formal education but received an invaluable schooling in the native lore and traditions of his country from his mother and father. These ballads and legends of the powers of darkness he committed to paper with dedicated fervour— and then in 1801, through a chance meeting with Sir Walter Scott, was invited to contribute material for inclusion in the great writer's forthcoming publication,* Border Minstrelsy (*1803*). *This was not an automatic passport to success for Hogg, however, and after a number of unsuccessful collections of verse—and an attempt at farming—he moved to Edinburgh and there concentrated on prose. In 1813 he at last found recognition with the publication of* The Queen's Wake *and his fortunes never looked back. In the closing years of his life he was a familiar figure in Edinburgh society and even rather grandly titled himself* '*The King of the Mountain and Fairy School*'. *The story here is taken from* The Shepherd's Calendar (*1829*) *and combines many of the elements which Hogg depicted so well in his work, local lore, retribution and natural and supernatural evil; even the author himself said of it,* '*I never*

*heard any story like it and however ridiculous it may
appear it has made a dreadful impression on my mind'.*

When the Sprots were Lairds of Wheelhope, which is
now a long time ago, there was one of the ladies who was
very badly spoken of in the country. People did not just
openly assert that Lady Wheelhope (for every landward
laird's wife was then styled Lady) was a witch, but every
one had an aversion even at hearing her named; and when
by chance she happened to be mentioned, old men would
shake their heads and say, 'Ah! let us alane o' her! The
less ye meddle wi' her the better.' Old wives would give
over spinning, and, as a pretence for hearing what might
be said about her, poke in the fire with the tongs, cocking
up their ears all the while; and then, after some meaning
coughs, hems, and haws, would haply say, 'Hech-wow, sirs!
An a' be true that's said!' or something equally wise and
decisive.

In short, Lady Wheelhope was accounted a very bad
woman. She was an inexorable tyrant in her family, quarrelled with her servants, often cursing them, striking them,
and turning them away; especially if they were religious,
for she could not endure people of that character, but
charged them with every thing bad. Whenever she found
out that any of the servant men of the Laird's establishment
were religious, she gave them up to the military, and got
them shot; and several girls that were regular in their
devotions, she was supposed to have got rid of by poison.
She was certainly a wicked woman, else many good people
were mistaken in her character; and the poor persecuted
Covenanters were obliged to unite in their prayers against
her.

As for the Laird, he was a big, dun-faced, pluffy body,
that cared neither for good nor evil, and did not well
know the one from the other. He laughed at his lady's
tantrums and barley-hoods; and the greater the rage that
she got into, the Laird thought it the better sport. One day,
when two maid-servants came running to him, in great

73

agitation, and told him that his lady had felled one of their companions, the Laird laughed heartily, and said he did not doubt it.

'Why, sir, how can you laugh?' said they. 'The poor girl is killed.'

'Very likely, very likely,' said the Laird. 'Well, it will teach her to take care who she angers again.'

'And, sir, your lady will be hanged.'

'Very likely; well, it will teach her not to strike so rashly again—Ha, ha, ha! Will it not, Jessy?'

But when this same Jessy died suddenly one morning, the Laird was greatly confounded, and seemed dimly to comprehend that there had been unfair play going. There was little doubt that she was taken off by poison; but whether the Lady did it through jealously or not, was never divulged; but it greatly bamboozled and astonished the poor Laird, for his nerves failed him, and his whole frame became paralytic. He seems to have been exactly in the same state of mind with a colley that I once had. He was extremely fond of the gun as long as I did not kill anything with it (there being no game laws in Ettrick Forrest in those days), he got a grand chase after the hares when I missed them. But there was one day that I chanced for a marvel to shoot one dead, a few paces before his nose. I'll never forget the astonishment that the poor beast manifested. He stared one while at the gun, and another while at the dead hare, and seemed to be drawing the conclusion, that if the case stood thus, there was no creature sure of its life. Finally, he took his tail between his legs and ran away home, and never would face a gun all his life again.

So was it precisely with Laird Sprot of Wheelhope. As long as his lady's wrath produced only noise and uproar among the servants, he thought it fine sport; but when he saw what he believed the dreadful effects of it, he became like a barrel organ out of tune, and could only discourse one note, which he did to every one he met. 'I wish she mayna hae gotten something she had been the waur of.' This note he repeated early and late, night and day, sleeping

74

and waking, alone and in company, from the moment that Jessy died till she was buried; and on going to the churchyard as chief mourner, he whispered it to her relatives by the way. When they came to the grave, he took his stand at the head, nor would he give place to the girl's father; but there he stood, like a huge post, as though he neither saw nor heard; and when he had lowered her head into the grave and dropped the cord, he slowly lifted his hat with one hand, wiped his dim eyes with the back of the other, and said, in a deep tremulous tone, 'Poor lassie! I wish she didna get something she had been the waur of.'

This death made a great noise among the common people; but there was little protection for the life of the subject in those days; and provided a man or woman was a real Anti-Covenanter, they might kill a good many without being quarrelled for it. So there was no one to take cognizance of the circumstances relating to the death of poor Jessy.

After this the Lady walked softly for the space of two or three years. She saw that she had rendered herself odious, and had entirely lost her husband's countenance, which she liked worst of all. But the evil propensity could not be overcome; and a poor boy, whom the Laird out of sheer compassion had taken into his service, being found dead one morning, the country people could no longer be restrained; so they went in a body to the Sheriff, and insisted on an investigation. It was proved that she detested the boy, had often threatened him, and had given him brose and butter the afternoon before he died; but notwithstanding of all this, the cause was ultimately dismissed, and the pursuers fined.

No one can tell to what height of wickedness she might now have proceeded, had not a check of a very singular kind been laid upon her. Among the servants that came home at the next term, was one who called himself Merodach; and a strange person he was. He had the form of a boy, but the features of one a hundred years old, save that his eyes had a brilliancy and restlessness, which were

75

very extraordinary, bearing a strong resemblance to the eyes of a well-known species of monkey. He was forward and perverse, and disregarded the pleasure or displeasure of any person; but he performed his work well and with apparent ease. From the moment he entered the house, the lady conceived a mortal antipathy against him, and besought the laird to turn him away. But the Laird would not consent; he never turned away any servant, and moreover he had hired this fellow for a trival wage, and he neither wanted activity nor perseverance. The natural consequence of this refusal was, that the Lady instantly set herself to embitter Merodach's life as much as possible, in order to get early quit of a domestic every way so disagreeable. Her hatred of him was not like a common antipathy entertained by one human being against another—she hated him as one might hate a toad or an adder; and his occupation of jotteryman (as the Laird termed his servant of all work) keeping him always about her hand, it must have proved highly annoying.

She scolded him, she raged at him; but he only mocked her wrath, and giggled and laughed at her, with the most provoking derision. She tried to fell him again and again, but never, with all her address, could she hit him; and never did she make a blow at him, that she did not repent it. She was heavy and unwieldy, and he as quick in his motions as a monkey; besides, he generally contrived that she should be in such an ungovernable rage, that when she flew at him, she hardly knew what she was doing. At one time she guided her blow towards him, and he at the same instant avoided it with such dexterity that she knocked down the chief hind, or foresman; and then Merodach giggled so heartily, that, lifting the kitchen poker, she threw it at him with a full design of knocking out his brains; but the missile only broke every article of crockery on the kitchen dresser.

She then hasted to the Laird, crying bitterly, and telling him she would not suffer that wretch Merodach, as she called him, to stay another night in the family.

76

'Why, then, put him away, and trouble me no more about him,' said the Laird.

'Put him away!' exclaimed she, 'I have already ordered him away a hundred times, and charged him never to let me see his horrible face again; but he only grins, and answers with some intolerable piece of impertinence.'

The pertinacity of the fellow amused the Laird; his dim eyes turned upwards into his head with delight; he then looked two ways at once, turned round his back, and laughed till the tears ran down his dun cheeks; but he could only articulate, 'You're fitted now.'

The Lady's agony of rage still increasing from his derision, she upbraided the laird bitterly, and said he was not worthy the name of man, if he did not turn away that pestilence, after the way he had abused her.

'Why, Shusy, my dear, what has he done to you?'

'What done to me! has he not caused me to knock down John Thomson? and I do not know if ever he will come to life again!'

'Have you felled your favourite John Thomson?' said the Laird, laughing more heartily than before; 'you might have done a worse deed than that.'

'And has he not broke every plate and dish on the whole dresser?' continued the Lady; 'and for all this devastation, he only mocks at my displeasure—absolutely mocks me— and if you do not have him turned away, and hanged or shot for his deeds, you are not worthy the name of man.'

'O alack! What a devastation among the cheena metal!' said the laird; and calling on Merodach, he said, 'Tell me, thou evil Merodach of Babylon, how thou daredst knock down thy Lady's favourite servant, John Thomson?'

'Not I, your honour. It was my Lady herself, who got into such a furious rage at me, that she mistook her man, and felled Mr Thomson; and the good man's skull is fractured.'

'That was very odd,' said the Laird, chuckling; 'I do not comprehend it. But then, what set you on smashing all my

77

Lady's delft and cheena ware?—That was a most infamous and provoking action.'

'It was she herself, your honour. Sorry would I be to break one dish belonging to the house. I take all the house servants to witness, that my Lady smashed all the dishes with a poker; and now lays the blame on me!'

The Laird turned his dim eyes on his lady, who was crying with vexation and rage, and seemed meditating another personal attack on the culprit, which he did not at all appear to shun, but rather to court. She, however, vented her wrath in threatenings of the most deep and desperate revenge, the creature all the while assuring her that she would be foiled, and that in all her encounters and contest with him, she would uniformly come to the worst; he was resolved to do his duty, and there before his master he defied her.

The Laird thought more than he considered it prudent to reveal; he had little doubt that his wife would find some means of wreaking her vengeance on the object of her displeasure; and he shuddered when he recollected on who had taken 'something that she had been the waur of'.

In a word, the Lady of Wheelhope's inveterate malignity against this one object, was like the rod of Moses, that swallowed up the rest of the serpents. All her wicked and evil propensities seemed to be superseded if not utterly absorbed by it. The rest of the family now lived in comparative peace and quietness; for early and late her malevolence was venting itself against the jotteryman, and against him alone. It was a delirium of hatred and vengeance, on which the whole bent and bias of her inclination was set. She could not stay from the creature's presence, or, in the intervals when absent from him, she spent her breath in curses and execrations; and then, not able to rest, she ran again to seek him, her eyes gleaming with the anticipated delights of vengeance, while, ever and anon, all the ridicule and the harm rebounded on herself.

Was it not strange that she could not get quit of this sole annoyance of her life? One would have thought she

78

easily might. But by this time there was nothing farther from her wishes; she wanted vengeance, full, adequate, and delicious vengeance, on her audacious opponent. But he was a strange and terrible creature, and the means of retaliation constantly came, as it were, to his hand.

Bread and sweet milk was the only fare that Merodach cared for, and having bargained for that, he would not want it, though he often got it with a curse and with ill will. The Lady having, upon one occasion, intentionally kept back his wonted allowance for some days, on the Sabbath morning following, she set him down a bowl of rich sweet milk, well drugged with a deadly poison; and then she lingered in a little ante-room to watch the success of her grand plot, and prevent any other creature from tasting of the potion. Merodach came in, and the housemaid said to him, 'There is your breakfast, creature.'

'Oho! my Lady has been liberal this morning,' said he; 'but I am beforehand with her. Here, little Missie, you seem very hungry today—take you my breakfast.' And with that he set the beverage down to the Lady's little favourite spaniel. It so happened that the Lady's only son came at that instant into the ante-room seeking her, and teasing his mamma about something, which withdrew her attention from the hall-table for a space. When she looked again, and saw Missie lapping up the sweet milk, she burst from her hiding-place like a fury, screaming as if her head had been on fire, kicked the remainder of its contents against the wall, and lifting Missie in her bosom, retreated hastily, crying all the way.

'Ha, ha, ha—I have you now!' cried Merodach, as she vanished from the hall.

Poor Missie died immediately, and very privately; indeed, she would have died and been buried, and never one have seen her, save her mistress, had not Merodach, by a luck that never failed him, looked over the wall of the flower garden, just as his lady was laying her favourite in a grave of her own digging. She, not perceiving her tormentor, plied on at her task, apostrophising the insensate little

79

carcass—'Ah! poor dear little creature, thou hast had a hard fortune, and has drank of the bitter potion that was not intended for thee; but he shall drink it three times double for thy sake!'

'Is that little Missie?' said the eldrich voice of the jottery-man, close at the lady's ear. She uttered a loud scream, and sank down on the bank. 'Alack for poor Missie!' continued the creature in a tone of mockery, 'my heart is sorry for Missie. What has befallen her—whose breakfast cup did she drink?'

'Hence with thee, fiend!' cried the Lady; 'what right hast thou to intrude on thy mistress's privacy? Thy turn is coming yet; or may the nature of woman change within me!'

'It is changed already,' said the creature, grinning with delight; 'I have thee now, I have thee now! And were it no to show my superiority over thee, which I do every hour, I should soon see thee strapped like a mad cat, or a worrying bratch. What wilt thou try next?'

'I will cut thy throat, and if I die for it, will rejoice in the deed; a deed of charity to all that dwell on the face of the earth.'

'I have warned thee before, dame, and I now warn thee again, that all thy mischief meditated against me will fall double on thine own head.'

'I want none of your warning, fiendish cur. Hence with your elvish face, and take care of yourself.'

It would be too disgusting and horrible to relate or read all the incidents that fell out between this unaccountable couple. Their enmity against each other had no end, and no mitigation; and scarcely a single day passed over on which the Lady's acts of malevolent ingenuity did not terminate fatally for some favourite thing of her own. Scarcely was there a thing, animate or inanimate, on which she set a value, left to her, that was not destroyed; and yet scarcely one hour or minute could she remain absent from her tormentor, and all the while, it seems, solely for the purpose of tormenting him. While all the rest of the

80

establishment enjoyed peace and quietness from the fury of their termagant dame, matters still grew worse and worse between the fascinated pair. The Lady haunted the menial, in the same manner as the raven haunts the eagle, for a perpetual quarrel, though the former knows that in every encounter she is to come off the loser. Noises were heard on the stairs by night, and it was whispered among the servants, that the lady had been seeking Merodach's chamber, on some horrible intent. Several of them would have sworn that they had seen her passing and repassing on the stair after midnight, when all was quiet; but then it was likewise well known that Merodach slept with well-fastened doors, and a companion in another bed in the same room, whose bed, too, was nearest the door. Nobody cared much what became of the jotteryman, for he was an unsocial and disagreeable person; but someone told him what they had seen, and hinted a suspicion of the Lady's intent. But the creature only bit his upper lip, winked with his eyes, and said, 'She had better let that alone; she will be the first to rue that.'

Not long after this, to the horror of the family and the whole countryside, the laird's only son was found murdered in his bed one morning, under circumstances that manifested the most fiendish cruelty and inveteracy on the part of his destroyer. As soon as the astrocious act was divulged, the Lady fell into convulsions, and lost her reason; and happy had it been for her had she never recovered the use of it, for there was blood upon her hand, which she took no care to conceal, and there was little doubt that it was the blood of her own innocent and beloved boy, the sole heir and hope of the family.

This blow deprived the laird of all power of action; but the lady had a brother, a man of the law, who came and instantly proceeded to an investigation of this unaccountable murder. Before the Sheriff arrived, the housekeeper took the lady's brother aside, and told him he had better not go on with the scrutiny, for she was sure the crime would be brought home to her unfortunate mistress; and after examining into several corroborative circumstances, and viewing the state of the raving maniac, with the blood on her hand and arm, he made the investigation a very short one, declaring the domestics all exculpated.

The Laird attended his boy's funeral, and laid his head in the grave, but appeared exactly like a man walking in a trance, an automaton, without feelings or sensations, oftentimes gazing at the funeral procession, as on something he could not comprehend. And when the deathbell of the parish church fell a-tolling, as the corpse approached the kirk-stile, he cast a dim eye up towards the belfry, and said hastily, 'What, what's that? Och ay, we're just in time, just in time.' And often was he hammering over the name of 'Evil Merodach, King of Babylon', to himself. He seemed to have some farfetched conception that his un- accountable jotteryman was in some way connected with the death of his only son, and other lesser calamities, although the evidence in favour of Merodach's innocence was as usual quite decisive.

This grievous mistake of Lady Wheelhope can only be accounted for, by supposing her in a state of derangement, or rather under some evil influence, over which she had no control; and to a person in such a state, the mistake was not so very unnatural. The mansion-house of Wheel- hope was old and irregular. The stair had four acute turns, and four landing-places, all the same. In the uppermost chamber slept the two domestics—Merodach in the bed farthest in, and in the chamber immediately below that, which was exactly similar, slept the Young Laird and his tutor, the former in the bed farthest in; and thus, in the turmoil of her wild and raging passions, her own hand made herself childless.

Merodach was expelled by the family forthwith, but refused to accept of his wages which the man of law pressed upon him, for fear of further mischief; but he went away in apparent sullenness and discontent, no one knowing whither.

When his dismissal was announced to the Lady, who

was watched day and night in her chamber, the news ha
such an effect on her, that her whole frame seemed electri-
fied: the horrors of remorse vanished, and another passion,
which I neither can comprehend nor define, took the sole
possession of her distempered spirit. 'He *must* not go!—
He *shall* not go!' she exclaimed. 'No, no, no—he shall
not—he shall not—he shall not!' and then she instantly set
herself about making ready to follow him, uttering all the
while the most diabolical expressions, indicative of anticipated vengeance. 'Oh, could I but snap his nerves one by
one, and birl among his vitals! Could I but slice his heart
off piecemeal in small messes, and see his blood lopper,
and bubble, and spin away in purple slays: and then to
see him grin, and grin, and grin, and grin! Oh—oh—oh—
How beautiful and grand a sight it would be to see him
grin, and grin, and grin!' And in such a style would she
run on for hours together.

She thought of nothing, she spake of nothing, but the
discarded jotteryman, whom most people now began to
regard as a creature that was 'not canny'. They had seen
him eat and drink, and work, like other people; still he
had that about him that was not like other men. He was
a boy in form, and an antediluvian in feature. Some thought
he was a mongrel, between a Jew and an ape; some a
wizard, some a kelpie, or a fairy, but most of all, that he
was really and truly a Brownie. What he was I do not know,
and therefore will not pretend to say; but be that as it
may, in spite of locks and keys, watching and waking, the
Lady of Wheelhope soon made her escape, and eloped
after him. The attendants, indeed, would have made oath
that she was carried away by some invisible hand, for it
was impossible, they said, that she could have escaped on
foot like other people; and this edition of the story took
in the country; but sensible people viewed the matter in
another light.

As for instance, when Wattie Blythe, the Laird's old
shepherd, came in from the hill one morning, his wife
Bessie thus accosted him. 'His presence be about us,

83

Wattie Blythe! have ye heard what has happened at the ha'? Things are aye turning waur and waur there, and it looks like as if Providence had gi'en up our Laird's house to destruction. This grand estate maun now gang frae the Sprots; for it has finished them.'

'Na, na, Bessie, it isna the estate that has finished the Sprots, but the Sprots that hae finished the estate, and themsells into the boot. They hae been a wicked and degenerate race, and aye the langer the waur, till they hae reached the utmost bounds o' earthly wickedness; and it's time the deil were looking after his ain.'

'Ah, Wattie Blythe, ye never said a truer say. And that's just the very point where your story ends, and mine begins; for hasna the deil, or the fairies, or the brownies, ta'en away our Leddy bodily! and the hail country is running and riding in search o' her; and there is twenty hunder merks offered to the first that can find her, and bring her safe back. They hae ta'en her away, skin and bane, body and soul, and a', Wattie!'

'Hech-wow! but that is awesome! And where is it thought they have ta'en her to, Bessie?'

'O, they hae some guess at that frae her ain hints afore. It is thought they hae carried her after that satan of a creature, wha wrought sae muckle wae about the house. It is for him they are a' looking, for they ken weel, that where they get the tane they will get the tither.'

'Whew! is that the gate o't, Bessie? Why, then, the awfu' story is nouther mair nor less than this, that the Leddy has made a 'lopement, as they ca't, and run away after a blackguard jotteryman. Heck-wow! wae's me for human frailty! But that's just the gate! When aince the deil gets in the point o' his finger, he will soon have in his haill hand. Ay, he wants but a hair to make a tether of, ony day! I hae seen her a braw sonsy lass; but even then I feared she was devoted to destruction, for she aye mockit at religion, Bessie, and that's no a good mark of a young body. And she made a' its servants her enemies; and think you these good men's prayers were a' to blaw away i' the

wind, and be nae mair regarded? Na, na, Bessie, my woman
take ye this mark baithe o' our bairns and other folk's—
If ever ye see a young body that disregards the Sabbath,
and makes a mock at the ordinances o' religion, ye will
never see that body come to muckle good. A braw hand
our Leddy has made o' her gives and jeers at religion, and
her mockeries o' the poor persecuted hill-folk!—sunk down
by degrees into the very dregs o' sin and misery! Run
away after a scullion!'

'Fy, fy, Wattie, how can ye say sae? It was weel kenn'd
that she hatit him wi' a perfect and mortal hatred, and
tried to make away wi' him mae ways nor ane.'

'Aha, Bessie; but nipping and scarting is Scots folk's
wooing; and though it is but right that we suspend our
judgments, there will naebody persuade me if she be found
alang wi' the creature, but that she has run away after him
in the natural way, on her twa shanks, without help either
frae fairy or brownie.'

'I'll never believe sic a thing of ony woman born, let be
a leddy weel up in years.'

'Od help ye, Bessie! ye dinna ken the stretch o' corrupt
nature. The best o' us, when left to oursells, are nae better
than strayed sheep, that will never find the way back to
their ain pastures; and of a' things made o' mortal flesh, a
wicked woman is the warst.'

'Alack-a-day! we got the blame o' muckle that we little
deserve. But, Wattie, keep ye a geyan sharp lookout about
the cleuchs and the caves o' our hope; for the Leddy kens
them a' geyan weel; and gin the twenty hunder merks wad
come our way, it might gang a waur gate. It wad tocher a'
our bonny lasses.'

'Ay, weel I wat, Bessie, that's nae lee. And now, when ye
bring me amind o't, I'm sair mista'en if I didna hear a
creature up in the Brockholes this morning, skirling as if
something were cutting its throat. It gars a' the hairs stand
on my head when I think it may hae been our Leddy, and
the droich of a creature murdering her. I took it for a
battle of wulcats, and wished they might pu' out ane

anither's thrapples; but when I think on it again, they war
unco like some o' our Leddy's unearthly screams.'

'His presence be about us, Wattie! Haste ye—pit on
your bonnet—tak' your staff in your hand, and gang and
see what it is.'

'Shame fa' me, if I daur gang, Bessie.'

'Hout, Wattie, trust in the Lord.'

'Aweel, sae I do. But ane's no to throw himsell ower a
linn, and trust that the Lord will kep him in a blanket.
And it's nae muckle safer for an auld stiff man like me to
gang away out to a wild remote place, where there is ae
body murdering another. What is that I hear, Bessie?
Haud the lang tongue o' you, and rin to the door, and see
what noise that is.'

Bessie ran to the door, but soon returned, with her
mouth wide open, and her eyes set in her head.

'It is them, Wattie! it is them! His presence be about us!
What will we do?'

'Them? whaten them?'

'Why, that blackguard creature, coming here, leading
our Leddy by the hair o' the head, and yerking her wi' a
stick. I am terrified out o' my wits. What will we do?'

'We'll *see* what they *say*,' said Wattie, manifestly in as
great terror as his wife; and by a natural impulse, or as a
last resource, he opened the Bible, not knowing what he
did, then hurried on his spectacles; but before he got two
leaves turned over, the two entered, a frightful-looking
couple indeed. Merodach, with his old withered face, and
ferret eyes, leading the Lady of Wheelhope by the long
hair, which was mixed with grey, and whose face was all
bloated with wounds and bruises, and having stripes of
blood on her garments.

'How's this!—How's this, sirs?' said Wattie Blythe.

'Close that book, and I will tell you, goodman,' said
Merodach.

'I can hear what you hae to say wi' the beuk open, sir,'
said Wattie, turning over the leaves, pretending to look for
some particular passage, but apparently not knowing what

86

he was doing. 'It is a shamefu' business this; but some will hae to answer for't. My Leddy, I am unco grieved to see you in sic a plight. Ye hae surely been dooms sair left to yoursell.'

The Lady shook her head, uttered a feeble hollow laugh, and fixed her eyes on Merodach. But such a look! It almost frightened the simple aged couple out of their senses. It was not a look of love nor of hatred exclusively; neither was it of desire or disgust, but it was a combination of them all. It was such a look as one fiend would cast on another, in whose everlasting destruction he rejoiced. Wattie was glad to take his eyes from such countenances, and look into the Bible, that firm foundation of all his hopes and all his joy.

'I request that you will shut that book, sir,' said the horrible creature; 'or if you do not, I will shut it for you with a vengeance'; and with that he seized it, and flung it against the wall. Bessie uttered a scream, and Wattie was quite paralysed; and although he seemed disposed to run after his best friend, as he called it, the hellish looks of the Brownie interposed, and glued him to his seat.

'Hear what I have to say first,' said the creature, 'and then pore your fill on that precious book of yours. One concern at a time is enough. I came to do you a service. Here, take this cursed, wretched woman, whom you style your Lady, and deliver her up to the lawful authorities, to be restored to her husband and her place in society. She has followed one that hates her, and never said one kind word to her in his life; and though I have beat her like a dog, still she clings to me, and will not depart, so enchanted is she with the laudable purpose of cutting my throat. Tell your master and her brother, that I am not to be burdened with their maniac. I have scourged—I have spurned and kicked her, afflicting her night and day, and yet from my side she will not depart. Take her. Claim the reward in full, and your fortune is made; and so farewell!'

The creature went away, and the moment his back was turned, the Lady fell a-sreaming and struggling, like one

87

in an agony, and, in spite of all the couple's exertions, she forced herself out of their hands, and ran after the retreating Merodach. When he saw better would not be, he turned upon her, and, by one blow with his stick, struck her down; and, not content with that, continued to maltreat her in such a manner, as to all appearance would have killed twenty ordinary persons. The poor devoted dame could do nothing, but now and then utter a squeak like a half-worried cat, and writhe and grovel on the sward, till Wattie and his wife came up, and withheld her tormentor from further violence. He then bound her hands behind her back with a strong cord, and delivered her once more to the charge of the old couple, who contrived to hold her by that means, and take her home.

Wattie was ashamed to take her into the hall, but led her into one of the out-houses, whither he brought her brother to receive her. The man of the law was manifestly vexed at her reappearance, and scrupled not to testify his dissatisfaction; for when Wattie told him how the wretch had abused his sister, and that, had it not been for Bessie's interference and his own, the Lady would have been killed outright, he said, 'Why, Walter, it is a great pity that he did *not* kill her outright. What good can her life now do to her, or of what value is her life to any creature living? After one has lived to disgrace all connected with them, the sooner they are taken off the better.'

The man, however, paid old Walter down his two thousand merks, a great fortune for one like him in those days; and not to dwell longer on this unnatural story, I shall only add, very shortly, that the Lady of Wheelhope soon made her escape once more, and flew, as if drawn by an irresistible charm, to her tormentor. Her friends looked no more after her; and the last time she was seen alive, it was following the uncouth creature up the water of Daur, weary, wounded, and lame, while he was all the way beating her, as a piece of excellent amusement. A few days after that, her body was found among some wild haggs, in a place called Crook-burn, by a party of the persecuted

Covenanters that were in hiding there, some of the very men whom she had exerted herself to destroy, and who had been driven, like David of old, to pray for a curse and earthly punishment upon her. They buried her like a dog at the Yetts of Keppel, an rolled three huge stones upon her grave, which are lying there to this day. When they found her corpse, it was mangled and wounded in a most shocking manner, the fiendish creature having manifestly tormented her to death. He was never more seen or heard of in this kingdom, though all that countryside was kept in terror of him for many years afterwards; and to this day, they will tell you of THE BROWNIE OF THE BLACK HAGGS, which title he seems to have acquired after his disappearance.

THE GHOST WITH THE GOLDEN CASKET

by Allan Cunningham

ALLAN CUNNINGHAM *(1784–1842) had an early introduction to Scottish literature as his father was for a time a neighbour and admirer of Robert Burns when the poet lived at Ellisland, and together the two attended Burns' funeral. Born in Dumfriesshire, Allan Cunningham was apprenticed to a stonemason but cared little for this work and devoted the major part of his energies to collecting the traditional ballads and songs. Eventually, deciding to seek a livelihood in this pursuit, he was rewarded with the publication of his first book in 1810. Then a meeting with Sir Walter Scott (who dubbed him 'Honest Allan') lead to his decision to move to London where his storytelling ability soon made him a popular contributor to the much respected* London Magazine. *His best known work is* Traditional Tales of the English and Scottish Peasantry *(1822) which contains 'The Haunted Ships', probably one of the most anthologised macabre stories of all time! Avoiding the temptation to reprint this story yet again—although its quality and power are unique—I have re-read the original collection (now of some rarity) and picked the following tale which seems to me to have been completely overlooked by earlier anthologists. Like 'The Haunted Ships', it again demonstrates Cunningham's dual knowledge of the sea and the supernatura!.*

From the coast of Cumberland the beautiful old castle of Caerlaverock is seen standing on the point of a fine green promontory, bounded by the river Nith on one side, by the deep sea on another, by the almost impassable morass of

Solway on a third; while, far beyond, you observe the three spires of Dumfries, and the high green hills of Dalswinton and Keir. It was formerly the residence of the almost princely names of Douglas, Seaton, Kirkpatrick, and Maxwell: it is now the dwelling-place of the hawk and the owl; its courts are a lair for cattle, and its walls afford a midnight shelter to the passing smuggler; or, like those of the city doomed in Scripture, are places for the fisherman to dry their nets. Between this fine old ruin and the banks of the Nith, at the foot of a grove of pines, and within a stone-cast of tide-mark, the remains of a rude cottage are yet visible to the curious eye; the bramble and the wild plum have in vain tried to triumph over the huge, grey granite blocks, which composed the foundations of its walls. The vestiges of a small garden may still be traced, more particularly in summer, when roses and lilies, and other relics of its former beauty, begin to open their bloom, clinging, amid the neglect and desolation of the place, with something like human affection, to the soil. This rustic ruin presents no attractions to the eye of the profound antiquary, compared to those of its more stately companion, Caerlaverock Castle; but with this rude cottage and its garden tradition connects a tale so wild and so moving, as to elevate it, in the contemplation of the peasantry, above all the princely feasts and feudal atrocities of its neighbour.

It is now some fifty years since I visited the parish of Caerlaverock; but the memory of its people, its scenery, and the story of the Ghost with the Golden Casket, are as fresh with me as matters of yesterday. I had walked out to the river bank one sweet afternoon of July, when the fishermen were hastening to dip their nets in the coming tide, and the broad waters of the Solway sea were swelling and leaping against bank and cliff, as far as the eye could reach. It was studded over with boats, and its more unfrequented bays were white with water-fowl. I sat down on a small grassy mound between the cottage ruins and the old garden plat, and gazed, with all the hitherto untasted pleasure of a stranger, on the beautiful scene before me. On the right, and beyond the river, the mouldering relics of the ancient religion of Scotland ascended, in unassimilating beauty, above the humble kirk of New-Abbey and its squalid village; farther to the south rose the white sharp cliffs of Barnhourie, while on the left stood the ancient keeps of Cumlongan, and Torthorald, and the castle of Caerlaverock. Over the whole looked the stately green mountain of Criffel, confronting its more stately but less beautiful neighbour, Skiddaw; while between them flowed the deep wide sea of Solway, hemmed with cliff, and castle, and town.

As I sat looking on the increasing multitudes of waters, and watching the success of the fishermen, I became aware of the approach of an old man, leading, as one will conduct a dog on a string, a fine young milch cow, in a halter of twisted hair, which passing through the ends of two pieces of flat wood, fitted to the animal's cheek-bones, pressed her nose, and gave her great pain whenever she became dis-obedient. The cow seemed willing to enjoy the luxury of a browze on the rich pasture which surrounded the little ruined cottage; but in this humble wish she was not to be indulged, for the aged owner, coiling up the tether, and seizing her closely by the head, conducted her past the tempting herbage, towards a small and close-cropt hillock, a good stone-cast distant. In this piece of self-denial the animal seemed reluctant to sympathise—she snuffed the fresh green pasture, and plunged, and startled, and nearly broke away. What the old man's strength seemed nearly unequal to, was accomplished by speech:

'Bonnie lady, bonnie lady,' said he, in a soothing tone, 'it canna be, it mauna be—hinnie! hinnie! what would become of my three bonnie grand-bairns, made fatherless and mitherless by that false flood afore us, if they supped milk, and tasted butter, that came from the greensward of this doomed and unblessed spot?'

The animal appeared to comprehend something in her own way from the speech of her owner: she abated her resis-tance; and indulging only in a passing glance at the rich deep herbage, passed on to her destined pasture.

92

I had often heard of the singular superstitions of the Scottish peasantry, and that every hillock had its song, every hill its ballad and every valley its tale. I followed with my eye the old man and his cow; he went but a little way, till, seating himself on the ground, retaining still the tether in his hand, he said, 'Now bonnie lady, feast thy fill on this good greensward—it is halesome and holy, compared to the sward at the doomed cottage of auld Gibbie Gyrape—leave that to smugglers' nags: Willie o' Brandyburn and Roaring Jock o' Kempstane will ca' the haunted ha' a hained bit—they are godless fear-noughts.' I looked at the person of the peasant: he was a stout hale old man, with a weather-beaten face, furrowed something by time, and, perhaps, by sorrow. Though summer was at its warmest, he wore a broad chequered mantle, fastened at the bosom with a skewer of steel, a broad bonnet, from beneath the circumference of which straggled a few thin locks, as white as driven snow, shining like amber, and softer than the finest flax, while his legs were warmly cased in blue-ribbed boothose. Having laid his charge to the grass, he looked leisurely around him, and espying me—a stranger, and dressed above the manner of the peasantry, he acknowledged my presence by touching his bonnet; and, as if willing to communicate something of importance, he struck the tether stake in the ground, and came to the old garden fence.

Wishing to know the peasant's reasons for avoiding the ruins, I thus addressed him: 'This is a pretty spot, my aged friend, and the herbage looks so fresh and abundant, that I would advise thee to bring thy charge hither; and while she continued to browze, I would gladly listen to the history of thy white locks, for they seem to have been bleached in many tempests.'

'Aye, aye,' said the peasant, shaking his white head with a grave smile, 'they have braved sundry tempests between sixteen and sixty; but, touching this pasture, sir, I know nobody who would like their cows to crop it—the aged cattle shun the place, the bushes bloom but bear no fruit, the birds never build in the branches, the children never come near to

93

play, and the aged never choose it for a resting-place but pointing it out, as they pass, to the young, tell them the story of its desolation. Sae ye see, sir, having nae good will to such a spot of earth myself, I like little to see a stranger sitting in such an unblessed place and I would as good as advise ye to come owre with me to the cowslip knoll—there are reasons mony that an honest man should nae sit there.'

I arose at once, and seating myself beside the peasant, on the cowslip knoll, desired to know something of the history of the spot from which he had just warned me. The Caledonian looked on me with an air of embarrassment.

'I am just thinking,' said he, 'that as ye are an Englishman, I should nae acquaint ye with such a story. Ye'll make it, I'm doubting, a matter of reproach and vaunt, when ye gae hame, how Willie Borlan o' Caerlaverock told ye a tale of Scottish iniquity, that cowed all the stories in Southron book or history.'

This unexpected obstacle was soon removed. 'My sage and considerate friend,' I said, 'I have the blood in my bosom will keep me from revealing such a tale to the scoffer and scorner. I am something of a Caerlaverock man—the grandson of Marion Stobe of Dookdub.'

The peasant seized my hand—'Marion Stobie! bonnie Marion Stobie o' Dookdub—whom I wooed sae sair, and loved sae lang!—Man, I love ye for her sake; and well was it for her braw English bridegroom, that William Borlan—frail and faded now, but strong and in manhood then—was a thousand miles from Caerlaverock, rolling on the salt sea, when she was brided: ye have the glance of her ee—I could ken't yet amang ten thousand, grey as my head is. I will tell the grandson of bonnie Mary Stobie ony tale he likes to ask for; and the Story of the Ghost and the Gowd Casket shall be foremost.'

'You may imagine, then,' said the old Caerlaverock peasant, rising at once with the commencement of his story from his native dialect into very passable English—'you may imagine these ruined walls raised again in their beauty—whitened and covered with a coating of green broom; that garden, now desolate, filled with herbs in their season, and with flowers, hemmed round with a fence of cherry and plum-trees; and the whole possessed by a young fisherman, who won a fair subsistence for his wife and children from the waters of the Solway sea; you may imagine it, too, as far from the present time as fifty years. There are only two persons living now, who remember when the *Bonne-Homme-Richard*, the first ship ever Richard Faulder commanded, was wrecked on the Pellock sand—one of these persons now addresses you, the other is the fisherman who once owned that cottage, whose name ought never to be named, and whose life seems lengthened as a warning to the earth, how fierce God's judgments are. Life changes—all breathing things have their time and their season; but the Solway flows in the same beauty—Criffel rises in the same majesty—the light of morning comes, and the full moon arises now, as they did then;—but this moralising matters little. It was about the middle of harvest—I remember the day well— it had been sultry and suffocating, accompanied by rushings of wind, sudden convulsions of the water, and cloudings of the sun: I heard my father sigh, and say, "Dool—dool to them found on the deep sea tonight—there will happen strong storm and fearful tempest." The day closed, and the moon came over Skiddaw: all was perfectly clear and still— frequent dashings and whirling agitations of the sea were soon heard mingling with the hasty clang of the water-fowls' wings, as they forsook the waves, and sought shelter among the hollows of the rocks. The storm was nigh. The sky darkened down at once—clap after clap of thunder followed —and lightning flashed so vividly, and so frequent, that the wide and agitated expanse of Solway was visible from side to side—from St. Bees to Barnhourie. A very heavy rain, mingled with hail, succeeded; and a wind accompanied it, so fierce, and so high, that the white foam of the sea was showered as thick as snow on the summit of Caerlaverock Castle.

'Through this perilous sea, and amid this darkness and tempest, a bark was observed coming swiftly down the middle of the sea; her sails rent, and her decks crowded with people. The carry, as it is called, of the tempest, was direct from St. Bees to Caerlaverock; and experienced swains could see that the bark would be driven full on the fatal shoals of the Scottish side; but the lightning was so fierce that few dared venture to look on the approaching vessel, or take measures for endeavouring to preserve the lives of the unfortunate mariners. My father stood on the threshold of his door, and beheld all that passed in the bosom of the sea. The bark approached fast—her canvas rent to threads, her masts nearly levelled with the deck, and the sea foaming over her so deep, and so strong, as to threaten to sweep the remains of her crew from the little refuge the broken masts and splintered beams still afforded them. She now seemed within half a mile of the shore, when a strong flash of lightning, that appeared to hang over the bark for a moment, showed the figure of a lady, richly dressed, clinging to a youth who was pressing her to his bosom. My father exclaimed, "Saddle me my black horse, and saddle me my grey, and bring them down to the Dead-man's bank"—and, swift in action as he was in resolve, he hastened to the shore, his servants following with his horses. The shore of Solway presented then, as it does now, the same varying line of coast; and the house of my father stood in the bosom of a little bay, nearly a mile from where we sit. The remains of an old forest interposed between the bay at Dead-man's bank, and the bay at our feet; and mariners had learnt to wish, that if it were their doom to be wrecked, it might be in the bay of douce William Borlan, rather than that of Gilbert Gyrape, the proprietor of that ruined cottage. But human wishes are vanities, wished either by sea or land. I have heard my father say he could never forget the cries of the mariners, as the bark smote on the Pellock-bank, and the flood rushed through the chasms made by the concussion; but he would far less forget the agony of a lady—the loveliest that could be looked upon, and the calm and affectionate courage of the young man who supported her, and endeavoured to save her from destruction. Richard Faulder, the only man who survived, has often

96

sat at my fireside, and sung me a very rude, but a very moving ballad, which he made on this young and unhappy pair; and the old mariner assured me he had only added rhymes, and a descriptive line or two, to the language in which Sir William Musgrave endeavoured to soothe and support his wife.'

It seemed a thing truly singular, that at this very moment two young fishermen, who sat on the margin of the sea below us, watching their halve-nets, should sing, and with much sweetness, the very song the old man had described. They warbled verse and verse alternately—and rock and bay seemed to retain and then release the sound. Nothing is so sweet as a song by the sea-side on a tranquil evening.

The young fishermen having concluded their song, my companion proceeded—'The lightning still flashed vivid and fast, and the storm raged with unabated fury; for between the ship and the shore the sea broke in frightful undulation, and leaped on the greensward several fathoms deep abreast. My father, mounted on one horse, and holding another in his hand, stood prepared to give all the aid that a brave man could to the unhappy mariners; but neither horse nor man could endure the onset of that tremendous surge. The bark bore for a time the fury of the element—but a strong eastern wind came suddenly upon her, and, crushing her between the wave and the freestone bank, drove her from the entrance of my father's little bay towards the dwelling of Gibbie Gyrape, and the thick forest intervening, she was out of sight in a moment. My father saw, for the last time, the lady and her husband looking shoreward from the side of the vessel, as she drifted along; and as he galloped round the head of the forest, he heard for the last time the outcry of some, and the wail and intercession of others. When he came before the fisherman's house, a fearful sight presented itself—the ship, dashed to atoms, covered the shore with its wreck, and with the bodies of the mariners—not a living soul escaped, save Richard Faulder, whom the fiend who guides the spectre-shallop of Solway had rendered proof to perils on the deep. The fisherman himself came suddenly from his cottage, all

97

dripping and drenched, and my father addressed him: "O Gilbert, Gilbert, what a fearful sight is this!—has Heaven blessed thee with making thee the means of saving a human soul?"—"Nor soul nor body have I saved," said the fisherman, doggedly: "I have done my best—the storm proved too stark, and the lightning too fierce for me—their boat alone came near with a lady and a casket of gold—but she was swallowed up with the surge." My father confessed afterwards that he was touched with the tone in which these words were delivered, and made answer, "If thou hast done thy best to save souls tonight, a bright reward will be thine—if thou hast been fonder for gain than for working the mariners' redemption, thou hast much to answer for." As he uttered these words, an immense wave rolled landward as far as the place where they stood—it almost left its foam on their faces, and suddenly receding, deposited at their feet the dead body of the lady. As my father lifted her in his arms, he observed that the jewels which had adorned her hair, at that time worn long—had been forcibly rent away—the diamonds and gold that enclosed her neck, and ornamented the bosom of her rich satin dress, had been torn off—the rings removed from her fingers—and on her neck, lately so lily-white and pure, there appeared the marks of hands—not laid there in love and gentleness, but with a fierce and deadly grasp.

'The lady was buried with the body of her husband, side by side, in Caerlaverock burial-ground. My father never openly accused Gilbert the fisherman of having murdered the lady for her riches as she reached the shore, preserved, as was supposed, from sinking, by her long, wide, and stiff satin robes—but from that hour till the hour oı his death, my father never broke bread with him—never shook him or his by the hand, nor spoke with them in wrath or in love. The fisherman, from that time, too, waxed rich and prosperous—and from being the needy proprietor of a halve-net, and the tenant at will of a rude cottage, he became, by purchase, lord of a handsome inheritance, proceeded to build a bonny mansion, and called it Gyrape-ha'; and became a leading man in a flock of a purer kind of Presbyterians—and a precept and example to the community.

'Though the portioner of Gyrape-ha' prospered wondrously, his claims to parichial distinction, and the continuance of his fortune, were treated with scorn by many, and with doubt by all: though nothing open or direct was said—looks, more cutting at times than the keenest speech, and actions still more expressive, showed that the hearts of honest men were alienated—the cause was left to his own interpretation. The peasant scrupled to become his servant—sailors hesitated to receive his grain on board, lest perils should find them on the deep—the beggar ceased to solicit alms—the drover and horse-couper, an unscrupling generation, found out a more distant mode of concluding bargains than by shaking his hand—his daughters, handsome and blue-eyed, were neither wooed nor married—no maiden would hold tryst with his sons—though maidens were then as little loth as they are now; and the aged peasant, as he passed his new mansion, would shake his head and say—"The voice of spilt blood will be lifted up against thee—and a spirit shall come up from the waters and make the corner stone of thy habitation tremble and quake."

'It happened, during the summer which succeeded this unfortunate shipwreck, that I accompanied my father to the Solway, to examine his nets. It was near midnight—the tide was making, and I sat down by his side, and watched the coming of the waters. The shore was glittering in starlight as far as the eye could reach. Gilbert the fisherman had that morning removed from his cottage to his new mansion—the former was, therefore, untenanted; and the latter, from its vantage ground on the crest of the hill, threw down to us the sound of mirth and music and dancing, a revelry common in Scotland on taking possession of a new house. As we lay quietly looking on the swelling sea, and observing the waterfowl swimming and ducking in the increasing waters, the sound of the merriemnt became more audible. My father listened to the mirth, looked to the sea, looked to the deserted cottage, and then to the new mansion, and said: "My son, I

99

have a counsel to give thee—treasure it in thy heart, and practise it in thy life—the daughters of *him* of Gyrape-ha' are fair, and have an eye that would wile away the wits of the wisest—their father has wealth—I say nought of the way he came by it—they will have golden portions doubtless. But I would rather lay thy head aneath the gowans in Caerlaverock kirkyard, and son have I none beside thee, than see thee lay it on the bridal pillow with the begotten of that man, though she had Nithsdale for her dowry. Let not my words be as seed sown on the ocean—I may not now tell thee why this warning is given. Before that fatal shipwreck, I would have said Prudence Gyrape, in her kirtle, was a better bride than some who have golden dowers. I have long thought some one would see a sight—and often, while holding my halve-net in the midnight tide, have I looked for something to appear—for where blood is shed, there doth the spirit haunt for a time' and give warning to man. May I be strengthened to endure the sight!"

'I answered not—being accustomed to regard my father's counsel as a matter not to be debated, as a solemn command: we heard something like the rustling of wings on the water, accompanied by a slight curling motion of the tide. "God haud His right hand about us!" said my father, breathing thick with emotion and awe, and looking on the sea with a gaze so intense that his eyes seemed to dilate, and the hair of his forehead to project forward, and bristle into life. I looked, but observed nothing, save a long line of thin and quivering light, dancing along the surface of the sea: it ascended the bank, on which it seemed to linger for a moment, and then entering the fisherman's cottage, made roof and rafter gleam with a sudden illumination. "I'll tell thee what, Gibbie Gyrape," said my father, "I wouldna be the owner of thy heart, and the proprietor of thy right hand, for all the treasures in earth and ocean." A loud and piercing scream from the cottage made us thrill with fear, and in a moment the figures of three human beings rushed into the open air, and ran towards us with a swiftness which supernatural dread alone could inspire. We instantly knew them

100

to be three noted smugglers, who infested the country; and rallying when they found my father maintain his ground, they thus mingled their fears and the secrets of their trade—for terror fairly overpowered their habitual caution.

' "I vow by the night tide, and the crooked timber," said Willie Weethause, "I never beheld sic a light as yon since our distillation pipe took fire, and made a burnt, instead of a drink-offering of our spirits; I'll uphold it comes for nae good—a warning may be—sae ye may gang on, Wattie Bouseaway, wi' yere wickedness; as for me, I'se gae hame and repent." "Saulless bodie!" said his companion, whose natural hardihood was considerably supported by his communion with the brandy cup—"Saulless bodie, for a flaff o' fire and a maiden's shadow, would ye forswear the gallant trade? Saul to gude! but auld Miller Morison shall turn yere thrapple into a drain-pipe to wyse the waste water from his mill, if ye turn back now, and help us nae through with as strong an importation as ever cheered the throat, and cheeped in the crapin. Confound the fizzenless bodie! he glowers as if this fine starlight were something frae the warst side of the world, and thae staring een o' his are busy shaping heaven's sweetest and balmiest air in the figures of wraiths and goblins." "Robert Telfer," said my father, addressing the third smuggler, "tell me nought of the secrets of your perilous craft—but tell me what you have seen, and why ye uttered that fearful scream, that made the wood-doves start from Caerlaverock pines." "I'll tell ye what, goodman," said the mariner, "I have seen the fires o' heaven running as thick along the sky, and on the surface of the ocean, as ye ever saw the blaze on a bowl o' punch at a merry-making, and neither quaked nor screamed; but ye'll mind the light that came to that cottage tonight was one for some fearful purport, which let the wise expound; sae it lessened nae one's courage to quail for sic an apparation. Od! if I thought living soul would ever make the start I gied an upcast to me, I'd drill his breast-bane wi' my dirk like a turnip lantern."

'My father mollified the wrath of this maritime desperado, by assuring him he beheld the light go from the sea to the cottage, and that he shook with terror, for it seemed no common light. "Ou God! then," said hopeful Robin, "since it was one o' our ain cannie sea apparitions, I care less about it—I took it for some landward sprite! and now I think on't, where were my een? did it no stand amang its ain light, with its long hanks of hair dripping, and drenched; with a casket of gold in ae hand, and the other guarding its throat? I'll be bound it's the ghost o' some sonsie lass that has had her neck nipped for her gold—and had she stayed till I emptied the bicker o' brandy, I would have asked a cannie question or twae." Willie Weethause had now fairly overcome his consternation, and began to feel all his love for the gallant trade, as his comrade called it, return. "The tide serves, lads! the tide serves; let us slip our drap o' brandy into the bit bonnie boat, and tottle away amang the sweet starlight as far as the Kingholm or the town quarry—ye ken we have to meet Bailie Gardevine, and Laird Soukaway o' Ladle-mouth." They returned, not without hesitation and fear, to the old cottage; carried their brandy to the boat; and as my father and I went home, we heard the dipping of their oars in the Nith, along the banks of which they sold their liquor, and told their tale of fear, magnifying its horror at every step, and introducing abundance of variations.

'The story of the Ghost with the Golden Casket flew over the countryside with all its variations, and with many comments: some said they saw her, and some thought they saw her—and those who had the hardihood to keep watch on the beach at midnight, had their tales to tell of terrible lights and strange visions. With one who delighted in the marvellous, the spectre was decked in attributes that made the circle of auditors tighten round the hearth; while others, who allowed to a ghost only a certain quantity of thin air to clothe itself in, reduced it in their description to a very unpoetic shadow, or a kind of better sort of will-o'-the-wisp, that could for its own amusement counterfeit the human shape. There were many who, like my father, beheld the singular illumination appear at midnight on the coast; saw also something sailing along with it in the form of a lady in bright garments, her hair long and wet, and shining in diamonds; and heard a struggle, and the shriek as of a creature drowning.

'The belief of the peasantry did not long confine the apparation to the sea coast; it was seen sometimes late at night far inland, and following Gilbert the Fisherman, like a human shadow—like a pure light—like a white garment—and often in the shape, and with the attributes, in which it disturbed the carousel of the smugglers. I heard douce Davie Haining—a God-fearing man, and an elder of the Burgher congregation, and on whose word I could well lippen, when drink was kept from his head—I heard him say that as he rode home late from the Roodfair of Dumfries—the night was dark, there lay a dusting of snow on the ground, and no one appeared on the road but himself—he was lilting and singing the cannie end of the auld sang, "There's a cuttie stool in our Kirk," which was made on some foolish quean's misfortune, when he heard the sound of horses' feet behind him at full gallop, and ere he could look round, who should flee past, urging his horse with whip and spur, but Gilbert the Fisherman! "Little wonder that he galloped," said the elder, "for a fearful form hovered around him, making many a clutch at him, and with every clutch uttering a shriek most piercing to hear." But why should I make a long story of a common tale? The curse of spilt blood fell on him, and on his children, and on all he possessed; his sons and daughters died, his flocks perished, his grain grew, but never filled the ear; and fire came from heaven, or rose from hell, and consumed his house, and all that was therein. He is now a man of ninety years—a fugitive and a vagabond on the earth, without a house to put his white head in, with the unexpiated curse still clinging to him.'

While my companion was making this summary of human wretchedness, I observed the figure of a man, stooping to the earth with extreme age, gliding through among the bushes of the ruined cottage, and approaching the advancing tide. He wore a loose greatcoat, patched to the ground, and fastened round his waist by a belt and buckle—the remains of stock-ings and shoes were on his feet; a kind of fisherman's cap surmounted some remaining white hairs, while a long peeled stick supported him as he went. My companion gave an involuntary shudder when he saw him 'Lo, and behold, now, here comes Gilbert the Fisherman! once every twenty-four hours doth he come, let the wind and the rain be as they will, to the nightly tide, to work o'er again, in imagination, his auld tragedy of unrighteousness. See how he waves his hand, as if he welcomed someone from the sea—he raises his voice, too, as if something in the water required his counsel; and see how he dashes up to the middle, and grapples with the water as if he clutched a human being!'

I looked on the old man, and heard him call, in a hollow and broken voice, 'O hoy! the ship, O hoy,—turn your boat's head ashore!—and my bonnie lady, keep haud o' yere casket. Hech be't! that wave would have sunk a three-decker, let be a slender boat—see—see an' she binna sailing aboon the water like a wild swan!'—and, wading deeper in the tide as he spoke, he seemed to clutch at something with both hands, and struggle with it in the water.

'Na! na! dinna haud your white hands to me—ye wear ower mickle gowd in your hair, and o'er many diamonds on your bosom, to 'scape drowning. There's as mickle gowd in this casket as would have sunk thee seventy fathom deep.' And he continued to hold his hands under the water, muttering all the while.

'She's half gane now—and I'll be a braw laird, and build a bonnie house, and gang crousely to kirk and market—now I may let the waves work their will—my work will be ta'en for theirs.'

He turned to wade to the shore, but a large and heavy wave came full dash on him, and bore him off his feet, and ere any assistance reached him, all human aid was too late; for nature was so exhausted with the fullness of years, and with his exertions, that a spoonful of water would have drowned him. The body of this miserable old man was interred, after some opposition from the peasantry, beneath the wall of the kirkyard; and from that time, the Ghost with the Golden Casket was seen no more, and only continued to haunt the evening tale of the hind and the farmer.

THE SEA-MAIDEN

by J. F. Campbell

JOHN FRANCIS CAMPBELL (*1822–1885*) *has been
described as the greatest of Scotland's folk lore collectors,
and certainly his work in this area has saved a vast
treasury of oral tales and legends from complete oblivion.
It is impossible to praise too highly the labours of men
like him who travelled into the wildest and most isolated
places of Scotland to first win the confidence of the local
people and then induce them to retell for posterity the
old stories of men and deeds of long ago. John Campbell
was born on Islay and was educated at Eton and Edinburgh University. He first entered the legal profession
but then abandoned this to become secretary to the lighthouse and coal commissions. His dual passion for the
Highlands and folk lore early took him on travels to
collect the oral stories of the local people. The culmina-
tion of this work was the four volumes of* Popular Tales
of the West Highlands, *published in 1890. Laymen and
critics alike considered them among the finest of their
kind to be found anywhere in the world. In introducing
the work, Campbell said it was 'a museum of curious
rubbish about to perish, given as it was gathered in the
rough, for it seemed to me as barbarous to "polish" a
genuine popular tale as it would be to gild a rare old copper
coin'. He noted, also, that it had not always been easy to
obtain the stories as the people did not speak readily and
were 'shy and proud and peculiarly sensitive to ridicule'.
He found, too, that 'many have a lurking belief in the
truth of the stories which they tell'. Here, then, from the
body of Campbell's magnificent collection of* Sgialachdan

(folk stories) is an item which I think is particularly outstanding because it contains so many of the components of fantasy usually found in such tales: a sea-maiden, a giant, a king and his beautiful daughter, a poor, handsome hero (of course) and even a loch monster! This story was told to the recorder by John MacKenie, a fisherman at Inverary in 1850.

There was ere now a poor old fisher, but on this year he was not getting much fish. On a day of days, and he fishing, there rose a sea-maiden at the side of his boat, and she asked him if he was getting fish. The old man answered, and he said that he was not. 'What reward wouldst thou give me for sending plenty of fish to thee?' 'Ach!' said the old man, 'I have not much to spare.' 'Wilt thou give me the first son thou hast?' said she. 'It is I that would give thee that, if I were to have a son; there was not, and there will not be a son of mine,' said he, 'I and my wife are grown so old.' 'Name all thou hast.' 'I have but an old mare of a horse, an old dog, myself and my wife. There's for thee all the creatures of the great world that are mine.' 'Here, then, are three grains for thee that thou shalt give thy wife this very night, and three others to the dog, and these three to the mare, and these three likewise thou shalt plant behind thy house, and in their own time thy wife will have three sons, the mare three foals, and the dog three puppies, and there will grow three trees behind thy house, and the trees will be a sign, when one of the sons dies, one of the trees will wither. Now, take thyself home, and remember me when thy son is three years of age, and thou thyself wilt get plenty of fish after this.' Everything happened as the sea-maiden said, and he himself was getting plenty of fish; but when the end of the three years was nearing, the old man was growing sorrowful, heavy hearted, while he failed each day as it came. On the namesake of the day, he went to fish as he used, but he did not take his son with him.

The sea-maiden rose at the side of the boat, and asked, 'Didst thou bring thy son with thee hither to me?' 'Och! I did not bring him. I forgot that this was the day.' 'Yes! yes! then,' said the sea-maiden; 'thou shalt get four other years of him, to try if it be easier for thee to part from him. Here thou hast his like age,' and she lifted up a big bouncing baby. 'Is thy son as fine as this one?' He went home full of glee and delight, for that he had got four other years of his son, and he kept on fishing and getting plenty of fish, but at the end of the next four years sorrow and woe struck him, and he took not a meal, and he did not a turn, and his wife could not think what was ailing him. This time he did not know what to do, but he set it before him, that he would not take his son with him this time either. He went to fish as at the former times, and the sea-maiden rose at the side of the boat, and she asked him, 'Didst thou bring thy son hither to me?' 'Och! I forgot him this time too,' said the old man. 'Go home then,' said the sea-maiden, 'and at the end of seven years after this, thou art sure to remember me, but then it will not be the easier for thee to part with him, but thou shalt get fish as thou used to do.'

The old man went home full of joy; he had got seven other years of his son, and before seven years passed, the old man thought that he himself would be dead, and that he would see the sea-maiden no more. But no matter, the end of those seven years was nearing also, and if it was, the old man was not without care and trouble. He had rest neither day nor night. The eldest son asked his father one day if any one were troubling him? The old man said that some one was, but that belonged neither to him nor to any one else. The lad said he *must* know what it was. His father told him at last how the matter was between him and the sea-maiden. 'Let not that put you in any trouble,' said the son; 'I will not oppose you.' 'Thou shalt not; thou shalt not go, my son, though I should not get fish for ever.' 'If you will not let me go with you, go to the smithy, and let the smith make me a great strong sword, and I will go to the end of fortune.' His father went to the smithy, and the smith made a doughty sword for him. His father came home with the sword. The lad grasped it and gave it a shake or two, and it went in a hundred splinters. He asked his father to go to the smithy and get him another sword in which there should be twice as much weight; and so did his father, and so likewise it happened to the next sword—it broke in two halves. Back went the old man to the smithy; and the smith made a great sword, its like he never made before. 'There's thy sword for thee,' said the smith, 'and the fist must be good that plays this blade.' The old man gave the sword to his son, he gave it a shake or two. 'This will do,' said he; 'it's high time now to travel on my way.' On the next morning he put a saddle on the black horse that the mare had, and he put the world under his head,* and his black dog was by his side. When he went on a bit, he fell in with the carcass of a sheep beside the road. At the carrion were a great dog, a falcon, and an otter. He came down off the horse, and he dvided the carcass amongst the three. Three third shares to the dog, two third shares to the otter, and a third share to the falcon. 'For this,' said the dog, 'if swiftness of foot or sharpness of tooth will give thee aid, mind me, and I will be at thy side.' Said the otter, 'If the swimming of foot on the ground of a pool will loose thee, mind me, and I will be at thy side.' Said the falcon, 'If hardship comes on thee, where swiftness of wing or crook of a claw will do good, mind me, and I will be at thy side.' On this he went onward till he reached a king's house, and he took service to be a herd, and his wages were to be according to the milk of the cattle. He went away with the cattle, and the grazing was but bare. When lateness came (in the evening), and when he took (them) home they had not much milk, the place was so bare, and his meat and drink was but spare this night.

On the next day he went on farther with them; and at last he came to a place exceedingly grassy, in a green glen, of which he never saw the like.

But about the time when he should go behind the cattle, for taking homewards, who is seen coming but a great giant with his sword in his hand. 'Hiu! Hau! Hogaraich!!!' says the giant. 'It is long since my teeth were rusted seeking thy

* Took the world for his pillow. Editor's note.

109

flesh. The cattle are mine; they are on my march; and a dead man art thou.' 'I said, not that,' says the herd; 'there is no knowing, but that may be easier to say than to do.'

To grips they go—himself and the giant. He saw that he was far from his friend, and near his foe. He drew the great clean-sweeping sword, and he neared the giant; and in the play of the battle the black dog leaped on the giant's back. The herd drew back his sword, and the head was off the giant in a twinking. He leaped on the black horse, and he went to look for the giant's house. He reached a door, and in the haste that the giant made he had left each gate and door open. In went the herd, and that's the place where there was magnificence and money in plenty, and dresses of each kind on the wardrobe with gold and silver, and each thing finer than the other. At the mouth of night he took himself to the king's house, but he took not a thing from the giant's house. And when the cattle were milked this night there *was* milk. He got good feeding this night, meat and drink without stint, and the king was hugely pleased that he had caught such a herd. He went on for a time in this way, but at last the glen grew bare of grass, and the grazing was not so good.

But he thought he would go a little further forward in on the giant's land; and he sees a great park of grass. He returned for the cattle, and he puts them into the park.

They were but a short time grazing in the park when a great wild giant came full of rage and madness. 'Hia! Haw! Hogaraich!!!' said the giant. 'It is a drink of thy blood that quenches my thirst this night.' 'There is no knowing,' said the herd, 'but that's easier to say than to do.' And at each other went the men. *There* was the shaking of blades! At length and at last it seemed as if the giant would get the victory over the herd. Then he called on his dog, and with one spring the black dog caught the giant by the neck, and swiftly the herd struck off his head.

He went home very tired this night, but it's a wonder if the king's cattle had not milk. The whole family was delighted that they had got such a herd.

He followed herding in this way for a time; but one night

110

after he came home, instead of getting 'all hail' and 'good luck' from the dairymaid, all were at crying and woe.

He asked what cause of woe there was this night. The dairymaid said that a great beast with three heads was in the loch, and she was to get (some) one every year, and the lots had come this year on the king's daughter, 'and in the middle of the day (tomorrow) she is to meet the Uile Bheist at the upper end of the loch, but there is a great suitor yonder who is going to rescue her.'

'What suitor is that?' said the herd. 'Oh, he is a great General of arms,' said the dairymaid, 'and when he kills the beast, he will marry the king's daughter, for the king has said, that he who could save his daughter should get her to marry.'

But on the morrow when the time was nearing, the king's daughter and this hero of arms went to give a meeting to the beast, and they reached the black corrie at the upper end of the loch. They were but a short time there when the beast stirred in the midst of the loch; but on the general's seeing this terror of a beast with three heads, he took fright, and he slunk away, and he hid himself. And the king's daughter was under fear and under trembling with no one at all to save her. At a glance, she sees a doughty handsome youth, riding a black horse, and coming where she was. He was marvellously arrayed, and full armed, and his black dog moving after him. 'There is gloom on thy face, girl,' said the youth. 'What dost thou here?' 'Oh! that's no matter,' said the king's daughter. 'It's not long I'll eb here at all events.' 'I said not that,' said he. 'A worthy fled as likely as thou, and not long since,' said she. 'He is a worthy who stands the war,' said the youth. He lay down beside her, and he said to her, if he should fall asleep, she should rouse him when she should see the beast making for shore. 'What is rousing for thee?' said she. 'Rousing for me is to put the gold ring on thy finger on my little finger.' They were not long there when she saw the beast making for shore. She took a ring off her finger, and put it on the little finger of the lad. He awoke and to meet the beast he went with his sword and his dog. But there was the spluttering and splashing between himself and the beast! The dog was doing all he might, and the king's daughter was palsied by fear of the noise of the beast. They would now be under, and now above. But at last he cut one of the heads off her. She gave one roar RAIVIC, and the son of earth, MACTALLA of the rocks (echo), called to her screech, and she drove the loch in spindrift from end to end, and in a twinkling she went out of sight. 'Good luck and victory that were following thee, lad!' said the king's daughter. 'I am safe for one night, but the beast will come again, and for ever, until the other two heads come off her.' He caught the beast's head, and he drew a withy through it, and he told her to bring it with her there tomorrow. She went home with the head on her shoulder, and the herd betook himself to the cows, but she had not gone far when this great General saw her, and he said to her that he would kill her, if she would not say that 'twas he took the head off the beast. 'Oh!' says she, ' 'tis I will say it, who else took the head off the beast but thou!' They reached the king's house, and the head was on the General's shoulder. But here was rejoicing, that she should come home alive and whole, and this great captain with the beast's head full of blood in his hand. On the morrow they went away, and there was no question at all but that this hero would save the king's daughter.

They reached the same place, and they were not long there when the fearful Uile Bheist stirred in the midst of the loch, and the hero slunk away as he did on yesterday, but it was not long after this when the man of the black horse came, with another dress on. No matter, she knew that it was the very same lad. 'It is I am pleased to see thee,' said she. 'I am in hopes thou wilt handle thy great sword today as thou didst yesterday. Come up and take breath.' But they were not long there when they saw the beast steaming in the midst of the loch.

The lad lay down at the side of the king's daughter, and he said to her, 'If I sleep before the beast comes, rouse me.' 'What is rousing for thee?' 'Rousing for me is to put the

ear-ring that is in thine ear in mine.' He had not well fallen
asleep when the king's daughter cried, 'rouse! rouse!' but
wake he would not; but she took the ear-ring out of her ear,
and she put it in the ear of the lad. At once he woke, and to
meet the beast he went, but *there* was Tloopersteich and
Tlaperstich, rawceil s'tawceil, spluttering, splashing, raving
and roaring on the beast! They kept on thus for a long time,
and about the mouth of night, he cut another head off the
beast. He put it on the withy, and he leaped on the black
horse, and he betook himself to the herding. The king's
daughter went home with the heads. The General met her,
and took to heads from her, and he said to her, that she
must tell that it was he who took the head off the beast this
time also. 'Who else took the head off the beast but thou?'
said she. They reached the king's house with the heads.
Then there was joy and gladness. If the king was hopeful
the first night, he was now sure that this great hero would
save his daughter, and there was no question at all but that
the other head would be off the beast on the morrow.

About the same time on the morrow, the two went away.
The officer hid himself as he usually did. The king's daughter
betook herself to the bank of the loch. The hero of the black
horse came, and he lay at her side. She woke the lad, and
put another ear-ring in his other ear and at the beast he
went. But if rawceil and tawceil, roaring and raving were
on the beast on the days that were passed, this day she was
horrible. But no matter, he took the third head off the beast;
and if he did, it was not without a struggle. He drew it
through the withy, and she went home with the heads.
When they reached the king's house, all were full of smiles,
and the General was to marry the king's daughter the next
day. The wedding was going on, and every one about the
castle longing till the priest should come. But when the
priest came, she would marry but the one who could take
the heads off the withy without cutting the withy. 'Who
should take the heads off the withy but the man that put
the heads on?' said the king.

The General tried them, but he could not loose them;

113

and at last there was no one about the house but had tried to take the heads off the withy, but they could not. The king asked if there were any one else about the house that would try to take the heads off the withy? They said that the herd had not tried them yet. Word went for the herd; and he was not long throwing them hither and thither. 'But stop a bit, my lad,' said the king's daughter, 'the man that took the heads off the beast, he has my ring and my two ear-rings.' The herd put his hand in his pocket, and he threw them on the board. 'Thou art my man,' said the king's daughter. The king was not so pleased when he saw that it was a herd who was to marry his daughter, but he ordered that he should be put in a better dress; but his daughter spoke, and she said that he had a dress as fine as any that ever was in his castle; and thus it happened. The herd put on the giant's golden dress, and they married that same night.

They were now married, and everything going on well. They were one day sauntering by the side of the loch, and there came a beast more wonderfully terrible than the other, and takes him away to the loch without fear, or asking. The king's daughter was now mournful, tearful, blind-sorrowful for her married man; she was always with her eye on the loch. An old smith met her, and she told how it had befallen her married mate. The smith advised her to spread everything that was finer than another in the very same place where the beast took away her man; and so she did. The beast put up her nose, and she said, 'Fine is thy jewellery, king's daughter.' 'Finer than that is the jewel that thou tookest from me,' said she. 'Give me one sight of my man, and thou shalt get any one thing of all these thou seest.' The beast brought him up. 'Deliver him to me, and thou shalt get all thou seest,' said she. The beast did as she said. She threw him alive and whole on the bank of the loch

A short time after this, when they were walking at the side of the loch, the same beast took away the king's daughter. Sorrowful was each one that was in the town on this night. Her man was mournful, tearful, wandering down and up about the banks of the loch, by day and night. The old

114

smith met him. The smith told him that there was no way of killing the Uile Bheist but the one way, and this is it— 'In the island that is in the midst of the loch is Eillid Chaisfhion—the white footed hind, of the slenderest legs, and the swiftest step, and though she should be caught, there would spring a hoodie out of her, and though the hoodie should be caught, there would spring a trout out of her, but there is an egg in the mouth of the trout, and the soul of the beast is in the egg, and if the egg breaks, the beast is dead.

Now, there was no way of getting to this island, for the beast would sink each boat and raft that would go on the loch. He thought he would try to leap the strait with the black horse, and even so he did. The black horse leaped the strait, and the black dog with one bound after him. He saw the Eillid, and he let the black dog after her, but when the black dog would be on one side of the island, the Eillid would be on the other side. 'Oh! good were now the great dog of the carcass of flesh here!' No sooner spoke he the word than the generous dog was at his side; and after the Eillid he took, and the worthies were not long in bringing her to earth. But he no sooner caught her than a hoodie sprang out of her. ' 'Tis now, were good the falcon grey, of sharpest eye and swiftest wing!' No sooner said he this than the falcon was after the hoodie, and she was not long putting her to earth; and as the hoodie fell on the bank of the loch, out of her jumps the trout. 'Oh, that thou wert by me now, oh otter!' No sooner said than the otter was at his side, and out on the loch she leaped, and brings the trout from the midst of the loch; but no sooner was the otter on shore with the trout than the egg came from his mouth. He sprang and he put his foot on it. 'Twas then the beast let out a roar, and she said, 'Break not the egg, and thou gettest all thou askest.' 'Deliver to me my wife!' In the wink of an eye she was by his side. When he got hold of her hand in both his hands he let his foot (down) on the egg and the beast died.

The beast was dead now, and now was the sight to be seen. She was horrible to look upon. The three heads were off her doubtless, but if they were, there were heads under and heads over head on her, and eyes, and five hundred feet. But no matter, they left her there, and they went home, and there was delight and smiling in the king's house that night. And till now he had not told the king how he killed the giants. The king put great honour on him, and he was a great man with the king.

Himself and his wife were walking one day, when he noticed a little castle beside the loch in a wood; he asked his wife who was dwelling in it? She said that no one would be going near that castle, for that no one had yet come back to tell the tale, who had gone there.

'The matter must not be so,' said he; 'this very night I will see who is dwelling in it.' 'Go not, go not,' said she; 'there never went man to this castle that returned.' 'Be that as it pleases,' says he. He went; he betakes himself to the castle. When he reached the door, a little flattering crone met him standing in the door. 'All hail and good luck to thee, fisher's son; 'tis I myself am pleased to see thee; great is the honour for this kingdom, thy like to be come into it— thy coming in is fame for this little bothy; go in first; honour to the gentles; go on, and take breath.' In he went, but as he was going up, she drew the Slachdan druidhach on him, on the back of his head, and at once—there he fell.

On this night there was woe in the king's castle, and on the morrow there was a wail in the fisher's house. The tree is seen withering, and the fisher's middle son said that his brother was dead, and he made a vow and oath, that he would go, and that he would know where the corpse of his brother was lying. He put saddle on a black horse, and rode after his black dog; (for the three sons of the fisher had a black horse and a black dog), and without going hither or thither he followed on his brother's step till he reached the king's house.

This one was so like his elder brother, that the king's daughter thought it was her own man. He stayed in the castle. They told him how it befell his brother; and to the little castle of the crone, go he must—happen hard or soft

116

as it might. To the castle he went; and just as befell the eldest brother, so in each way it befell the middle son, and with one blow of the Slachdan druidhach, the crone felled him stretched beside his brother.

On seeing the second tree withering, the fisher's youngest son said that now his two brothers were dead, and that he must know what death had come on them. On the black horse he went, and he followed the dog as his brothers did, and he hit the king's house before he stopped. 'Twas the king who was pleased to see him; but to the black castle (for that was its name) they would not let him go. But to the castle he must go; and so he reached the castle. 'All hail and good luck to thyself, fisher's son: 'tis I am pleased to see thee; go in and take breath,' said she (the crone). 'In before me thou crone: I don't like flattery out of doors; go in and let's hear thy speech.' In went the crone, and when her back was to him he drew his sword and whips her head off; but the sword flew out of his hand. And swift the crone gripped her head with both hands, and puts it on her neck as it was before. The dog sprung on the crone, and she struck the generous dog with the club of magic; and there he lay. But this went not to make the youth more sluggish. To grips with the crone he goes; he got a hold of the Slachdan druidhach, and with one blow on the top of the head, she was on the earth in the wink of an eye. He went forward, up a little, and he sees his two brothers lying side by side. He gave a blow to each one with the Slackdan druidhach and on foot they were, and there was the spoil! Gold and silver, and each thing more precious than another, in the crone's castle. They came back to the king's house, and then there was rejoicing! The king was growing old. The eldest son of the fisherman was crowned king, and the pair of brothers stayed a day and a year in the king's house, and then the two went on their journey home, with the gold and silver of the crone, and each other grand thing which the king gave them; and if they have not died since then, they are alive to this very day.

THE DOOM OF SOULIS

by John Mackay Wilson

JOHN MACKAY WILSON (*1804–1835*) *started Scotland's first weekly journal for the collection and reprinting of stories and legends,* Tales of the Borders. *The son of a poor millwright, Wilson was none the less determined to earn himself a good education—and having done so gained an apprenticeship in the printing trade. This first brought him into contact with the world of letters and also caused him, after qualification, to move to London. Here he began the absorption with prose and drama which was to last him all his tragically short life. His own early attempts at authorship—mainly poetry—were unsuccessful, and despairing of life in England he returned to Scotland and was shortly afterwards appointed as editor of the* Berwick Advertiser. *Wilson's love of tradition soon became evident in his journalism and was then allowed full rein when he ventured to start a weekly journal retelling the tales and ballads of the North (1834). From an initial printing of 2,000 copies, the figure for* Tales of the Borders *soon leapt to 16,000 (a very considerable sale at this time) and success was assured. Wilson's own triumph was short-lived, however, for in the following year with forty-eight issues behind him and sales both at home and abroad booming, he died suddenly at his home—just thirty-one years old. The* Tales, *fortunately, did not die with him and after a short period in which his brother occupied the editorial chair, the series passed into the capable hands of Alexander Leighton (1800-1874) who continued the founder's work and recruited still more distinguished contributors.* Tales of the Borders *was finally completed in 1840, though new editions and revisions appeared until the end of the century. In 'The Doom of Soulis,' by Wilson himself, we find as fine a piece of writing as any to have appeared in its pages.* (The footnotes are the author's own.)

A gazetteer would inform you that Denholm is a village beautifully situated near the banks of the Teviot, about midway between Jedburgh and Hawick, and in the Parish of Cavers; and perhaps, if of modern date, it would add, it has the honour of being the birth-place of Dr. Leyden. However, it was somewhat early on a summer morning, a few years ago, that a young man, a stranger, with a fishing-rod in his hand, and a creel fastened to his shoulders, entered the village. He stood in the midst of it, and, turning round—'This, then,' said he, 'is the birth-place of Leyden— the son of genius—the martyr of study—the friend of Scott!'

Few of the villagers were astir; and at the first he met— who carried a spade over his shoulder, and appeared to be a ditcher—he inquired if he would show him the house in which the bard and scholar was born.

'Ou, ay, sir,' said the man, 'I wat I can; I'll show ye that instantly and proud to show you it, too.'

'That is good,' thought the stranger: 'the prophet is dead, but he yet speaketh—he hath honour in his own country.'

The ditcher conducted him across the green, and past the end of a house, which was described as being the schoolhouse, and was newly built, and led him towards a humble building, the height of which was but a single storey, and which was found occupied by a millwright as a workshop. Yet again, the stranger rejoiced to find that the occupier venerated his premises for the poet's sake, and that he honoured the genius of him who was born in their precincts.

'Dash it!'* said the stranger, quoting the habitual phrase of poor Leyden, 'I shall fish none today.'

---

* This was a common expression of Leyden's, and, perhaps, was in some degree expressive of his headlong and determined character.

119

And I wonder not at his having so said; for it is not every day that we can stand beneath the thatch-clad roof—or any other roof—where was born one whose name time will bear written in undying characters on its wings, until those wings droop in the darkness of eternity.

The stranger proceeded up the Teviot, oftentimes thinking of Leyden, of all that he had written, and occasionally repeating passages aloud. He almost forgot that he had a rod in his hand—his eyes did anything but follow the fly, and, I need hardly say, his success was not great.

About mid-day, he sat down on the green bank in solitariness, to enjoy a sandwich, and he also placed by his side a small flask, containing spirits, which almost every angler, who can afford it, carries with him. But he had not sat long, when a venerable-looking old man saluted him with—

'Here's a bonny day, sir.'

The old man stood as he spoke. There was something prepossessing in his appearance: he had a weatherbeaten face, with thin white hair; blue eyes, that had lost somewhat of their former lustre; his shoulders were rather bent; and he seemed a man who was certainly neither rich nor affluent, but who was at ease with the world, and the world was at ease with him.

They entered into conversation, and they sat down together. The old man appeared exactly one of those characters whom you will occasionally find fraught with the traditions of the Borders, and still tainted with, and half believing in, their ancient superstitions. I wish not to infer that superstition was carried to a greater height of absurdity on the Borders than in other parts of England and Scotland, nor even that the inhabitants of the North were as remarkable in early days for their superstitions, as they now are for their intelligence; for every nation had its superstitions, and I am persuaded that most of them might be traced to a common origin. Yet, though the same in origin, they change their likeness with the character of a nation or district. People unconsciously made their superstitions to suit themselves, though their imaginary effects still terrified them.

120

There was, therefore, a something characteristic in the fables of our forefathers which fables they believed as facts. The cunning deceived the ignorant—the ignorant were willing to deceive themselves; and what we now laugh at as the clever trick of a *hocus-pocus* man, was, scarce more than a century ago, received as a miracle—as a thing performed by the hand of the 'prince of the powers of the air'. Religion without knowledge, and still swaddled in darkness, fostered their idle fear; yea, there are few superstitions, though prostituted by wickedness, that did not own their existence to some glimmering idea of religion. They had not seen the lamp which lightens the soul, and leadeth it to knowledge; but, having perceived its far-off reflection, plunged into the quagmire of error—and hence proceeded superstition.

But I digress into a descant on the superstitions of our fathers, nor should I have done so, but that it is impossible to write a Border tale of the olden time without bringing them forward; and, when I do so, it is not with the intention of instilling into the minds of my readers the old idea of sorcery, witchcraft, and visible spirits, but of showing what was the belief and conduct of our forefathers. Therefore, without further comment, I shall cut short these remarks, and simply observe, that the thoughts of the young stranger still running upon Leyden, he turned to the elder, after they had sat together for some time, and said—

'Did you know Dr. Leyden, sir?'

'Ken him!' said the old man: 'fifty years ago, I've wrought day'swark beside his father for months together.'

They continued their conversation for some time, and the younger inquired of the elder if he were acquainted with Leyden's ballad of 'Lord Soulis'.

'Why, I hae heard a verse or twa o' the ballant, sir,' said the old man; 'but I'm sure everybody kens the story. However, if ye're no perfectly acquaint wi' it, I'm sure I'm willing to let ye hear it wi' great pleasure; and a remarkable story it is—and just as true, sir, ye may tak my word on't, as that I'm raising this bottle to my lips.'

So saying, the old man raised the flask to his mouth, and, after a regular fisher's draught, added—

'Weel, sir, I'll let ye hear the story about Lord Soulis: You have no doubt heard of Hermitage Castle, which stands upon the river of that name, at no great distance from Hawick. In the days of the great and good King Robert the Bruce, that castle was inhabited by Lord Soulis.* He was a man whose very name spread terror far and wide; for he was a tyrant and a sorcerer. He had a giant's strength, an evil eye,† and a demon's heart; and he kept his *familiar*‡ locked in a chest. Peer and peasant became pale at the name of Lord Soulis. His hand smote down the strong, his eye blasted the healthy; he oppressed the poor, and he robbed the rich. He ruled over his vassals with a rod of iron. From the banks of the Tweed, the Teviot, and the Jed, with their tributaries, to beyond the Lothians, an incessant cry was raised against him to heaven and to the king. But his life was protected by a charm, and mortal weapons could not prevail against him.'

The seriousness with which the narrator said this, showed that he gave full credit to the tradition, and believed in Lord Soulis as a sorcerer.

'He was a man of great stature, and his person was exceeding powerful. He had also royal blood in his veins, and laid claim to the crown of Scotland, in opposition to the Bruce. But two things troubled him: and the one was, to place the crown of Scotland on his head; the other, to possess the hand of a fair and rich maiden, named Marion, who was about to wed with Walter, the young heir of Branxholm, the stoutest and the boldest youth on all the wide

* He was also proprietor of Eccles, in Berwickshire, and, according to history, was seized in the town of Berwick; but tradition saith otherwise.

† There is, perhaps, no superstition more widely diffused than the belief in the fascination of an evil eye, or a malignant glance; and, I am sorry to say, the absurdity has still its believers.

‡ Each sorcerer was supposed to have his familiar spirit, that accompanied him; but Soulis was said to keep his locked in a chest.

122

Borders. Soulis was a man who was not only of a cruel heart, but it was filled with forbidden thoughts; and, to accomplish his purpose, he went down into the dungeon of his castle, in the dead of night, that no man might see him perform the "deed without a name". He carried a small lamp in his hand, which threw around a lurid light, like a glowworm in a sepulchre; and as he went, he locked the doors behind him. He carried a cat in his arms; behind him a dog followed timidly, and before him, into the dungeon, he drove a young bull, that had "never nipped the grass". He entered the deep and the gloomy vault, and, with a loud voice, he exclaimed—

' "Spirit of darkness! I come!"

'He placed the feeble lamp upon the ground, in the middle of the vault; and with a pick-axe, which he had previously prepared, he dug a pit, and buried the cat alive; and as the poor suffocating creature mewed, he exclaimed the louder—

' "Spirit of darkness! come!"

'He then leapt upon the grave of the living animal, and, scizing the dog by the neck, he dashed it violently against the wall, towards the left corner where he stood, and, unable to rise, it lay howling long and piteously on the floor. Then did he plunge his knife into the throat of the young bull, and, while its bleatings mingled with the howling of the dying dog, amidst what might be called the blue darkness of the vault, he received the blood on the palms of his hands, and he stalked around the dungeon, sprinkling it in circles, and crying with a loud voice—

' "Spirit of darkness! hear me!"

'Again he digged a pit, and, seizing the dying animal, he hurled it. into the grave, feet upwards;* and again he groaned, while the sweat stood on his brow, "Come, spirit, come!"

'He took a horse-shoe, which had lain in the vault for years, and which was called, in the family, the *spirit's shoe*,

---

* These are the recorded practices which sorcerers resorted to, when they wished to have a *glimpse* of *invisible* spirits.

and he nailed it against the door, so that it hung obliquely;*
and, as he gave the last blow to the nail, again he cried—
"Spirit, I obey thee! come!"

'Afterwards, he took his place in the middle of the floor,
and nine times he scattered around him a handful of salt,
at each time exclaiming—

' "Spirit! arise!"

'Then did he strike thrice nine times with his hands upon
a chest which stood in the middle of the floor, and by its
foot was the pale lamp, and at each blow he cried—

' "Arise, spirit! arise!"

'Therefore, when he had done these things, and cried
twenty-and-seven times, the lid of the chest began to move,
and a fearful figure, with a red cap† upon its head, and
which resembled nothing in heaven above, or on earth
below, rose, and, with a hollow voice,‡ inquired—

' "What want ye, Soulis?"

' "Power, spirit! power!" he cried, "that mine eyes may
have their desire, and that every weapon formed by man
may fall scatheless on my body, as the spent light of a
waning moon!"

' "Thy wish is granted, mortal!" groaned the fiend;
"tomorrow eve, young Branxholm's bride shall sit within
thy bower, and his sword return bent from thy bosom, as
though he had lashed it against a rock. Farewell! invoke me
not again for seven years, nor open the door of the vault,
but then knock thrice upon the chest, and I will answer thee.
Away! follow thy course of sin, and prosper; *but beware of a
coming wood!*"

* In the account of the trial of Elizabeth Bathgate, wife of Alexander
Pae, maltman in Eyemouth, one of the accusations in the indictment
against her was, that she had 'ane horse-schoe in ane darnet and secriet
pairt of your dur, keepit by you thairopoun, as ane devilish meanis
and instructions from the devill'.

† Red-cap is a name given to spirits supposed to haunt castles.

‡ In the proceedings regarding Sir George Maxwell, it is gravely set
forth that the voice of evil spirits is 'rough and goustie'; and, to crown
all, Lilly, in his *Life and Times*, informs us that they speak Erse; and,
adds he, 'when they do so, it's like Irishmen, much in the throat!'

'With a loud and sudden noise, the lid of the massy chest fell, and the spirit disappeared, and from the floor of the vault issued a deep sound, like the reverbing of thunder. Soulis took up the flickering lamp, and, leaving the dying dog still howling in the corner whence he had driven it, he locked the iron door, and placed the huge key in his bosom.

'In the morning, his vassals came to him, and they prayed him on their bended knees that he would lessen the weight of their hard bondage; but he laughed at their prayers, and answered them with stripes. He oppressed the widow, and persecuted the fatherless; he defied the powerful, and trampled on the weak. His name spread terror wheresoever it was breathed, and there was not in all Scotland a man more feared than the Wizard Soulis, the Lord of Hermitage.

'He rode forth in the morning, with twenty of his chosen men behind him; and wheresoever they passed, the castle or the cottage, where the occupier was the enemy of Soulis or denied his right to the crown,* they fired the latter, destroyed the cattle around the former, or he sprinkled upon them the dust of a dead man's hand, that a murrain might come amongst them.

'But, as they rode by the side of the Teviot, he beheld fair Marion, the betrothed bride of young Walter, the heir of Branxholm, riding forth with her maidens, and pursuing the red-deer.

' "By this token, spirit!" muttered Soulis, joyously, "thou hast not lied—tonight young Branxholm's bride shall sit within my bower!"

'He dashed the spur into the side of his fleet steed, and, although Marion and her attendants forsook the chase, and fled, as they perceived him, yet, as though his *familiar* gave speed to his horse's feet, in a few seconds he rode by the side of Marion, and, throwing out his arm, he lifted her from the saddle, while her horse yet flew at its fastest speed, and continued its course without its fair rider.

* If legitimacy could have been proved on the part of the grandmother of Lord Soulis, he certainly was a nearer heir to the crown than either Bruce or Baliol.

'She screamed aloud, she struggled wildly, but her attendants had fled afar off, and her strength was feeble as an insect's web in his terrible embrace. He held her upon the saddle before him—

' "Marion!—fair Marion!" said the wizard and ruffian lover, "scream not —struggle not—be calm, and hear me. I love thee, pretty one!—I love thee!" and he rudely raised her lips to his. "Fate hath decreed thou shalt be mine, Marion, and no human power shall take thee from me. Weep not—strive not. Hear ye not, I love thee—love thee fiercely, madly, maiden, as a she-wolf doth its cubs. As a river seeketh the sea, so have I sought thee, Marion: and now, thou art mine—fate hath given thee unto me, and thy fair cheek shall rest upon a manlier bosom than that of Branxholm's beardless heir." Thus saying, and still grasping her before him, he again plunged his spurs into his horse's sides, and he and his followers rode furiously towards Hermitage Castle.

'He locked the gentle Marion within a strong chamber, he

"Woo'd her as the lion woos his bride".

And now she wept, she wrung her hands, she tore her raven hair before him, and it hung dishevelled over her face and upon her shoulders. She implored him to save her, to restore her to liberty; and again finding her tears wasted and her prayers in vain, she defied him, she invoked the vengeance of Heaven upon his head; and, at such moments, the tyrant and the reputed sorcerer stood awed and stricken in her presence. For there is something in the majesty of virtue, and the holiness of innocence, as they flash from the eyes of an injured woman, which deprives guilt of its strength, and defeats its purpose, as though Heaven lent its electricity to defend the weak.

'But, wearied with importunity, and finding his threats of no effect, on the third night that she had been within his castle, he clutched her in his arms, and, while his vassals slept, he bore her to the haunted dungeon, that the spirit might throw its spell over her, and compel her to love him.

He unlocked the massy door. The faint howls of the dog were still heard from a corner of the vault. He placed the lamp upon the ground. He still held the gentle Marion to his side, and her terror had almost mastered her struggles. He struck his clenched hand upon the huge chest—he cried aloud, "Spirit! come forth!"

'Thrice he repeated the blow—thrice he uttered aloud his invocation. But the spirit arose not at his summons. Marion knew the tale of his sorcery—she knew and believed it—and terror deprived her of consciousness. On recovering, she found herself again in the strong chamber where she had been confined, but Soulis was not with her. She strove to calm her fears, she knelt down and told her beads and, she begged that her Walter might be sent to her deliverance.

'It was scarce daybreak when the young heir of Branxholm, whose bow no man could bend, and whose sword was terrible in battle, with twice ten armed men, arrived before Hermitage Castle, and demanded to speak with Lord Soulis. The warder blew his horn, and Soulis and his attendants came forth and looked over the battlement.

' "What want ye, boy," inquired the wizard chief, "that, ere the sun be risen, ye come to seek the lion in his den?"

' "I come," replied young Walter, boldly, "in the name of our good king, and by his authority, to demand that ye give into my hands, safe and sound, my betrothed bride, lest vengeance come upon thee."

' "Vengeance, beardling!" rejoined the sorcerer; "who dare speak of vengeance on the house of Soulis?—or whom call ye king? The crown is mine—thy bride is mine, and thou also shalt be mine; and a dog's death shalt thou die in thy morning's boasting."

' "To arms!" he exclaimed, as he disappeared from the battlement, and within a few minutes a hundred men rushed from the gate.

'Sir Walter's little band qualied as they beheld the superior force of their enemies, and they were in dread also of the sorcery of Soulis. But hope revived within them when they beheld the look of confidence on the countenance of their young leader, and thought of the strength of his arm, and the terror which his sword spread.

'As hungry tigers spring upon their prey, so rushed Soulis and his vassals upon Sir Walter and his followers. No man could stand before the sword of the sorcerer. Antagonists fell as impotent things before his giant strength. Even Walter marvelled at the havoc he made, and he pressed forwards to measure swords with him. But, ere he could reach him, his few followers who had escaped the hand of Soulis and his host fled, and left him to maintain the battle single-handed. Every vassal of the sorcerer, save three, pursued them; and against these three, and their charmed lord, young Walter was left to maintain the unequal strife. But, as they pressed around him, "Back!" cried Soulis, trusting to his strength and to his charm; "from my hand alone must Branxholm's young boaster meet his doom. It is meet that I should give his head as a toy to my bride, fair Marion."

' "Thy bride, fiend!" exclaimed Sir Walter; "thine—now perish!" and he attacked him furiously.

' "Ha! ha!" cried Soulis, and laughed at the impetuosity of his antagonist, while he parried his thrusts; "take rushes for thy weapon, boy; steel falls feckless upon me."

' "Vile sorcerer!" continued Walter, pressing upon him more fiercely, "this sword shall sever thy enchantment."

'Again Soulis laughed; but he found that his contempt availed him not, for the strength of his enemy was equal to his own, and, in repelling his fierce assaults, he almost forgot the charm which rendered his body invulnerable. They fought long and desperately, when one of the followers of Soulis, suddenly and unobserved, thrusting his spear into the side of Sir Walter's horse, it reared, stumbled, and fell, and brought him to the ground.

' "An arrow-schot!"* exclaimed Soulis. "Wherefore, boy, didst thou presume to contend with me?" And suddenly

---

* When cattle died suddenly, it was believed to be by an arrowshot—that is, shot or struck down by the invisible dart of a sorcerer.

springing from his horse, he pressed his iron heel upon the breast of his foe, and turning also the point of his sword towards his throat, "Thou shalt not die yet," said he; and turning to the three attendants who had not followed in the pursuit, he added, "Hither—bind him fast and sure." Then did the three hold him on the ground, and bind his hands and his feet, while Soulis held his naked sword over him.

' "Coward and wizard!" exclaimed Walter, as they dragged him within the gate, "ye shall rue this foul treachery."

' "Ha! ha! vain, boasting boy!" returned Soulis, "thou indeed shalt rue thy recklessness."

'He caused his vassals to bear Walter into the strong chamber where fair Marion was confined, and, grasping him by the neck, while he held his sword to his breast, he dragged him towards her, and said, sternly, "Consent thee now, maiden, to be mine, and this boy shall live; refuse, and his head shall roll before thee on the floor as a plaything."

' "Monster!" she exclaimed, and screamed aloud. "would ye harm my Walter?"

' "Ha! my Marion!—Marion!" cried Walter, struggling to be free. And, turning his eyes fiercely upon Soulis—"Destroy me, fiend," he added, "but harm not her."

' "Think on it, maiden," cried the sorcerer, raising his sword; "the life of thy bonny bridegroom hangs upon thy word. But ye shall have until midnight to reflect on it. Be mine, then, and harm shall not come upon him or thee; but a man shall be thy husband, and not the boy whom he hath brought to thee in bonds."

' "Beshrew thee, vile sorcerer!" rejoined Walter. "Were my hands unbound, and unarmed as I am, I would force my way from thy prison, in spite of thee and thine!"

'Soulis laughed scornfully, and again added, "Think on it, fair Marion."

'Then did he drag her betrothed bridegroom to a corner of the chamber, and ordering a strong chain to be brought, he fettered him against the wall; in the same manner, he fastened her to the opposite side of the apartment—but the chains with which he bound her were made of silver.

'When they were left alone, "Mourn not, sweet Marion," said Walter, "and think not of saving me—before tomorrow our friends will be here to thy rescue; and, though I fall a victim to the vengeance of the sorcerer, still let me be the bridegroom of thy memory."

'Marion wept bitterly, and said that she would die with him.

'Throughout the day, the spirit of Lord Soulis was troubled, and the fear of coming evil sat heavy on his heart. He wandered to and fro on the battlements of his castle, anxiously looking for the approach of his retainers, who had followed in pursuit of the followers of Branxholm's heir. But the sun set, and the twilight drew on, and still they came not; and it was drawing towards midnight when a solitary horseman spurred his jaded steed towards the castle gate. Soulis admitted him with his own hand into the courtyard; and, ere the rider had dismounted, he inquired of him hastily, and in a tone of apprehension—

' "Where be thy fellows, knave? and why come alone?"

' "Pardon me, my lord," said the horseman, falteringly, as he dismounted; "thy faithful bondsman is the bearer of evil tidings."

' "Evil, slave!" exclaimed Soulis, striking him as he spoke; "speak ye of evil to me? What of it?—where are thy fellows?"

'The man trembled and added—"In pursuing the followers of Branxholm, they sought refuge in the wilds of Tarras, and being ignorant of the winding paths through its bottomless morass, horses and men have been buried in it—they who sank not fell beneath the swords of those they had pursued, and I only have escaped."

' "And wherefore did ye escape, knave?" cried the fierce sorcerer; "why did ye live to remind me of the shame of the house of Soulis?" And, as he spoke, he struck the trembling man again.

130

'He hurried to the haunted dungeon, and again performed his incantations, with impatience in his manner and fury in his looks. Thrice he violently struck the chest, and thrice he exclaimed, impetuously—

' "Spirit! come forth!—arise and speak with me!"

'The lid was lifted up, and a deep and angry voice said, "Mortal! Wherefore hast thou summoned me before the time I commanded thee? Was not thy wish granted? Steel shall not wound thee—cords bind thee—hemp hang thee— nor water drown thee. Away!"

' "Stay!" exclaimed Soulis—"add, nor fire consume me!"

' "Ha! ha!" cried the spirit, in a fit of horrid laughter, that made even the sorcerer tremble. "*Beware of a coming wood*!" And, with a loud clang, the lid of the chest fell, and the noise as of thunder beneath his feet was repeated.

' "Beware of a coming wood!" muttered Soulis to himself; "what means the fiend?"

'He hastened from the dungeon without locking the door behind him, and as he hurried from it, he drew the key from his bosom, and flung it over his left shoulder, crying, "Keep it, spirit!"

'He shut himself up in his chamber to ponder on the words of his familiar, and on the extirpation of his followers; and he thought not of Marion and her bridegroom until daybreak, when, with a troubled and a wrathful countenance, he entered the apartment where they were fettered.

' "How now, fair maiden?" he began; "hast thou considered well my words?—wilt thou be my willing bride, and let young Branxholm live? or refuse, and look thy fill on his smooth face as his head adorns the point of my good spear?"

' "Rather than see her thine," exclaimed Walter, "I would thou shouldst hew me in pieces, and fling my mangled body to your hounds."

' "Troth! and 'tis no bad thought," said the sorcerer; "thou mayest have thy wish. Yet, boy, ye think that I have no mercy: I will teach thee that I have, and refined mercy too. Now, tell me truly, were I in thy power as thou art in mine, what fate would ye award to Soulis?"

131

' "Then truly," replied Walter, "I would hang thee on the highest tree in Branxholm woods."

' "Well spoken, young Strong-bow," returned Soulis; "and I will show thee, though ye think I have no mercy, that I am more merciful than thou. Ye would choose for me the highest tree, but I shall *give thee the choice of the tree from which you may prefer your body to hang*, and from whose top the owl may sing its midnight song, and to which the ravens shall gather for a feast. And thou, pretty face," added he, turning to Marion, "because you will not, even to save him, give me thine hand, i'faith, if I may not be thy husband, I will be thy priest, and celebrate your marriage, for I will bind your hands together, and ye shall hang on the next branch to him."

' "For that I thank thee," said the undaunted maiden.

'He then called together his four remaining armed men, and placing halters round the necks of his intended victims, they were dragged forth to the Hermitage, where Walter was to choose the fatal tree.

'Now a deep mist covered the face of the earth, and they could perceive no object at the distance of half a bow-shot before them; and ere he had approached the wood where he was to carry his merciless project into execution—

' "The wood comes towards us!" exclaimed one of his followers.

' "What!—*the wood comes*!" cried Soulis, and his cheek became pale, and he thought on the words of the demon— "*Beware of a coming wood*!"—and, for a time, their remembrance, and the forest that seemed to advance before him, deprived his arm of strength, and his mind of resolution, and, before his heart recovered, the followers of the house of Branxholm, to the number of fourscore, each bearing a tall branch of a rowan-tree in their hands,* as a charm

* It is probable that the legend of the '*coming wood*', referred to in the tradition respecting Lord Soulis, is the same as that from which Shakespeare takes Macbeth's charm—'Till Birnam Wood shall come to Dunsinane'. The circumstances are similar.

against his sorcery, perceived, and raising a loud shout, surrounded him.

'The cords with which the arms of Marion and Walter were bound, were instantly cut asunder. But, although the odds against him were as twenty to one, the daring Soulis defied them all. Yea, when his followers were overpowered, his single arm dealt death around.

'Now, there was not a day passed that complaints were not brought to King Robert, from those residing on the Borders, against Lord Soulis, for his lawless oppression, his cruelty, and his wizard-craft. And, one day, there came before the monarch, one after another, some complaining that he had brought diseases on their cattle, or destroyed their houses by fire, and a third, that he had stolen away the fair bride of Branxholm's heir, and they stood before the king, and begged to know what should be done unto him. Now, the king was wearied with their importunities and complaints, and he exclaimed, peevishly and unthinkingly, "*Boil him, if you please, but let me hear no more about him.*" But,

"It is the curse of kings to be attended
    By slaves that take their humour for a warrant",
and, when the enemies of Soulis heard these words from the lips of the king, they hastened away to put them in execution; and with them they took a wise man, one who was learned in breaking the spells of sorcery,* and with him he carried a scroll, on which was written the secret wisdom of Michael the Wizard; and they arrived before Hermitage Castle, while its lord was contending single-handed against the retainers of Branxholm, and their swords were blunted on his buckler, and his body received no wounds. They

---

* Dr. Leyden represents this personage as being 'True Thomas, Lord of Ersylton'; but the Rhymer was dead before the time fixed by tradition of the death of Lord Soulis, which took place in the time of Robert the Bruce, who came to the crown in 1308, and the Rhymer was dead before 1299 for in that year his son and heir granted a charter to the convent of Soltra, and in it he describes himself *Filius et haeres Thomae Rymour de Erceldon.*

struck him to the ground with their lances; and they endeavoured to bind his hands and his feet with cords, but his spell snapped them asunder as threads.

' "Wrap him in lead," cried the wise man, "and boil him therewith, according to the command of the king; for water and hempen cords have no power over his sorcery."

'Many ran towards the castle, and they tore the lead from the turrets, and they held down the sorcerer, and rolled the sheets around him in many folds, till he was powerless as a child, and the foam fell from his lips in the impotency of his rage. Others procured a caldron, in which it was said many of his incantations were performed, and the cry was raised—

' "Boil him on the Nine-stane rig!"

'And they bore him to where the stones of the Druids are to be seen till this day, and the two stones are yet pointed out from which the caldron was suspended. They kindled piles of faggots beneath it, and they bent the living body of Soulis within the lead; and thrust it into the caldron, and, as the flames arose, the flesh and the bones of the wizard were consumed in the boiling lead. Such was the doom of Soulis.

'The king sent messengers to prevent his hasty words being carried into execution, but they arrived too late.

'In a few weeks there was mirth, and music, and a marriage feast in the bowers of Branxholm, and fair Marion was the bride.'

THE HOUSE OF ELD

by Robert Louis Stevenson

ROBERT LOUIS BELFOUR STEVENSON (*1850–1894*) *is, of course, one of the greatest of all Scottish literary figures. His stories of high adventure have appealed continuously to generations of young readers, while his novels such as* Dr. Jekyll and Mr. Hyde *and essays such as* Virginibus Puerisque *have assured him a place in the forefront of world literature. Stevenson's unhappy life of illness and his recurring nightmares undoubtedly contributed in making his tales of fantasy and evil outstanding examples of their kind. (More than one biographer has also cited an influence in the vivid tales of dark forces which were told to him as a child by his nurse.) While much of his work is widely known—and indeed readily available—this is not true of his fables, a story-form which attracted him on and off throughout his life. In 1888 he discussed a collection of these tales with a publisher while in New York, and already had in hand the nucleus of a book. However, further travels and absorption in the major work still to come caused him to shelve the project, and it was not until after his death that the half-forgotten group of fables found their way into print. It is difficult to tell what impact the collection might have had on later assessments of Stevenson's work if it had been completed as originally planned—yet by the selection of just one story here the reader can soon see how the master of so many areas of literature shows himself no less skilled and inventive in the area of fantasy and moral allegory.*

So soon as the child began to speak, the gyve (fetter) was riveted; and the boys and girls limped about their play like convicts. Doubtless it was more pitiable to see and more painful to bear in youth; but even the grown folk, besides being very unhandy on their feet, were often sick with ulcers.

About the time when Jack was ten years old, many strangers began to journey through that country. These he beheld going lightly by on the long roads, and the thing amazed him. 'I wonder how it comes,' he asked, 'that all these strangers are so quick afoot, and we must drag about our fetter?'

'My dear boy,' said his uncle, the catechist, 'do not complain about your fetter, for it is the only thing that makes life worth living. None are happy, none are good, none are respectable, that are not gyved like us. And I must tell you, besides, it is very dangerous talk. If you grumble of your iron, you will have no luck; if ever you take it off, you will be instantly smitten by a thunderbolt.'

'Are there no thunderbolts for these strangers?' asked Jack.

'Jupiter is longsuffering to the benighted,' returned the catechist.

'Upon my word, I could wish I had been less fortunate,' said Jack. 'For if I had been born benighted, I might now be going free; and it cannot be denied the iron is inconvenient, and the ulcer hurts.'

'Ah!' cried his uncle, 'do not envy the heathen! Theirs is a sad lot! Ah, poor souls, if they but knew the joys of being fettered! Poor souls, my heart yearns for them. But the truth is they are vile, odious, insolent, ill-conditioned, stinking brutes, not truly human—for what is a man without a fetter?—and you cannot be too particular not to touch or speak with them.'

After this talk, the child would never pass one of the unfettered on the road but what he spat at him and called him names, which was the practice of the children in that part.

136

It chanced one day, when he was fifteen, he went into the woods, and the ulcer pained him. It was a fair day, with a blue sky; all the birds were singing; but Jack nursed his foot. Presently, another song began; it sounded like the singing of a person, only far more gay; at the same time there was a beating on the earth. Jack put aside the leaves; and there was a lad of his own village, leaping, and dancing and singing to himself in a green dell; and on the grass beside him lay the dancer's iron.

'Oh!' cried Jack, 'you have your fetter off!'

'For God's sake, don't tell your uncle!' cried the lad.

'If you fear my uncle,' returned Jack, 'why do you not fear the thunderbolt?'

'That is only an old wives' tale,' said the other. 'It is only told to children. Scores of us come here among the woods and dance for nights together, and are none the worse.'

This put Jack in a thousand new thoughts. He was a grave lad; he had no mind to dance himself; he wore his fetter manfully, and tended his ulcer without complaint. But he loved the less to be deceived or to see others cheated. He began to lie in wait for heathen travellers, at covert parts of the road, and in the dusk of the day, so that he might speak with them unseen; and these were greatly taken with their wayside questioner, and told him things of weight. The wearing of gyves (they said) was no command of Jupiter's. It was the contrivance of a white-faced thing, a sorcerer, that dwelt in that country in the Wood of Eld. He was one like Glaucus that could change his shape, yet he could be always told; for when he was crossed, he gobbled like a turkey He had three lives; but the third smiting would make an end of him indeed; and with that his house of sorcery would vanish, the gyves fall, and the villagers take hands and dance like children.

'And in your country?' Jack would ask.

But at this the travellers, with one accord, would put him off; until Jack began to suppose there was no land entirely happy. Or, if there were, it must be one that kept its folk at home; which was natural enough.

But the case of the gyves weighed upon him The sight of the children limping stuck in his eyes; the groans of such as dressed their ulcers haunted him. And it came at last in his mind that he was born to free them.

There was in that village a sword of heavenly forgery, beaten upon Vulcan's anvil. It was never used but in the temple, and then the flat of it only; and it hung on a nail by catechist's chimney. Early one night, Jack rose, and took the sword, and was gone out of the house and the village in the darkness.

All night he walked at a venture; and when day came, he met strangers going to the fields. Then he asked after the Wood of Eld and the house of sorcery; and one said north, and one south; until Jack saw that they deceived him. So then, when he asked his way of any man, he showed the bright sword naked; and at that the gyve on the man's ankle rang, and answered in his stead; and the word was still *Straight on*. But the man, when his gyve spoke, spat and struck at Jack, and threw stones at him as he went away; so that his head was broken.

So he came to that wood, and entered in, and he was aware of a house in a low place, where funguses grew, and the trees met, and the steaming of the marsh arose about it like a smoke. It was a fine house, and very rambling; some parts of it were ancient like the hills, and some but of yesterday, and none finished; and all the ends of it were open, so that you could go in from every side. Yet it was in good repair, and all the chimneys smoked.

Jack went in through the gable; and there was one room after another, all bare, but all furnished in part, so that a man could dwell there; and in each there was a fire burning, where a man could warm himself, and a table spread where he might eat. But Jack saw nowhere any living creature; only the bodies of some stuffed.

'This is a hospitable house,' said Jack; 'but the ground must be quaggy underneath, for at every step the building quakes.'

He had gone some time in the house, when he began to be

138

hungry. Then he looked at the food, and at first he was afraid; but he bared the sword, and by the shining of the sword, it seemed the food was honest. So he took the courage to sit down and eat, and he was refreshed in mind and body.

'This is strange,' thought he, 'that in the house of sorcery there should be food so wholesome.'

As he was yet eating, there came into that room the appearance of his uncle, and Jack was afraid because he had taken the sword. But his uncle was never more kind, and sat down to meat with him, and praised him because he had taken the sword. Never had these two been more pleasantly together, and Jack was full of love for the man.

'It was very well done,' said his uncle, 'to take the sword and come yourself into the House of Eld; a good thought and a brave deed. But now you are satisfied; and we may go home to dinner arm in arm.'

'Oh, dear, no!' said Jack. 'I am not satisfied yet.'

'How!' cried his uncle. 'Are you not warmed by the fire? Does not this food sustain you?'

'I see the food to be wholesome,' said Jack: 'and still it is no proof that a man should wear a gyve on his right leg.'

Now at this the appearance of his uncle gobbled like a turkey.

'Jupiter!' cried Jack, 'is this the sorcerer?'

His hand held back and his heart failed him for the love he bore his uncle; but he heaved up the sword and smote the appearance on the head; and it cried out aloud with the voice of his uncle; and fell to the ground; and a little bloodless white thing fled from the room.

The cry rang in Jack's ears, and his knees smote together, and conscience cried upon him; and yet he was strengthened, and there woke in his bones the lust of that enchanter's blood. 'If the gyves are to fall,' said he, 'I must go through with this, and when I get home I shall find my uncle dancing.'

So he went on after the bloodless thing. In the way, he met the appearance of his father; and his father was incensed,

139

and railed upon him, and called to him upon his duty, and bade him be home, while there was yet time. 'For you can still,' said he, 'be home by sunset; and then all will be forgiven.'

'God knows,' said Jack, 'I fear your anger; but yet your anger does not prove that a man should wear a gyve on his right leg.'

And at that the appearance of his father gobbled like a turkey.

'Ah, heaven,' cried Jack, 'the sorcerer again!'

The blood ran backward in his body and his joints rebelled against him for the love he bore his father; but he heaved up the sword, and plunged it in the heart of the appearance; and the appearance cried out aloud with the voice of his father; and fell to the ground, and a little bloodless white thing fled from the room.

The cry rang in Jack's ears, and his soul was darkened; but now rage came to him. 'I have done what I dare not think upon,' said he. 'I will go to an end with it, or perish. And when I get home, I pray God this may be a dream, and I may find my father dancing.'

So he went on after the bloodless thing that had escaped; and in the way he met the appearance of his mother, and she wept. 'What have you done?' she cried. 'What is this that you have done? Oh, come home (where you may be by bedtime) ere you do more ill to me and mine; for it is enough to smite my brother and your father.'

'Dear mother, it is not these that I have smitten,' said Jack; 'it was but the enchanter in their shape. And even if I had, it would not prove that a man should wear a gyve on his right leg.'

And at this the appearance gobbled like a turkey.

He never knew how he did that; but he swung the sword on the one side, and clove the appearance through the midst; and it cried out aloud with the voice of his mother; and fell to the ground; and with the fall of it, the house was gone from over Jack's head, and he stood alone in the woods, and the gyve was loosened from his leg.

'Well,' said he, 'the enchanter is now dead, and the fetter gone.' But the cries rang in his soul, and the day was like night to him. 'This has been a sore business,' said he. 'Let me get forth out of the wood, and see the good that I have done to others.'

He thought to leave the fetter where it lay, but when he turned to go, his mind was otherwise. So he stooped and put the gyve in his bosom; and the rough iron galled him as he went, and his bosom bled.

Now when he was forth of the wood upon the highway, he met folk returning from the field; and those he met had no fetter on the right leg, but, behold! they had one upon the left. Jack asked them what it signified; and they said, 'that was the new wear, for the old was found to be a superstition.' Then he looked at them nearly; and there was a new ulcer on the left ankle, and the old one on the right was not yet healed.

'Now, may God forgive me!' cried Jack. 'I would I were well home.'

And when he was home, there lay his uncle smitten on the head, and his father pierced through the heart, and his mother cloven through the midst. And he sat in the lone house and wept beside the bodies.

Moral

Old is the tree and the fruit good,
Very old and thick the wood.
Woodman, is your courage stout?
Beware! the root is wrapped about
Your mother's heart, your father's bones;
And like the mandrake comes with groans.

THE MAN IN THE BELL

by W. E. Aytoun

WILLIAM EDMONSTOUNE AYTOUN (*1813–1865*) *was one of the earliest and most distinguished contributors to* Blackwood's Magazine—*the immortal* Maga, *now over 150 years old and still read all round the world. Professor Aytoun, who was born and educated in Edinburgh, was first called to the bar, but later turned to teaching and in 1845 became professor of Rhetoric and Belles-Lettres at the city's University. At this time he was also writing a great deal of poetry and had a reputation for delivering brilliant lectures on famous poets. During his social round he met and became friendly with William Blackwood (1776–1834), the Edinburgh bookseller who started* Blackwood's Magazine *in 1817. He was invited to contribute to the new publication, did so, and was soon an intimate of the other contributors to the magazine, including John Wilson ('Christopher North'), John Gibson Lockhart and James Hogg. Professor Aytoun earns his place here as representative of the macabre fiction which has appeared in* Blackwood's Magazine, *not because of the weight of material of this type which he contributed to the journal (in fact, he wrote very little fiction) but rather because this tale, of all those I have studied, is a near perfect example of controlled, suspenseful horror. Reminiscent somewhat of Poe's* The Pit and the Pendulum, *it may well have been based on a real occurrence, but in its grim retelling of a ghastly experience sets a standard of terror few even of today's masters could hope to better.*

In my younger days bell-ringing was much more in fashion among the young men of —— than it is now. Nobody, I believe, practises it there at present except the servants of the church, and the melody has been much injured in consequence. Some fifty years ago about twenty of us who dwelt in the vicinity of the cathedral formed a club, which used to ring every peal that was called for; and from continual practice and a rivalry which arose between us and a club attached to another steeple, and which tended considerably to sharpen our zeal, we became very Mozarts on our favorite instruments. But my bell-ringing practice was shortened by a singular accident, which not only stopped my performance, but made even the sound of a bell terrible to my ears.

One Sunday I went with another into the belfry to ring for noon prayers, but the second stroke we had pulled showed us that the clapper of the bell we were at was muffled. Some one had been buried that morning, and it had been prepared, of course, to ring a mournful note. We did not know of this, but the remedy was easy.

'Jack,' said my companion, 'step up to the loft and cut off the hat'; for the way we had of muffling was by typing a piece of an old hat, or of cloth (the former was preferred), to one side of the clapper, which deadened every second toll.

I complied, and mounting into the belfry, crept as usual into the bell, where I began to cut away. The hat had been tied on in some more complicated manner than usual, and I was perhaps three or four minutes in getting it off, during which time my companion below was hastily called away, by a message from his sweetheart, I believe; but that is not material to my story.

The person who called him was a brother of the club, who, knowing that the time had come for ringing for service, and not thinking that any one was above, began to pull. At this moment I was just getting out, when I felt the bell moving; I guessed the reason at once—it was a moment of terror; but by a hasty, and almost convulsive effort, I succeeded in jumping down, and throwing myself on the flat of my back under the bell.

143

The room in which it was was little more than sufficient to contain it, the bottom of the bell coming within a couple of feet of the floor of lath. At that time I certainly was not so bulky as I am now, but as I lay it was within an inch of my face. I had not laid myself down a second when the ringing began. It was a dreadful situation. Over me swung an immense mass of metal, one touch of which would have crushed me to pieces; the floor under me was principally composed of crazy laths, and if they gave way, I was precipitated to the distance of about fifty feet upon a loft, which would, in all probability, have sunk under the impulse of my fall, and sent me to be dashed to atoms upon the marble floor of the chancel, a hundred feet below.

I remembered—for fear is quick in recollection—how a common clock-wright, about a month before, had fallen, and bursting through the floors of the steeple, driven in the ceilings of the porch, and even broken into the marble tombstone of a bishop who slept beneath. This was my first terror, but the ringing had not continued a minute before a more awful and immediate dread came on me. The deafening sound of the bell smote into my ears with a thunder which made me fear their drums would crack. There was not a fibre of my body it did not thrill through! it entered my very soul; thought and reflection were almost utterly banished; I only retained the sensation of agonising terror.

Every moment I saw the bell sweep within an inch of my face; and my eyes—I could not close them, though to look at the object was bitter as death—followed it instinctively in its oscillating progress until it came back again. It was in vain I said to myself that it could come no nearer at any future swing than it did at first; every time it descended I endeavoured to shrink into the very floor to avoid being buried under the down-sweeping mass; and then reflecting on the danger of pressing too weightily on my frail support, would cower up again as far as I dared.

At first my fears were mere matter of fact. I was afraid the pulleys above would give way and let the bell plunge

144

on me. At another time the possibility of the clapper being shot out in some sweep, and dashing through my body, as I had seen a ramrod glide through a door, flitted across my mind. The dread also, as I have already mentioned, of the crazy floor, tormented me; but these soon gave way to fears not more unfounded, but more visionary, and of course more tremendous. The roaring of the bell confused my intellect, and my fancy soon began to teem with all sorts of strange and terrifying ideas. The bell pealing above, and opening its jaws with a hideous clamour, seemed to me at one time a ravening monster, raging to devour me; at another, a whirlpool ready to suck me into its bellowing abyss.

As I gazed on it, it assumed all shapes; it was a flying eagle, or rather a roc of the Arabian story-tellers, clapping its wings and screaming over me. As I looked upwards into it, it would appear sometimes to lengthen into indefinite extent, or to be twisted at the end into the spiral folds of the tail of a flying-dragon. Nor was the flaming breath, or fiery glance of that fabled animal, wanting to complete the picture. My eyes, inflamed, bloodshot, and glaring, invested the supposed monster with a full proportion of unholy light.

It would be endless were I to merely hint at all the fancies that possessed my mind. Every object that was hideous and roaring presented itself to my imagination. I often thought that I was in a hurricane at sea, and that the vessel in which I was embarked tossed under me with the most furious vehemence. The air, set in motion by the swinging of the bell, blew over me, nearly with the violence, and more than the thunder, of a tempest; and the floor seemed to reel under me, as under a drunken man.

But the most awful of all the ideas that seized on me were drawn from the supernatural. In the vast cavern of the bell hideous faces appeared, and glared down on me with terrifying frowns, or with grinning mockery still more appalling. At last the devil himself, accoutred, as in the common description of the evil spirit, with hoof, horn, and tail, and eyes of infernal lustre, made his appearance, and called on

145

me to curse God and worship him, who was powerful to save me. This dread suggestion he uttered with the full-toned clangour of the bell. I had him within an inch of me, and I thought on the fate of the Santon Barsisa. Strenuously and desperately I defied him, and bade him begone.

Reason then, for a moment, resumed her sway, but it was only to fill me with fresh terror, just as the lightning dispels the gloom that surrounds the benighted mariner, but to show him that his vessel is driving on a rock, where she must inevitably be dashed to pieces, I found I was becoming delirious, and trembled lest reason should utterly desert me. This is at all times an agonising thought, but it smote me then with tenfold agony. I feared lest, when utterly deprived of my senses, I should rise, to do which I was every moment tempted by that strange feeling which calls on a man, whose head is dizzy from standing on the battlement of a lofty castle, to precipitate himself from it, and then death would be instant and tremendous.

When I thought of this I became desperate. I caught the floor with a grasp which drove the blood from my nails; and I yelled with the cry of despair. I called for help, I prayed, I shouted, but all the efforts of my voice were, of course, drowned in the bell. As it passed over my mouth it occasionally echoed my cries, which mixed not with its own sound, but preserved their distinct character. Perhaps this was but fancy. To me, I know, they then sounded as if they were the shouting, howling, or laughing of the fiends with which my imagination had peopled the gloomy cave which swung over me.

You may accuse me of exaggerating my feelings; but I am not. Many a scene of dread have I since passed through, but they are nothing to the self-inflicted terrors of this half hour. The ancients have doomed one of the damned in their Tartarus to lie under a rock, which every moment seems to be descending to annihilate him—and an awful punishment it would be. But if to this you add a clamour as loud as if ten thousand furies were howling about you—a deafening uproar banishing reason, and driving you to madness, you

146

must allow that the bitterness of the pang was rendered more terrible. There is no man, firm as his nerves may be, who could retain his courage in this situation.

In twenty minutes the ringing was done. Half of that time passed over me without power of computation—the other half appeared an age. When it ceased, I became gradually more quiet, but a new fear retained me. I knew that five minutes would elapse without ringing, but at the end of that short time the bell would be rung a second time, for five minutes more. I could not calculate time. A minute and an hour were of equal duration. I feared to rise, lest the five minutes should have elapsed, and the ringing be again commenced, in which case I should be crushed, before I could escape, against the walls or framework of the bell. I therefore still continued to lie down, cautiously shifting myself, however, with a careful gliding, so that my eye no longer looked into the hollow.

This was of itself a considerable relief. The cessation of the noise had, in a great measure, the effect of stupefying me, for my attention being no longer occupied by the chimeras I had conjured up, began to flag. All that now distressed me was the constant expectation of the second ringing, for which, however, I settled myself with a kind of stupid resolution. I closed my eyes, and clenched my teeth as firmly as if they were screwed in a vice. At last the dreaded moment came, and the first swing of the bell extorted a groan from me, as they say the most resolute victim screams at the sight of the rack, to which he is for a second time destined. After this, however, I lay silent and lethargic, without a thought. Wrapped in the defensive armour of stupidity, I defied the bell and its intonations. When it ceased, I was roused a little by the hope of escape. I did not, however, decide on this step hastily, but, putting up my hand with the utmost caution, I touched the rim.

Though the ringing had ceased, it still was tremulous from the sound, and shook my hand, which instantly recoiled as from an electric jar. A quarter of an hour probably elapsed before I again dared to make the experiment, and

147

then I found it at rest. I determined to lose no time, fearing that I might have delayed already too long, and that the bell for evening service would catch me. This dread stimulated me, and I slipped out with the utmost rapidity and arose. I stood, I suppose, for a minute, looking with silly wonder on the place of my imprisonment, penetrated with joy at escaping, but then rushed down the stony and irregular stair with the velocity of lightning, and arrived in the bell-ringer's room. This was the last act I had power to accomplish. I leaned against the wall, motionless and deprived of thought, in which posture my companions found me, when, in the course of a couple of hours, they returned to their occupation.

They were shocked, as well they might, at the figure before them. The wind of the bell had excoriated my face, and my dim and stupefied eyes were fixed with a lack-lustre gaze in my raw eyelids. My hands were torn and bleeding, my hair dishevelled, and my clothes tattered. They spoke to me, but I gave no answer. They shook me, but I remained insensible. They then became alarmed, and hastened to remove me. He who had first gone up with me in the forenoon met them as they carried me through the churchyard, and through him, who was shocked at having, in some measure, occasioned the accident, the cause of my misfortune was discovered. I was put to bed at home, and remained for three days delirious, but gradually recovered my senses.

You may be sure the bell formed a prominent topic of my ravings, and if I heard a peal, they were instantly increased to the utmost violence. Even when the delirium abated, my sleep was continually disturbed by imagined ringings, and my dreams were haunted by the fancies which almost maddened me while in the steeple. My friends removed me to a house in the country, which was sufficiently distant from any place of worship to save me from the apprehensions of hearing the church-going bell; for what Alexander Selkirk, in Cowper's poem, complained of as a misfortune, was then to me as a blessing.

Here I recovered; but, even long after recovery, if a gale

wafted the notes of a peal towards me, I started with nervous apprehension. I felt a Mahometan hatred to all the bell tribe, and envied the subjects of the Commander of the Faithful the sonorous voice of their Muezzin. Time cured this, as it docs the most of our follies; but, even at the present day, if, by chance, my nerves be unstrung, some particular tones of the cathedral bell have power to surprise me into a momentary start.

RED HAND

by Neil Munro

NEIL MUNRO (*1864–1930*) *has become recognised as one of Scotland's modern masters of the short story and his tales of Gaelic lore are unique in the country's literature. Born in Inveraray, he entered journalism as a young man and a notable career in newspapers was crowned when he served as editor of the much respected Glasgow* Evening News. *His love of Scotland and Scottish traditions was evident in most of his books, but probably nowhere to greater effect than in the collection of tales published under the title* The Lost Pibroch (*1896*). *From this book I have selected 'Red Hand', which introduces us to the Scots' great love of music—and in particular the instrument which is associated with them throughout the world; the bagpipes. In this story, however, they are not played to the tune of a joyful skirl, but rather a lament of hatred and vengeance.*

The smell of wet larch was in the air, and Glenaora was aburst to the coaxing of spring. Paruig Dall the piper—son of the son of Iain Mor—filled his broad chest with two men's wind, and flung the drones over his shoulder. They dangled a little till the bag swelled out, and the first blast rang in the ear of the morning. Rough and noisy, the reeds cried each other down till a master's hand held them in check, and the long soft singing of the *piobaireachad* floated out among the tartan ribbons. The grey peak of Drimfern heard the music; the rock that wards the mouth of Carnus let it pass through the gap and over the hill and down to the isles below; Dun Corrbhile and Dunchuach, proud Kilmune, the Paps of

Salachary, and a hundred other braes around, leaned over to listen to the vaunting notes that filled the valley. 'The Glen, the Glen is mine!' sang the blithe chanter; and, by Finne's sword, Macruimen himself could not have fingered it better!

It was before Paruig Dall left for Half Town; before the wars that scorched the glens; and Clan Campbell could cock its bonnet in the face of all Albainn. Raruig was old, and Paruig was blind, as the name of him tells, but he swung with a king's port up and down on the short grass, his foot firm to every beat of the tune, his kilt tossing from side to side like a bard's song, his sporran leaping gaily on his brown knees. Two score of lilting steps to the burnside, a slow wheel on a brogue-heel, and then back with the sun-glint on the buckles of his belt.

The men, tossing the caber and hurling the *clachneart* against the sun beyond the peat-bog, paused in their stride at the chanter's boast, jerked the tartan tight on their loins, and came over to listen; the women, posting blankets for the coming sheiling, stopped their splashing in the little linn, and hummed in a dream; and men and women had mind of the days that were, when the Glen was soft with the blood of men, for the Stewarts were over the way from Appin.

'God's splendour! but he can play too,' said the piper's son, with his head areel to the fine tripling.

Then Paruig pushed the bag further into his oxter, and the tune changed. He laid the ground of 'Bodaich nam Briogais' and such as knew the story saw the 'carles with the breeks' broken and flying before Glenurchy's thirsty swords, far north of Morven, long days of weary march through spoiled glens.

'It's fine playing, I'll allow,' said the blind man's son, standing below a saugh-tree with the bag of his bannered pipes in the crook of his arm. He wore the dull tartan of the Diarmaids, and he had a sprig of gall in his bonnet, for he was in Black Duncan's tail. 'Son of Paruig Dall,' said the Chief seven years ago come Martinmas, 'if you're to play like your father, there's but Dunvegan for you, and the

151

schooling of Patrick Macruimen.' So Tearlach went to Skye—cold isle of knives and caves—and in the college of Macruimen he learned the *piob-mhor*. Morning and evening, and all day between, he fingered the *feadan* or the full set— gathering and march, massacre and moaning, and the stately salute. Where the lusty breeze comes in salt from Vaternish across Loch Vegan, and the purple loom of Uist breaks the sunset's golden bars, he stood on the braes over against Borearaig and charmed the brumdling tide. And there came a day that he played 'The Lament of the Harp- Tree' with the old years of sturdy fight and strong men all in the strain of it, and Patrick Macruimen said, 'No more, lad; go home: Lochow never heard another like you.' As a cock with its comb uncut, came the stripling from Skye.

'Father,' he had said, 'you play not ill for a blind man, but you miss the look on the men's faces, and that's half the music. Forbye, you are old, and your fingers are slow on the grace-notes. Here's your own flesh and blood can show you fingering there was never the like of anywhere east the Isles.'

The stepmother heard the brag. '*A pheasain!*' she snapped, with hate in her peat-smoked face. 'Your father's a man, and you are but a boy with no heart for a long day. A place in Black Duncan's tail, with a gillie to carry your pipes and knapsack, is not, mind ye, all that's to the making of a piper.'

Tearlach laughed in her face. 'Boy or man,' said he, 'look at me! north, east, south, and west, where is the one to beat me? Macruimen has the name, but there were pipers before Macruimen, and pipers will come after him.'

'It's maybe as you say,' said Paruig. 'The stuff's in you, and what is in must out; but give me *cothrom na Feinne*, and old as I am, with Finne's chance, and that's fair play, I can maybe make you crow less crouse. Are ye for trying?'

'I am at the training of a new chanter-reed,' said Tearlach; 'but let it be when you will.'

They fixed a day, and went out to play against each other for glory, and so it befell that on this day Paruig Dall was

152

playing 'The Glen is Mine' and 'Bodaich nam Briogais' in a way to make stounding hearts.

Giorsal snapped her fingers in her stepson's face when her husband closed the *crunluadh* of his *piobaireachd*.

'Can you better it, bastard?' snarled she.

'Here goes for it, whatever!' said Tearlach, and over his back went the banner with its boar's head sewn on gold. A pretty lad, by the cross! clean-cut of limb and light of foot, supple of loin, with the toss of the shoulder that never a decent piper lacked. The women who had been at the linn leaned on each other all in the soft larch-scented day, and looked at him out of deep eyes; the men on the heather arose and stood nigher.

A little tuning, and then

> *Is comadh leam's comadh leam, cogadh na sithe,*
> *Marbhar 'sa chogadh na crochar's an t-sith mi.*

'Peach or war! cried Giorsal, choking in anger, to her man—'peace or war! the black braggart! it's an asp ye have for a son, goodman!'

The lad's fingers danced merry on the chanter, and the shiver of something to come fell on all the folk around. The old hills sported with the prancing tune; Dun Corrbhile tossed it to Drimfern, and Drimfern sent it leaping across the flats of Kilmune to the green corries of Lecknamban. 'Love, love, the old tune; come and get flesh!' rasped a crow to his mate far on misty Ben Bhreac, and the heavy black wings flapped east. The friendly wind forgot to dally with the pine-tuft and the twanging bog-myrtle, the plash of Aora in its brown linn was the tinkle of wine in a goblet. 'Peace or war, peace or war; come which will, we care not,' sang the pipe-reeds, and there was the muster and the march, hot-foot rush over the rotting rain-wet moor, the mingle of iron, the dunt of pike and targe, the choked roar of hate and hunger, batter and slash and fall, and behind, the old, old feud with Appin!

Leaning forward, lost in a dream, stood the swank lads

153

of Aora. They felt at their hips, where were only empty belts, and one said to his child, 'White love, get me yon long knife with the nicks on it, and the basket-hand, for I am sick of shepherding.' The bairn took a look at his face and went home crying.

And the music still poured on. 'Twas 'I got a Kiss o' the King's Hand' and 'The Pretty Dirk', and every air better than another. The fairy pipe of the Wee Folk's Knowe never made a sweeter fever of sound, yet it hurt the ears of the women, who had reason to know the payment of pipers' springs.

'Stop, stop, O Tearlach og!' they cried; 'enough of war: have ye not a reel in your budget?'

'There was never a reel in Borearaig,' said the lad, and he into 'Duniveg's Warning', the tune Coll Ciotach heard his piper play in the west on a day when a black bitch from Dunstaffnage lay panting for him, and his barge put nose about in time to save his skin.

'There's the very word itself in it,' said Paruig, forgetting the taunting of Giorsal and all but a father's pride.

'Twas in the middle of the 'Warning' Black Duncan, his toe on the stirrup, came up from Castle Inneraora, with a gillie-wet-foot behind, on his way to Lochow.

'It's down yonder you should be, Sir Piper, and not blasting here for drink,' said he, switching his trews with his whip and scowling under black brows at the people. 'My wife is sick of the *clarsach* and wants the pipes.'

'I'm no woman's piper, Lochow; your wife can listen to the hum of her spinning-wheel if she's weary of her harp,' said the lad; and away rode the Chief, and back to the linn went the women, and the men to the *cabar* and the stone, and Tearlach, with an extra feather in his bonnet, home to Inneraora, leaving a gibe as he went, for his father.

Paruig Dall cursed till the evening at the son he never saw, and his wife poisoned his mind.

'The Glen laughs at you, from Carnus to Croitbhile. It's a black, burning day of shame for you, Paruig Dall!'

154

'Lord, it's a black enough day for me at the best!' said the blind man.

'It's disgraced by your own ill-got son you are, by a boy with no blood on his *biodag*, and the pride to crow over you.'

And Paruig cursed anew, by the Cross and the Dogs of Lorn, and the White Glaive of Light the giants wear, and the Seven Witches of Cothmar. He was bad though he was blind, and he went back to the start of time for his language. 'But *Dhé!* the boy can play!' he said at the last.

'Oh, *amadain dhoill!*' cried the woman; 'if it was I, a claw was off the cub before the mouth of day.'

'Witless woman, men have played the pipes before now, lacking finger; look at Alasdair Corrag!'

'Allowing; but a hand's as easy to cut as a finger for a man who has gralloched deer with a keen *sgain-dubh*. Will ye do't or no'?'

Paruig would hearken no more, and took to his pillow.

Rain came with the gloaming. Aora, the splendid river, roared up the dark glen from the Salmon Leap; the hills gathered thick and heavy round about the scattered townships, the green new tips of fir and the copper leaves of the young oaks moaned in the wind. Then salt airs came tearing up from the sea, grinding branch on branch, and the whole land smoked with the drumming of rain that slanted on it hot and fast.

Giorsal arose, her clothes still on her, put a plaid on her black head, and the thick door banged back on the bed as she dived into the storm. Her heavy feet sogged through the boggy grass, the heather clutched at her draggled coat-tails to make her stay, but she filled her heart with one thought, and that was hate, and behold! she was on the slope of the Black Bull before her blind husband guessed her meaning. Castle Inneraora lay at the foot of the woody dun, dozing to the music of the salt loch that made tumult and spume north and south in the hollow of the mountains. Now and then the moon took a look at things, now and then a night-hag in the dripping wood hooted as the rain whipped her

155

breast feathers; a roe leaped out of the gloom and into it with a feared hoof-plunge above Carlonan; a thunderbolt struck in the dark against the brow of Ben Ime and rocked the world.

In the cold hour before the mouth of day the woman was in the piper's room at the gate of Inneraora, where never a door was barred against the night while Strong Colin the warder could see from the Fort of Dunchuach to Cladich. Tearlach the piper lay on his back, with the glow of a half-dead peat on his face and hands. 'Paruig, Paruig!' said the woman to herself, as she softly tramped out the peat-fire and turned to the bed. And lo! it was over. Her husband's little black knife made a fast sweep on the sleeper's wrist, and her hand was drenched with the hot blood of her husband's son.

Tearlach leaped up with a roar in the dark and felt for his foe; but the house was empty, for Giorsal was running like a hind across the soaked stretch of Cairnban. The lightning struck at Glenaora in Dubh; in a turn of the pass at the Three Bridges the woman met her husband.

'Daughter of hell!' said he, 'is't done? and was't death?'

'Darling,' said she, with a fond laugh, ''twas only a brat's hand. You can give us "The Glen is Mine!" in the morning.'

156

THROUGH THE VEIL

by Sir Arthur Conan Doyle

SIR ARTHUR CONAN DOYLE (*1859–1930*), *as creator of the archetypal fictional detective, Sherlock Holmes, remains to this day one of the best read of all Scottish popular fiction writers. Born of Irish parents in Edinburgh, he studied medicine as a young man and went into practice at Southsea. Financial difficulties forced him to develop a second source of income and he decided to try his hand at writing. As a natural storyteller, his work was soon being eagerly accepted by two of the then most popular periodicals*, Chamber's Journal *and the* Strand Magazine. *This in turn was to lead to hardcover publication for both his general tales and the early adventures of Sherlock Holmes. Despite the popularity of the Baker Street detective, Conan Doyle tried to kill him off in 1893 in favour of the historical romances, which he considered superior work. Public demand, however, forced him to revive Holmes in 1903 and continue his activities until the end of his life. In the years immediately after the First World War, Conan Doyle became interested in, and then a convert to, Spiritualism. His enquiries in this area, which still come in for periodic discussion, caused him to Write several books, the best of these probably being* The Wanderings of a Spiritualist (*1921*) *and a two-volume* History of Spiritualism *published in 1926. His convictions about this topic could not but help find their way into some of his tales, and the little known short story which follows recounts how a visit to the site of an ancient Roman camp turns into a nightmare situation for two people.*

He was a great shock-headed, freckle-faced Borderer, the lineal descendant of a cattle-thieving clan in Liddesdale. In spite of his ancestry he was as solid and sober a citizen as one would wish to see, a town councillor of Melrose, an elder of the Church, and the chairman of the local branch of the Young Men's Christian Association. Brown was his name—and you saw it printed up as 'Brown and Handiside' over the great grocery stores in the High Street. His wife, Maggie Brown, was an Armstrong before her marriage, and came from an old farming stock in the wilds of Teviothead. She was small, swarthy, and dark-eyed, with a strangely nervous temperament for a Scotch woman. No greater contrast could be found than the big tawny man the dark little woman, but both were of the soil as far back as any memory could extend.

One day—it was the first anniversary of their wedding—they had driven over together to see the excavations of the Roman Fort at Newstead. It was not a particularly picturesque spot. From the northern bank of the Tweed, just where the river forms a loop, there extends a gentle slope of arable land. Across it run the trenches of the excavators, with here and there an exposure of old stonework to show the foundations of the ancient walls. It had been a huge place, for the camp was fifty acres in extent, and the fort fifteen. However, it was all made easy for them since Mr. Brown knew the farmer to whom the land belonged. Under his guidance they spent a long summer evening inspecting the trenches, the pits, the ramparts, and all the strange variety of objects which were waiting to be transported to the Edinburgh Museum of Antiquities. The buckle of a woman's belt had been dug up that very day, and the farmer was discoursing upon it when his eyes fell upon Mrs. Brown's face.

'Your good leddy's tired,' said he. 'Maybe you'd best rest a wee before we gang further.'

Brown looked at his wife. She was certainly very pale, and her dark eyes were bright and wild.

158

'What is it, Maggie? I've wearied you. I'm thinkin' it's time we went back.'

'No, no, John, let us go on. It's wonderful! It's like a dreamland place. It all seems so close and so near to me. How long were the Romans here, Mr. Cunningham?'

'A fair time, mam. If you saw the kitchen midden-pits you would guess it took a long time to fill them.'

'And why did they leave?'

'Well, mam, by all accounts they left because they had to. The folk round could thole them no longer, so they just up and burned the fort aboot their lugs. You can see the fire marks on the stanes.'

The woman gave a quick little shudder. 'A wild night—a fearsome night,' said she. 'The sky must have been red that night—and these grey stones, they may have been red also.'

'Aye, I think they were red,' said her husband. 'It's a queer thing, Maggie, and it may be your words that have done it; but I seem to see that business aboot as clear as ever I saw anything in my life. The light shone on the water.'

'Aye, the light shone on the water. And the smoke gripped you by the throat. And all the savages were yelling.'

The old farmer began to laugh. 'The leddy will be writin' a story aboot the old fort,' said he. 'I've shown many a one ower it, but I never heard it put so clear afore. Some folk have the gift.'

They had strolled along the edge of the foss, and a pit yawned upon the right of them.

'That pit was fourteen foot deep,' said the farmer. 'What d'ye think we dug oot from the bottom o't? Weel, it was just the skeleton of a man wi' a spear by his side. I'm thinkin' he was grippin' it when he died. Now, how cam' a man wi' a spear doon a hole fourteen foot deep. He wasna' buried there, for they aye burned their dead. What make ye o' that, mam?'

'He sprang doon to get clear of the savages,' said the woman.

159

'Weel, it's likely enough, and a' the professors from Edinburgh couldna gie a better reason. I wish you were aye here, mam, to answer a' oor deeficulties sae readily. Now, here's the altar that we foond last week. There's an inscreeption. They tell me it's Latin, and it means that the men o' this fort give thanks to God for their safety.'

They examined the old worn stone. There was a large deeply-cut 'VV' upon the top of it.

'What does "VV" stand for?' asked Brown.

'Naebody kens,' the guide answered.

'*Valeria Victrix*,' said the lady softly. Her face was paler than ever, her eyes far away, as one who peers down the dim aisles of over-arching centuries.

'What's that?' asked her husband sharply.

She started as one who wakes from sleep. 'What were we talking about?' she asked.

'About this "VV" upon the stone.'

'No doubt it was just the name of the Legion which put the altar up.'

'Aye, but you gave some special name.'

'Did I? How absurd! How should I ken what the name was?'

'You said something—"*Victrix*," I think.'

'I suppose I was guessing. It gives me the queerest feeling, this place, as if I were not myself, but someone else.'

'Aye, it's an uncanny place,' said her husband, looking round with an expression almost of fear in his bold grey eyes. 'I feel it mysel'. I think we'll just be wishin' you good evening', Mr. Cunningham, and get back to Melrose before the dark sets in.'

Neither of them could shake off the strange impression which had been left upon them by their visit to the excavations. It was as if some miasma had risen from those damp trenches and passed into their blood. All the evening they were silent and thoughtful, but such remarks as they did make showed that the same subject was in the minds of each. Brown had a restless night, in which he dreamed a strange connected dream, so vivid that he woke sweating and

160

shivering like a frightened horse. He tried to convey it all to his wife as they sat together at breakfast in the morning.

'It was the clearest thing, Maggie,' said he. 'Nothing that has ever come to me in my waking life has been more clear than that. I feel as if these hands were sticky with blood.'

'Tell me of it—tell me slow,' said she.

'When it began, I was oot on a braeside. I was laying flat on the ground. It was rough, and there were clumps of heather. All round me was just darkness, but I could hear the rustle and the breathin' of men. There seemed a great multitude on every side of me, but I could see no one. There was a low chink of steel sometimes, and then a number of voices would whisper "Hush!" I had a ragged club in my hand, and it had spikes o' iron near the end of it. My heart was beatin' quickly, and I felt that a moment of great danger and excitement was at hand. Once I dropped my club, and again from all round me the voices in the darkness cried, "Hush!" I put oot my hand, and it touched the foot of another man lying in front of me. There was some one at my very elbow on either side. But they said nothin'.

'Then we all began to move. The whole braeside seemed to be crawlin' downwards. There was a river at the bottom and a high-arched wooden bridge. Beyond the bridge were many lights—torches on a wall. The creepin' men all flowed towards the bridge. There had been no sound of any kind, just a velvet stillness. And then there was a cry in the darkness, the cry of a man who has been stabbed suddenly to the hairt. That one cry swelled out for a moment, and then the roar of a thoosand furious voices. I was runnin'. Every one was runnin'. A bright red light shone out, and the river was a scarlet streak. I could see my companions now. They were more like devils than men, wild figures clad in skins, with their hair and beards streamin'. They were all mad with rage, jumpin' as they ran, their mouths open, their arms wavin', the red light beatin' on their faces. I ran, too, and yelled out curses like the rest. Then I heard a great cracklin' of wood, and I knew that the palisades were doon. There was a loud whistlin' in my ears, and I was aware that arrows

161

were flyin' past me. I got to the bottom of a dyke, and I saw a hand stretched doon from above. I took it, and was dragged to the top. We looked doon, and there were silver men beneath us holdin' up their spears. Some of our folk sprang on to the spears. Then we others followed, and we killed the soldiers before they could draw the spears oot again. They shouted loud in some foreign tongue, but no mercy was shown them. We went ower them like a wave, and trampled them doon into the mud, for they were few, and there was no end to our numbers.

'I found myself among buildings, and one of them was on fire. I saw the flames spoutin' through the roof. I ran on, and then I was alone among the buildings. Some one ran across in front o' me. It was a woman. I caught her by the arm, and I took her chin and turned her face so as the light of the fire would strike it. Whom think you that it was, Maggie?'

His wife moistened her dry lips. 'It was I,' she said.

He looked at her in surprise. 'That's a good guess,' said he. 'Yes, it was just you. Not merely like you, you understand. It was you—you yourself. I saw the same soul in your frightened eyes. You looked white and bonny and wonderful in the firelight. I had just one thought in my head—to get you awa' with me; to keep you all to mysel' in my own home somewhere beyond the hills. You clawed at my face with your nails. I heaved you over my shoulder, and I tried to find a way oot of the light of the burning hoose and back into the darkness.

'Then came the thing that I mind best of all. You're ill, Maggie. Shall I stop? My God! you have the very look on your face that you had last night in my dream. You screamed. He came runnin' in the firelight. His head was bare; his hair was black and curled; he had a naked sword in his hand, short and broad, little more than a dagger. He stabbed at me, but he tripped and fell. I held you with one hand, and with the other—'

His wife had sprung to her feet with writhing features.

'Marcus!' she cried. 'My beautiful Marcus! Oh, you

162

brute! you brute! you brute!' There was a clatter of tea-cups as she fell forward senseless upon the table.

They never talk about that strange isolated incident in their married life. For an instant the curtain of the past had swung aside, and some strange glimpse of a forgotten life had come to them. But it closed down, never to open again. They live their narrow round—he in his shop, she in her household—and yet new and wider horizons have vaguely formed themselves around them since that summer evening by the crumbling Roman fort.

THE OUTGOING OF THE TIDE*

by John Buchan

JOHN BUCHAN, *First Baron Tweedsmuir (1875–1940),
was by his own admission brought up in a 'noted household for fairy tales' in Perth, and throughout his life had
an abiding interest in the supernatural. Numbered among
the half-dozen most well-known of Scottish authors,
Buchan's colourful life began when he became private
secretary to the High Commissioner of South Africa,
continued as a director of a London publishing house, a
Member of Parliament, a highly regarded Governor-
General of Canada, and finally as a privy counsellor.
Despite the tremendous demands these jobs made on his
time, he wrote over fifty books: many of high adventure,
destined to become classics of their kind, read and enjoyed
all over the world. According to his biographers, Buchan
felt that human beings combined 'both heavenly and
hellish elements' and when the dark side was allowed to
predominate in any man, conspiracy and evil were the
result. Several of his novels expound this theme, as does
a collection of fantasy and horror tales,* The Watcher by
the Threshold *(1902), which has constantly been overshadowed by his other work. From this volume I have
taken the following story, which is full of Buchan's knowledge of the land of his birth—and his great ability at
weaving a tale of ancient forces and 'unco' evil.*

Men come from distant parts to admire the tides of Solloway, which race in at flood and retreat at ebb with a greater
speed than a horse can follow. But nowhere are there

* From the unpublished Remains of the Reverend John Dennistoun,
sometime minister of the Gospel in the parish of Caulds, and author of
Satan's Artifices against the Elect.

queerer waters than in our own parish of Caulds at the place called the Sker Bay, where between two horns of land a shallow estuary receives the stream of the Sker. I never daunder by its shores, and see the waters hurrying like messengers from the great deep, without solemn thoughts and a memory of Scripture words on the terror of the sea. The vast Atlantic may be fearful in its wrath, but with us it is no clean open rage, but the deceit of the creature, the unholy ways of quicksands when the waters are gone, and their stealthy return like a thief in the night-watches. But in the times of which I write there were more awful fears than any from the violence of nature. It was before the day of my ministry in Caulds, for then I was a bitcallant in short clothes in my native parish of Lesmahagow; but the worthy Doctor Chrystal, who had charge of spiritual things, has told me often of the power of Satan and his emissaries in that lonely place. It was the day of warlocks and apparitions, now happily driven out by the zeal of the General Assembly. Witches pursued their wanchancy calling, bairns were spirited away, young lassies selled their souls to the evil one, and the accuser of the brethren in the shape of a black tyke was seen about cottage-doors in the gloaming. Many and earnest were the prayers of good Doctor Chrystal, but the evil thing, in spite of his wrestling, grew and flourished in his midst. The parish stank of idolatry, abominable rites were practised in secret, and in all the bounds there was no one had a more evil name for this black traffic than one Alison Sempill, who bode at the Skerburnfoot.

The cottage stood nigh the burn in a little garden with lilyoaks and grosart-bushes lining the pathway. The Sker ran by in a linn among hollins, and the noise of its waters was ever about the place. The highroad on the other side was frequented by few, for a nearer-hand way to the west had been made through the Lowe Moss. Sometimes a herd from the hills would pass by with sheep, sometimes a tinkler or a wandering merchant, and once in a long while the laird of Heriotside on his grey horse riding to Gledsmuir. And they who passed would see Alison hirpling in her garden, speaking to herself like the ill wife she was, or sitting on a suttystool by the doorside with her eyes on other than mortal sights. Where she came from no man could tell. There were some said she was no woman, but a ghost haunting some mortal tenement. Others would threep she was gentrice, come of a persecuting family in the west, that had been ruined in the Revolution wars. She never seemed to want for siller; the house was as bright as a new preen, the yaird better delved than the manse garden; and there was routh of fowls and doos about the small steading, forbye a wheen sheep and milk-kye in the fields. No man ever saw Alison at any market in the countryside, and yet the Skerburnfoot was plenished yearly in all proper order. One man only worked on the place, a doited lad who had long been a charge to the parish, and who had not the sense to fear danger or the wit to understand it. Upon all other the sight of Alison, were it but for a moment, cast a cold grue, not to be remembered without terror. It seems she was not ordinarily ill-faured. as men use the word. She was maybe sixty years in age, small and trig, with her grey hair folded neatly under her mutch. But the sight of her eyes was not a thing to forget. John Dodds said they were the een of a deer with the devil ahint them, and indeed they would so appal an onlooker that a sudden unreasoning terror came into his heart, while his feet would impel him to flight. Once John, being overtaken in drink on the road-side by the cottage, and dreaming that he was burning in hell, woke, and saw the old wife hobbling towards him. Thereupon he fled soberly to the hills, and from that day became a quiet-living humble-minded Christian. She moved about the country like a wraith, gathering herbs in dark loanings, lingering in kirkyards, and casting a blight on innocent bairns. Once Robert Smillie found her in a ruinous kirk on the Lang Muir where of old the idolatrous rites of Rome were practised. It was a hot day, and in the quiet place the flies buzzed in crowds, and he noted that she sat clothed in them as with a garment, yet suffering no discomfort. Then he, having mind of Beelzebub, the god of flies, fled without a halt homewards; but, falling in the Coo's Loan,

166

broke two ribs and a collar-bone, the whilk misfortune was much blessed to his soul. And there were darker tales in the countryside, of weans stolen, of lassies misguided, of innocent beasts cruelly tortured, and in one and all there came in the name of the wife of the Skerburnfoot. It was noted by them that kenned best that her cantrips were at their worst when the tides in the Sker Bay ebbed between the hours of twelve and one. At this season of the night the tides of mortality run lowest, and when the outgoing of these unco waters fell in with the setting of the current of life, then indeed was the hour for unholy revels. While honest men slept in their beds, the auld rudas carlines took their pleasure. That there is a delight in sin no man denies, but to most it is but a broken glint in the pauses of their conscience. But what must be the hellish joy of those lost beings who have forsworn God and trysted with the Prince of Darkness, it is not for a Christian to say. Certain it is that it must be great, though their master waits at the end of the road to claim the wizened things they call their souls. Serious men, notably Gidden Scott in the Back of the Hill and Simon Wauch in the Sheiling of Chasehope, have seen Alison wandering on the wet sands, dancing to no earthly music, while the heaven, they said, were full of lights and sounds which betokened the presence of the prince of the powers of the air. It was a season of heart-searching for God's saints in Caulds, and the dispensation was blessed to not a few.

It will seem strange that in all this time the presbytery was idle, and no effort was made to rid the place of so fell an influence. But there was a reason, and the reason, as in most like cases, was a lassie. For by Alison there lived at the Skerburnfoot a young maid, Ailie Sempill, who by all accounts was as good and bonnie as the other was evil. She passed for a daughter of Alison's, whether born in wedlock or not I cannot tell; but there were some said she was no kin to the auld witch-wife, but some bairn spirited away from honest parents. She was young and blithe, with a face like an April morning and a voice in her that put the lave-rocks to shame. When she sang in the kirk folk have told me that they had a foretaste of the music of the New Jerusalem, and when she came in by the village of Caulds old men stottered to their doors to look at her. Moreover, from her earliest days the bairn had some glimmerings of grace. Though no minister would visit the Skerburnfoot, or if he went, departed quicker than he came, the girl Ailie attended regular at the catechising at the Mains of Sker. It may be that Alison thought she would be a better offering for the devil if she were given the chance of forswearing God, or it may be that she was so occupied in her own dark business that she had no care of the bairn. Meanwhile the lass grew up in the nurture and admonition of the Lord. I have heard Doctor Chrystal say that he never had a communicant more full of the things of the Spirit. From the day when she first declared her wish to come forward to the hour when she broke bread at the table, she walked like one in a dream. The lads of the parish might cast admiring eyes on her bright cheeks and yellow hair as she sat in her white gown in the kirk, but well they knew she was not for them. To be the bride of Christ was the thought that filled her heart; and when at the fencing of the tables Doctor Chrystal preached from Matthew nine and fifteen, 'Can the children of the bride-chamber mourn, as long as the bridegroom is with them?' it was remarked by sundry that Ailie's face was liker the countenance of an angel than of a mortal lass.

It is with the day of her first communion that this narrative of mine begins. As she walked home after the morning table she communed in secret and her heart sang within her. She had mind of God's mercies in the past, how He had kept her feet from the snares of evil-doers which had been spread around her youth. She had been told unholy charms like the seven south streams and the nine rowan berries, and it was noted when she went first to the catechising that she prayed 'Our Father which wert in heaven', the prayer which the ill wife Alison had taught her, meaning by it Lucifer who had been in heaven and had been cast out therefrom. But when she had come to years of discretion she had freely chosen the better part, and evil had ever been repelled from her soul like Gled water from the stones of Gled brig. Now she was in a rapture of holy content. The drucken bell—for the ungodly fashion lingered in Caulds—was ringing in her ears as she left the village, but to her it was but a kirk-bell and a goodly sound. As she went through the woods where the primroses and the whitethorn were blossoming, the place seemed as the land of Elam, wherein there were twelve wells and threescore and ten palm-trees. And then, as it might be, another thought came into her head, for it is ordained that frail mortality cannot long continue in holy joy. In the kirk she had been only the bride of Christ; but as she same through the wood, with the birds lilting and the winds of the world blowing, she had mind of another lover. For this lass, though so cold to men, had not escaped the common fate. It seemed that the young Heriotside, riding by one day, stopped to speir something or other, and got a glisk of Ailee's face, which caught his fancy. He passed the road again many times, and then he would meet her in the gloaming or of a morning in the field as she went to fetch the kye. 'Blue are the hills that are far away' is an owercome in the countryside, and while at first on his side it may have been but a young man's fancy, to her he was like the god Apollo descending from the skies. He was good to look on, brawly dressed, and with a tongue in his head that would have wiled the bird from the tree. Moreover, he was of gentle kin, and she was a poor lass biding in a cot-house with an ill-reputed mother. It seems that in time the young man, who had begun the affair with no good intentions, fell honestly in love, while she went singing about the doors as innocent as a bairn, thinking of him when her thoughts were not on higher things. So it came about that long ere Ailie reached home it was on young Heriotside that her mind dwelt, and it was the love of him that made her eyes glow and her cheeks redden.

Now it chanced that at that very hour her master had been with Alison, and the pair of them were preparing a deadly pit. Let no man say that the devil is not a cruel tyrant. He

169

may give his folk some scrapings of unhallowed pleasure; but he will exact tithes, yea of anise and cummin, in return, and there is aye the reckoning to pay at the hinder end. It seems that now he was driving Alison hard. She had been remiss of late, fewer souls sent to hell, less zeal in quenching the Spirit, and above all the crowning offence that her bairn had communicated in Christ's kirk. She had waited over-long, and now it was like that Ailie would escape her toils. I have no skill of fancy to tell of that dark collogue, but the upshot was that Alison swore by her lost soul and the pride of sin to bring the lass into thrall to her master. The field had bare departed when Ailie came over the threshold to find the auld carline glunching by the fire.

It was plain she was in the worst of tempers. She flyted on the lass till the poor thing's cheek paled. 'There you gang,' she cried, 'troking wi' thae wearifu' Pharisees o' Caulds, whae daurna darken your mither's door. A bonnie dutiful child, quotha! Wumman, hae ye nae pride?—no even the mense o' a tinkler-lass?' And then she changed her voice, and would be as soft as honey. 'My puir wee Ailie! was I thrawn till ye? Never mind, my bonnie. You and me are a' that's left, and we maunna be ill to ither.' And then the two had their dinner, and all the while the auld wife was crooning over the lass. 'We maun 'gree weel,' she says, 'for we're like to be our lee-lane for the rest o' our days. They tell me Heriotside is seeking Joan o' the Croft, and they're sune to be cried in Gledsmuir kirk.'

It was the first the lass had heard of it, and you may fancy she was struck dumb. And so with one thing and other the auld witch raised the fiends of jealousy in that innocent heart. She would cry out that Heriotside was an ill-doing wastral, and had no business to come and flatter honest lasses. And then she would speak of his gentle birth and his leddy mother, and say it was indeed presumption to hope that so great a gentleman could mean all that he said. Before long Ailie was silent and white, while her mother rhymed on about men and their ways. And then she could thole it no longer, but must go out and walk by the burn to

170

cool her hot brow and calm her thoughts, while the witch indoors laughed to herself at her devices.

For days Ailie had an absent eye and a sad face, and it so fell out that in all that time young Heriotside, who had scarce missed a day, was laid up with a broken arm and never came near her. So in a week's time she was beginning to hearken to her mother when she spoke of incantations and charms for restoring love. She kenned it was sin; but though not)seven days syne she had sat at the Lord's table, so strong is love in a young heart that she was on the very brink of it. But the grace of God was stronger than her weak will. She would have none of her mother's runes and philters, though her soul cried out for them. Always when she was most disposed to listen some merciful power stayed her consent. Alison grew thrawner as the hours passed. She kenned Heriotside's broken arm, and she feared that any day he might recover and put her stratagems to shame. And then it seems that she collogued with her master and heard word of a subtler device. For it was approaching that uncanny time of year, the festival of Beltane, when the auld pagans were wont to sacrifice to their god Baal. In this season warlocks and carlines have a special dispensation to do evil, and Alison waited on its coming with graceless joy. As it happened, the tides in the Sker Bay ebbed at this time between the hours of twelve and one, and, as I have said, this was the hour above all others when the powers of darkness were most potent. Would the lass but consent to go abroad in the unhallowed place at this awful season and hour of the night, she was as firmly handfasted to the devil as if she had signed a bond with her own blood. For there, it seemed, the forces of good fled far away, the world for one hour was given over to its ancient prince, and the man or woman who willingly sought the spot was his bond-servant for ever. There are deadly sins from which God's people may recover. A man may even communicate unworthily, and yet, so be it he sin not against the Holy Ghost, he may find forgiveness. But it seems that for this Beltane sin there could be no pardon, and I can testify from my own knowledge that they

171

who once committed it became lost souls from that day. James Deuchar, once a promising professor, fell thus out of sinful bravery and died blaspheming; and of Kate Mallison, who went the same road, no man can tell. Here, indeed, was the witch-wife's chance, and she was the more keen, for her master had warned her that this was her last chance. Either Ailie's soul would be his, or her auld wrinkled body and black heart would be flung from this pleasant world to their apportioned place.

Some days later it happened that young Heriotside was stepping home over the lang Muir about ten at night—it being his first jaunt from home since his arm had mended. He had been to the supper of the Forest Club at the Cross Keys in Gledsmuir, a clamjamfry of wild young blades who passed the wine and played at cards once a-fortnight. It seems he had drunk well, so that the world ran around and he was in the best of tempers. The moon came down and bowed to him, and he took off his hat to it. For every step he travelled miles, so that in a little he was beyond Scotland altogether and pacing the Arabian desert. He thought he was the Pope of Rome, so he held out his foot to be kissed, and rolled twenty yards to the bottom of a small brae. Syne he was the King of France, and fought hard with a whin-bush till he had banged it to pieces. After that nothing would content him but he must be a bogle, for he found his head dunting on the stars and his legs were knocking the hills together. He thought of the mischief he was doing to the auld earth, and sat down and cried at his wickedness. Then he went on, and maybe the steep road to the Moss Rig helped him, for he began to get soberer and ken his where-abouts.

On a sudden he was aware of a man linking along at his side. He cried 'A fine night,' and the man replied. Syne, being merry from his cups, he tried to slap him on the back. The next he kenned he was rolling on the grass, for his hand had gone clean through the body and found nothing but air.

His head was so thick with wine that he found nothing droll in this. 'Faith, friend,' he sayd, 'that was a nasty fall

172

for a fellow that has supped weel. Where might your road be gaun to?'

'To the World's End,' said the man; 'but I stop at the Skerburnfoot.'

'Bide the night at Heriotside,' says he. 'It's a thought out of your way, but it's a comfortable bit.'

'There's mair comfort at the Skerburnfoot,' said the dark man.

Now the mention of the Skerburnfoot brought back to him only the thought of Ailie and not of the witch-wife, her mother. So he jaloused no ill, for at the best he was slow in the uptake.

The two of them went on together for a while, Heriotside's fool head filled with the thought of the lass. Then the dark man broke silence. 'Ye're thinkin' o' the maid Ailie Sempill,' says he.

'How ken ye that?' asked Heriotside.

'It is my business to read the herts o' men,' said the other.

'And who may ye be?' said Heriotside, growing eerie.

'Just an auld packman,' said he—'nae name ye wad ken, but kin to mony gentle houses.'

'And what about Ailie, you that ken sae muckle?' asked the young man.

'Naething,' was the answer—'naething that concerns you, for ye'll never get the lass.'

'By God, and I will!' says Heriotside, for he was a profane swearer.

'That's the wrong name to seek her in, any way,' said the man.

At this the young laird struck a great blow at him with his stick, but found nothing to resist him but the hill-wind.

When they had gone on a bit the dark man spoke again. 'The lassie is thirled to holy things,' says he. 'She has nae care for flesh and blood, only for devout contemplation.'

'She loves me,' says Heriotside.

'Not you,' says the other, 'but a shadow in your stead.'

At this the young man's heart began to tremble, for it

173

seemed that there was truth in what his companion said, and he was ower drunk to think gravely.

'I kenna whatna man ye are,' he says, 'but ye have the skill of lassies' hearts. Tell me truly, is there no way to win her to common love?'

'One way there is,' said the man, 'and for our friendship's sake I will tell it you. If ye can ever tryst wi' her on Beltane's Eve on the Sker sands, at the green link o' the burn where the sands begin, on the ebb o' the tide when the midnight is bye but afore cockcrow, she'll be yours, body and soul, for this world and for ever.'

And then it appeared to the young man that he was walking his lone up the grass walk of Heriotside with the house close by him. He thought no more of the stranger he had met, but the word stuck in his heart.

It seems that about this very time Alison was telling the same tale to poor Ailie. She cast up to her every idle gossip she could think of. 'It's Joan o' the Croft,' was aye her owercome, and she would threep that they were to be cried in kirk on the first Sabbath of May. And then she would rhyme on about the black cruelty of it, and cry down curses on the lover, so that her daughter's heart grew cauld with fear. It is terrible to think of the power of the world even in a redeemed soul. Here was a maid who had drunk of the well of grace and tasted of God's mercies, and yet there were moments when she was ready to renounce her hope. At those awful seasons God seemed far off and the world very nigh, and to sell her soul for love looked a fair bargain. At other times she would resist the devil and comfort herself with prayer; but aye when she woke there was the sore heart, and when she went to sleep there were the weary eyes. There was no comfort in the goodliness of spring or the bright sunshine weather, and she who had been wont to go about the doors lightfoot and blithe was now as dowie as a widow woman.

And then one afternoon in the hinder end of April came young Heriotside riding to the Skerburnfoot. His arm was healed, he had got him a fine new suit of green, and his horse

174

was a mettle beast that well set off his figure. Ailie was standing by the doorstep as he came down the road, and her heart stood still with joy. But a second thought gave her anguish. This man, so gallant and braw, would never be for her; doubtless the fine suit and the capering horse were for Joan o' the Croft's pleasure. And he in turn, when he remarked her wan cheek and dowie eyes, had mind of what the dark man said on the muir, and saw in her a maid sworn to no mortal love. Yet the passion for her had grown fiercer than ever, and he swore to himself that he would win her back from her phantasies. She, one may believe, was ready enough to listen. As she walked with him by the Sker water his words were like music to her ears, and Alison within-doors laughed to herself and saw her devices prosper.

He spoke to her of love and his own heart, and the girl hearkened gladly. Syne he rebuked her coldness and cast scorn upon her piety, and so far was she beguiled that she had no answer. Then from one thing and another he spoke of some true token of their love. He said he was jealous, and craved something to ease his care. 'It's but a small thing I ask,' says he; 'but it will make me a happy man, and nothing ever shall come atween us. Tryst wi' me for Beltane's Eve on the Sker sands, at the green link o' the burn where the sands begin, on the ebb o' the tide when midnight is bye but afore cockcrow. For,' said he, 'that was our forebears' tryst for true lovers, and wherefore no for you and me?'

The lassie had grace given her to refuse, but with a woeful heart, and Heriotside rode off in black discontent, leaving poor Ailie to sigh her lone. He came back the next day and the next, but aye he got the same answer. A season of great doubt fell upon her soul. She had no clearness in her hope, nor any sense of God's promises. The Scriptures were an idle tale to her, prayer brought her no refreshment, and she was convicted in her conscience of the unpardonable sin. Had she been less full of pride she would have taken her troubles to good Doctor Chrystal and got comfort; but her grief made her silent and timorous, and she found no help anywhere. Her mother was ever at her side, seeking

175

with coaxings and evil advice to drive her to the irrevocable step. And all the while there was her love for the man riving in her bosom and giving her no ease by night or day. She believed she had driven him away and repented her denial. Only her pride held her back from going to Heriotside and seeking him herself. She watched the road hourly for a sight of his face, and when the darkness came she would sit in a corner brooding over her sorrows.

At last he came, speiring the old question. He sought the same tryst, but now he had a further tale. It seemed he was eager to get her away from the Skerburnside and auld Alison. His aunt, the Lady Balcrynie, would receive her gladly at his request till the day of their marriage. Let her but tryst with him at the hour and place he named, and he would carry her straight to Balcrynie, where she would be safe and happy. He named that hour, he said, to escape men's observation for the sake of her own good name. He named that place, for it was near her dwelling, and on the road between Balcrynie and Heriotside, which fords the Sker Burn. The temptation was more than mortal heart could resist. She gave him the promise he sought, stifling the voice of conscience; and as she clung to his neck it seemed to her that heaven was a poor thing compared with a man's love.

Three days remained till Beltane's Eve, and throughout the time it was noted that Heriotside behaved like one possessed. It may be that his conscience pricked him, or that he had a glimpse of his sin and its coming punishment. Certain it is that, if he had been daft before, he now ran wild in his pranks, and an evil report of him was in every mouth. He drank deep at the Cross Keys, and fought two battles with young lads that had angered him. One he let off with a touch on the shoulder, the other goes lame to this day from a wound he got in the groin. There was word of the procurator-fiscal taking note of his doings, and troth, if they had continued long he must have fled the country. For a wager he rode his horse down the Dow Craig, wherefore the name of the place is the Horseman's Craig to this day. He laid a hundred guineas with the laird of Slipperfield that he would drive four horses through the Slipperfield loch, and in the prank he had his bit chariot dung to pieces and a good mare killed. And all men observed that his eyes were wild and his face grey and thin, and that his hand would twitch as he held the glass, like one with the palsy.

The eve of Beltane was lown and hot in the low country, with fire hanging in the clouds and thunder grumbling about the heavens. It seems that up in the hills it had been an awesome deluge of rain, but on the coast it was still dry and lowering. It is a long road from Heriotside to the Skerburnfoot. First you go down the Heriot Water, and syne over the Lang Muir to the edge of Mucklewhan. When you pass the steadings of Mirehope and Cockmalane you turn to the right and ford the Mire Burn. That brings you on to the turnpike road, which you will ride till it bends inland, while you keep on straight over the Whinny Knowes to the Sker Bay. There, if you are in luck, you will find the tide out and the place fordable dryshod for a man on a horse. But if the tide runs, you will do well to sit down on the sands and content yourself till it turn, or it will be the solans and scarts of the Solloway that will be seeing the next of you. On this Beltane's Eve the young man, after supping with some wild young blades, bade his horse be saddled about ten o'clock. The company were eager to ken his errand, but he waved them back. 'Bide here,' he says, 'and birl the wine till I return. This is a ploy of my own on which no man follows me.' And there was that in his face as he spoke which chilled the wildest, and left them well content to keep to the good claret and the soft seat and let the daft laird go his own ways.

Well and on, he rode down the bridlepath in the wood, along the top of the Heriot glen, and as he rode he was aware of a great noise beneath him. It was not wind, for there was none, and it was not the sound of thunder, and aye as he speired at himself what it was it grew the louder till he came to a break in the trees. And then he saw the cause, for Heriot was coming down in a furious flood, sixty yards wide, tearing at the roots of the aiks, and flinging red waves against the drystone dykes. It was a sight and sound

177

to solemnise a man's mind, deep calling unto deep, the great waters of the hills running to meet with the great waters of the sea. But Heriotside recked nothing of it, for his heart had but one thought and the eye of his fancy one figure. Never had he been so filled with love of the lass, and yet it was not happiness but a deadly secret fear.

As he came to the Lang Muir it was geyan dark, though there was a moon somewhere behind the clouds. It was little he could see of the road, and ere long he had tried many moss-pools and sloughs, as his braw new coat bare witness. Aye in front of him was the great hill of Mucklewhan, where the road turned down by the Mire. The noise of the Heriot had not long fallen behind him ere another began, the same eerie sound of burns crying to ither in the darkness. It seemed that the whole earth was overrun with waters. Every little runnel in the bog was astir, and yet the land around him was as dry as flax, and no drop of rain had fallen. As he rode on the din grew louder, and as he came over the top of Mirehope he kenned by the mighty rushing noise that something uncommon was happening with the Mire Burn. The light from Mirehope Mill twinkled on his left, and had the man not been dozened with his fancies he might have observed that the steading was deserted and men were crying below in the fields. But he rode on, thinking of but one thing, till he came to the cot-house of Cockmalane, which is nigh the fords of the Mire.

John Dodds, the herd who bode in the place, was standing at the door, and he looked to see who was on the road so late.

'Stop,' says he, 'stop, Laird Heriotside. I kenna what your errand is, but it is to no holy purpose that ye're out on Beltane Eve. D'ye no hear the warning o' the waters?'

And then in the still night came the sound of Mire like the clask of armies.

'I must win over the ford,' says the laird quietly, thinking of another thing.

'Ford!' cried John in scorn. 'There'll be nae ford for you the nicht unless it be the ford o' the river Jordan. The burns are up, and bigger than man ever saw them. It'll be a Beltane's Eve that a' folk will remember. They tell me that Gled valley is like a loch, and that there's an awesome folk drooned in the hills. Gin ye were ower the Mire, what about crossin' the Caulds and the Sker?' says he, for he jaloused he was going to Gledsmuir.

And then it seemed that that word brought the laird to his senses. He looked the airt the rain was coming from, and he saw it was the airt the Sker flowed. In a second, he has told me, the works of the devil were revealed to him. He saw himself a tool in Satan's hands, he saw his tryst a device for the destruction of the body, as it was assuredly meant for the destruction of the soul, and there came on his mind the picture of an innocent lass borne down by the waters with no place for repentance. His heart grew cold in his breast. He had but one thought, a sinful and reckless one—to get to her side, that the two might go together to their account. He heard the roar of the Mire as in a dream, and when John Dodds laid hands on his bridle he felled him to the earth. And the next seen of it was the laird riding the floods like a man possessed.

The horse was the grey stallion he aye rode, the very beast he had ridden for many a wager with the wild lads of the Cross Keys. No man but himself durst back it, and it had lamed many a hostler lad and broke two necks in its day. But it seemed it had the mettle for any flood, and took the Mire with little spurring. The herds on the hillside looked to see man and steed swept into eternity; but though the red waves were breaking about his shoulders and he was swept far down, he aye held on for the shore. The next thing the watchers saw was the laird struggling up the far bank, and casting his coat from him, so that he rode in his sark. And then he set off like a wildfire across the muir towards the turnpike road. Two men saw him on the road and have recorded their experience. One was a gangrel, by name M'Nab, who was travelling from Gledsmuir to Allerkirk with a heavy pack on his back and a bowed head. He heard a sound like wind afore him, and, looking up, saw coming

179

down the road a grey horse stretched out to a wild gallop and a man on its back with a face like a soul in torment. He kenned not whether it was devil or mortal, but flung himself on the roadside, and lay like a corpse for an hour or more till the rain aroused him. The other was one Sim Doolittle, the fish-hawker from Allerfoot, jogging home in his fish-cart from Gledsmuir fair. He had drunk more than was fit for him, and he was singing some light song, when he saw approaching, as he said, the pale horse mentioned in the Revelations, with Death seated as the rider. Thoughts of his sins came on him like a thunder-clap, fear loosened his knees, he leaped from the cart to the road, and from the road to the back of a dyke. Thence he flew to the hills, and was found the next morning far up among the Mire Craigs, while his horse and cart were gotten on the Aller sands, the horse lamed and the cart without the wheels.

At the tollhouse the road turns inland to Gledsmuir, and he who goes to Sker Bay must leave it and cross the wild land called the Whinny Knowes, a place rough with bracken and foxes' holes and old stone cairns. The tollman, John Gilzean, was opening his window to get a breath of air in the lown night when he heard or saw the approaching horse. He kenned the beast for Heriotside's, and, being a friend of the laird's, he ran down in all haste to open the yett, wondering to himself about the laird's errand on this night. A voice came down the road to him bidding him hurry; but John's old fingers were slow with the keys, and so it happened that the horse had to stop, and John had time to look up at the gash and woeful face.

'Where away the nicht sae late, laird?' says John.

'I go to save a soul from hell,' was the answer.

And then it seems that through the open door there came the chapping of a clock.

'Whatna hour is that?' asks Heriotside.

'Midnicht,' says John, trembling, for he did not like the look of things.

There was no answer but a groan, and horse and man went racing down the dark hollows of the Whinny Knowes.

How he escaped a broken neck in that dreadful place no human being will ever tell. The sweat, he has told me, stood in cold drops upon his forehead; he scarcely was aware of the saddle in which he sat; and his eyes were stelled in his head, so that he saw nothing but the sky ayont him. The night was growing colder, and there was a small sharp wind stirring from the east. But, hot or cold, it was all one to him, who was already cold as death. He heard not the sound of the sea nor the peesweeps startled by his horse, for the sound that ran in his ears was the roaring Sker Water and a girl's cry. The thought kept goading him, and he spurred the grey till the creature was madder than himself. It leaped the hole which they call the Devil's Mull as I would step over a thistle, and the next he kenned he was on the edge of the Sker Bay.

It lay before him white and ghastly, with mist blowing in wafts across it and a slow swaying of the tides. It was the better part of a mile wide, but save for some fathoms in the middle where the Sker current ran, it was no deeper even at flood than a horse's fetlocks. It looks eerie at bright midday when the sun is shining and whaups are crying among the seaweeds; but think what it was on that awesome night with the powers of darkness brooding over it like a cloud. The rider's heart quailed for a moment in natural fear. He stepped his beast a few feet in, still staring afore him like a daft man. And then something in the sound or the feel of the waters made him look down, and he perceived that the ebb had begun and the tide was flowing out to sea.

He kenned that all was lost, and the knowledge drove him to stark despair. His sins came in his face like birds of night, and his heart shrank like a pea. He knew himself for a lost soul, and all that he loved in the world was out in the tides. There, at any rate, he could go too, and give back that gift of life he had so blackly misused. He cried small and soft like a bairn, and drove the grey out into the waters. And aye as he spurred it the foam should have been flying as high as his head; but in that uncanny hour there was no foam, only the waves running sleek like oil. It was not long

181

ere he had come to the Sker channel, where the red moss-waters were roaring to the sea, an ill place to ford in mid summer heat, and certain death, as folks reputed it, at the smallest spate. The grey was swimming, but it seemed the Lord had other purposes for him than death, for neither man nor horse could drown. He tried to leave the saddle, but he could not; he flung the bridle from him, but the grey held on, as if some strong hand were guiding. He cried out upon the devil to help his own, he renounced his Maker and his God; but whatever his punishment, he was not to be drowned. And then he was silent, for something was coming down the tide.

It came down as quiet as a sleeping bairn, straight for him as he sat with his horse breasting the waters, and as it came the moon crept out of a cloud and he saw a glint of yellow hair. And then his madness died away and he was himself again, a weary and stricken man. He hung down over the tides and caught the body in his arms, and then let the grey make for the shallows. He cared no more for the devil and all his myrmidons, for he kenned brawly he was damned. It seemed to him that his soul had gone from him and he was as toom as a hazel-shell. His breath rattled in his throat, the tears were dried up in his head, his body had lost its strength, and yet he clung to the drowned maid as to a hope of salvation. And then he noted something at which he marvelled dumbly. Her hair was drookit back from her clay-cold brow, her eyes were shut, but in her face there was the peace of a child. It seemed even that her lips were smiling. Here, certes was no lost soul, but one who had gone joyfully to meet her Lord. It may be in that dark hour at the burn-foot, before the spate caught her, she had been given grace to resist her adversary and flung herself upon God's mercy.

And it would seem that it had been granted, for when he came to the Skerburnfoot there in the corner sat the weird-wife Alison dead as a stone and shrivelled like a heatherbirn.

For days Heriotside wandered the country or sat in his own house with vacant eye and trembling hands. Conviction of sin held him like a vice; he saw the lassie's death laid at his door, her face haunted him by day and night, and the word of the Lord dirled in his ears telling of wrath and punishment. The greatness of his anguish wore him to a shadow, and at last he was stretched on his bed and like to perish. In his extremity worthy Doctor Chrystal went to him unasked and strove to comfort him. Long, long the good man wrestled, but it seemed as if his ministrations were to be of no avail. The fever left his body, and he rose to stotter about the doors; but he was still in his torments, and the mercy-seat was far from him. At last in the back-end of the year came Mungo Muirhead to Caulds to the autumn communion, and nothing would serve him but he must try his hand at this storm-tossed soul. He spoke with power and unction, and a blessing came with his words, the black cloud lifted and showed a glimpse of grace, and in a little the man had some assurance of salvation. He became a pillar of Christ's Kirk, prompt to check abominations, notably the sin of witchcraft, foremost in good works; but with it all a humble man, who walked contritely till his death. When I came first to Caulds I sought to prevail upon him to accept the eldership, but he aye put me by, and when I heard his tale I saw that he had done wisely. I mind him well as he sat in his chair or daundered through Caulds, a kind word for every one and sage counsel in time of distress, but withal a severe man to himself and a crucifier of the body. It seems that this severity weakened his frame, for three years syne come Martinmas he was taken ill with a fever, and after a week's sickness he went to his account, where I trust he is accepted.

THE WOLVES OF GOD

by Algernon Blackwood

ALGERNON HENRY BLACKWOOD (*1869–1951*), *whose ancestors were Scots—though he himself was born in Kent—holds a position of pre-eminence in the field of macabre literature. As a young man he formed an abiding interest in Scotland, while a scholar at Edinburgh University, and during his forays into the Highlands gave vent to the spirit of adventure which was later to take him to the far corners of the earth. He spent some years in Canada and this became a setting for many of his tales. Today the bulk of his work is easily available in hardcover and paperback volumes, so a relatively unknown story is something of a rarity. I have been fortunate enough to find such a one—and one which deals with an important aspect of Scottish life. 'The Wolves of God' is about a Scot returning to his native land ater a generation away—a silent, changed man, locked in a private nightmare which he will not discuss. It clearly shows Blackwood's own feeling for the country, and through its remarkable portrayal of an unseen power which can transcend time and distance, must surely be classified as one of the best tales he wrote.*

As the little steamer entered the bay of Kettletoft in the Orkneys the beach at Sanday appeared so low that the houses almost seemed to be standing in the water; and to the big, dark man leaning over the rail of the upper deck the sight of them came with a pang of mingled pain and pleasure. The scene, to his eyes, had not changed. The houses, the low shore, the flat treeless country beyond, the vast open sky, all looked exactly the same as when he left the island thirty years ago to work for the Hudson Bay Company in distant N.W. Canada. A lad of eighteen then, he was now a man of forty-eight, old for his years, and this was the home-coming he had so often dreamed about in the lonely wilderness of trees where he had spent his life. Yet his grim face wore an anxious rather than a tender expression. The return was perhaps not quite as he had pictured it.

Jim Peace had not done too badly, however, in the Company's service. For an islander, he would be a richman now; he had not married, he had saved the greater part of his salary, and even in the far-away Post where he had spent so many years there had been occasional opportunities of the kind common to new, wild countries where life and law are in the making. He had not hesitated to take them. None of the big Company Posts, it was true, had come his way, nor had he risen very high in the service; in another two years his turn would have come ,yet he had left of his own accord before those two years were up. His decision, judging by the strength in the features, was not due to impulse; the move had been deliberately weighed and calculated; he had renounced his opportunity after full reflection. A man with those steady eyes, with that square jaw and determined mouth, certainly did not act without good reason.

A curious expression now flickered over his weather-hardened face as he saw again his childhood's home, and the return, so often dreamed about, actually took place at last. An uneasy light flashed for a moment in the deep-set grey eyes, but was quickly gone again, and the tanned visage recovered its accustomed look of stern composure. His keen sight took in a dark knot of figures on the landing-pier—his brother, he knew, among them. A wave of home-sickness swept over him. He longed to see his brother again, the old farm, the sweep of open country, the sand-dunes,

185

and the breaking seas. The smell of long-forgotten days came to his nostrils with its sweet, painful pang of youthful memories.

How fine, he thought, to be back there in the old familiar fields of childhood, with sea and sand about him instead of the smother of endless woods that ran a thousand miles without a break. He was glad in particular that no trees were visible, and that rabbits scampering among the dunes were the only wild animals he need ever meet. . . .

Those thirty years in the woods, it seemed, oppressed his mind; the forests, the countless multitudes of trees, had wearied him. His nevers, perhaps, had suffered finally. Snow, frost and sun, stars, and the wind had been his companions during the long days and endless nights in his lonely Post, but chiefly—trees. Trees, trees, trees! On the whole, he had perferred them in stormy weather, though, in another way, their rigid hosts, 'mid the deep silence of still days, had been equally oppressive. In the clear sunlight of a windless day they assumed a waiting, listening, watching aspect that had something spectral in it, but when in motion—well, he preferred a moving animal to one that stood stock-still and stared. Wind, moreover, in a million trees, even the lighest breeze, drowned all other sounds— the howling of the wolves, for instance, in winter, or the ceaseless harsh barking of the husky dogs he so disliked.

Even on this warm September afternoon a slight shiver ran over him as the background of dead years loomed up behind the present scene. He thrust the picture back, deep down inside himself. The self-control, the strong, even violent will that the face betrayed, came into operation instantly. The background was background; it belonged to what was past, and the past was over and done with. It was dead. Jim meant it to stay dead.

The figure waving to him from the pier was his brother. He knew Tom instantly; the years had dealt easily with him in this quiet island; there was no startling, no unkindly change, and a deep emotion, though unexpressed, rose in his heart. It was good to be home again, he realised, as he

186

sat presently in the cart, Tom holding the reins, driving slowly back to the farm at the north end of the island. Everything he found familiar, yet at the same time strange. They passed the school where he used to go as a little bare-legged boy; other boys were now learning their lessons exactly as he used to do. Through the open window he could hear the droning voice of the schoolmaster, who, though invisible, wore the face of Mr. Lovibond, his own teacher.

'Lovibond?' said Tom, in reply to his question. 'Oh, he's been dead these twenty years. He went south, you know—Glasgow, I think it was, or Edinburgh. He got typhoid.'

Stands of golden plover were to be seen as of old in the fields, or flashing overhead in swift flight with a whir of wings, wheeling and turning together like one huge bird. Down on the empty shore a curlew cried. Its piercing note rose clear above the noisy clamour of the gulls. The sun played softly on the quiet sea, the air was keen but pleasant, the tang of salt mixed sweetly with the clean smells of open country that he knew so well. Nothing of essentials had changed, even the low clouds beyond the heaving uplands were the clouds of childhood.

They came presently to the sand-dunes, where rabbits sat at their burrow-mouths, or ran helter-skelter across the road in front of the slow cart.

'They're safe till the colder weather comes and trapping begins,' he mentioned. It all came back to him in detail.

'And they know it, too—the canny little beggars,' replied Tom. 'Any rabbits out where you've veen?' he asked casually.

'Not to hurt you,' returned his brother shortly.

Nothing seemed changed, although everything seemed different. He looked upon the old, familiar things, but with other eyes. There were, of course, changes, alterations, yet so slight, in a way so odd and curious, that they evaded him; not being of the physical order, they reported to his soul, not to his mind. But his soul, being troubled, sought to

187

deny the changes; to admit them meant to admit a change in himself he had determined to conceal even if he could not entirely deny it.

'Same old place, Tom,' came one of his rare remarks. 'The years ain't done much to it.' He looked into his brother's face a moment squarely. 'Nor to you, either, Tom,' he added, affection and tenderness just touching his voice and breaking through a natural reserve that was almost taciturnity.

His brother returned the look; and something in that instant passed between the two men, something of understanding that no words had hinted at, much less expressed. The tie was real, they loved each other, they were loyal, true, steadfast fellows. In youth they had known no secrets. The shadow that now passed and vanished left a vague trouble in both hearts.

'The forests,' said Tom slowly, 'have made a silent man of you, Jim. You'll miss them here, I'm thinking.'

'Maybe,' was the curt reply, 'but I guess not.'

His lips snapped to as though they were of steel and could never open again, while the tone he used made Tom realise that the subject was not one his brother cared to talk about particularly. He was surprised, therefore, when, after a pause, Jim returned to it of his own accord. He was sitting a little sideways as he spoke, taking in the scene with hungry eyes. 'It's a queer thing,' he observed, 'to look round and see nothing but clean empty land, and not a single tree in sight. You see, it don't look natural quite.'

Again his brother was struck by the tone of voice, but this time by something else as well he could not name. Jim was excusing himself, explaining. The manner, too, arrested him. And thirty years disappeared as though they had not been, for it was thus Jim acted as a boy when there was something unpleasant he had to say and wished to get it over. The tone, the gesture, the manner, all were there. He was edging up to something he wished to say, yet dared not utter.

'You've had enough of trees then?' Tom said sympathetically, trying to help, 'and things?'

The instant the last two words were out he realised that they had been drawn from him instinctively, and that it was the anxiety of deep affection which had prompted them. He had guessed without knowing he had guessed, or rather, without intention or attempt to guess. Jim had a secret. Love's clairvoyance had discovered it, though not yet its hidden terms.

'I have—' began the other, then paused, evidently to choose his words with care. 'I've had enough of trees.' He was about to speak of something that his brother had unwittingly touched upon in his chance phrase, but instead of finding the words he sought, he gave a sudden start, his breath caught sharply. 'What's that?' he exclaimed, jerking his body round so abruptly that Tom automatically pulled the reins. 'What is it?'

'A dog barking,' Tom answered, much surprised. 'A farm dog barking. Why? What did you think it was?' he asked, as he flicked the horse to go on again. 'You made me jump,' he added, with a laugh. 'You're used to huskies, ain't you?'

'It sounded so—not like a dog, I mean,' came the slow explanation. 'It's long since I heard a sheep-dog bark, I suppose it startled me.'

'Oh, it's a dog al right,' Tom assured him comfortingly, for his heart told him infallibly the kind of tone to use. And presently, too, he changed the subject in his blunt, honent fashion, knowing that, also, was the right and kindly thing to do. He pointed out the old farms as they drove along, his brother silent again, sitting stiff and rigid at his side. 'And it's good to have you back, Jim, from those outlandish places. There are not too many of the family left now—just you and I, as a matter of fact.'

'Just you and I,' the other repeated gruffly, but in a sweetened tone that proved he appreciated the ready sympathy and tact. 'We'll stick together, Tom, eh? Blood's thicker than water, ain't it? I've learnt that much, anyhow.'

The voice had something gentle and appealing in it, something his brother heard now for the first time. An elbow nudged into his side, and Tom knew the gesture was not solely a sign of affection, but grew partly also from the comfort born of physical contact when the heart is anxious. The touch, like the last words, conveyed an appeal for help. Tom was so surprised he couldn't believe it quite.

Scared! Jim scared! The thought puzzled and afflicted him who knew his brother's character inside out, his courage, his presence of mind in danger, his resolution. Jim frightened seemed an impossibility, a contradiction in terms; he was the kind of man who did not know the meaning of fear, who shrank from nothing, whose spirits rose highest when things appeared most hopeless. It must, indeed, be an uncommon, even a terrible danger that could shake such nerves; yet Tom saw the signs and read them clearly. Explain them he could not, nor did he try. All he knew with certainty was that his brother, sitting now beside him in the cart, hid a secret terror in his heart. Sooner or later, in his own good time, he would share it with him.

He ascribed it, this simple Orkney farmer, to those thirty years of loneliness and exile in wild desolate places, without companionship, without the society of women, with only Indians, husky dogs, a few trappers or fur-dealers like himself, but none of the wholesome, natural influences that sweeten life within reach. Thirty years was a long, long time. He began planning schemes to help. Jim must see people as much as possible, and his mind ran quickly over the men and women available. In women the neighbour-hood was not rich, but there were several men of the right sort who might be useful, good fellows all. There was John Rossiter, another old Hudson Bay man, who had been factor at Cartwright, Labrador, for many years, and had returned long ago to spend his last days in civilisation. There was Sandy McKay, also back from a long spell of rubber-planting in Malay. . . . Tom was still busy making plans when they reached the old farm and presently sat

190

down to their first meal together since that early breakfast thirty years ago before Jim caught the steamer that bored him off to exile—an exile that now returned him with nerves unstrung and a secret terror hidden in his heart.

'I'll ask no questions,' he decided. 'Jim will tell me in his own good time. And, meanwhile, I'll get him to see as many folks as possible.' He meant it too; yet not only for his brother's sake. Jim's terror was so vivid it had touched his own heart too.

'Ah, a man can open his lungs here and breathe!' exclaimed Jim, as the two came out after supper and stood before the house, gazing across the open country. He drew a deep breath as though to prove his assertion, exhaling with slow satisfaction again. 'It's good to see a clear horizon and to know there's all that water between— between me and where I've been.' He turned his face to watch the plover in the sky, then looked towards the distant shore-line where the sea was just visible in the long evening light. 'There can't be too much water for me,' he added, half to himself. 'I guess they can't cross water—not that much water at any rate.'

Tom stared, wondering uneasily what to make of it.

'At the trees again, Jim?' he said laughingly. He had overheard the last words, though spoken low, and thought it best not to ignore them altogether. To be natural was the right way, he believed, natural and cheery. To make a joke of anything unpleasant, he felt, was to make it less serious. 'I've never seen a tree come across the Atlantic yet, except as a mast—dead,' he added.

'I wasn't thinking of the trees just then,' was the blunt reply, 'but of—something else. The damned trees are nothing, though I hate the sight of 'em. Not of much account, anyway'—as though he compared them mentally with another thing. He puffed at his pipe a moment.

'They certainly can't move,' put in his brother, 'nor swim either.'

'Nor another thing,' said Jim, his voice thick suddenly, but not with smoke, and his speech confused, though the

191

idea in his mind was certainly clear as daylight. 'Things can't hide behind 'em—can they?'

'Not much cover hereabouts, I admit,' laughed Tom, though the look in his brother's eyes made his laughter as short as it sounded unnatural.

'That's so,' agreed the other. 'But what I meant was'— he threw out his chest, looked about him with an air of intense relief, drew in another deep breath, and again exhaled with satisfaction—'if there are no trees, there's no hiding.'

It was the expression on the rugged, weathered face that sent the blood in a sudden gulping rush from his brother's heart. He had seen men frightened, seen men afraid before they were actually frightened; he had slso seen men stiff with terror in the face both of natural and so-called supernatural things; but never in his life before had he seen the look of unearthly dread that now turned his brother's face as white as chalk and yet put the glow of fire in two haunted burning eyes.

Across the darkening landscape the sound of distant barking had floated to them on the evening wind.

'It's only a farm-dog barking.' Yet it was Jim's deep, quiet voice that said it, one hand upon his brother's arm.

'That's all,' replied Tom, ashamed that he had betrayed himself, and realising with a shock of surprise that it was Jim who now played the role of comforter—a startling change in their relations. 'Why, what did you think it was?

He tried hard to speak naturally and easily, but his voice shook. So deep was the brothers' love and intimacy that they could not help but share.

Jim lowered his great head. 'I though,' he whispered, his grey beard touching the other's cheek, 'maybe it was the wolves'—an agony of terror made both voice and body tremble—'the Wolves of God!'

The interval of thirty years had been bridged easily enough; it was the secret that left the open gap neither of them cared or dared to cross. Jim's reason for hesitation lay within reach of guesswork, but Tom's silence was more complicated.

With strong, simple men, strangers to affectation or pretence, reserve is a real, almost a sacred thing. Jim offered nothing more; Tom asked no single question. In the latter's mind lay, for one thing, a singular intuitive certainty: that if he knew the truth he would lose his brother. How, why, wherefore, he had no notion; whether by death, or because, having told an awful thing, Jim would hide—physically or mentally—he knew not, nor even asked himself. No subtlety lay in Tom, the Orkney farmer. He merely felt that a knowledge of the truth involved separation which was death.

Day and night, however, that extraordinary phrase which, at its first hearing, had frozen his blood, ran on beating in his mind. With it came always the original, nameless horror that had held him motionless where he stood, his brother's bearded lips against his ear: *The Wolves of God*. In some dim way, he sometimes felt—tried to persuade himself, rather—the horror did not belong to the phrase alone, but was a sympathetic echo of what Jim felt himself. It had entered his own mind and heart. They had always shared in this same strange, intimate way. The deep brotherly tie accounted for it. Of the possible transference of thought and emotion he knew nothing, but this was what he meant perhaps.

At the same time he fought and strove to keep it out, not because it brought uneasy and distressing feelings to him, but because he did not wish to pry, to ascertain, to discover his brother's secret as by some kind of subterfuge that seemed too near to eavesdropping almost. Also, he wished most earnestly to protect him. Meanwhile, in spite of himself, or perhaps because of himself, he watched his brother as a wild animal watches its young. Jim was the only tie he had on earth. He loved him with a brother's love, and Jim, similarly, he knew, loved him. His job was difficult. Love alone could guide him.

He gave openings, but he never questioned:

'Your letter did surprise me, Jim. I was never so delighted in my life. You had still two years to run.'

'I'd had enough,' was the short reply. 'God, man, it was good to get home again!'

This, and the blunt talk that followed their first meeting, was all Tom had to go upon, while those eyes that refused to shut watched ceaselessly always. There was improvement, unless, which never occurred to Tom, it was self-control; there was no more talk of trees and water, the barking of the dogs passed unnoticed, no reference to the loneliness of the backwoods life passed his lips; he spent his days fishing, shooting, helping with the work of the farm, his evenings smoking over a glass—he was more than temperate—and talking over the days of long ago.

The signs of uneasiness still were there, but they were negative, far more suggestive, therefore, than if open and direct. He desired no company, for instance—an unnatural thing, thought Tom, after so many years of loneliness.

It was this and the awkward fact that he had given up two years before his time was finished, renouncing, therefore, a comfortable pension—it was these two big details that stuck with such unkind persistence in his brother's thoughts. Behind both, moreover, ran ever the strange whispered phrase. What the words meant, or whence they were derived, Tom had no possible inkling. Like the wicked refrain of some forbidden song, they haunted him day and night, even his sleep was not free from them entirely. All of which, to the simple Orkney farmer, was so new an experience that he knew not how to deal with it at all. Too strong to be flustered, he was at any rate bewildered. And it was for Jim, his brother, he suffered most.

What perplexed him chiefly, however, was the attitude his brother showed towards old John Rossiter. He could

194

almost have imagined that the two men had met and known each other out in Canada, though Rossiter showed him how impossible that was, both in point of time and of geography as well. He had brought them together within the first few days, and Jim, silent, gloomy, morose, even surly, had eyed him like an enemy. Old Rossiter, the milk of human kindness as thick in his veins as cream, had taken no offence. Grizzled veteran of the wilds, he had served his full term with the Company and now enjoyed his well-earned pension. He was full of stories, reminiscences, adventures of every sort and kind; he knew men and values, had seen strange things that only the true wilderness delivers, and he loved nothing better than to tell them over a glass. He talked with Jim so genially and affably that little response was called for luckily, for Jim was glum and unresponsive almost to rudeness. Old Rossiter noticed nothing. What Tom noticed was, chiefly perhaps, his brother's acute uneasiness. Between his desire to help his attachment to Rossiter, and his keen personal distress, he knew not what to do or say. The situation was becoming too much for him.

The two families, besides—Peace and Rossiter—had been neighbours for generations, had intermarried freely, and were related in various degrees. He was too fond of his brother to feel ashamed, but he was glad when the visit was over and they were out of their host's house. Jim had even declined to drink with him.

'They're good fellows on the island,' said Tom on their way home, 'but not specially entertaining, perhaps. We all stick together though. You can trust 'em mostly.'

'I never was a talker, Tom,' came the gruff reply. 'You know that.' And Tom, understanding more than he understood, accepted the apology and made generous allowances.

'John likes to talk,' he helped him. 'He appreciates a good listener.'

'It's the kind of talk I'm finished with,' was the rejoinder. 'The Company and their goings-on don't interest me any more. I've had enough.'

195

Tom noticed other things as well with those affectionate eyes of his that did not want to see yet would not close. As the days drew in, for instance, Jim seemed reluctant to leave the house towards evening. Once the full light of day had passed, he kept indoors. He was eager and ready enough to shoot in the early morning, no matter at what hour he had to get up, but he refused point blank to go with his brother to the lake for an evening flight. No excuse was offered; he simply declined to go.

The gap between them thus widened and deepened, while yet in another sense it grew less formidable. Both knew, that is, that a secret lay between them for the first time in their lives, yet both knew also that at the right and proper moment it would be revealed. Jim only waited till the proper moment came. And Tom understood. His deep, simple love was equal to all emergencies. He respected his brother's reserve. The obvious desire of John Rossiter to talk and ask questions, for instance, he resisted staunchly as far as he was able. Only when he could help and protect his brother did he yield a little. The talk was brief, even monosyllabic; neither the old Hudson Bay fellow nor the Orkney farmer ran to many words:

'He ain't right with himself,' offered John, taking his pipe out of his mouth and leaning forward. 'That's what I don't like to see.' He put a skinny hand on Tom's knee, and looked earnestly into his face as he said it.

'Jim!' replied the other. 'Jim ill, you mean!' It sounded ridiculous.

'His mind is sick.'

'I don't understand,' Tom said, though the truth bit like roughedged steel into the brother's heart.

'His soul, then, if you like that better.'

Tom fought with himself a moment, then asked him to be more explicit.

More'n I can say,' rejoined the laconic old backwoodsman. 'I don't know myself. The woods heal some men and make others sick.'

'Maybe, John, maybe.' Tom fought back his resentment.

196

'You've lived, like him, in lonely places. You ought to know.' His mouth shut with a snap, as though he had said too much. Loyalty to his suffering brother caught him strongly. Already his heart ached for Jim. He felt angry with Rossiter for his divination, but perceived, too, the the old fellow meant well and was trying to help him. If he lost Jim, he lost the world—his all.

A considerable pause followed, during which both men puffed their pipes with reckless energy. Both, that is, were a bit excited. Yet both had their code, a code they would not exceed for worlds.

'Jim,' added Tom presently, making an effort to meet the sympathy half way, 'ain't quite up to the mark, I'll admit that.'

There was another long pause, while Rossiter kept his eyes on his companion steadily, though without a trace of expression in them—a habit that the woods had taught him.

'Jim,' he said at length, with an obvious effort, 'is skeered. And it's the soul in him that's skeered.'

Tom wavered dreadfully then. He saw that old Rossiter, experienced backwoodsman and taught by the Comapny as he was, knew where the secret lay, if he did not yet know its exact terms. It was easy enough to put the question, yet he hesitated, because loyalty forbade.

'It's a dirty outfit somewheres,' the old man mumbled to himself.

Tom sprang to his feet. 'If you talk that way,' he exclaimed angrily, 'you're no friend of mine—or his.' His anger gained upon him as he said it. 'Say that again,' he cried, 'and I'll knock your teeth——'

He sat back, stunned a moment.

'Forgive me, John,' he faltered, shamed yet still angry. 'It's pain to me, it's pain. Jim,' he went on, after a long breath and a pull at his glass, 'Jim *is* scared, I know it.' He waited a moment, hunting for the words that he could use without disloyalty. 'But it's nothing he's done himself,' he said, 'nothing to his discredit. I know *that*.'

Old Rossiter looked up, a strange light in his eyes.

'No offence,' he said quietly.

'Tell me what you know,' cried Tom suddenly, standing up again.

The old factor met his eye squarely, steadfastly. He laid his pipe aside.

'D'ye really want to hear?' he asked in a lowered voice. 'Because, if you don't—why, say so right now. I'm all for justice,' he added, 'and always was.'

'Tell me,' said Tom, his heart in his mouth. 'Maybe, if I knew—I might help him.' The old man's words woke fear in him. He well knew his passionate, remorseless sense of justice.

'Help him,' repeated the other. 'For a man skeered in his soul there ain't no help. But—if you want to hear—I'll tell you.'

'Tell me,' cried Tim. 'I *will* help him,' while rising anger fought back rising fear.

John took another pull at his glass.

'Jest between you and me like.'

'Between you and me,' said Tom. 'Get on with it.'

There was a deep silence in the little room. Only the sound of the sea came in, the wind behind it.

'The Wolves,' whispered old Rossiter. 'The Wolves of God.'

Tom sat still in his chair, as though struck in the face. He shivered. He kept silent and the silence seemed to him long and curious. His heart was throbbing, the blood in his veins played strange tricks. All he remembered was that old Rossiter had gone on talking. The voice, however, sounded far away and distant. It was all unreal, he felt, as he went homewards across the bleak, wind-swept upland, the sound of the sea for ever in his ears. . . .

Yes, old John Rossiter, damned be his soul, had gone on talking. He had said wild, incredible things. Damned be his soul! His teeth should be smashed for that. It was outrageous, it was cowardly, it was not true.

198

'Jim,' he thought, 'my brother, Jim!' as he ploughed his way wearily against the wind. 'I'll teach him. I'll teach him to spread such wicked tales!' He referred to Rossiter. 'God blast these fellows! They come home from their outlandish places and thing they can say anything! I'll knock his yellow dog's teeth . . . !'

While, inside, his heart went quailing, crying for help, afraid.

He tried hard to remember exactly what old John had said. Round Garden Lake—that's where Jim was located in his lonely Post—there was a tribe of Redskins. They were of unusual type. Malefactors among them—thieves, criminals, murderers—were not punished. They were merely turned out by the Tribe to die.

But how?

The Wolves of God took care of them. What were the Wolves of God?

A pack of wolves the Redskins held in awe, a sacred pack, a spirit pack—God curse the man! Absurd, outlandish nonsense! Superstitious humbug! A pack of wolves that punished malefactors, killing but never eating them. 'Torn but not eaten,' the words came back to him, 'white men as well as red. They could even cross the sea. . . .'

'He ought to be strung up for telling such wild yarns. By God—I'll teach him!'

'Jim! My brother, Jim! It's monstrous!'

But the old man, in his passionate cold justice, had said a yet more terrible thing, a thing that Tom would never forget, as he never could forgive it: 'You mustn't keep him here; you must send him away. We cannot have him on the island.' And for that, though he could scarcely believe his ears, wondering afterwards whether he heard aright, for that, the proper answer to which was a blow in the mouth, Tom knew that his old friendship and affection had turned to bitter hatred.

'If I don't kill him, for that cursed lie, my God—and Jim—forgive me!'

II,

It was a few days later that the storm caught the islands, making them tremble in their sea-born bed. The wind tearing over the treeless expanse was terrible, the lightning lit the skies. No such rain had ever been known. The building shook and trembled. It almost seemed the sea had burst her limits, and the waves poured in. Its fury and the noises that the wind made affected both the brothers, but Jim disliked the uproar most. It made him gloomy, silent, morose. It made him—Tom perceived it at once—uneasy. 'Scared in his soul'—the ugly phrase came back to him.

'God save anyone who's out tonight,' said Jim anxiously, as the old farm rattled about his head. Whereupon the door opened as of itself. There was no knock. It flew wide, as if the wind had burst it. Two drenched and beaten figures showed in the gap against the lurid sky—old John Rossiter and Sandy. They laid their fowling pieces down and took off their capes; they had been up at the lake for the evening flight and six birds were in the game bag. So suddenly had the storm come up that they had been caught before they could get home.

And, while Tom welcomed them, looked after their creature wants, and made them feel at home as in duty bound, no visit, he felt at the same time, could have been less opportune. Sandy did not matter—Sandy never did matter anywhere, his personality being negligible—but John Rossiter was the last man Tom wished to see just then. He hated the man; hated that sense of implacable justice that he knew was in him; with the slightest excuse he would have turned him out and sent him on to his own home, storm or no storm. But Rossiter provided no excuse; he was all gratitude and easy politeness, more pleasant and friendly to Jim even than to his brother. Tom set out the whisky and sugar, sliced the lemon, put the kettle on, and furnished dry coats while the soaked garments hung up before the roaring fire that Orkney makes customary even when days are warm.

'It might be the equinoctials,' observed Sandy, 'if it wasn't late October.' He shivered, for the tropics had thinned his blood.

'This ain't no ordinary storm,' put in Rossiter, drying his drenched boots. 'It reminds me a bit'—he jerked his head to the window that gave seawards, the rush of rain against the panes half drowning his voice—'reminds me a bit of yonder.' He looked up, as though to find someone to agree with him, only one such person being in the room.

'Sure, it ain't,' agreed Jim at once, but speaking slowly, 'no ordinary storm.' His voice was quiet as a child's. Tom, stooping over the kettle, felt something cold go trickling down his back. 'It's from across the Atlantic too.'

'All our big storms come from the sea,' offered Sandy, saying just what Sandy was expected to say. His lank red hair lay matted on his forehead, making him look like an unhappy collie dog.

'There's no hospitality,' Rossiter changed the talk, 'like an islander's,' as Tom mixed and filled the glasses. 'He don't even ask "Say when?"' He chuckled in his beard and turned to Sandy, well pleased with the compliment to his host. 'Now, in Malay,' he added dryly, 'it's probably different, I guess.' And the two men, one from Labrador, the other from the tropics, fell to bantering one another with heavy humour, while Tom made things comfortable and Jim stood silent with his back to the fire. At each blow of the wind that shook the building, a suitable remark was made, generally by Sandy: 'Did you hear that now?' 'Ninety miles an hour at least!' 'Good thing you build solid in this country!' while Rossiter occasionally repeated that it was an 'uncommon storm' and that 'it reminded' him of the northern tempests he had known 'out yonder'.

Tom said little, one thought and one thought only in his heart—the wish that the storm would abate and his guests depart. He felt uneasy about Jim. He hated Rossiter. In the kitchen he had steadied himself already with a good stiff drink, and was now half-way through a second; the feeling was in him that he would need their help before the evening was out. Jim, he noticed, had left his glass untouched. His attention, clearly, went to the wind and the outer night; he added little to the conversation.

'Hark!' cried Sandy's shrill voice. 'Did you hear that? That wasn't wind, I'll swear.' He sat up, looking for all the world like a dog pricking its ears to something no one else could hear.

'The sea coming over the dunes,' said Rossiter. 'There'll be an awful tide tonight and a terrible sea off the Swarf. Moon at the full, too.' He cocked his head sideways to listen. The roaring was tremendous, waves and wind combining with a result that almost shook the ground. Rain hit the glass with incessant volleys like duck shot.

It was then that Jim spoke, having said no word for a long time.

'It's good there's no trees,' he mentioned quietly. 'I'm glad of that.'

'There'd be fearful damage, wouldn't there?' remarked Sandy. 'They might fall on the house too.'

But it was the tone Jim used that made Rossiter turn stiffly in his chair, looking first at the speaker, then at his brother. Tom caught both glances and saw the hard keen glitter in the eyes. This kind of talk, he decided, had got to stop, yet how to stop it he hardly knew, for his were not subtle methods, and rudeness to his guests ran too strong against the island customs. He refilled the glasses, thinking in his blunt fashion how best to achieve his object, when Sandy helped the situation without knowing it.

'That's my first,' he observed, and all burst out laughing. For Sandy's tenth glass was equally his 'first', and he absorbed his liquor like a sponge, yet showed no effects of it until the moment when he would suddenly collapse and sink helpless to the ground. The glass in question, however, was only his third, the final moment still far away.

'Three in one and one in three,' said Rossiter, amid the general laughter, while Sandy, grave as a judge, half emptied it at a single gulp. Good-natured, obtuse as a cart-horse, the tropics, it seemed, had first worn out his

202

nerves, then removed them entirely from his body. 'That's Malay theology, I guess,' finished Rossiter. And the laugh broke out again. Whereupon, setting his glass down, Sandy offered his usual explanation that the hot lands had thinned his blood, that he felt the cold in these 'artic islands', and that alcohol was a necessity of life with him. Tom, grateful for the unexpected help, encouraged him to talk, and Sandy accustomed to neglect as a rule, responded readily. Having saved the situation, however, he now unwittingly led it back into the danger zone.

'A night for tales, eh?' he remarked, as the wind came howling with a burst of strange noises against the house. 'Down there in the States,' he went on, 'they'd say the evil spirits were out. They're a superstitious crowd, the natives. I remember once—' And he told a tale, half foolish, half interesting, of a mysterious track he had seen when following buffalo in the jungle. It ran close to the spoor of a wounded buffalo for miles, a track unlike that of any known animal, and the natives, though unable to name it, regarded it with awe. It was a good sign, a kill was certain. They said it was a spirit track.

'You got your buffalo?' asked Tom.

'Found him two miles away, lying dead. The mysterious spoor came to an end close beside the carcass. It didn't continue.'

'And that reminds me—' began old Rossiter, ignoring Tom's attempt to introduce another subject. He told them of the haunted island at Eagle River, and a tale of the man who would not stay buried on another island off the coast. From that he went on to describe the strange man-beast that hides in the deep forests of Labrador, manifesting but rarely, and dangerous to men who stray too far from camp, men with a passion for wild life overstrong in their blood—the great mythical Wendigo. And while he talked, Tom noticed that Sandy used each pause as a good moment for a drink, but that Jim's glass still remained untouched.

The atmosphere of incredible things, thus, grew in the little room, much as it gathers among the shadows round a forest campfire when men who have seen strange places of the world give tongue about them, knowing they will not be laughed at—an atmosphere, once established, it is vain to fight against. The ingrained superstition that hides in every mother's son comes up at such times to breathe. It came up now. Sandy, closer by several glasses to the moment, Tom saw, when he would be suddenly drunk, gave birth again, a tale this time of a Scottish planter who had brutally dismissed a native servant for no other reason than that he disliked him. The man disappeared completely, but the villagers hinted that he would—soon indeed that he had—come back, though 'not quite as he went'. The planter armed, knowing that vengeance might be violent. A black panther, meanwhile, was seen prowling about the bungalow. One night a noise outside his door on the veranda roused him. Just in time to see the black brute leaping over the railings into the compound, he fired, and the beast fell with a savage growl of pain. Help arrived and more shots were fired into the animal, as it lay, mortally wounded already, lashing its tail upon the grass. The lanterns, however, showed that instead of a panther, it was the servant they had shot to shreds.

Sandy told the story well, a certain odd conviction in his tone and manner, neither of them at all to the liking of his host. Uneasiness and annoyance had been growing in Tom for some time already, his inability to control the situation adding to his anger. Emotion was accumulating in him dangerously; it was directed chiefly against Rossiter, who, though saying nothing definite, somehow deliberately encouraged both talk and atmosphere. Given the conditions, it was natural enough the talk should take the turn it did take, but what made Tom more and more angry was that, if Rossiter had not been present, he could have stopped it easily enough. It was the presence of the old Hudson Bay man that prevented his taking decided action. He was afraid of Rossiter, afraid of putting his back up. That was the truth. His recognition of it made him furious.

'Tell us another, Sandy McKay,' said the veteran.

'There's a lot in such tales. They're found the world over—men turning into animals and the like.'

And Sandy, yet nearer to his moment of collapse, but still showing no effects, obeyed willingly. He noticed nothing; the whisky was good, his tales were appreciated, and that sufficed him. He thanked Tom, who just then refilled his glass, and went on with his tale. But Tom, hatred and fury in his heart, had reached the point where he could no longer contain himself, and Rossiter's last words inflamed him. He went over, under cover of a tremendous clap of wind, to fill the old man's glass. The latter refused, covering the tumbler with his big, lean hand. Tom stood over him a moment, lowering his face. 'You keep still,' he whispered ferociously, but so that no one else heard it. He glared into his eyes with an intensity that held danger, and Rossiter, without answering, flung back that glare with equal, but with a calmer, anger.

The wind, meanwhile, had a trick of veering, and each time it shifted, Jim shifted his seat too. Apparently, he preferred to face the sound, rather than have his back to it.

'Your turn now for a tale,' said Rossiter with purpose, when Sandy finished. He looked across at him, just as Jim, hearing the burst of wind at the walls behind him, was in the act of moving his chair again. The same moment the attack rattled the door and windows facing him. Jim, without answering, stood for a moment still as death, not knowing which way to turn.

'It's beatin' up from all sides,' remarked Rossiter, 'like it was goin' round the building.'

There was a moment's pause, the four men listening with awe to the roar and power of the terrific wind. Tom listened too, but at the same time watched, wondering vaguely why he didn't cross the room and crash his fist into the old man's chattering mouth. Jim put out his hand and took his glass, but did not raise it to his lips. And a lull came abruptly in the storm, the wind sinking into a moment's dreadful silence. Tom and Rossiter turned their heads in the same instant and stared into each other's eyes. For Tom the instant seemed enormously prolonged. He realised the challenge in the other and that his rudeness had roused it into action. It had become a contest of wills— Justice battling against Love.

Jim's glass had now reached his lips, and the chattering of his teeth against its rim was audible.

But the lull passed quickly and the wind began again, though so gently at first, it had the sound of innumerable swift footsteps treading lightly, of countless hands fingering the doors and windows, but then suddenly with a mighty shout as it swept against the walls, rushed across the roof and descended like a battering-ram against the farther side.

'God, did you hear that?' cried Sandy. 'It's trying to get in!' and having said it, he sank in a heap beside his chair, all of a sudden completely drunk. 'It's wolves or panthersh,' he mumbled in his stupor on the floor, 'but whatsh's happened to Malay?' It was the last thing he said before unconsciousness took him, and apparently he was insensible to the kick on the head from a heavy farmer's boot. For Jim's glass had fallen with a crash and the second kick was stopped midway. Tom stood spellbound, unable to move or speak, as he watched his brother suddenly cross the room and open a window into the very teeth of the gale.

'Let be! Let be!' came the voice of Rossiter, an authority in it, a curious gentleness too, both of them new. He had risen, his lips were still moving, but the words that issued from them were inaudible, as the wind and rain leaped with a galloping violence into the room, smashing the glass to atoms and dashing a dozen loose objects helter-skelter on to the floor.

'I saw it!' cried Jim, in a voice that rose above the din and clamour of the elements. He turned and faced the others, but it was at Rossiter he looked. 'I saw the leader.' He shouted to make himself heard, although the tone was quiet. 'A splash of white on his great chest. I saw them all!'

At the words, and at the expression in Jim's eyes, old

Rossiter, white to the lips, dropped back into his chair as if a blow had struck him. Tom, petrified, felt his own heart stop. For through the broken window, above yet within the wind, came the sound of a wolf-pack running, howling in deep, full-throated chorus, mad for blood. It passed like a whirlwind and was gone. And, of the three men so close together, one sitting and two standing, Jim alone was in that terrible moment wholly master of himself.

Before the others could move or speak, he turned and looked full into the eyes of each in succession. His speech went back to his wilderness days:

'I done it,' he said calmly. 'I killed him—and I got ter go.'

With a look of mystical horror on his face, he took one stride, flung the door wide, and vanished into the darkness.

So quick were both words and action, that Tom's paralysis passed only as the draught from the broken window banged the door behind him. He seemed to leap across the room, old Rossiter, tears on his cheeks and his lips mumbling foolish words, so close upon his heels that the backward blow of fury Tom aimed at his face caught him only in the neck and sent him reeling sideways to the floor instead of flat upon his back.

'Murderer! My brother's death upon you!' he shouted as he tore the door open again and plunged out into the night.

And the odd thing that happened then, the thing that touched old John Rossiter's reason, leaving him from that moment till his death a foolish man of uncertain mind and memory, happened when he and the unconscious, drink-sodden Sandy lay alone together on the stone floor of that farm-house room.

Rossiter, dazed by the blow and his fall, but in full possession of his senses, and the anger gone out of him owing to what he had brought about, this same John Rossiter sat up and saw Sandy was sober as a judge, his eyes and speech both clear, even his face unflushed.

'John Rossiter,' he said, 'it was not God who appointed

207

you executioner. It was the devil.' And his eyes, thought Rossiter, were like the eyes of an angel.

'Sandy McKay,' he stammered, his teeth chattering and breath failing him. 'Sandy McKay!' It was all the words that he could find. But Sandy, already sunk back into his stupor again, was stretched drunk and incapable upon the farm-house floor, and remained in that condition till the dawn.

Jim's body lay hidden among the dunes for many months and in spite of the most careful and prolonged searching. It was another storm that laid it bare. The sand had covered it. The clothes were gone, and the flesh, torn but not eaten, was naked to the December sun and wind.

THE CLOCK

by Neil M. Gunn

NEIL MILLER GUNN (*1891–1973*) *a master at depicting the fantasy of the unknown through vivid, engrossing prose, remains sadly unknown to too many readers outside Scotland. Born in Dunbeath, Caithness, he grew to understand the life and tempo of Scottish fishing and crofting villages from intimate contact, and his best work is set against these backgrounds. For a time a Civil Servant—latterly as a Customs Officer—Gunn had his first book,* The Grey Coast, *published in 1926. In subsequent years he demonstrated the range of his talent with books such as* Butcher's Broom (*1934*), *in which he showed how the Highlands were being spoiled by the eviction of crofters to make way for sheep, and in* Second Sight (*1940*), *how certain people with 'the gift' can see future events. The old lore and superstitions are, however, never far from his stories and in* The Well at the World's End (*1951*) *he combined ancient fantasy and modern reality with consummate skill. The short story here is likewise rooted in fact, but moves inexorably towards the borderlands of hallucination and terror.*

Putting an edge on a razor is a fascinating task, demanding a precision at once mathematical and infernal. Moreover, from the steady edge-grinding on the oiled hone to the brisk slapping of the leather the process requires time and a fine sense of leisure, while the final testing of the glittering steel on a hair plucked violently from the head has in it a consciousness of artistry not at all of the flesh nor altogether of the devil.

As, perfectly satisfied, I caressed my palm with the cool blade my eyes were drawn across my little sitting-room to the clock. The hands lay along each other at midnight. I waited for the striking with a sense of self-deception that was only half-cynical. For under its glass dome the clock was noiseless, with a noiselessness that was intimate and mocking and unending. The minute hand moved to an acute angle with the hour hand. I closed my razor and laid it on the table. Then I crossed to my armchair, and, watching the clock, began to fill my pipe.

Watching the clock had become for me an absorbing occupation. Indeed, at times and in places the most odd, I could see its round pendulum of burnished brass twist noiselessly through nearly two revolutions, then twist noiselessly back, with always the corresponding twisting of the supporting ribbon of steel, the untwisting, and the twisting back. I understood from it, through long periods of reverie, the sensations that move the hearts of devil worshippers. I became aware of the mockery that is the hidden soul of all perfect mechanism; I knew the carven cruelty of unheeding Time.

I thought again of my morning's conversation with my landlady. It troubled me, because in this matter of the clock I knew that I had, by some malevolent impulse, overstepped the boundary line of that good taste that is born of understanding and sympathy. Suddenly, as she smoothed the tea-cosy over the teapot, I had said:

'I was looking at that blessed clock last night till it sent me to sleep in my chair. Then if it didn't come along and sit tight on my chest, and refuse to let me wake up! We had a fight and a half, I can tell you.'

I stretched for a pat of butter, smiling at the obvious idiocy of all dreams; but all the time at the back of my mind I was acutely aware of a state of tension. She said nothing, and I hurried on:

'The fun of it was that I thought the clock didn't know that I knew that its heart was a coiled spring. You've no idea how I struggled to get at that heart—till all at once the

210

spring whizzed out and cut my hand off!' I laughed. 'I awoke with a jump,' I added, 'to find that my hot pipe had merely dropped from my mouth on to the back of my hand!'

But her smile was pale, and she went out without a word.

Before the door had closed a swift wave of annoyance decided me that I had been paying too much attention to that clock. I glared at it, at its silent twisting and glittering in the fresh morning light. Why in the name of the devil didn't she lock it up, and put in its place a decent thing that would tick-tock, tick-tock with cheerful folly! . . . Then I laughed at myself.

But all day the little affair had kept cropping up in my mind. Indeed, at moments, with a queer sense of incredulity, I even began to glimpse shapes of something actually sinister: a twist, a flicker, a vanishing expression of something mockingly real; as though fantasy hinted at an existence in fact, as though the creature of the imagination could take on a life of its own with curious, inimical intent. It was really too much.

Yet its interest was persistent, undeniable, and not without its fascination.. . .

No, not without its fascination now that I consider it comfortably, in complete leisure, and without any distractions. The night was so still that the trees in the garden did not even sigh. The tobacco smoke curled lazily, fantastically, and the light from the shaded oil-lamp had a yellowish tinge. The midnight hour is the hour of inanimate things, the legs and the arms of furniture, for example, or photographs on a wall at such a moment nothing can be more grotesque than a wedding group, or more persistent than a round knob, or more evilly mesmeric than the toils of an arabesque.

The steel ribbon winked every time it straightened itself, but the upright gleam on the revolving brass was actively constant. My mind began working again, but now in a more direct, human way than the clock had yet prompted.

After all, there was a lot to be said for my landlady's attitude. The facts were in a way tremendous when considered exclusively. Here was a woman round about forty, an active woman, finely built, dark hair, dark interesting eyes and smooth intelligent features, to be credited surely with most mother instincts a woman may possess.

No doubt of it. And because there was no doubt of it I felt I should be able to fathom most things. Born and brought up as she was in this typically Scots country parish, capable, for instance, of laying a spotless tea-table to the final butter-knife without my being quite aware of the operation till called to table—surely, I felt, there could be nothing behind these steady eyes, that level brow, savouring of the esoteric, of hidden, dark things—in a Scots country parish—and a Scotswoman! It was plainly impossible. My knowledge of landladies between London and Caithness was, I considered, fairly extensive. Yet, in spite of all, I had to admit to myself there was on her part a curious attitude to the clock, conscious or subconscious, fearful or antagonistic or both, that I could not fathom.

And I knew a lot about the clock, positive facts about its material history, that is—not mere fanciful projections of midnight thought. I had asked her one day in the early stages of my tenancy, and quite idly, where in the world she had got the marvellous piece of mechanism. And in a few appalling words, uttered more quietly than any observation about the weather, she told me the manner of its arrival. Exactly what could have prompted her to tell it in the way she did, what incredible simplicity or strange perversity, I failed utterly to grasp.

Two days after her marriage, I learned, her husband had contracted double pneumonia by diving off the pier of the little harbour to save the life of a man who was three parts drunk. One afternoon, round about the crisis of his illness, the doctor having just left the sick-room after expressing the comforting hope that the turn appeared to have been successfully negotiated, she was called downstairs by a gentle knocking at the front door. The postman handed her a parcel. It was the clock—a marriage present. When she went upstairs again she found her husband dead.

212

The recital in her simple, direct language was so short and stark that I must positively have gaped at her. It certainly left me without a single word, without even a mutter.

The incident haunted me for a long time, so much so that almost unconsciously I began groping around for more facts, but this time not of my landlady. And in time stray bits of information seemed to gather almost of their own volition and to group themselves into a sort of intelligible scheme that more than hinted at a story human enough.

But the process of collation of gradual perception, need not be elaborated, for like most stories of human happenings the outline can be given simply enough. In the first place, then, it was the man her husband had saved from drowning who had presented the clock. It was thus both a marriage present and a token of gratitude for having saved a life, even though, with all of life's bitterest irony, it had been presented at the door of death. In the next place, it appeared she had at one time been 'in service' in the house of the very man who had presented the clock, a man who was the last of a line of big farmers whose family name had been established a sufficient number of generations to ensure parochial respect. In the third place, between this man and my landlady (whilst still in his service) there had been some clashing of wills. So much was clear.

Then the outline gets blurred. Throughout the countryside it was inevitable that this farmer's character should get known more or less in its main features, and certainly his drunken bouts were notorious. A hard-living, hard-riding type of man, and, in his cups, imperious to a degree that was not only overbearing but frequently verging on a momentary madness, yet always, to those around him, with a certain insolent, aristocratic sanction. When added to this imperiousness were a personal fearlessness and generosity, almost a spendthrift prodigality, the total compound may be understood to have struck the more timid parish souls with a royal and fearful air of greatness. Further, a few months after the heroic incident of the pier, his drowned body was discovered one morning in the little harbour. How the

213

fatality had occurred, what had attracted him to the pier during a night of storm when no other living soul was abroad, what his possible state of mind, no one would hazard an opinion, however many heads might be shaken.

As has been said, between my landlady and this man there had been a clashing of wills, and though nothing definite appeared to be known concerning whatever incidents there may have been, it is certain that she fled his service before a pursuit that was not too honourable. As a definite statement of mere fact it may be left at that.

I lay back in my chair considering the history. It was interesting, decidedly interesting. I was aware that my education in the subtle had been neglected. The literature of the Continent proved it to me. In the mere obscurity of motive there was a world of enthralling interest. Admitting, for instance, that one may appreciate evil without being either ashamed of it or attracted by it, what an underworld of curious fascination, of feelings pitiful or poisonous but ever elusive, spreads its fatal shadows, shot with such strange light-glimmerings!

So I permitted myself to come under the full sway of that noiseless, mesmeric pendulum, while I searched for motives to my landlady's pale smile. . . . I sank gradually into the bodiless deeps of thought. Presently I found myself visualising possible scenes in her past, and from the scenes I went to what must have followed—the palpitating hopes, the tumultous uncertainties, the myriad fears of her mind. Has not every life at least dreamt of its secret and great adventure? Deep answering to deep, height to height? Her country upbringing with its barriers of convention and conscience so holy, so fearful; the mystery to herself of her untried womanhood so alluring, so tantalising; the fire of youth at its dawn, so unquenchable. To every woman has there not come at one time or another if not some man's love at least some man's gesture, some flash of a naked mind lighting up her inmost shrine with a fearful radiance? Who but a woman can understand Cleopatra—or the Magdalene? Did that hard-thinking fearless type of man ever strike an elemental chord? Did he

214

pursue her, haunting the deeps—even the deeps of fear? . . .
The love of her husband—obviously a thing as clear and
dear as a piece of statuary. . . . The arrival of the clock at
such a moment—almost as an omen, if not an interpretation.
Or was all my thought in its one dimension becoming too
far-fetched, too finical? Probably. And yet the clock was
there—still there—on its grim silent journey through time.
Why? After all, was there really something hidden here of
the nature of fine tragedy, even here—in this little house on
the outskirts of a country village, at this very moment? . . .

My heart leapt. The midnight silence seemed to have been
touched by the slightest of sounds. I smiled at myself whilst
yet my ears listened with desperate intentness. I had noticed
this peculiarity about my midnight education before that it
left my mind with a sensitiveness that was extreme to sudden
material intrusions—the creaking of a chair, for instance,
or the sudden tapping of a swaying twig on a window pane.
But one mastered these things by an effort of clear common
sense. . . .

And now the sound came like a slow, regular padding of
bare feet descending the stairs. And now in the passage-way.
A thin shudder moved over my skin. There were fingers
against the door. The knob turned visibly, and slowly the
door opened. I gripped the arms of my chair convulsively.
First an arm, then gradually the whole body. My landlady!
I ceased to breathe. Her white nightdress fell straightway
from the curves of her breast, her head was erect, her face
wide-eyed and terribly calm. In a moment I saw she was
asleep.

She looked across the room directly at the clock and
moved towards it. As she came to the table her fingers crept
lightly over its corner surface as though to guide her around
it, came in contact with my razor, hesitated, and slowly
closed over it.

She lifted the razor, and, without looking at it, opened it.
I saw the blade suddenly gleam against the lamplight. In the
slow, automatic manner in which this action was accomplished there was something so deadly and indescribably horrible

215

that my throat clove against all sound, my body froze against all movement. Her gaze never strayed for a second from the clock, yet her eyes were almost expressionless in their full, unwinking solemnity of purpose. As she moved on again towards the clock I had an agonising desire to cry out, to stop her, that merely left me more rigid, paralysed. I have a feeling now that the way she held that razor with the blade swinging free must have left my jaws agape, for of all the impressions that have remained it is one of the most horribly distinct.

As she came over against the clock something sinister, imperceptibly crouching, moved in her body and face, and I think without knowing it I must have risen in my chair. For a few seconds she stood motionless, taut, and I felt that she was speaking terrible words in a perfect agony of intensity. Then of a sudden a violence of energy swept over her body, and the arm with the razor swung up—and in that instant somehow I managed to close with her.

Two impressions remain vividly: the astonishing and un-expected looseness of her body so that I could get no firm hold of it, and her incredible strength. But I hung on desper-ately to the razor arm, madly. Altogether the struggle was probably over in half a minute, for I was presently swung against the sideboard with a terrific, side-long impact that swept the clock, glass dome and all, smashing to the floor.

And instantly she was still, like a figure of victorious doom. The razor dropped from her fingers. Instinctively I glanced for it and became aware of my left wrist gushing blood. Without doubt the result of the blade swinging loose on its axis. Swift cunning made me hide the wound, for I had an intuition that before red blood her eyes would dilate and her voice find itself in madness. Her breast heaved with each gasping breath, but already the fever of intensity was dying in her eyes. The fear that she would awake, which had dog-ged me mercilessly ever since she had entered the room, now became acute, but the expression on her face was gradually becoming more remote, fixed. Something of fateful inevita-bility was there, revealing a deep consciousness of a secret

216

purpose, or of some unsearchable process of the mind, at last brought to accomplishment.

She turned and walked slowly round the table and out at the door. I heard the soft padding of her feet on the stairs. Against an overpowering weariness and exhaustion I fought till I had stanched the gash on my wrist, then I dragged myself to my arm-chair.

TAM MACKIE'S TRIAL

by Hugh MacDiarmid

HUGH MACDIARMID (*1892–1978*), *the pen name of Christopher Murray Grieve, was one of the great influences on modern Scottish writing. Born in Dumfries, MacDiarmid first came to prominence in the twenties as a journalist in Montrose; he then turned to poetry and for a time edited the* Scottish Chapbook. *His fierce patriotism was already very evident at this period, and with publication of a series of poems in the Lallans dialect he demonstrated the beauty of word and metre that could be obtained from use of traditional Scottish sources without recourse to the English language. Overnight a Scottish literary renaissance was born. Later works were to continue this style, but some—according to his critics—are clouded by strong political undertones. (MacDiarmid was a founder member of the Scottish National Party.) His influence on Scottish letters has been immense and was marked in 1957 with the award of an honorary doctorate at Edinburgh University. MacDiarmid has written relatively little prose, and of his stories few—with the exception of 'Tam Mackie's Trial'—have any reference to the weird and the supernatural. Yet here he shows in one swift, certain stroke most of the skills that tellers of macabre tales strive all their lives to achieve.*

Maria was gaun to dee. 'But it'll no likely be till some time through the nicht,' he'd heard his mither say. Still, that wasna lang. It was an unco queer thing to think aboot; there she was, takin' and to a' appearances gey near in her usual—as he'd aye kent her; and even jokin' and lauchin' whiles. Did she ken she was gaun to dee? She didna seem the least bit feart. Ye'd think the prospects o' the weather and the clish-clash o' the toon wadna maitter muckle to a wuman that wadna see the morn. He wondered at his mither. She kent Maria was 'at daith's door', and yet she was as bad as Maria—her tongue gaen sixteen to the dizzen aboot nocht o' ony consequence, and rallyin' and cairryin' on as if deein' was the maist ordinary thing imaginable. He'd expected something a'thegither different—hushed voices and lang faces, and a terrible solemn kind o' feelin' ower a'body and a' thing. He felt disappointed. To a' ootward appearances there was neist to naething oot o' the common in't ava. Maria micht be gaun' to dee, but she certainly didna look like it. Yet a' at aince—accordin' to his maither—something 'ud happen, and Maria 'ud be 'nae mair'; the blinds 'ud be pu'd doon, and syne the men 'ud come and pit Maria's body in a lang black coffin and tak' it awa' and bury it in the grun', and she'd never be seen or heard tell o' again. What a queer thing! What did a body feel like, deein'? He'd hae liked to speir at Maria, but something tell't him that he mauna. That was hoo Maria and his mither were gibble-gabblin' the way they were daein'—to keep awa' frae the thing that was uppermaist in baith o' their minds.

Mebbe he'd see Maria deein' and ken a' aboot it. His mither had to rin hame for a wee; and he'd to bide wi' Maria till she cam' back. 'Ye'll no' be feart?' she'd speirted him, and he'd said he wadna—but he'd felt feart eneuch, till he cam' in and saw Maria lookin' juist as she'd aye lookit.

But, tho' he'd felt real feart, he'd managed to smile a brave wee smile and say, 'Na, na! I'll be a'richt,' for he kent weel eneuch that it wasna ilka laddie o' his age that had the chance o' sittin' by a daith-bed—alane at that. It wadna be a thing to brag aboot—but to haud his tongue aboot, and that 'ud mak' him a' the mair mysterious and important. He could hear folk sayin': 'There was naebody wi' her when she deed—but Tam Mackie. His mither had had to

219

gang hame, but Tam volunteered to bide till she cam' back. She wasna lang gane afore the cheenge cam'. Puir Maria; she'd a sair struggle at the end. The laddie did a' he could. It maun hae been a gey trial for him. He disna like to talk aboot it, but ye canna wonder at that.'

Sae, altho' it was a relief in a way to find Maria sae like hersel', it was disappointin' in anither. There was only a'e thing oot o' the ordinar'. Maria was lyin' in the best bedroom—what had been Mary's room—instead o' in the kitchen bed. It was a bonny room—a' licht colours, juist like the water-colour paintings hingin' on the wa's in their gowd frames. He mindit Mary. She'd been an awfu' ladybody; Maria had aye dune a' the wark. It seemed queer to see Maria in Mary's bed. It gied ye the same sensation as when ye crackit open a chestnut. O' a' the unexpectit things in the warl' shairly there's naething mair unexpectit than to crack open sic a pale green shell and see yon bricht broon chestnut inside it—like a muckle doonsin' e'e. Maria lookit juist as oot o' place in Mary's bed. She was that dark o' the skin. Mary had been a' pink and white—like a rose. And, if Maria lookit a kennin' paler than usual it was mebbe owin' to the whiteness o' the sheets reflectin' in her face. If there had been naething but the blankets, there micht hae been nae cheenge at a'.

'Weel, weel, I'll no' be lang,' his mither was sayin'. 'Juist lie back and see if ye canna get a wee sleep. I wadna talk ony mair. . . . Tam'll juist sit owre here by the winda and if there's onything ye want he'll get it for ye. . . . Sit here, Tam.'

And she gar'd him sit beside the winda. 'Gie her a look ilka noo and then,' she whispered, 'I'll no' be lang. I think she'll be a'richt till I come back. Keep quiet an' she'll mebbe fa' owre.'

His mither was gane. As sune as the door closed ahint her, he lookit owre; Maria was lyin' back wi' her e'en shut. She lookit afa' aur awa' tho' and he could haurdly mak oot her face at a' for a shaft o' sunlicht that cam' slantin' in. Bairns were playin' in the street ootside. It was queer to

220

think his brither was up on the golf course somewhere caddyin'. He wadna come and sit like this. Nae fear. 'Tam was his mither's boy.' What gar'd folk say that in sic a way as to mak' ye feel a wee thing ashamed—as if ye were a kind o' lassie-boy? Shairly it took mair courage to sit like this aside a deein' wumman than to cairry a kit o' clubs roon' the hill. Hoo quiet it was in here—like bein' cut off frae like a'thegithere. He was mair feart noo; he felt his hair risin'. He wished Maria 'ud wauken again. It hadna been sae bad when she was talkin' awa' to his mither. If he moved and made a wee noise mebbe she'd wauken. He lookit owre to the bed again, movin' his heid forrit to get clear o' the sunbeam. She hadna stirred. There wasna a soon' o' ony kind. It seemed a lang time since his mither gaed awa'. Mebbe she'd met somebody an' was standin' talkin'. He wished she'd come noo.

. . . Wheesht! Was that her? He thocht he'd heard a door openin'. Could it be Daith comin'? His hert was dirlin' inside him at an awfu' rate. He felt like runnin' owre to the bedside for protection—but he couldna move. The bedroom door was openin'—tho' you could haurdly see it move; it couldna be a human bein' that was open'n't. His mither's heid keeked in; he'd been sittin' wi stelled e'en, haudin' his braith—he could haurdly believe it was really her and no'—no' what? He couldna conjure up ony picter o' the terrible sicht he'd expecit to see.

His mither stepped owre to the bedside. Had she seen hoo frichtened he was?

'Wheesht,' he felt lik sayin', 'She's sleepin',' but something hindered him. And his mither turned roon'. He kent at aince frae her look that it was a' owre. Maria was deed!

THE STRANGE MEETING

by A. J. Cronin

ARCHIBALD JOSEPH CRONIN (1896–1981) has an enduring place in the hearts of readers all over the world through his series of novels about the two Scottish medical practitioners Dr. Finlay and Dr. Cameron. Born in Cardross, A. J. Cronin studied medicine himself as a young man and graduated at Glasgow in 1919. He later abandoned his practice to write and scored an immediate success with his first novel, Hatter's Castle *(1931). The piece which follows here—one of the very few short stories which Dr. Cronin has written—is barely a fantasy or horror tale, but has long been one of my favourite 'uncanny experience' tales. In the simplest, yet most effective way, it conveys the emotions of a man confronted again by a person he once brought back from the dead. 'The Strange Meeting' is a haunting episode in prose which I believe will stay in your mind long after you have finished reading it.*

On the second day out from New York, while making the round of the promenade deck, I suddenly became aware that one of the other passengers was watching me closely, following me with his gaze every time I passed, his eyes filled with a queer, almost pathetic intensity.

I have crossed the Atlantic many times. And on this occasion, tired after a prolonged piece of work, I wanted to rest, to avoid the tedium of casual and importunate shipboard contacts. I gave no sign of having noticed the man.

Yet there was nothing importunate about him. On the contrary, he seemed affected by a troubled, rather touching diffidence. He was in his early forties, I judged—out of the corner of my eye—rather short in build, with a fair complexion, a good forehead from which his thin hair had begun to recede, and clear blue eyes. His dark suit, sober tie and rimless spectacles gave evidence of a serious and reserved disposition.

At this point the bugle sounded for dinner and I went below.

On the following forenoon, I again observed my fellow voyager watching me earnestly from his deck-chair.

Now a lady was with him, obviously his wife. She was about his age, quiet and restrained, with brown eyes and slightly faded brown hair, dressed in a grey skirt and grey woollen cardigan.

The situation by this time had begun to intrigue me and from my steward I discovered that they were Mr. and Mrs. John S—, from a small suburb of London. Yet when another day passed without event, I began to feel certain that Mr. S— would remain too shy to carry out his obvious desire to approach me. However, on our final evening at sea, Mrs. S— decided the matter. With a firm pressure on his arm and a whispered word in his ear, she urged her husband towards me as I passed along the deck.

'Excuse me, Doctor. I wonder if I might introduce myself.' He spoke almost breathlessly, offering me the visiting card which he held in his hand and studying my face to see if the name meant anything to me. Then, as it plainly did not, he went on with the same awkwardness. 'If you could spare a few minutes . . . my wife and I would so like to have a word with you.'

A moment later I was occupying the vacant chair beside them. Haltingly he told me that this had been their first visit to America. It was was not entirely a holiday trip. They had been making a tour of the New England states, inspecting many of the summer recreational camps provided for young people there. Afterwards, they had visited settlement houses in New York and other cities to study the

223

methods employed in dealing with youth groups, especially backward, maladjusted and deliquent cases.

There was in his voice and manner, indeed in his whole personality, a genuine enthusaism which was disarming. I found myself liking him instinctively. Questioning him further, I learned that he and his wife had been active for the past fifteen years in the field of youth welfare. He was, by profession, a solicitor but, in addition to his practice, found time to act as director of a charitable organisation devoted to the care of boys and girls, mostly from city slums, who had fallen foul of the law.

As he spoke with real feeling, I got a vivid picture of the work which these two people were doing—how they took derelict adolescents from the juvenile courts and, placing them in a healthy environment, healed them in mind and body, sent them back into the world, trained in a useful handicraft and fit to take their places as worthy members of the community.

It was a work of redemption which stirred the heart and I asked what had directed his life into this channel. The question had a strange effect upon him; he took a sharp breath and exclaimed:

'So you still do not remember me?'

I shook my head: to the best of belief I had never in my life seen him before.

'I've wanted to get in touch with you for many years,' he went on, under increasing stress. 'But I was never able to bring myself to do so.' Then, bending near, he spoke a few words, tensely, in my ear. At that, slowly, the veils parted, my thoughts sped back a quarter of a century and, with a start, I remembered the sole occasion when I had seen this man before.

I was a young doctor at the time and had just set up in practices in a working-class district of London. On a foggy November night, towards one o'clock, I was awakened by a loud banging at the door. In those days of economic necessity any call even at this unearthly hour, was a welcome one. Hurriedly, I threw on some clothes, went downstairs. It was a sergeant of police, in dripping helmet and cape, mistily outlined on the doorstep. A suicide case, he told me abruptly, in the lodgings round the corner—I had better come at once.

Outside it was raw and damp, the traffic stilled, the street deserted, quiet as the tomb. We walked the short distance in silence, even our footsteps muffled by the fog, and turned into the narrow entrance of an old building.

As we mounted the creaking staircase, my nostrils were stung by the sick-sweet odour of gas. On the upper storey the agitated landlady showed us to a bare little attic where, stretched on a narrow bed, lay the body of a young man.

Although apparently lifeless, ther remained the barest chance that the youth was not quite beyond recall. With the sergeant's help, I began the work of resuscitation. For an entire hour we laboured without success. A further fifteen minutes and, despite our most strenuous exertions, it appeared useless. Then, as we were about to give up, completely exhausted, there broke from the patient a shallow, convulsive gasp. It was like a resurrection from the grave, a miracle, this stirring of life under our hands. Half an hour of redoubled efforts and we had the youth sitting up, gazing at us dazedly and, alas, slowly realising the horror of his situation.

He was a round-cheeked lad, with a simple, countrified air, and the story that he told us, as he slowly regained strength in the bleak morning hours, was simple too. His, parents were dead. An uncle in the provinces, anxious, no doubt, to be rid of an unwanted responsibility, had found him a position as clerk in a London solicitor's office. He had been in the city only six months. Utterly friendless, he had fallen victim to the loose society of the streets, had made bad companions, and like a young fool, eager to taste pleasures far beyond his means, had bugun to bet on horses. Soon he had lost all his small savings, had pledged his belongings, and owed the bookmaker a disastrous amount, In an effort to recoup, he had taken a sum of money from the office safe for a final gamble which, he was assured, was certain to win.

225

But this last resort had failed, Terrified of the prosecution which must follow, sick at heart, sunk in despair, he had shut himself in his room and turned on the gas.

A long bar of silence throbbed in the little attic when he concluded this halting confession. Then, gruffly, the sergeant asked how much he had stolen. Pitifully, almost, the answer came: seven pounds ten shillings. Yes, incredible though it seemed, for this paltry sum this poor misguided lad had almost thrown away his life.

Again there came a pause in which, plainly, the same unspoken thought was uppermost in the minds of the three of us who were the sole witness of this near tragedy. Almost of one accord, we voiced our desire to give the youth—whose defenceless nature rather than any vicious tendencies had brought him to this extremity—a fresh start. The sergeant, at considerable risk to his job, resolved to make no report upon the case, so that no court proceedings would result. The landlady offered a month's free board until he should get upon his feet again. While I, making perhaps the least contribution, came forward with seven pounds ten shillings for him to put back in the office safe.

The ship moved on through the still darkness of the night. There was no need of speech. With a tender gesture Mrs. S— had taken her husband's hand. And as we sat in silence, hearing the sounding of the sea and the sighing of the breeze, a singular emotion overcame me. I could not but reflect that, against all the bad investments I had made throughout the years—those foolish speculations for material gain, producing only anxiety, disappointment and frustration— here at last was one I need not regret, one that has paid no dividends in worldly goods, yet which might stand, nevertheless, on the profit side, in the final reckoning.

226

MUSIC WHEN SOFT VOICES DIE...

by John Keir Cross

JOHN KEIR CROSS (*1911–1967*) *was one of the early influences on my own interest in the supernatural and in macabre literature in particular and it gives me particular pleasure to be able to include one of his stories in this volume. Born and brought up in Scotland—with a special love of the Highlands—he was a writer still in his teens and a well-known broadcaster in his late twenties. Scottish readers may well remember his famous Hallowe'en night radio programme when he attempted to summon up the Devil by performing a Medieval Magic ritual; others probably associate his name with a series of authoritative ghost and horror story anthologies which are models of their kind. John Keir Cross was also a writer of weird tales himself, and probably the best of his collections is* The Other Passenger *published in 1946. He believed the most effective horror stories were those which made use of simple objects like eyes or hands or any of the myriad small objects found in the home, for in this way the reader did not even need to look behind his back after reading a tale—it, the object of fear, could be right under his nose. He died in 1967 and would, I hope, like to be remembered for stories such as 'Music When Soft Voices Die' which is full of his special 'terror in needle-point'.*

I

I heard of the death of Sir Simon Erskine some five years ago, when I was taking a long holiday in my beloved

Scotland. I had known him quite well—a terrible man, moody, powerful, irascible. They said he was only forty-eight when he died. Yet, when I had last seen him, about two years before, at the time of the tragic death of his young wife, he had seemed at least eighty. I remember him then, standing in the porch of that huge, bleak house of his, a brooding and lonely figure, holding tight about him the black cloak he favoured, his already white hair blowing round his temples in the eternal winds of that wild corner of Perthshire. He was the last survivor of the Pitvrackie Erskines—the Black Erskines, as they had been called in the old Covenanting days: stern, merciless, religious men, who believed (if truth be faced) in hellfire and damnation and not much else. It was one of the Black Erskines who, with one mad stroke, had swept the head from the shoulder of a young officer who, in his cups, had questioned some religious truths. And another of the clan, on discovering his wife in adultery, had hanged the woman with his own hands, after immolating her lover most dreadfully before her eyes. A terrible, half-beastly family they were, with a long history of bloodshed and cruelty behind them.

About a month after the death of Sir Simon, the factors announced an auction of his properties and effects at Vrackie Hall. I was sufficiently interested to travel in the creaking old bus from Perth to Pitvrackie that day: not only was I keen to see the curious old house again on its storm-swept promontory among the hills, but there was the chance of picking up a treasure of two. Sir Simon had been a man of many accomplishments. He had been interested in a thousand things—in seventeenth-century Dutch painting, in Romantic English literature of the late eighteenth and early nineteenth centuries, and, above all, in unusual musical instruments. He had, too, done much big game hunting in Africa. It was in Africa, in fact, that he met Bridgid Cannell, whom he later married, and whose strange death affected him so terribly. Indeed, let me be honest and say that it affected him almost to the point of madness. There were wild tales of his behaviour during the last two lonely years

228

of his life—tales of how he shut himself up for days on end in the big library of Vrackie Hall, of how the scared servants heard him sometimes weeping aloud, sometimes laughing, and sometimes, as it were in a disconsolate frenzy, beating on a collection of native drums he had brought back from one of his African expeditions. The wild, primitive rhythms, going on through the hours and throbbing into the farthest corners of the dark house, hypnotised him, perhaps, into forgetting his bitterness and the terrible sense of his loss. He was a man whose mind was delicately enough poised as it was, God knows—a man who feared loneliness for what it might do to him, yet who nursed his passions jealously and secretly. Neither Bridgid nor his first wife had near-succeeded in fathoming him—it was as if he needed them, he needed their company and the comfort of their bodies, yet was unwilling to let them have access to the innermost parts of him—a Bluebeard who kept one chamber eternally secret. His first wife, a young Scotswoman of good family, had, after five years of him, run off incontinently with a middle-aged American doctor. The fact that she had no child by him but had been delivered of a son within a year of meeting the American, weighed bitterly with Sir Simon. And when Bridgid died childless, so that he saw the line of the Black Erskines ending with him, he raged vilely against the destinies: and so shut himself up in the decaying house, seeing no one, brooding jealously among those priceless possessions of his, weeping like a spoilt child over his failures, beating insanely on those damnable drums and sending the throbbing restless voices, of them across the valley and against the forbidding harsh face of old Ben Vrackie itself. . . .

I reached the house that day of the sale in a battered, irritable condition. Gusts of wet, mist-laden wind had worried at me as I mounted the mud-raddled roads to the Hall from Pitvrackie. Dull clouds sagged over the peaks of the hills that surrounded the house, the pine forests that flanked my path were silent and evil seeming, heavily adrip with moisture. I saw no one, save, at one point, an old cross-eyed tinker who carried, over his shoulder, a long pole slung with dead rabbits, all matted and patchy from the damp. A fawn-coloured, evil-eyed ferret stared at me out of his pocket. I had a fleeting remembrance of an old childhood fear—that ferrets were capable of springing at human throats and sucking the blood there-from: but the beast, I saw, was chained to the tinker's wrist. I gave the man a greeting but he did not reply—passed on his silent way, his squinting eyes fixed on the roadway before him as he walked.

Vrackie Hall stood back from the road in a large park full of trees and gardens that at one time had been carefully laid out. There was a drive of red gravel, The entrance gates were made of elaborate wrought-iron and there were, above the pillars of them, two eagles, staring at each other with their heads turned sideways. They were made of soft stone that had been eaten away by the weathers, so that they seemed to have a frightful and painful disease, The big house itself, built three-quarters of a century ago on the site of the old Erskine Castle, was a mixture of many styles and periods. There was, first, a large porchway flanked with smooth Grecian pillars, the arch of it embellished by a florid frieze consisting of festoons of fruits and flowers with, occasionally in the midst of them, pot-bellied nymphs in modest attitudes. There were festoons above some of the windows too, any many tiles, glazed in yellow and green, with small fat cupids on them and long formal garlands of flowers. The windows themselves were large, and some of them had inset panes of stained glass at each corner. Those on the front of the house had narrow barred shutters in the French style folded back from them, some a dingy cream colour, others painted in flaky green with white underneath. On the south wall there was an exuberant creeper of a rich glossy brown that merged into fresh green at the top and sides; on the back wall there were espalier fruit trees, pegged symmetrically to the lime-eaten bricks. The roof was tiles with slates of varying shapes, some square, others pointed like diamonds and others curved and scalloped—the layers of these last ones looking like enormous fish scales. And on top of all, overtowering the chimneys, was domed belfry decorated with still more stone festoons and with, inside it, a small rusted bell that had come from an old monastery of St. Fechan, the ruins of which could be seen among the trees in a corner of the park. That old bell had been rung for three days after the death of Bridgid Erskine—not as a sign of mourning: as a last forlorn hope that its clamour, borne out over the hills would guide he back through the thick mountain mist that was her death-pall to the house where her distracted husband awaited her.

It was a hideous house, this home of the Erskines. I had often speculated, in the old days, on how it was possible for a man of Sir Simon's fastidiousness to live among its rococo carvings. But he seemed singularly attached to it— it was, he once sardonically said, an embodiment, a projection of his own over-elaborate and tortured mind.

When I arrived that day at Vrackie Hall for the auction sale it was to find a small silent company already gathered in the big lobby. The auctioneer had not yet appeared—he was, I understood, a Glasgow man, one Gregory, famed for his dry wit. But it appeared to me, as I looked round the group in the dark hall, that he would have little opportunity that day for the exercise of it. There were about a dozen serious-faced men and two women, and they talked quietly together in twos and threes. I recognised some acquaintances —one of the women was a dealer in Perth, a Miss Logan: I had been introduced to her the year before in my mother's house. Standing alone in a corner was an old man I had seen at several sales in Scotland before (I was, you must understand, profoundly interested in such things, with an eye for old tapestries). This man, I had the fancy, came from Dundee, where he had a business of some strange sort—we none of us had ever discovered quite what it was, though we knew it to be lucrative and had the impression that it had something to do with drawing or designing. His name was Menasseh, and he was a small, wizened fellow with a large head covered with an obvious toupee.

I roamed about the tables for some ten minutes. There

231

were, I could perceive, even at a cursory glance, some exquisite things. Among the paintings were two minatures by Koninck that I coveted instantly, and a small landscape by Samuel van Hoogstraaten that I would fain have seen in my rooms in London as a companion to the de Hooch *Study of a Hillside Town* I had acquired at Christie's a year before. There were some beautiful vases from the Delft potteries and a Mortlake tapestry—a copy, unless I was heavily mistaken, of one of Le Brun's Gobelin cartoons. In a corner I saw a most masterly carved limewood cravat, attributed, according to the notice on it, to Grinling Gibbons. Among the books was a first edition of Lewis's *The Monk* and a copy, signed by Maturin himself, of that strangest of works, *Melmoth the Wanderer*. There were some Blake drawings too, and some of the Master's hand-coloured prints for the *Songs of Innocence*. And among all these beautiful things, curiously out of place even in that strange house, was Erskine's collection of African drums. I shudder-ed as I looked at them, recalling the man's mad, grief-wracked thumping of them during the last two years of his life. They were, in their way, I suppose, beautiful enough. The largest ones were made of parchment stretched on hollow hardwood trunks, with primitive designs carved round them. There were two enchanting but repulsive small drums, however, that had for sounding boards polished human skulls. I could see, from a close examination of the larger one, the low brow and long cranium of the primitive. The parchments of these (as were also the parchments of some of the large drums) were held tight by means of small carved ivory pegs, driven in at an angle. The stretched surfaces of them bore a design in coloured dyes— a serpent coiled in a curious way: three coils at the tail end, an erratic figure eight in the centre of the body, and two coils again at the head, with the long fangs pointing downwards. It was the mounting of these skull-drums that particularly attracted me. A small hole had been bored in the forehead of each and the end of a long bent bar of chased silver inserted therein, so that the drums inclined at a convenient angle for the player. The drumsticks—long, polished bones—rested in hollows in the bases of the silver bars. Yes, beautiful things in their way, they were, as they stood there on the table beneath Erskine's trophy heads of buffalo and lions and his crossed game rifles. It was impossible not to be fascinated by them, though they contrasted so strangely with the more delicate products of the less barbaric civilisation.

I wandered upstairs, since there still seemed little chance of the arrival of Gregory, the auctioneer. One or two of the buyers were looking at their watches and I heard one of them say something about the 'Glasga'' express being late as usual, he supposed. I looked into some of the rooms on the first floor, but most of the portable things had been carried downstairs and the bigger pieces were covered with dustsheets—they were being sold with the house.

I was standing at the long stained glass window at the end of the corridor looking at the mist-cloaked hills, first through the clear panes and then, to give more interest, through the red and the blue ones, when I heard a step behind me and a cheerful deep voice.

'Hullo, Mr. Ferguson. I didn't know you were coming to the auction of I'd have suggested we travelled up from Perth together.'

I looked round and found myself confronting Miss Logan, the dealer I had met the year before at my mother's house. I greeted her civilly and we stood together chatting— talking of my mother first and of what we had both done since our last meeting, and then going on naturally to the things downstairs and Sir Simon.

'You knew him, didn't you?' the big woman asked, and I nodded.

'Oh yes—quite well. A curious man. Impossible to understand.'

'I met him once,' said Miss Logan thoughtfully. 'He made me very uncomfortable—so bleak and cruel, somehow. I was at school with his first wife, you know.'

I expressed myself as interested—as indeed I was.

'Was she—well, as volatile in those days? I mean—you know how she went off with the American doctor—'

'Oh yes, I know about that,' said Miss Logan quickly. 'No—it was really a most curious thing. She wasn't at all like that at school—rather serious and unenterprising, in fact. I could never quite understand it all. . . .'

She fell silent, staring out at the hills. The she added ruminatively:

'A tragic man—tragic. And the last one of that terrible family. What exactly was the story about his second wife?— do you know it? I've heard odd rumours, of course, but I was in France at the time. I never heard the real truth of what happened to her.'

'Nor did anyone,' I said shortly. 'You're looking now at the only one who does know the truth of it all.'

'What do you mean?' asked Miss Logan, turning for a moment from the window, at which she had been standing firmly implanted in the expensive brogues.

'Ben Vrackie. That old mountain is her graveyard—and her only father confessor. There were two of them, you know,' I went on, 'Bridgid and on old friend of Sir Simon's— a well-educated South African Negro called David Strange, a lawyer, I think. Simon met him in Cape Town about the same time that he met Bridgid. He was holidaying here with the Erskine's and one Sunday afternoon he went out for a walk in the hills with Bridgid. Simon would have gone too. but he had a headache and went to lie down instead. . . .'

I paused for a moment, looking through the red pane at the clammy mist creeping and twisting round the summit of the old mountain. Then I continued:

'They never returned. They stayed out longer than they had intended, and in the evening one of those sudden and terrible mountain mists came down. Simon sent out search parties—he rang the old bell in the belfry for as long as the mist lasted—three whole days—as some sort of signal to them. But they never came. They must have wandered for miles—you know how it is when you are lost in a fog—and

234

then slipped and fallen into a gully, perhaps. Their bodies were never found. . .'

'Horrible,' said Miss Logan with a shudder. 'And that was it, then. . . . It must have been appalling for Sir Simon—appalling!'

I nodded.

'It was. He had set such store on this second marriage—the last of the line, you know. Particularly after the tragic disappointment his first wife had been to him. . . .'

We were silent. There came a slight commotion from downstairs and, looking over the banister into the hall, I saw that Gregory had arrived. He was divesting himself of his coat—a large, red-faced man, benevolent in appearance: singularly out of place in that over-crowded room with his, big, bucolic personality. He was joking with some of the buyers.

Miss Logan and I went downstairs. The buyers were collecting round the dais that had been set up for Gregory. We joined the solemn, whispering group.

II

I stop my narrative here for a moment. It is not easy for me to write—I am no literary man. The sheer manual labour of setting things down is enormous, to say nothing of the wearing effort of coordinating one's facts and arranging them in reasonable coherence for the reader. The pen moves over the paper, the ink flows, the page fills up. Words and more words, yet somehow all the things one had hoped to say remain unsaid. I sit here at my desk in my sequestered room in London, five hundred miles away from Pilvrackie, struggling to set down something about the beastly things that happened in that hideous house. Why? Is it, with those pothooks on paper, to exorcise the ghosts that have been haunting me since ever I learned the truth about Simon Erskine? I don't know. I only know that for five years I have wanted to do this, I have looked forward to doing this.

235

It may never be read—secretly, I hardly want it to be read. If it is, it can harm no one now. They are all dead—old Samuel Menasseh is dead: even Miss Logan, I learned about six months ago in a letter from my mother, died suddenly of heart-failure in her shop.

And there it all is—all those miles away and all those years away. Above my desk now is the van Hoogstraaten landscape I saw and coveted that day of the sale at Vrackie Hall. I bite the end of my pen as I contemplate it. It stands as a symbol for all the horror I have felt through the years—it is impossible for me to look at the peaceful hillside scene without thinking of old Ben Vrackie as I saw him that day through the stained glass with the blood-red mists all about him. And I seem to hear, in my heart, a throbbing echo of the forlorn music thumped out in the empty, soulless rooms of Vrackie Hall by the grief-torn man who was, so tragically against his will, the last of the Black Erskines. . . . Well, it is all an old tale now—older with the writing of it, whether that writing is good or ill. How should I know how best to set the story down? How should I know how to arrange in sequence that will give the utmost dramatic value to them? I may emphasise unimportant things, I may hold back on things that should be thrown into relief. I am not a professional. I write for one reason and for one reason only—because I must.

So. I light a cigarette. I return to Vrackie Hall on that day of the auction.

We stood round Gregory, the auctioneer, in a small depressed group. Bidding was good, though the scene was so curiously lifeless in the grey light that came in from the hills through the big windows. Gregory made some valiant efforts to exercise his famous wit, but we were unresponsive —his voice rolled away into the recesses of the hall and the stairway. In the end he gave up. He became mechanical. He lowered his voice, he took to nodding and signalling, the tap of his gavel was almost inaudible. I lost interest after I had bought the van Hoogstraaten and the Mortlake tapestry I had my eye on. I wandered away from the froup

236

of bidders and began to glance through the books. I was turning over the leaves of an early copy of *Vathek* when my eye was distracted by the figure of the strange old man, Menasseh.

He was standing a little to my left, before the table displaying Sir Simon's big game trophies. His attitude was one of extreme horror—yet the horror was grotesque: his small wizened body was rigid, so that the musty black cloth of his coat was stretched tight across his shoulder-blades, his pale eyes seemed to protrude, his toupee had slipped a little awry, giving him an irrelevantly rakish aspect. I went on observing him for some time, then moved over beside him.

'Good morning, sir,' I said. 'You seem, like myself, to have lost interest in the proceedings over there.'

He started, then, adjusting his old wire-frame spectacles with, I noticed, a trembling hand, he said:

'Yes . . . I—I'm afraid I have. I . . .'

His voice trailed away. He glanced back at the table and I followed his gaze—to the drums that were among the African trophies. He coughed, Then he suddenly took off his glasses altogether and started to polish them with an old silk handkerchief.

'I know you sir,' he said quaveringly, 'I've seen you before —several times.'

'I'm often in Scotland,' I replied. 'And when I'm in Scotland I'm often at the sales. My name is Ferguson. I know that your name is Menasseh—I've seen you frequently too. I take it you're a dealer?—or are you only an amateur, as I am?'

'Eh?' he stammered (it was as if his mind were not focusing properly—he was thinking all the time of something else). 'No—not a dealer. Only an amateur, Mr. Ferguson.'

He put on his spectacles again and started back at the drums on the table. His gaze was particularly drawn to the two small drums with the silver mountings. He passed his hand over his brow—his toupee fell even further askew.

'Horrible—horrible,' he muttered. 'God of Abraham, it's horrible . . . .'

237

He seemed to go into a trance for a moment or two. Then he put out his finger and traced, with the trembling point of it, the singular design of the coiled serpent on the parchment of the small drums. I watched him, fascinated.

'Hideously attractive things,' I said, by the way of an opening. 'Typical of Sir Simon to have had them—a man of curious tastes. You know how he is said to have beaten on them frantically for hours on end after the disappearance of his second wife?'

'Yes,' said Menasseh, in a whisper. 'Yes. I know. . . .'

'A strange sign of grief.' (I was still searching to bring him out—he was, there was no doubt, affected to the very roots by something.)

'A strange sign of grief indeed,' he muttered. then once more he fell distrait. It was a long time before he added, in an almost inaudible undertone: 'A terrible sign of grief— terrible and horrible. . . .'

I looked at him, drawing my brows together. He was white. He kept moistening his thin lisp with the point of a colourless tongue. I wanted extremely to ask him what it was that was upsetting him, yet after all I hardly knew him. I found myself, in the long silence that ensued after his last remark, wondering who he was and what he did (I had forgotten, when I asked him if he was a dealer, how, in the old days, we had speculated on his occupation.) Printing, was it—or drawing? Something of that nature, I recalled. Perhaps it was a little publishing business? Yet it was more than likely I would know of it if it was publishing: that was my own line of business—I knew most of the trade in Scotland. Whatever it was it was lucrative—I remembered having heard that he was a wealthy old fellow.

Suddenly we became aware—simultaneously—that two of Gregory's assistants were moving towards us. Apparently the African trophies were next item on the catalogue. I glanced quickly at Menasseh.

'Now's the time,' I said smiling. 'You seem interested in these drums of Erskine's. They're going up, I fancy. Are you buying?'

He gazed at me, his eyes large behind the thick glass of his spectacles.

'Oh no,' he whispered. 'Oh no. God forbid it. . . .'

The two men in green baize aprons were lifting some of the larger drums, preparatory to carrying them over to Gregory's dais. Menasseh, I saw by this time, was looking quickly backwards and forwards in an access of nervous apprehension of some sort. He suddenly leaned close up to me.

'Ferguson,' he said, 'I can't keep it, I can't. I must tell someone. I want to see you—I must see you.'

'We could go outside,' I said, a little disturbed, I had to confess, by his urgency. 'I shall not be bidding again. Will you?

'No. No. Not here,' he muttered. 'Not here—I can't stay here. It has upset me too much—I must go away from here, quickly.'

He fumbled in his waistcoat pocket and thrust a card into my hand.

'If you are in Dundee,' he said, 'if you should be in Dundee—'

'I have to be there at the end of this week, as it happens,' I answered. 'I have a little business which I am mixing with my holiday. Thursday, I should say—or possibly Friday.'

'Good. Good. Then could you call on me? For God's sake could you call on me?'

I nodded: and he, in his nervousness, set his old head nodding up and down too. I fingered his card, looking at the address on it:

SAMUEL MENASSEH
39, THE PORTWAY
DUNDEE

'My business address,' he said, reading my thoughts. 'But come anytime, anytime this week. I shall be there. I have a little room behind the shop where I live—I only go to my house outside the city at weekends and so on.' Then,

239

reading my thoughts still more deeply, he added: 'My business is strange—very strange. Don't be surprised. It's a little—unpleasant. I don't tell people about it—I won't mention it here. . . . But come, sir—oh for God's sake I beg you to come! It will haunt me, this—I'll have no peace!'

He said these last words quickly, in a hoarse, strained whisper. Then he turned and was gone. I was left holding his card, staring after him as he hastened over to the massive door. He had left me with an intolerable curiosity—a sense of dismay over his hurried and half-finished sentences.

I was brought back to my senses by the deep, healthy tones of Miss Logan's voice. She was standing, a sane, coherent figure in her brogues and tweed costume, watching the men as they carried the little skull-drums to Gregory's dais.

'Ferguson,' she called. 'Come quickly. Look at these—they're lovely. I'm having these—by Jove, I'm certainly having these.'

I slipped the old man's card into my pocket and went over to join her. She was by this time holding the smaller drum up to the light and examining the silver base.

'Look here,' she said excitedly. 'What an odd thing. Someone's scratched some verse on the silver—look at it, Shelley of all strange things!'

She read out solemnly:

> '*Music, when soft voices die,*
> *Vibrates in the memory . . .*

And she laughed.

'Odd thing to find on the mounting of an African drum, I must say. Your old Sir Simon was a devilish queer fish, if ever there was one. . . .'

I had to agree. Above all I have to agree to that. . . .

III

Almost midnight, Incredible how quickly the time has gone. I started writing shortly before seven, and since then have interrupted myself only for long enough to brew some tea at about ten. My pen hand is cramped and painful and my eyes ache terribly from staring at the white paper. Yet I cannot stop—I must go on now.

I look back at what I have written. I feel a sinking in the stomach. How imperfectly I have set things down! A rambling introduction, too much description, a conversation which, on paper, seems disjointed and insane. Yet I have tried faithfully enough to keep a clear head over this nightmare. I have tried to set things in their order, to conjure up some sense of atmosphere. The old house, the death of Bridgid and David Strange in the terrible hill mist, the tragic last months of that haunted lost, man. . . . You see, I know it all now, I know every shade of it. And this informs every word I write, every thought I have in this quiet room. My pen moves over the paper slowly and carefully—I stop to think before every word. I know all of it—all of it. . . .

My rememberances go, irrelevantly, to Miss Logan. By her very inconsequence in this nightmare she is the most grotesque figure of them all. Tweeds, brogues, untinted lip-salve. The more select journals, the Scottish Nationalist movement, long walks on the moors with one of those sticks with spikes on the end and handles that fold open to form a little seat. And her shop with the Chelsea china, the old spinning wheels, the pictures on wood, the church-warden pipes in bundles, the little ornamental shepherd crooks of green Nailsea glass. And somewhere among all these things, tucked away in a corner, perhaps, when her first enthusiasm for them had waned, the little drums. I do not suppose she even knew of those insane weeping fits of Sir Simon's, when he sent the sound of those drums across the valley. . . .

She had met him once, I remember she said. He had made her uncomfortable. She had been at school with his

241

first wife. A quiet girl. She had never been able to understand——

What? How *could* she understand? Miss Logan in her
little shop, dying of heart failure. Yet had her heart ever
started? A man to her was a companion for a walk on the
moors. Of course she had never been able to understand,
with her babbling of Shelly. How could she?

No matter, though. She had her shop with its green Nailsea glass. And over the door of it, in guilt, old-style lettering,
one word: *Antiques*.

And now, as I near the end of the story, I think of another
shop, a stranger shop. I found it, in the twilight, in a side-
street near the docks in Dundee. It was low-fronted, ill-lit
by a flickering gas standard at the kerb of the pavement. The
window had nothing in it, above the door was no sign to
announce the trade or occupation of its tennant. The name,
no more, in faded block capitals:

SAMUEL MENASSEH

I knocked, and heard the echo of my knock go rolling
into the dust and darkness inside. I waited, impatient. A
sailor stumbled in the dusk farther along the street, singing
in the drawn-out, lugubrious tones of a drunken man. I
knocked again, and from inside this time there came the
sound of shuffling feet and the undoing of a chain.

He seemed smaller now, the old man, as I looked down
on him from the pavement. He wore a loose, grey-wool
cardigan and, on his head, instead of the toupee, was a
skullcap of black velvet—a little biretta of the sort the
cantors wear in the synagogues. I greeted him and he nodded.
Then he motioned me to follow him and I went inside.

It would be a mockery to say that I was not, in all desperation, impatient and curious. I remembered too acutely
the old man's broken conversation in the hall at Vrackie,
the whole sense of dismay and nervous horror that had
come from him. In the intervening days since that interview
I had seen too often, in my mind's eye, that white wizened

242

face, those long trembling fingers of parchment tracing the design of the snake on the other parchment of the drums. I was consumed by impatience. As I followed him through the dim corridor to the sitting-room at the back of the shop, I searched feverishly about me for some sign, some illumination of the mystery of him. But there was nothing. Halfway along the corridor we passed an open door that led into the shop proper. I peered anxiously through it. Dimly glimpsed in the light from the gas standard outside as it flickered through the window, was a counter, exceptionally low. Suspended above it from the ceiling was a long, flexible, snake-like thing—a piece of gas tubing I thought at first, and then had the curious fancy that it was a drill—the cable lead of a pedal drill, such as old-fashioned dentists use. But fantastic to suppose that the man was a dentist. Besides, I had no more than glimpsed the appliance in the gloom. . . .

We reached the small sitting-room. I stood for a moment opening and shutting my eyes, accustoming them to the light that came from the gas-bracket above the mantelshelf. The room was poorly furnished—a table, a basket-chair by the fireplace, an old dresser, a wardrobe. In the corner a divan bed. Some books in a hanging shelf, a fretwork pipe-rack. And for pictures—

I, so accustomed to the beautiful in pictures, so used to the shaded tones, the colours in harmony, the designs so subtle, so balanced—all the magic of the Masters: I, with my fastidious passion for tapestries and delicate needlework panels—what could I make of the monstrous things on the walls of that room of Menasseh's? Unframed, stuck to the plaster with rusted drawing pins, glazed with layers of size varnish—those rioting tortured dragons in wild reds and blues those posies of purple flowers, those bleeding hearts transfixed with arrows, those fleshy nudes in violent pink, with bellies sagged and scarlet-nippled breasts—what could I make of them? And yet, I knew that I knew them—they were, in their style, unmistakable. I searched my memory and then, in a moment, could have laughed aloud. For I had, by a wild coincidence, been thinking just outside,

243

while I had listened to the drunken sailor go stumbling along the street—as it goes, you will understand, when one's mind wanders inconsequently in its own secret places and among old associations—I had been thinking then of a fascination of my childhood: whether that sailor were, as had been the only sailor I had known as a child—tattooed! And I understood the meaning of the drill that hung from the ceiling of Menasseh's shop— I had an image of the dye-charged needle at the end of it stabbing again and again into white, tight flesh. . . .

I turned and looked at the old man.

'Yes,' he nodded. 'Not pleasant, not pleasant. Not a very —*select* job, tattooing. I keep it a secret. I have money, you see—it makes money for me. I can gratify my passions for the beautiful things in the sale-rooms. You should see my house outside the town—beautiful, beautiful. Different from this,' he added, sweeping his arm vaguely round the room. 'Oh different, much different. . . . But it makes money, this. You haven't an idea—the people who want it—big men: lawyers—I did a lawyer from Glasgow last week—he came up specially. Women too. I'm busy—all the time. There's a sort of fascination in it for some people—all sorts of strange and unexpected people. . . .'

He went on, rubbing his hands together. It was incredible and fantastic—too much. But at the back of my back of my mind was beginning to throb the idea that has haunted me through these years. On the table in that little room, smaller than those other charts on the walls, but like them painted in brilliant water colours and covered with size, was a design I had seen before. A serpent coiled in a curious way: three coils at the tail end, an erratic figure eight in the centre of the body, and two coils again at the head, with the long fangs pointing downwards. . . .

Half-past one. Almost finished. A century, since I started to write. How did it go?—

'I heard of the death of Sir Simon Erskine some five

244

years ago . . . I had known him quite well—a terrible man, moody, powerful, irascible. . . .'

I had known him quite well. . . . How did I dare to write that? How could I—or anyone—know him? No one in the world—no one but those half-beast forebears of his. And they, thank God, have gone out of the world—as he has. The line of the Black Erskines is ended, and for ever.

I look at the quiet picture above me. Samuel van Hoogstraaten—a still man, unpreturbed. His world a hillside scene in Holland: small square houses, lines on canvas. To my right, on the wall there, is the Mortlake tapestry. And what association have these things with the things Menasseh told me in that room of his behind the shop? . . .

David Strange, the young Negro lawyer—the descendant, he claimed, of Kings Cetewayo and Dingaan; for he had, as he showed Menasseh, the royal serpent of the Zulus needled into the dark skin of his breast. And the woman with him in the shop that day, with Menasseh copying the design on to *her* breast, while she flinched at every needle-prick, holding tight with her white hand to the dark hand of the Negro. . . . The sign of blood-kinship among the Zulus, that serpent. Menasseh had been intrigued by the design of it and had made, on paper, one copy: but no other copy, at any time, on any human skin but hers. . . .

My hand aches terribly. I sit back. I look at my fingers as I stretch them out to ease them. . . .

I think—oh God knows what I think! Of the two skulls that were the sounding boards of those hellish drums. Of Miss Logan tramping over the moors. Of those other two—of blood-kinship—setting off that Sunday afternoon for a walk on Ben Vrackie. Of Sir Simon saying he had a headache and so being unable to accompany them. Of the neat round holes in the skulls in which were inserted the ends of the silver mounts. Of the rifles on the walls of Vrackie Hall. Of the bodies that were never found. Of the shape of the larger skull, the low brow and long cranium of the primitive—the Negro. Of the merciful hill mist that came down on the

245

grim old mountain—red and terrible seen through the glass of that hideous house. . . .

Yes, what do I think. . . .

Of the two last years of the last of the Erskines, his fits of weeping, his fits of laughing, his fits of—

No. The image fades. The ghost goes out of me. I think of nothing. Except, coming over the years, the echo, terrible in this quiet room, of Miss Logan's cheerful voice:

'Someone's scratched some verse on the silver—Shelly, of all strange things. . . .'

Yes. Shelly, of all strange things.

SEALSKIN TROUSERS

by Eric Linklater

ERIC LINKLATER (*1899–1974*) *was born at Dounby in the Orkney Islands, and recalled in a recent autobiography that ancient lore entered early into his life in the shape of his grandmother who was ':reputed to be a witch and ill-wished her rivals'. He was also as a child introduced to the legends of the Norsemen and this influence can be seen in certain of his work. Educated at Aberdeen, he first studied medicine before turning to English language and literature. After World War One he was for a time a journalist in India, later returning to Scotland to lecture at his old university. Travel has always fascinated him, and stays in America and the South Seas were particularly profitable in terms of novels—*Poet's Pub (*1929*), resulting from the first, and* The Faithful Ally (*1954*) from the second. His international reputation was secured with* Private Angelo *which was made into a successful film in 1949. His devotion and love for his country shines through much of his work. One of his abiding interests has been seals—now in danger of extinction on the Scottish coast through indiscriminate slaughter—and in this classic short story he mingles fact and fantasy with a sure and brilliant touch.*

I am not mad. It is necessary to realise that, to accept it as a fact about which there can be no dispute. I have been seriously ill for some weeks, but that was the result of shock. A double or conjoint shock: for as well as the obvious concussion of a brutal event, there was the more dreadful necessity of recognising the material evidence of a happening so monstrously implausible that even my friends here, who in general are quite extraordinary kind and understanding, will not believe in the occurrence, though they cannot deny it or otherwise explain—I mean explain away—the clear and simple testimony of what was left.

I, of course, realised very quickly what had happened, and since then I have more than once remembered that poor Coleridge teased his unquiet mind, quite unnecessarily in his case, with just such a possibility; or impossibility, as the world would call it. 'If a man could pass through Paradise in a dream,' he wrote, 'and have a flower presented to him as a pledge that his soul had really been there, and if he found that flower in his hand when he woke—Ay, and what then?'

But what if he had dreamt of Hell and wakened with his hand burnt by the fire? Or of Chaos, and seen another face stare at him from the looking-glass? Coleridge does not push the question far. He was too timid. But I accepted the evidence, and while I was ill I thought seriously about the whole proceeding, in detail and in sequence of detail. I thought, indeed, about little else. To begin with, I admit, I was badly shaken, but gradually my mind cleared and my vision improved, and because I was patient and persevering —that needed discipline—I can now say that I know what happened. I have indeed, by a conscious intellectual effort, *seen and heard* what happened. This is how it bagan. . . .

How very unpleasant! she thought.

She had come down the great natural steps on the seacliff to the ledge that narrowly gave access, round the angle of it, to the western face which today was sheltered from the breeze and warmed by the afternoon sun. At the beginning of the week she and her fiance, Charles Sellin, had found their way to an almost hidden shelf, a deep veranda sixty feet above the white-veined water. It was rather bigger than a billiard-table and nearly as private as an abandoned lighthouse. Twice they had spent some blissful hours there. She had a good head for heights, and Sellin was indifferent to

248

scenery. There had been nothing vulgar, no physical contact, in their bliss together on this oceanic gazebo, for on each occasion she had been reading Healoin's *Studies in Biology* and he Lenin's *What is to be Done?*

Their relations were already marital, not because their mutual passion could brook no pause, but rather out of fear lest their friends might despise them for chastity and so conjecture some oddity or impotence in their nature. Their behaviour, however, was very decently circumspect, and they already conducted themselves, in public and out of doors, as if they had been married for several years. They did not regard the seclusion of the cliffs as an opportunity for secret embracing, but were content that the sun should warm and colour their skin; and let their anxious minds be soothed by the surge and cavernous colloquies of the sea. Now, while Charles was writing letters in the little fishing-hotel a mile away, she had come back to their sandstone ledge, and Charles would join her in an hour or two. She was still reading *Studies in Biology*.

But their gazebo, she perceived, was already occupied, and occupied by a person of the most embarrassing appearance. He was quite unlike Charles. He was not only naked, but obviously robust, brown-hued, and extremely hairy. He sat on the very edge of the rock, dangling his legs over the sea, and down his spine ran a ridge of hair like the dark stripe on a donkey's back, and on his shoulder-blades grew patches of hair like the wings of a bird. Unable in her disappointment to be sensible and leave at once, she lingered for a moment and saw to her relief that he was not quite naked. He wore trousers of a dark brown colour, very low at the waist, but sufficient to cover his haunches. Even so, even with that protection for her modesty, she could not stay and read biology in his company.

To show her annoyance, and let him become aware of it, she made a little impatient sound; and turning to go, looked back to see if he had heard.

He swung himself round and glared at her, more angry on the instant than she had been. He had thick eyebrows, large dark eyes, a broad snub nose, a big mouth. 'You're Roger Fairfield!' she exclaimed in surprise.

He stood up and looked at her intently. 'How do you know?' he asked.

'Because I remember you,' she answered, but then felt a little confused, for what she principally remembered was the brief notoriety he had acquired, in his final year at Edinburgh University, by swimming on a rough autumn day from North Berwick to the Bass Rock to win a bet of five pounds.

The story had gone briskly round the town for a week, and everybody knew that he and some friends had been lunching, too well for caution, before the bet was made. His friends, however, grew quickly sober when he took to the water, and in a great fright informed the police, who called out the lifeboat. But they searched in vain, for the sea was running high, until in calm water under the shelter of the Bass they saw his head, dark on the water, and pulled him aboard. He seemed none the worse for his adventure, but the police charged him with disorderly behaviour and he was fined two pounds for swimming without a regulation costume.

'We met twice,' she said, 'once at a dance and once in Mackie's when we had coffee together. About a year ago. There were several of us there, and we knew the man you came in with. I remember you perfectly.'

He stared the harder, his eyes narrowing, a vertical wrinkle dividing his forehead. 'I'm a little short-sighted too,' she said with a nervous laugh.

'My sight's very good,' he answered, 'but I find it difficult to recognise people. Human beings are so much alike.'

'That's one of the rudest remarks I've ever heard!'

'Surely not?'

'Well, one does like to be remembered. It isn't pleasant to be told that one's a nonentity.'

He made an impatient gesture. 'That isn't what I meant, and I do recognise you now. I remember your voice. You have a distinctive voice and a pleasant one. F sharp in the octave below middle C is your note.'

'Is that the only way in which you can distinguish people?'
'It's as good as any other.'
'But you don't remember my name?'
'No,' he said.
'I'm Elizabeth Barford.'
He bowed and said, 'Well, it was a dull party, wasn't it? The occasion, I mean, when we drank coffee together.'
'I don't agree with you. I thought it was very amusing, and we all enjoyed ourselves. Do you remember Charles Sellin?'
'No.'
'Oh, you're hopeless,' she exclaimed. 'What is the good of meeting people if you're going to forget all about them?'
'I don't know,' he said. 'Let us sit down, and you can tell me.'
He sat again on the edge of the rock, his legs dangling, and looking over his shoulder at her, said, 'Tell me: what is the good of meeting people?'
She hesitated and answered, 'I like to make friends. That's quite natural, isn't it?—But I came here to read.'
'Do you read standing?'
'Of course not,' she said, and smoothing her skirt tidily over her knees, sat down beside him. 'What a wonderful place this is for a holiday. Have you been here before?'
'Yes, I know it well.'
'Charles and I came a week ago. Charles Sellin, I mean, whom you don't remember. We're going to be married, you know. In about a year, we hope.'
'Why did you come here?'
'We wanted to be quiet, and in these islands one is fairly secure against interruption. We're both working quite hard.'
'Working!' he mocked. 'Don't waste time, waste your life instead.'
'Most of us have to work, whether we like it or not.'
He took the book from her lap, and opening it read idly a few lines, turned a dozen pages and read with a yawn another paragraph.
'Your friends in Edinburgh,' she said, 'were better-off

251

than ours. Charles and I, and all the people we know, have got to make our living.'

'Why?' he asked.

'Because if we don't we shall starve,' she snapped.

'And if you avoid starvation—what then?'

'It's possible to hope,' she said stiffly, 'that we shall be of some use in the world.'

'Do you agree with this?' he asked, smothering a second yawn, and read from the book: *'The physical factor in a germ-cell is beyond our analysis or assessment, but we can deny subjectively to the primordial initiatives? It is easier, perhaps, to assume that mind comes late in development, but the assumption must not be established on the grounds that we can certainly deny self-expression to the cell. It is common knowledge that the mind may influence the body both greatly and in little unseen ways; but how it is done, we do not know. Psychobiology is still in its infancy.'*

'It's fascinating, isn't it?' she said.

'How do you propose,' he asked, 'to be of use to the world?'

'Well, the world needs people who have been educated—educated to think—and one does hope to have a little influence in some way.'

'Is a little influence going to make any difference? Don't you think that what the world needs is to develop a new sort of mind? It needs a new primordial directive, or quite a lot of them, perhaps. But psychobiology is still in its infancy, and you don't know how such changes come about, do you? And you can't forsee when you *will* know, can you?'

'No, of course not. But science is advancing so quickly—'

'In fifty thousand years?' he interrupted. 'Do you think you will know by then?'

'It's difficult to say,' she answered seriously, and was gathering her thoughts for a careful reply when agian he interrupted, rudely, she thought, and quite irrelevantly. His attention had strayed from her and her book to the sea beneath, and he was looking down as though searching for something. 'Do you swim?' he asked.

'Rather well,' she said.

'I went in just before high water, when the weed down there was all brushed in the opposite direction. You never get bored by the sea, do you?'

'I've never seen enough of it,' she said. 'I want to live on an island, a little island, and hear it all round me.'

'That's very sensible of you,' he answered with more warmth in his voice. 'That's uncommonly sensible for a girl like you.'

'What sort of a girl do you think I am?' she demanded, vexation in her accent, but he ignored her and pointed his brown arm to the horizon: 'The colour has thickened within the last few minutes, The sea was quite pale on the skyline, and now it's a belt of indigo. And the writing has changed. The lines of foam on the water, I mean. Look at that! There's a submerged rock out there, and always, about half an hour after the ebb has started to run, but more clearly when there's an off-shore wind, you can see those two little whirlpools and the circle of white round them. You see the figure they make? It's like this, isn't it?'

With a splinter of stone he drew a diagram on the rock.

'Do you know what it is?' he asked. 'It's the figure the Chinese call the T'ai Chi. They say it represents the origin of all created things. And it's the sign manual of the sea.'

'But those lines of foam must run into every conceivable shape,' she protested.

'Oh, they do. They do indeed. But it isn't often you can read them. There he is!' he exclaimed, leaning forward and staring into the water sixty feet below. 'That's him, the old villain!'

From his sitting position, pressing hard down with his hands and thrusting against the face of the rock with his heels, he hurled himself into space, and straightening in mid-air broke the smooth green surface of the water with no more splash than a harpoon would have made. A solitary razorbill, sunning himself on a shelf below, fled hurriedly out to sea, and half a dozen white birds, startled by the

253

sudden movement, rose in the air crying 'Kittiwake! Kittiwake!'

Elizabeth screamed loudly, scrambled to her feet with clumsy speed, then knelt again on the edge of the rock and peered down. In the slowly heaving clear water she could see a pale shape moving, now striped by the dark weed that grew in tangles under the flat foot of the rock, now lost in the shadowy deepness where the tangles were rooted. In a minute or two his head rose from the sea, he shook bright drops from his hair, and looked up at her, laughing. Firmly grasped in his right hand, while he trod water, he held up an enormous blue-black lobster for her admiration. Then he threw it on to the flat rock beside him, and swiftly climbing out of the sea, caught it again and held it, cautious of its bite, till he found a piece of string in his trouser-pocket. He shouted to her, 'I'll tie its claws, and you can take it home for your supper!'

She had not thought it possible to climb the sheer face of the cliff, but from its forefoot he mounted by steps and handholds invisible from above, and pitching the tied lobster on to the floor of the gazebo, came nimbly over the edge.

'That's a bigger one than you've ever seen in your life before,' he boasted. 'He weighs fourteen pounds, I'm certain of it. Fourteen pounds at least. Look at the size of his right claw! He could crack a coconut with that. He tried to crack my ankle when I was swimming an hour ago, and got into his hole before I could catch him. But I've caught him now, the brute. He's had more than twenty years of crime,that black boy. He's twenty-four or twenty-five by the look of him. He's older than you, do you realise that? Unless you're a lot older than you look. How old are you?'

But Elizabeth took no interest in the lobster. She had retreated until she stood with her back to the rock, pressed hard against it, the palms of her hands fumbling on the stone as if feeling for a secret lock or bold that might give her entrance into it. Her face was white, her lips pale and tremulous.

254

He looked round at her, when she made no answer, and asked what the matter was.

Her voice was faint and frightened. 'Who are you?' she whispered, and the whisper broke into a stammer. 'What are you?'

His expression changed and his face, with the water-drops on it, grew hard as a rock shining undersea. 'It's only a few minutes,' he said, 'since you appeared to know me quite well. You addressed me as Roger Fairfield, didn't you?'

'But a name's not everything. It doesn't tell you enough.'

'What more do you want to know?'

Her voice was so strained and thin that her words were like the shadow of words, or words shivering in the cold: 'To jump like that, into the sea—it wasn't human!'

The coldness of his face wrinkled to a frown. 'That's a curious remark to make.'

'You would have killed yourself if—if—'

He took a seaward step again, looked down at the calm green depths below, and said, 'You're exaggerating, aren't you? It's not much more than fifty feet, sixty perhaps, and the water's deep.—Here, come back! Why are you running away?'

'Let me go!' she cried. 'I don't want to stay here. I—I'm frightened,'

'That's unfortunate. I hadn't expected this to happen.'

'Please let me go!'

'I don't think I shall. Not until you've told me what you're frightened of.'

'Why,' she stammered, 'why do you wear fur trousers?'

He laughed, and still laughing caught her round the waist and pulled her towards the edge of the rock. 'Don't be alarmed,' he said. 'I'm not going to throw you over. But if you insist on a conversation about trousers, I think we should sit down again. Look at the smoothness of the water, and its colour, and the light in the depths of it: have you ever seen anything lovelier? Look at the sky: that's calm enough, isn't it? Look at that fulmar sailing past: he's not worrying, so why should you?'

She leaned away from him, all her weight against the hand that held her waist, but his arm wass trong and he seemed unaware of any strain on it. Nor did he pay attention to the distress she was in—she was sobbing dryly, like a child who has cried too long—but continued talking in a light and pleasant conversational tone until the muscles of her body tired and relaxed, and she sat within his enclosing arm, making no more effort to escape, but timorously of his hand upon her side so close beneath her breast.

'I needn't tell you,' he said, 'the conventional reasons for wearing trousers. There are people, I know, who sneer at all conventions, and some conventions deserve their sneering. But not the trouser-convention. No, indeed! So we can admit the necessity of the garment, and pass to consideration of the material. Well, I like sitting on rocks, for one thing, and for such a hobby this is the best stuff in the world. It's very durable, yet soft and comfortable. I can slip into the sea for half an hour without doing it any harm, and when I come out to sun myself on the rock again, it doesn't feel cold and clammy. Nor does it fade in the sun or shrink with the wet. Oh, there are plenty of reasons for having one's trousers made of stuff like this.'

'And there's a reason,' she said, 'that you haven't told me.'

'Are you quite sure of that?'

She was calmer now, and her breathing was controlled. But her face was still white, and her lips were softly nervous when she asked him, 'Are you going to kill me?'

'Kill you? Good heavens, no! Why shou.d I do that?'

'For fear of my telling other people.'

'And what precisely would you tell them?'

'You know.'

'You jump to conclusions far too quickly: that's your trouble. Well it's a pity for your sake, and a nuisance for, me. I don't think I can let you take that lobster home for your supper after all. I don't, in fact, think you will go home for your supper.'

Her eyes grew dark again with fear, her mouth opened,

but before she could speak he pulled her to him and closed it, not asking leave, with a roughly occludent kiss.

'That was to prevent you from screaming. I hate to hear people scream,' he told her, smiling as he spoke. 'But this'—he kissed her again, now gently and in a more protracted embrace—'that was because I wanted to.'

'You mustn't!' she cried.

'But I have,' he said.

'I don't understand myself! I can't understand what has happened—'

'Very little yet,' he murmured.

'Something terrible has happened!'

'A kiss? Am I so repulsive?'

'I don't mean that. I mean something inside me. I'm not—at least I think I'm not—I'm not frightened now!'

'You have no reason to be.'

'I have every reason in the world. But I'm not! I'm not frightened—but I want to cry.'

'Then cry,' he said soothingly, and made her pillow her cheek against his breast. 'But you can't cry comfortably with that ridiculous contraption on your nose.'

He took from her the horn-rimmed spectacles she wore, and threw them into the sea.

'Oh!' she exclaimed. 'My glasses!—Oh, why did you do that? Now I can't see. I can't see at all without my glasses!'

'It's all right,' he assured her. 'You really won't need them. The refraction,' he added vaguely, 'will be quite different.'

As if this small but unexpected act of violence had brought to the boiling-point her desire for tears, they bubbled over, and because she threw her arms about him in a sort of fond despair, and snuggled close, sobbing vigorously still, he felt the warm drops trickle down his skin, and from his skin she drew into her eyes the saltness of the sea, which made her weep the more. He stroked her hair with a strong but soothing hand, and when she grew calm and lay still in his arms, her emotion spent, he sang quietly to a little enchanting tune a song that began:

257

> *I am a Man upon the land,*
> *I am a Selkie in the sea,*
> *And when I'm far from every strand*
> *My home it is on Sule Skerry.*

After the first verse or two she freed herself from his embrace, and sitting up listened gravely to the song. Then she asked him, 'Shall I ever understand?'

'It's not a unique occurrence,' he told her. 'It has happened quite often before, as I suppose you know. In Cornwall and Brittany and among the Western Isles of Scotland; that's where people have always been interested in seals, and understood them a little, and where seals from time to time have taken human shape. The one thing that's unique in our case, in my metamorphosis, is that I am the only seal-man who has ever become a Master of Arts of Edinburgh University, Or, I believe, of any university. I am the unique and solitary example of a sophisticated seal-man.'

'I must look a perfect fright,' she said. 'It was silly of me to cry. Are my eyes very red?'

'The lids are a little pink—not unattractively so—but your eyes are as dark and lovely as a mountain pool in October, on a sunny day in October. They're much improved since I threw your spectacles away.'

'I needed them, you know. I feel quite stupid without them. But tell me why you came to the University—and how? How could you do it?'

'My dear girl—what is your name, by the way? I've quite forgotten.'

'Elizabeth!' she said angrily.

'I'm so glad, it's my favourite human name. But you don't really want to listen to a lecture on psychobiology?'

'I want to know *how*. You must tell me!'

'Well, you remember, don't you, what your book says about the primordial initiatives? But it needs a footnote there to explain that they're not exhausted till quite late in life. The germ-cells, as you know, are always renewing themselves, and they keep their initiatives though they nearly

258

always follow the chosen pattern except in the case of certain illnesses, or under special direction. The direction of the mind, that is. And the glands have got a lot to do in a full metamorphosis, the renal first and then the pituitary, as you would expect. It is'nt approved of—making the change, I mean—but every now and then one of us does it, just for a frolic in the general way, but in my case there was a special reason.'

'Tell me,' she said again.

'It's too long a story.'

'I want to know.'

'There's been a good deal of unrest, you see, among my people in the last few years: doubt, and dissatisfaction with our leaders, and scepticism about traditional beliefs—all that sort of thing. We've had a lot of discussion under the surface of the sea about the nature of man, for instance. We had always been taught to believe certain things about him, and recent events didn't seem to bear out what our teachers told us. Some of our younger people got dissatisfied, so I volunteered to go ashore and investigate. I'm still considering the report I shall have to make, and that's why I'm living, at present, a double life. I come ashore to think, and go back to the sea to rest.

'And what do you think of us?' she asked.

'You're interesting. Very interesting indeed. There are going to be some curious mutations among you before long. Within three or four thousand years, perhaps.'

He stooped and rubbed a little smear of blood from his shin. 'I scratched it on a limpet,' he said. 'The limpets, you know, are the same today as they were four hundred thousand years ago. But human beings aren't nearly so stable.'

'Is that your main impression, that humanity's unstable?'

'That's part of it. But from our point of view there's something much more upsetting. Our people, you see, are quite simple creatures, and because we have relatively few beliefs, we're very much attached to them. Our life is a life of sensation—not entirely, but largely—and we ought to be extremely happy. We were, so long as we were satisfied

259

with sensation and a short undisputed creed. We have some advantages over human beings, you know. Human beings have to carry their own weight about, and they don't know how blissful it is to be unconscious of weight: to be wave-borne, to float on the idle sea, to leap without effort in a curving wave, and look up at the dazzle of the sky through a smother of white water, or dive so easily to the calmness far below and take a haddock from the weed-beds in a sudden rush of appetite. Talking of haddocks,' he said, 'it's getting late. It's nearly time for fish. And I must give you some instruction before we go. The preliminary phase takes a little while, about five minutes for you, I should think, and then you'll be another creature.'

She gasped, as though already she felt the water's chill, and whispered, 'Not yet! Not yet, please.'

He took her in his arms, and expertly, with a strong caressing hand, stroked her hair, stroked the roundness of her head and the back of her neck and her shoulders, feeling her muscles moving to his touch, and down the hollow of her back to her waist and hips. The head again, neck, shoulders, and spine. Again and again. Strongly and firmly his hand gave her calmness, and presently she whispered, 'Your're sending me to sleep.'

'My God!' he exclaimed, 'you must'nt do that! Stand up, stand up, Elizabeth!'

'Yes,' she said, obeying him. 'Yes, Roger. Why did you call yourself Roger? Roger Fairfield?'

'I found the name in a drowned sailor's pay-book. What does that matter now? Look at me, Elizabeth!'

She looked at him, and smiled.

His voice changed, and he said happily, 'Youll be the prettiest seal between Shetland and the Scillies. Now listen. Listen carefully.'

He held her lightly and whispered in her ear. Then kissed her on the lips and cheek, and bending her head back, on the throat. He looked, and saw the colour come deeply into her face.

'Good,' he said. 'That's the first stage. The adrenalin's

flowing nicely now. You know about the pituitary, don't you? That makes it easy then. There are two parts in the pituitary gland, the anterior and posterior lobes, and both must act together. It's not difficult, and I'll tell you how.'

Then he whispered again, most urgently, and watched her closely. In a little while he said, 'And now you can take it easy. Let's sit down and wait till you're ready. The actual change won't come till we go down.'

'But it's working,' she said, quietly and happily. 'I can feel it working.'

'Of course it is.'

She laughed triumphantly, and took his hand.

'We've got nearly five minutes to wait,' he said.

'What will it be like? What shall I feel, Roger?'

'The water moving against your side, the sea caressing you and holding you.'

'Shall I be sorry for what I've left behind?'

'No, I don't think so.'

'You didn't like us, then? Tell me what you discovered in the world.'

'Quite simply,' he said, 'that we had been deceived.'

'But I don't know what your belief had been.'

'Haven't I told you?—Well, we in our innocence respected you because you could work, and were willing to work. That seemed to us truly heroic. We don't work at all, you see, and you'll be much happier when you come to us. We who live in the sea don't struggle to keep our heads above water.'

'All my friends worked hard,' she said. 'I never knew anyone who was idle. We had to work, and most of us worked for a good purpose; or so we thought. But you didn't think so?'

'Our teachers had told us,' he said, 'that men endured the burden of human toil to create a surplus of wealth that would give them leisure from the daily task of breadwinning. And in their hard-won leisure, our teachers said, men cultivated wisdom and charity and the fine arts; and became aware of God.—But that's not a true description of the world, is it?'

261

'No,' she said, 'that's not the truth.'

'No,' he repeated, 'our teachers were wrong, and we've been deceived.'

'Men are always being deceived, but they get accustomed to learning the facts too late. They grow accustomed to deceit itself.'

'You are braver than we, perhaps. My people will not like to be told the truth.'

'I shall be with you,' she said, and took his hand. But still he stared gloomily at the moving sea.

The Minutes passed, and presently she stood up and with quick fingers put off her clothes. 'It's time,' she said.

He looked at her, and his gloom vanished like the shadow of a cloud that the wind has hurried on, and exultation followed like sunlight spilling from the burning edge of a cloud. 'I wanted to punish them,' he cried, 'for robbing me of my faith, and now, by God, I'm punishing them hard. I'm robbing their treasury now, the inner vault of all their treasury!—I hadn't guessed you were so beautiful! The waves when you swim will catch a burnish from you, the sand will shine like silver when you lie down to sleep, and if you can teach the red sea-ware to blush so well, I shan't miss the roses of your world.'

'Hurry,' she said.

He, laughing softly, loosened the leather thong that tied his trousers, stepped out of them, and lifted her in his arms. 'Are you ready?' he asked.

She put her arms round his neck and softly kissed his cheek. Then with a great shout he lept from the rock, from the little veranda, into the green silk calm of the water far below. . . .

I heard the splash of their descent—I am quite sure I heard the splash—as I came round the corner of the cliff, by the ledge that leads to the little rock veranda, our gazebo, as we called it, but the first thing I noticed, that really attracted my attention, was an enormous blue-black lobster, its huge claws tied with string, that was moving in a rather ludicrous fashion towards the edge. I think it fell over just before I left, but I wouldn't swear to that. Then I saw her book, the *Studies in Biology*, and her clothes.

Her white linen frock with the brown collar and the brown belt, some other garments, and her shoes were all there. And beside them, lying across her shoes, was a pair of sealskin trousers.

I realised immediately, or almost immediately, what had happened. Or so it seems to me now. And if, as I firmly believe, my apprehension was instantaneous, the faculty of intuition is clearly more important than I had previously supposed. I have, of course, as I said before, given the matter a great deal of thought during my recent illness, but the impression remains that I understood what had happened in a flash, to use a common but illuminating phrase. And no one, need I say? has been able to refute my intuition. No one, that is, has found an alternative explanation for the presence, beside Elizabeth's linen frock, of a pair of sealskin trousers.

I remember also my physical distress at the discovery. My breath, for several minutes I think, came into and went out of my lungs like the hot wind of a dust-storm in the desert. It parched my mouth and grated in my throat. It was, I recall, quite a torment to breathe. But I had to, of course.

Nor did I lose control of myself in spite of the agony, both mental and physical, that I was suffering. I didn't lose control till they began to mock me. Yes, they did, I assure you of that. I heard his voice quite clearly, and honesty compels me to admit that it was singularly sweet and the tune was the most haunting I have ever heard. They were about forty yards away, two seals swimming together, and the evening light was so clear and taut that his voice might have been the vibration of an invisible bow across its coloured bands. He was singing the song that Elizabeth and I had discovered in an album of Scottish music in the little fishing-hotel where we had been living:

I am a Man upon the land,
I am a Selkie in the sea,
And when I'm far from any strand
I am at home on Sule Skerry!

But his purpose, you see, was mockery. They were happy, together in the vast simplicity of the ocean, and I, abandoned to the terror of life alone, life among human beings, was lost and full of panic. It was then I began to scream. I could hear myself screaming, it was quite horrible. But I couldn't stop. I had to go on screaming. . . . .

DEAD MEN WALK

by Alex Hamilton

ALEX HAMILTON (*1930–*) *most suitably concludes this anthology as representative of the new school of young macabre story writers; indeed, a claim may well be advanced that he is the most subtly-unnerving of them all. Educated in South America and Oxford, he has had a variety of jobs, but turned exclusively to writing some five years ago. His interest in tales of the weird and the uncanny has led to his compiling four notable anthologies and producing a collection of his own work,* Beam of Malice, *which was greeted with enthusiasm. The critic Robert Nye accurately pin-pointed Alex Hamilton's absorption with conjuring horror out of the simplest situations when he wrote, 'He turns ordinariness inside out like a glove to show the darkness inside'. He is currently working on a new collection of his stories and, under the pseudonym of 'Pooter', writes a column on books and bookmen for* The Times. *It was while on an assignment for this column in Orkney to visit George Mackay Brown (a writer whose work he very much admires) that he had the idea for this story which is published for the first time.*

'*Orkney?*' said Smithson, unbelievingly.

The Features Editor swivelled through 330 degrees and, thereby meeting the phone again, placed the receiver against his chest, as if he were staking his oath on the entire network. 'Orkney,' he mouthed.

'Why not send Flett? He was born there.'

'That's why.'

'And when I get there?' challenged Smithson.

'Mill about in the stuff. Under the skin a bit. Drag in some history if you want.'

'Colour piece,' said Smithson colourlessly.

'Now listen,' said the Features Editor, absent-mindedly hanging up on his phone call, 'how often have you come in here . . . ?'

'All right, Orkney,' said Smithson quickly. 'Light and shade.'

'More of the latter, I think. You can bring out the darkness a bit if you want.'

'It's probably the wrong time of year for darkness, but all right. Only when I've got it, I hope you won't leave it lying round on overmatter until they declare their own U.D.I.'

'You should be so lucky. We'll want a newspaperman there then.'

'I am a camera,' intoned Smithson, on the way to the door, 'And also a quill, an I.B.M., a pair of ragged claws, scuttling across silent seas, a telex, a desk console, a dream of fair women. . . .'

'A poove.'

'All these things for just the one salary. But don't thank me, thank the Imperial Packaging Company who sent me.' He saw that he had lost his audience, began to open the door, and then quietly shut it again. He cleared his throat.

The Features Editior looked up. 'I thought you were in Orkney.'

'Just to clear up one point before I go. I read a piece the other day by Linklater. . . .'

'Eric?'

'Magnus, son of. Born there, like Flett. Wrote about the women there, how loving, how they came down to the boat, bearing gifts.'

'Reasonable expenses,' said the Features Editor. 'And by the way, Flett was telling me the other day how very reasonable expenses are up there.'

'Flett was born there,' said Smithson. 'That's always more reasonable.'

The phone rang. 'Ah glad, you got through again,' said the Features Editor. 'Some fool must have cut us off. I don't know how I get through the day with all the interruptions.'

'I'm not really at liberty to divulge,' said Smithson.

'I'm sorry for you,' said the elderly man on the boat. 'That's no life, to be keeping your fellow man at arm's lenght.'

'I'm going to stand in the middle of the boat,' said Smithson. 'They say it doesn't move about so much.'

'They blether that say it. The boat's all of a piece, and when it moves the middle moves with it.'

'I don't care to argue about it,' Smithson muttered. He calculated the middle and picked up his suitcase.

The elderly man moved off with him. 'Ye've no need to be taking the suitcase. It'll neither get sick nor stolen on a boat.'

'Do you mind?' said Smithson. 'I'm supposed to be looking at the scenery, not talking about suitcases.'

'Ye'll be a fillum executive no doubt. It's said fillum folk are aye searching for an island.'

'I am not, and I loathe islands. Islands have water round them, and I loathe water.'

'This bit water's placid enough today, so it is, I've seen the Pentland Firth when it was all one white agony, as though the de'il himself had gone into the lace business.'

'No doubt you had your work cut out handling your birch bark canoe?'

'There were no boats out that day, not for many days after. But many men have been drowned hereinabout on days like it. That was their privilege, but that they risked the lives of the lifeboatmen too. Perhaps ye've a mind to visit the wives of the Longhope men whiles ye're in Orkney?'

'Does everybody visit them? 'asked Smithson. 'Are they some sort of tourist attraction?'

'No, no. I'd no' go so far as that. But those from the television have been known to do so.'

267

'Television people fly,' murmured Smithson despondently. The old fellow crouched over to hear Smithson's words, and his coat tails stuck out like an insect's wings, as if he were about to take off himself. 'If I were to be sick now,' continued Smithson, 'I should have no choice but to spoil your shoes, which I see are of suede, and the nicest thing about you.'

The shoes moved a few prudent inches. 'It was better not to fly,' their owner remarked consolingly. 'This is the only true route into Orkney from the mainland. Ye'll aye remember the rocky wild profile of the Creator about you now.'

Smithson uttered nothing in reply but a sad little grunt, which altered in mid expression to a startled cry of pain, as the wizened little man smote him sharply between the shoulder blades. 'Look up, man!' cried his tormentor. 'take your mind off yoursel' wi a grand sight. The clouds are lifting off the brow of the cliffs. There they tower, in all their red majesty!'

Smithson jerked his head up, and gulped air. 'I suppose that stony stack all by itself is the Old Man of Hoy?' he forced himself to enquire. 'Didn't the TV people broadcast the first climb? A feat to rank with the sagas, took 'em days, nights, food and sleep on a dizzy ledge, wonderful stuff.'

'Aye!' replied the other. '*You* might call it that.'

'Didn't everybody?'

'More's the pity. For no sooner had they come down than three wee bairns ran up to the top and down again, wi'out a word of their intent to anybody. It's been a fright to every mother since every time she hears her weans talk of a picnic.'

'Still, you Orcadians must be glad to be able to boast that the old heroic blood of the norsemen is still running in young veins.'

'Don't call me Orcadian. If you please,' snorted the old man. I'm from Perth. There's nothing in Orkney but fish. They fetch me up against my better judgement, and the fish when you think of it live in the sea. And weans are the same the world over.'

268

'As you say,' said Smithson, as the chainmail grey of Stromness hove into view on the port bow, 'the kids are entitled to be mad here like anywhere else. But do they grow up mad?'

'I couldn't get in at Kirkwall,' said Smithson.
'I wonder at that,' returned the barman. 'There's nothing doing at Kirkwall. They'll not be that busy in Kirkwall that they could not take one more body in.'
'It has something to do with their experience of the Press. The last journalist in Kirkwall wrote the most terrible things about his hotel. Put them out of business, nearly.'
'Journalists are good company, but they get their facts wrong.'
'You have nothing to fear from me,' said Smithson. 'We aim to become a paper of record. We would much, much rather be dull than inaccurate. I take it that that moose was shot in about 1871, and the nickellodeon installed in the following year?'
'I could find out for you, Sir, but I would rather that my name were not brought into it.'
Smithson waved a deprecating hand. 'Oh, non-attributable, of course.'
'You'll be here to see Jo, perhaps?'
'Jo?'
'Jo Grimmond. Leader of the Liberals, that was.'
'That's not a bad idea. Where's he to be found?'
'At Westminster, I believe. But if you took the bus, you could see his house from the road. But if you mean to get out of the bus, for a proper look, then take a tip—catch an early bus, or you'll find that the last bus coming back the way is already safe here in Stromness for the night.'
Smithson urged his glass forward for a refill. 'Safe from what?'
'I can't tell you that, Sir. It wouldn't be facts.'
'Things happen at night?'
'They say they do.'
'That's a relief,' said Smithson.

269

'The hotel's a bit quiet just now. You should have been here last week. The place was hotching with facts.'

'And next week too, I suppose?'

'Packed out, Sir. The maids'll be doubling up next week. We'd not have been able to fit you in, not with a shoehorn wrapped in a five pound note.'

'Shows how astute they are in London,' said Smithson. 'Their only thought is that their reporters should bunk comfortably. Wherever possible we choose a quiet week. Do the waitresses double up too? That was a very pretty one with red hair that served me at dinner. Sharp too—recited the menu like a music hall turn.'

'That's very kind of you to say so, Sir. She's my daughter. Comes up from Edinburgh University for the season.'

'Does she, indeed? Well, I won't ask you about all the others. It's plain to see that they're your sisters.'

'Can you come up?' shrieked Smithson.

'You come on down!' roared back the painter.

Carried on the updraught, the words seemed to take physical shape as blobs and tatters of spume, wrenched from the yellow murk of the sea below.

'They said I might find you here,' temporised Smithson. Lying with only his head jutting out over the cliff edge, his vision swam with moving specks of black and white, in the remote background far below the painter. When the cramping vertigo relaxed its hold on him, he recognised them for kittiwakes, and puffins, and little auks and guillemots. The painter's head, pink and bald and nesting in a thick rolltop sweater, looked like the egg of some huge extinct bird. Smithson looked nervously around him as the idea occurred to him, fearing some troll might show up, casting about the crags for materials for an omelette, and seeing Smithson-filler as a *bonne bouche*.

The egg revealed a physiognomy again, as the painter looked up. 'Ye needna be feart,' he insisted. 'I'm used to people watching over my shoulder as I work.'

'I can't fly,' yelled Smithson.

270

'There's a rope in my car. Make it fast to the bumper.'

When he had lowered himself to the painter's side, Smithson was pleased to find that the relentless wind pinned him closely against the rockface, while his feet seemed to shoot nerves out through the leather of his shoes, palpating every interstice in the stone—until suddenly they found what they were hunting and, with an involuntary click like a plug entering its socket, both feet thrust simultaneously into holes. He turned his head at right angles and observed that the painter's canvas was lashed to a sort of natural easel, formed by a couple of cradling bush stumps and a knob of rock above. The painter himself swung as cheerfully in his cloth belay as if he had been a metropolitan window cleaner.

'I heard of your arrival last night,' said the painter. 'It's a terrible hotel that for gossip. It's said ye've an eye on Cathie. Ye'll need to be discreet. Her father's a mercenary old devil.'

'Good God!' exclaimed Smithson. 'Gossip isn't the word. After the sermon her old man gave me last night on facts! I haven't spoken two words out of place to the girl, beyond asking for an extra portion of chips when the kitchen was closed.'

The painter shook his head. 'It's a bit late to undo all that now', he said dubiously. 'It would cause ill feeling in the closes of Stromness if you went back in your shell after such a beginning. Besides, she's a good lass, Cathie, she and my second daughter were in school together, and I'd be as sorry to see the one with tears in her eyes as the other.'

The wind was whipping one continuous tear from the corner of Smithson's own right eye. 'I'll do my best to accommodate the common will,' he said.

The painter nodded and dabbed cloth at a mistake on the canvas. He walked up the rock a bit to tilt back and examine the result 'You're a good lad,' he said. 'Well now,' he continued, lying almost horizontal, 'I suppose you're after an interview on the fisheries situation?'

'Yes and no,' replied Smithson, as casually as the tearing

271

wind and his precarious balance would allow. 'I've not done the homework I should have on the fisheries situation.'

'I'll spoonfeed you. I'm just the man to do it. It's a scandal.'

'I can tell you have strong views on a number of subjects. Could we talk a bit about your painting first?'

'I paint what I see, you know, like any true artist.'

Smithson bent his head till it rested on the other's shoulder. He could now see the whole canvas. 'The intriguing thing is,' he said, 'that you don't . . .' A strange menacing sound rolled about in the painter's throat, like the sea booming in a cave. 'I mean,' continued Smithson hastily, 'it's like everything else since I came North, the real thing is just out of vision, or out of earshot. I mean, from where we are there's a whole lot of rock, and sky and sea and birds and some sort of inlet over there with what looks like a bashed-up boat. I don't see any of that on your canvas. You seem actually to be painting a croft, with a man coming home from work in the fields and a woman with a baby at her breast.'

'D'ye like it?'

'Yes, it's fine, but . . .'

'It's no.bad, is it? I've painted the subject a dozen times.'

'But you've gone to some considerable trouble to install yourself here, and I can't see anything remotely resembling a croft or these people for miles around. The whole land-scape's different from your picture.'

'Och, I only come here for the privacy. It's like Friday at the butcher's at home. I used to come here for eggs when I was a lad. I've painted that too, as a subject, more times than I could count, but now the inspiration for it has left me.'

'And these crofters, where did you see them?'

'Nowhere, boy. Ye'll maybe see a few crofts about still, standing with their roofs stripped away to the elements, but the way of life has gone. On these islands, dead men walk.'

'Dead men walk.' repeated Smithson. 'I think my editor

272

would like you to elaborate.' He ended the sentence on a panic-stricken squeal, as he perceived that he was voicing his request to the painter's boots. Then, as abruptly as he had descended, he felt himself rising again. As he passed the painter again, in a rapid ascent to the clifftop, the painter shouted after him—the words echoed weirdly as if they were spinning up from the sea itself—'And the living can't keep their hands off other men's motorcars. But don't worry. They'll be frightened to death when they see you coming up like a genie from a bottle.'

'Dead men walk,' said Smithson into his pillow. 'But nobody's said anything about them dancing.'

'Hush up,' said the girl with red hair (which on closer inspection had turned out to be a sort of deliriously rich auburn). 'The dance isn't till the day after tomorrow, and you'll be all right by then, except for a few bruises.'

'Would you massage the small of my back again, please.'

'There's not a thing wrong with the small of your back,' said the girl with red hair.

'I think that may be why I enjoyed it so much. Most of the rest was excruciatingly painful.'

'Be brave. Think of childbirth.'

'I'll meditate on it for an hour, unbroken,' he promised, 'if you will just first indulge me this whim.'

'Somebody might come.'

'Somebody might have come earlier, while the agony was on.'

'But I should have had a clear conscience.'

'All right then, I give in. Just pour a whisky down my left ear-hole, and leave me to my dreams of a frowsty bedsitter in Fulham, London, England, the World.'

'I'll give you a whisky,' said the girl with red hair, 'if you invite me to have one with you.'

'Among various linctuses and old herbal remedies on my night table,' said Smithson, 'you'll find a bottle labelled, unless my taste nerve was shattered with my kneecap, Park Royal. Please pour two bumpers, beakers or tooth-mugs of that blissful hippocrene, one for you and one for me.' With his eyes closed he listened to the viscid gurgle, and did not open them when he felt the mug placed between his outstretched fingers. 'You know,' he remarked, 'ever since I came to these islands, I've had the impression that it is not enought to paint, or report, merely what you see, and that just out of sight is something wonderful, mysterious, terrifying, beautiful or downright Orcadian. Which with a little more subtlety or a little more speed, I might just be in time to see one of these days. I have the idea that if I were to open my eyes this second, and turn my head as quickly as a puppet, I would see behind me a gorgeous woman, with long red hair glowing as red as the flames of the beacons when Rognvald Kolson returned from dalliance in the Mediterranean.'

'*Don't* open your eyes, *nor* move your head,' she said. He felt another glass of whisky being given him, in his left hand, then the swift flutter of her lips all across the small of his back.

'It burns more there, now, than anywhere,' proclaimed Smithson.

'I'll leave you to drink both whiskies, I think,' said the girl with red hair, and closed the door behind her.

'They said I wouldn't find you here,' said Smithson. 'They said you were away to Glasgow. Others said Perth, others Edinburgh. They all said you were away—the shopkeepers, I mean.'

'I've not been away for twenty years,' said the poet, standing aside from the doorway of his council flat. 'Will you come in?'

'Why did they say that, then?' asked Smithson, entering.

'Perhaps they wanted to protect me from the unexpected. It's not within mortal compass, but they try.'

'They warned you I was coming?'

'They did,' said the poet, turning his back on Smithson, and gazing through the window, out over the shoulder of

274

the museum towards Scapa. 'Jimmy Isbister told me in person.'

'Who's Jimmy Isbister?'

'He sells me things. He sold me that harpoon for half a crown. He found it in a dump, I believe. He keeps an eye out for things that might please me. You'll have met him in the closes, with his bicycle.'

'Of course. He pushes that bicycle everywhere, but I never see him riding it.'

'I believe he's still looking for the chain.'

'But it was he who told me where to find you.'

'He's my Public Relations Officer,' said the poet. He seemed, with a convulsive effort, to come to a decision. He wheeled round from the window and marched across the room, with his jaw thrust out, towards his little kitchen. 'You'll take a dish of coffee,' he ordered.

'Thank you kindly,' said Smithson, lowering himself with great care into a strawbacked rocking chair. For a rocking chair it was built on rather formal lines, and embraced him like a carnivorous mollusc. He instantly regretted his immobility, for he spied on the table by the window, held down by a porridge bowl, a marmalade pot and a sugar basin, sundry pieces of paper flapping in the draught. These should be the worksheets of a new epic concerning Vikings and Orkneymen, masons and crofters, fiddlers and bakers, before the Reformation corrupted the pure root of mythology which was the blood in the stone of the hard men of the North.

'I'd be sorry if I thought I was playing the person from Porlock,' called Smithson. But the poet was gazing down the sink, humming tunelessly. The person from Porlock would have made no impression on this one. When he had given Smithson his coffee, he turned away and communed with a picture of Rackwick on the wall.

'You're getting to be quite famous, even in America,' said Smithson at last. 'Are you never tempted to travel, out of Orkney?'

'Orkney exports whisky and eggs and professors,'

replied the poet, 'but I . . .' he broke off as he saw Smithson pull out pad and pencil. 'You're not thinking of writing it all down?'

'Just a note of two,' said Smithson. 'It makes a better interview if I do.'

A look of utter dejection lengthened the poet's countenance. 'I wouldn't know how to talk in an interview,' he said.

'You made a very promising beginning,' Smithson encouraged him.

The poet rubbed his hands together fretfully. 'Let's see then,' he said in a pessimistic tone.

'You never even cross to the mainland of Scotland?'

'No,' said the poet warily.

'You're content to write only about your own people?'

'Yes.'

'Their legends and myths, their heroes—like St. Magnus the Martyr.'

'He would be mentioned.'

'The clans that came out of the northern darkness? And put down roots of darnkess in this earth?'

'If you like.'

'Perhaps as a reminder to the people today of what they are in danger of losing?'

'You might put it like that.'

'Do you have a sense that here dead men walk?'

'Dead men . . .' The poet stopped. 'A sense. . . .' Perspiration stood out all over his brow. Smithson ostentatiously put pad and pencil back in his inside pocket. A faintly hopeful look lightened the poet's haggard expression. 'Is that all?' he asked.

'I think we've covered the main subjects,' said Smithson. 'I'll be in Orkney a few days yet. We might meet in one of the bars, and just drop in a few of the details.'

'We must, that,' said the poet enthusiastically, confirming the words with a vigorous twist of his head. 'But I hope you'll be getting into no more fisticuffs. You've had trouble enough with the Norwegians already, from the look of you.'

276

'Who told you that?' said Smithson. 'I haven't seen any Nor. . . .'

But his denials went unheard. The poet had launched into a series of waterfront stories and anecdotes, reaching farther and farther back into the past. Smithson listened, spellbound.

'Don't you find it eerie, a place like this right in your backyard?' asked Smithson.

The farm girl said nothing. She reached out a hand and a small girl sprang from nowhere to attach herself to it.

'It's pretty deserted,' said Smithson. 'We might be alone in the world.'

The farm girl, already plump as a pigeon, seemed to swell further. She compressed her lips, as if she had difficulty in holding utterance back.

'A few trees would help,' said Smithson doggedly. 'But I suppose the wind doesn't give them a chance.'

The farm picked up a lantern and held it ahead of her as she needed it to see the way ahead, although the sun was high in the sky. The mite held fiercely to a sheaf of postcards.

'I understand there's a tree in Kirkwall,' said Smithson.

With her little appendage skipping at her side, the sturdy wench forged briskly across the courtyard. Smithson caught with them at the edge of the highway which ran past the farm, where his two guides examined the road in both directions. As far as each of its horizons, no vehicle of any sort could be seen. After a pause, the pair of them scuttled across. 'Why don't you agitate for a zebra crossing?' Smithson called after them.

On the far side they bounced across the springy turf towards the entrance of the burial mound. Every time Smithson came up with them they accelerated. 'All right, I won't talk any more,' panted Smithson. 'I'll save my breath to cool my porridge.'

At the beginning of the shallow cutting which led to the mouth of the grass-covered tomb, they stopped and the little one finished a key out of her knickers. With a great air

277

of solemn officialdom she unlocked the iron gate, stood back to wave to her companion, then Smithson, and followed after into the vault. The elder girl put down her lantern and then stood as still as a graven image.

Standing erect under the dome, Smithson said, for the sake of a human voice, 'So this is the ancient Maeshowe, the chamber where the silent vanished races laid their chiefs to rest.'

There was a faint hiss from the farm girl at his elbow. Smithson turned in surpries from contemplation of the hieroglyphs around him, as he realised it was the prelude to speech. The farm girl then spoke for some ten minutes.

She delivered herself of her message in a high sing-song which, were it transcribed, could have no punctuation. She talked of high-born maidens and great heroes, of oppressors and defiance, of gold and jewels, mighty spirits and wretched vandals. She kept her head high all the time, never removing her eyes from a fixed spot at the apex of the ceiling. When she had come to the end, she lowered her head and for the first time her hitherto waxen features relaxed in a smile of sheer pride.

'Jolly good,' said Smithson. 'That sounded like word-perfect.' The little girl spread out a display of postcards on a slab for him to make a choice. 'They're sevenpence each,' she said. 'But some people give me a shilling.'

Smithson having aligned himself with some people, and effected several purchases, the farm girl said, 'Ye must accept my apology for remaining dumb. I canna concentrate on my history and the questions folk put to me all in the same while. But if there's anything ye want to know, ye can ask it now.'

'Well then,' said Smithson. 'Your great poet told me that on mid-winter's day, just before the year's midnight, the last of the setting sun actually comes down that passage for an instant and shines on the wall. Now, have you ever seen that?'

'I have not. And I dinna ken if it's so. For in December I'm always up and away to Switzerland for the skiing.'

278

At that moment the sound of a malicious little chuckle came from the external end of the passage. The iron gate clanged to, and the key turned in the padlock. In the silence that followed the farm girl sighed. Smithson dropped to a crouching stance and hurried down the passage. 'Come back, you little blighter!' he shouted.

But the little girl had vanished into the outside world, hidden from view by the curve in the cutting. Smithson came snarling and crouching back, like Caliban, to the farm girl. 'She's scapa'ed,' he said. 'Come to think of it, I wish she would, and drown herself.'

The farm girl had sat herself down, carefully spreading her skirts on the stone slab. 'She gets bored,' she said. 'It's only a phase. She needs a skelping, I suppose.'

'We're buried alive,' shrieked Smithson. 'With a lot of prehistoric bones!'

'They might find us, I think,' said the farm girl.

'Yes, but when? You said yourself ten minutes ago that at one period nothing but ghosts came near the place for several centuries.'

'Aye, but there wasn't a regular bus service in those days. There's generally somebody wanting to see the Maeshowe on every bus in the summer.'

'When's the next bus?'

'It's a two-hourly service.'

'Two hours! That's an eternity, ravelled up in a pagan crypt.'

'Ye're no'verra gallant.'

'There's a time and a place for everything,' said Smithson. 'And let me tell you that if that lamp isn't still burning when they dig us out of here, I'll sue the head off every modern descendant of your ancient earls that still haunt the place.'

'You're sitting just now on the bones of a warrior that lost his heid,' said the farm girl. 'It's a guid story, so it is, for those wi' a strong stomach. . . .'

'It's not the Maeshowe,' remarked Smithson sentenious-

279

ly, 'but it's a good site. I shouldn't think anything will disturb her there for a thousand years.' From the graveyard, on the other side of the wall, came the sound of the first sod being shovelled on to a coffin.

'She was in no hurry to come here, all the same,' observed the chemist.

'At 92?' exclaimed Smithson. 'There's a fair case for saying the angel of death must have passed her over a few times already.'

'Oh, I don't think she was greedy,' said the chemist. 'One more week, perhaps two, and she'd have been content As it was, I regret to say her last words were notable for their mood of indignation and a sense of injustice.'

'Some dear relative on the high seas couldn't quite make it?' suggested Smithson.

'Oh, not at all,' replied the chemist. 'She'd been a widow for nigh on fifty years, and there's moss already on the head-stone of the last of her family to be laid here. But you see, she took in lodgers to help the money along, and harvest celebration time, which falls next week, was always very fruitful for her.'

'From where we stand,' said Smithson, looking inward from the path which divided the cemetery from the sea, 'the harvest of death looks the richest of all. It's a beauti-fully kept estate. You're very conscious of death up here.'

'You re very conscious of our consciousness,' retorted the chemist. 'Furthermore the whisper says you spent a record four hours in the Maeshowe today, and it's even said there were tears in your eyes when you emerged.'

'Tears of desperation,' said Smithson. 'The first bus didn't even stop. I don't want to talk about it.'

'Yet here you are, straightaway down for the funeral of a poor old soul that spun out her history in a Stromness close. Did you follow the cortege down the hill from the kirk?'

'Pure accident,' said Smithson, who wished that he could believe that it had been woven in the loom of fate. 'I came round the shore looking for this wrecked freighter to take a photograph. . . .' They turned together to face the rusting

280

hulk, which lay canted over against the rocks, with its mainmast like a tall extra cross above the cemetery. Smithson looked into his viewfinder. 'It makes a dramatic shot, but I came down not even knowing the graveyard was here, much less that it would be operational at this moment.'

'There's sea wrack all about the coast,' said the chemist, scornfully. 'Many that would make better spectacles in a photograph than this one. I'm interested in the art of the camera myself, and could take you round the coast for some pictures. If you happened to use any of mine in your paper I wouldn't want payment—it's the credit to your name that's important when you're building up a reputation.'

'Exceedingly kind offer,' said Smithson. The mourners were beginning to move away, and he worked the lever with great speed. 'I think you'd need to belong to the union before we used your work. And anyway it's only this wreck I want. You see, your great poet based a story on it. He seeded in this freighter, that was his phrase.'

'It's no story to make public,' said the chemist witheringly. 'The crew were all drunk, or they'd never have lost her on a rock marked with a buoy.'

Smithson lowered his camera. 'Come again,' he said. 'I don't see any rock with a buoy.'

'No. It's up the way a bit. A couple of hundred yards yonder, perhaps a bit more.'

'And the wreck was in the way of shipping? She was pulled in tight by the shore?'

'No. She found her own way.'

'To a *graveyard*,' said Smithson in a hushed voice. 'Did anybody see this happen?'

'It happened one night.'

'Fantastic! Who saw it?'

'Nobody saw it. There was nothing to see. The crew had been taken off a long time.'

'Nothing to see!' echoed Smithson despairingly. 'Nobody saw it!'

'It was a natural happening. I don't understand your emotion.'

281

'I can't explain it,' replied Smithson. 'But if I can't see anything myself, I wish to heaven I could see something obliquely at least, through somebody else's eyes.'

'For a chemist, he's not a bad fiddler,' said Smithson.

'For an invalid, you're not a bad dancer,' said the girl with red hair.

'I've learnt that in Orkney everybody has to play two roles.'

'What else have you learnt?' she enquired, leading Smithson by the hand away from the concourse dancing in the barn.

'Read all about it in Thursday's edition. This year, next year, sometime, never.'

They passed down the central aisle of the adjacent cowshed. Every cubicle seemed to be occupoed by an amorous couple. She laughed when she saw the look on Smithson's face. 'Don't worry,' she whispered. 'I know you believe in A.A. comfort. Anyway, we're only going to fetch in the skog.'

The skog proved to be a dark brown liquid, getting its colour and viscid nature from a liberal ferment of sugar. They carried it back in small butter churns. She began to tell him the recipe but he stopped her after the first three items, 'Any moment you'll tell me it includes beastings.'

'It's very potent. It'll make them beastly drunk, but you can't have a barn dance without,' she said.

'A good many are three parts cut already.'

'They go on a pub crawl first,' said the girl with red hair.

'Yes, the poet showed me the way. I was afraid we'd soon run out of pubs, but he proved his genius by going in the public bar and saloon of each, thus doubling the number of stops.'

'You look sad. Is it because you're going tomorrow?'

'That of course,' said Smithson. 'And also because I didn't find what I was looking for, although I'm convinced it's here.'

282

'Perhaps you've been looking too hard. What were you looking for?'

'How can I put it?' wondered Smithson. 'Perhaps . . . what happens in the dark, only guessed at by most people.'

'You found a little of that, at least,' she said. 'Though I hope you won't write about it.'

'You have my word for that,' promised Smithson. 'But that's not what I meant.'

Three dances later the festival had become much noisier and the air was thick and sticky, as if it too were fermenting into skog. A young man and a girl were being pursued by shrill groups of youths, in and out of the barn, whooping and shrieking as they led their rout of pursuers. Both had their faces blacked.

'They've to be married tomorrow,' explained the girl with red hair. 'Tonight with their faces blacked they can do as they please and nobody knows who they are.'

'Everybody seems to know who we are,' said Smithson. 'At least, they keep looking. Perhaps we should have blacked our faces.'

'It doesn't work if you're not about to be wed.'

'Shall we just sit outside then?' suggested Smithson.

They sat on a knoll a hundred yards from the byre. The bare hills of Orkney lay all around in soft billows of charcoal, against a sky like polished eggshell. The dance behind them thumped and squeaked and skirled, with an occasional extra lift of irreverent, boisterous laughter. Sometimes a car door banged in the lane, and once a lad with a hip flask climbed on a metal roof and clanged out a solo dance, until he fell into the arms of his companions. The bride-to-be flashed by within a few yards of them like a firework, a small train of sparks still stubbornly after her, fizzled into a hollow, and was suddenly silent.

'But they won't sack you, will they?' asked the girl with red hair anxiously, 'if you didn't get what you came for?'

'Oh, Good Lord, no. I've got enough *copy*.'

'Then I don't understand.'

283

'Did you ever play Grandmother's Footsteps?' asked Smithson.
· 'Where one person stands with his back to everybody else, and they all try to creep up without being seen to move?'
'That's it. Exactly .Well, I haven't caught anybody moving. When I look directly, they're all standing like stone. As motionless as those stones, down there on the plain.'
The Standing Stones of Stenness, indecipherably ancient, were there in the bowl below, a wide circle of dolmens, on slightly raised turf between two tarns.
'This is the night when those stones are said to move,' she said quietly.
He sat and stared at the huge, roughly-hewn pieces of rock. It was impossible. 'They won't move if I'm looking,' he said
'Would you be content if I saw them move?'
'Have you seen them?'
'No, never. But I've never had cause.'
'Yes, I'd believe you.'
'It's coming up midnight,' she said. 'Stand with your back to the stones.'
She rose with him, and faced him. They stood there, unmoving. The sound of a police jeep came to them, making its way up the hill to the barn. A cat wound its way round Smithson's legs, but he did not look down. 'In the daytime you have green eyes,' said Smithson.
'Now! Now!' she cried. 'Don't look round!' In her eyes he saw the stones move. Then the vision trembled and was gone, as they filled with tears.
'I saw!' she said, swaying towards him.
'And I saw too,' said Smithson, catching her in a triumphant embrace.

'Most of it's padding,' said the Features Editor. 'And too damned dark at that.'
'You asked for darkness,' said Smithson.
'I don't know how you got that impression. We're not here to make people's flesh creep, except with facts. Anyway,

284

it doesn't matter. The Editor's very pleased with the stuff on the Fisheries Problem. There was a question asked in the House yesterday, so you can put in another two hundred words on that, and it'll do nicely for tomorrow's paper.'

'And the rest?'

'Forget the rest. You know, you make quite a good reporter, when you stick to the facts.'

'Thanks,' said Smithson. At the door he said, 'You know it's true about the girls. They do come down to the boat, bearing gifts.'

'So?'

'It's a fact.'

'Damned boring fact,' said the Features Editor. 'And quite irrelevant in the context of the fisheries problem.'

GLOSSARY

Because of the number of words in the Scottish dialect which appear in the early sections of this book, the following brief glossary has been prepared to make reading easier for those not familiar with the language.

The Secret Commonwealth
   Tossue: ruffle

Satan's Invisible World Discovered
   Warrand: go bail

A Night in the Grave
   Mear: a mare
   Whilk mair: which more
   Scowp: run
   Back-lill: hole of a wind instrument
   Flitt: to remove
   Siller: silver coin
   Leesome lane: quite alone
   Speerings: inquiry
   Grat: wept
   Graned: groaned
   Hesp: hank
   Bogle-wark: ghostly action
   Quean: young girl
   Dyvour: bankrupt, debtor
   Wanchancy: wicked
   Lhield: fellow
   Deray: uproar
   Birling: a drinking match
   Riped: searched

Skelloch: shriek
Dirdum: tumult
Douce: kind, gentle
Moulds: graves

The Brownie of the Black Haggs
Bratch: bitch hound
Birl: spin
Lopper: coagulate

The Ghost with the Golden Casket
Plat: plot of ground
Thrapple: windpipe
Crapin: bird's crop
Fizzenless: insipid, feeble
Hech: exclamation of surprise

Red Hand
Piobaireachad: bagpipe lament
Clachneart: putting stone
Piob-mhor: the great Highland bagpipe
Feadan: the chanter or pipe on which pipers practise
    tunes before playing them on the bagpipes
A pheasain: O Brat!
Cothrom na Feinne: man to man
Crunluadh: a movement in piping
Clarsach: harp
Cabar: tossing the caber
Biodag: a dirk, dagger
Dhe: God
Amadain dhoill: O blind fool!
Sgian-dubh: black knife worn in the stocking

Through the Veil
Thole: suffer, tolerate
Lugs: ears

The Outgoing of the Tide

Bitcallant: a lad
Hirpling: limping
Cantrips: magic spells, incantations
Rudas carlines: witches
Threep: assert pertinaciously
Gentrice: of good birth
Routh: abundance
Doited: foolish
Trig: active
Loanings: bypaths
Glisk: a passing glance
Brawly: well
Collogue: plot, conspiracy
Glunching: frowning
Troking: dealing
Thrawn: distorted
Lee-lane: lonely
Clamjamfry: company, mob
Jaloused: suspected
Thirled: under obligation
Mettle: spirited
Riving: raging
Gangrel: vagrant, tramp
Yett: gate
Gash: grim, dismal
Stelled: stuck
Toom: empty
Drookit: drenched
Dirled: vibrated